A Viral State

Degen Hill

Archer Publishing
E-book
ISBN-13: 978-1-7321364-3-4
Print
ISBN-13: 978-1-7321364-2-7

This book is dedicated to those willing to fight for what they believe in.

Acknowledgements

I'd first like to thank the many people who were patient enough to listen to me as I went into my tirade about a crazy conspiracy concerning a virus that later became this novel. Your insights, comments, and suggestions were most appreciated.

A big shoutout goes to Quincy Davenport, my mother, for her continual support and encouragement throughout the writing process. It's always nice to have someone in your corner, and no one better than my mom.

Finally, I'd like to thank Jarrod Williams and Mark McGinn for their edits, commentary, and provocative questions that helped iron out plot holes.

Chapter 1

August 2062

Bodies lay strewn across the streets with those still left alive sheltered in their homes. Broken glass from storefront windows and abandoned cars littered the once thriving city. Electricity had been out for over two weeks, and the stench of rotting food mixed with the sweltering summer heat hung in the air like a heavy fog. The Styre virus had infected the global population faster than any before it. The death toll amounted to millions in just the first week. The world was unprepared, and the human race was now struggling to prevent the eradication of its species. A new era had fallen upon Earth, and though there was no looking back, it was difficult to imagine a path forward.

June 2071

The white tram slithered through the city like a snake through tall grass. Solitary buildings flashed by as the soporific hum of the mag-lev tram echoed throughout the carriages. Finn Brantley looked at his watch—4:00 a.m. The city was not yet awake. He looked out the window at the same dimly lit streets he had seen countless times before. He wondered about the lives of the people in the buildings and whether they, too, had thoughts about the world they now found themselves in. But the early morning echoed back with resounding silence.

Finn looked down at the worn work boots that peeked out from his blue coveralls. He rubbed his hand over the discolored white "Conserta Engineer" emblem on his chest pocket and looked across the carriage at the other members of his crew, all wearing the same.

I hate that damn color, he thought. *We all look like mindless clones, no choice but to do what we're told, where we're told to do it.*

Some were asleep, some hunched over in thought, and others checked the morning news on their glass tablets. Though Finn felt nervous, there was nothing special about today. He couldn't put a finger on why, but the feeling was there, starting in his brain and working its way through his body.

The tram continued to wind its way through the city, passing through the city's slums, the housing projects, the financial district, and making its way toward the industrial zone. The sun was beginning to creep over the horizon, and it slowly cast its glow over the utilitarian box-shaped buildings that spread across what had once been known as New York City. Finn thought about the name *New York* and thought that *Central* was a pretty uninspired alternative.

After the Styre virus hit, things had changed. The U.S. had been renamed The United Federation, and many of its major cities also bore new names, which President Leon Burke had said, "…remind us of a past that is no longer a part of our future." Along with the name change, Central had been transformed into the nation's capital, and with that came renovations for the large and looming government buildings. The once-bustling streets of New York were now nothing more than a remnant of the past, and a constant reminder that life post-Styre was unlikely to return to the way things had been. The availability of meat, open borders, not having to wonder if the days to come might be the last. Now, in his thirties, the world Finn had known several years ago was nothing more than a memory in the minds of all those who had experienced it.

Finn's mind continued to wander, as it often did during his commute, wondering what he felt nervous about. He ran through the past few days in his mind and nothing unusual stood out to him, but he couldn't shake the feeling that had worked its way into his stomach. The sun poured over the quiet city outside until it crept through the window and caught his eye, waking him from his mindless thoughts. He looked out and saw the large orange pilings that, even after nine years of working for Conserta, still stood, as if frozen in time. Past the pilings, huge warehouses came into view, all marked with the clean white font of Conserta. The tram slowed, and the other engineers, techs, and assemblymen on the tram stood up and formed lines. Finn made his way into one of the lines when a gruff voice behind him said, "Another day, another dose, eh?"

"Another dose, another day," Finn said, turning around to shake hands with the stocky man. "All good, Wes?"

"You know me. Can't complain. Kids and wife are healthy if that's still an applicable term these days, and I've still got this job." Wes patted the white "Conserta Engineer" patch the same way Finn had done earlier. "Good weekend?"

"Tried to make the most of it. I'm still tinkering around with Tip's mechanical leg at home, but I'm not as close as I thought I'd be by now."

"You'll get there soon enough," Wes said, scratching his thick black beard. He leaned close to Finn, his green eyes shining. "But let me know if there's anything you need," he whispered. "I'll see what I can do."

"I appreciate that," Finn said as a bell rang throughout the tram.

The men in blue jumpsuits turned toward the doors, and an automated voice announced, "Proceed for authorization."

The tram doors opened, and in single file, the men pulled up the left sleeve of their blue uniform and touched it to a panel on the wall of the platform.

As Finn did the same, the panel lit up and displayed: "Finn Brantley - 31 - Conserta Engineer - Sector 3 - Authorized." After everyone was cleared, they made their way through the dimly lit platform and into the equipment room.

"Sector Three again, eh?" said Wes, as both he and Finn opened their lockers to grab the tools they'd need for the day.

"Just more soldering and tinkering. Grunt work, really," said Finn. "I've been assigned to Sector Three for years, repairing those damn bots. You'd think by now I'd get moved somewhere else, somewhere I could actually use my skills."

"So much for that engineering degree, huh?" Wes laughed. "Well, at least you've got a job."

Finn thought about all those who had died from Styre and knew that despite his feelings about his job, he was lucky to have one. The daily doses needed to survive were connected to employment and doled out on job sites. No job, no dose.

"I'm working to survive. What's the point?" Finn said looking over at Wes, his friend, and workmate for over nine years. When Finn started at Conserta, Wes had shown him the ropes, and they had grown close over the years.

"A chance at another life just means making a series of different choices."

"Where'd you hear that?" asked Finn. "The Dalai Lama?"

"Wife read it in her horoscope this morning," laughed Wes.

After grabbing their tools, the lights in the equipment room changed to green, and a door at the far end opened. "Please proceed to your sector," the mechanical voice announced over the intercom.

"I'll catch you later," said Finn as he and Wes made their way to the freight elevators marked with the corresponding sector. They exchanged nods as they entered their respective sector elevators. Inside the dirty metal lift, Finn looked around at the other men, all with the same "engineer" emblem, and wondered why Conserta would use such a title for a job that anyone could be taught to do. Solder this, weld that, grind these—the job was as repetitive as the days. The mechanical winch began to whir, and the elevator rose, giving Finn a view of the large industrial base that he had never wanted, or dreamed to work in.

As a bright-eyed engineering graduate a decade ago, Finn had aspired to work on something to better humanity. At the time, he wasn't sure exactly what that would be, but his dream was to work on things that benefitted society. After Styre hit and became a permanent part of the world, how people lived had shifted beyond recognition. Life became about survival, the paramount desire felt by all. His dreams of bettering the world remained with him until they became obsolete. He applied to Conserta, a global robotics producer that had promised stable pay and, more importantly, provided doses to stave off the deadly Styre virus that had infected everyone in the world. The implacable speed at which Styre infected the public had left little time to stop it.

Though not permanently effective, the doses were the closest any government around the world had come to stopping, or at best, delaying the effects of the Styre virus. Jobs now provided not only a salary but also an allotted number of doses for their employees based on the type of work. Much like the old world, companies gave more doses for jobs deemed "more essential for society." Finn's job in Sector Three at Conserta allotted him ten doses per week. One dose was taken each day while the other three were his to do with as he pleased. He could sell them, trade for goods, or stockpile them, as most did, to ensure life after work. For Finn, the doses represented time, another day to live, but time now had a more profound meaning.

As the elevator continued to ascend, Finn glanced at his workmates and wondered if they, too, felt that the work they were doing was beneath them, or if they were simply grateful to be employed. The world's population had dropped dramatically due to Styre, and although a cure still hadn't been found, the daily dose treatments they received along with their pay were the only things standing between them and inevitable death from the virus that now lived within everyone on Earth.

The elevator came to a halt. The large metal grate in front of the men descended, and they each made their way to their designated workstations. Piles of broken robots and mechanical devices lay in heaps next to a large metal table outfitted with tech panels to run diagnostics. With a lack of manpower to mine new resources, Conserta had risen to power as the leading tech company focused on repairs rather than manufacturing. It was cheaper to employ a massive labor force to fix outdated, broken, or malfunctioning robots than to produce new ones.

Finn had just set his tool bag on the table when a cheery voice rang out, "Finn, my man, what have we got for today?"

"The usual," he said, turning to look at his Sector Three workmate. Corbin Anvar had been with Conserta for a few years now and had worked his way up to Sector Three. Much like Finn, Corbin had been a young tech apprentice with hopes of greatness before realizing that an apprenticeship didn't provide doses. Coming to Conserta, for many, was out of necessity rather than desire.

"Where do they keep finding all this crap?" asked Corbin, picking up a robotic arm used for automotive manufacturing.

"Typical wear and tear, I suppose. With no new products, things break more often than not."

"Ready?" asked Corbin.

Finn looked at the pile of junk and realized that his level of interest corresponded exactly to the number of existing projects that would require at least some sense of creativity: none. He nodded slowly.

"Let's get to it then," said Corbin, also placing his tool bag on the table. Finn tapped one of the panels on the table, and numerous digital screens flickered on. Corbin put the robotic arm on the table, and the monitors began to run tests.

"Faulty wires," said Finn, as Corbin grabbed a holo-welder and began slicing open the arm to expose the internal wiring. The pair had settled into a comfortable routine and worked well together, both in sync with what needed to be done and who would do it. They worked with precision until each piece of equipment had been diagnosed, fixed, assessed, and placed on a cart outside their workplace. Occasionally, transporters in red jumpsuits would take the cart with the repaired tech and replace it with an empty one. The days were long and the work monotonous, but so long as they were employed, Conserta's workers lived to see another day.

"How's the wife?" asked Finn.

"Due any day now!" Corbin replied with a grin on his face. "Bit of a back and forth on the due date for a while, and finding prenatal vitamins ain't easy with our salary, but we're almost out of the woods."

"Congrats! You must be thrilled." Finn paused for a second and then asked, "Hey ... you're not worried about ...?"

Before he could finish, Corbin smiled and said, "It's the way things are now. I know the little one will have Styre when born, being dormant and all, but he, yep, a baby boy, will be safe until he's seventeen. Strange that the virus is latent until that age. Maybe something about the body still developing, who knows. But as my wife keeps telling me, where there is life, there is hope."

"You're a braver man than I am," said Finn. "I don't think I could bring a child into this world, let alone support one."

"Life must go on," said Corbin, while splitting open a guard drone on the table.

The sounds of electrical work and hammers echoed throughout Sector Three as the men in blue went about their work. Other sectors were also busy, recycling spare parts from retired pieces of tech, testing, and melting down old parts to create new ones. Conserta had become an integral part of the new society, providing it with the luxuries of the old world, despite not helping to advance it. *Maintain*, thought Finn, *life is now just about maintaining.*

As the day wore on, the pile of broken tech gradually got smaller. By the time Finn and Corbin had finished, and the red lights flashed to signal the end of the workday, Finn looked at their empty workshop and knew that there would be a new pile of junk to repair tomorrow, just as there had been every day for the last several years.

"Don't look so glum," said Corbin. "Payday tomorrow. Most of mine will go toward stuff for the new baby. Who knew kids could be so expensive? But I suppose if you were up for it, I could spare a few Units to grab a drink after work tomorrow."

"You're on," said Finn.

The two men collected their tools, then turned off the diagnostic table and light. They, along with the hundred or so other employees in

7

Sector Three, made their way back into the elevator and proceeded toward the tram.

The ride back home was much the same as it had been in the morning. The sun was setting, and the city seemed to fly by as if Finn were looking at a watercolor painting of some far-off land. The train was quiet, with most of the men lost in their thoughts, waiting to go home to the lives they worked so hard to sustain. Finn wondered what it would be like to have a family, maybe a daughter or a son. A wife to lay next to in bed. He had wanted those things but perpetuating his existence had become first priority in this new world, leaving no time for Finn to cultivate the life he had once dreamed of having.

As the train pulled into the station on the outskirts of town and slowly emptied, Finn waved goodbye to Corbin and made his way to the exit that led to the dark streets outside. The world around him was quiet as if the noise had been sucked from the air. He walked in silence through the streets and looked up at the buildings with sparsely lit rooms, wondering if they were filled with men like him or people like Corbin who were starting families.

As he approached his building in District Seven, he held out his wrist just as he had done at the entrance of Conserta, and the door opened after scanning the digital code under his skin. Keys and cards had fallen by the wayside in 2055, as technology had merged with humans under the guise of efficiency and convenience. Finn had always believed it to be an invasion of privacy, but without any position of power, he was just part of the masses that had had to quietly accept their fate.

The guard in the dilapidated lobby of his building nodded at Finn. "Busy day at Conserta?"

"The usual," Finn said as he walked toward the elevators.

Once inside, after the doors closed, a digital screen displayed the words, "A dose a day keeps Styre away. Work for your future." Finn shook his head. This was just one of President Burke's many public service announcements. *What does he care if people died?* thought Finn. After over a decade in office, it was hard to think of what he had accomplished. Much like the state of the world, Burke had maintained the country's existence, though not without changing its name and the entire system upon which it was founded. There hadn't been any breakthroughs concerning Styre, and despite the monthly updates stating that a cure was just on the horizon, nobody believed it. Styre was here to stay, and society carried on.

The Styre virus, which lived within every living soul on Earth, was like some unwelcome tenant who had moved in and refused to leave. The origins had caused and continued to cause international controversy over which country was responsible. Fingers were quickly pointed at China due to its history of starting global pandemics, but no matter how much research was done, no one could pinpoint where it had come from. One day, it was simply here and spread through the world like wildfire. There was nothing anyone could do to stop it. Babies were born with it, despite not requiring doses until they were seventeen, which was another thing scientists hadn't been able to figure out, and those older than seventeen lived with it like a ticking time bomb. Work, or an abundance of wealth to buy doses, were the only means to prolong life. The virus had not only infected the world; it had consumed it.

Finn scanned his wrist against the brown door of Apartment #5, and as soon as he opened the door, he saw Tipper, his jet-black Labrador, wagging his tail, eagerly awaiting his return.

"Were you a good boy today?" asked Finn, bending down to pet his dog. "Tear up any of my stuff while I was gone?" The dog licked his face and then hobbled into the kitchen, knowing it was dinnertime. With only three legs, walking on hardwood floors proved difficult, and Finn always smiled at Tipper's resolve to remain uninhibited by his disability. He'd always wondered if dogs knew they were disabled.

Dogs were a rarity these days. Breeding was limited, and people were too focused on survival to care for another living thing, but for Finn, having a dog had always been a part of his life. He'd grown up with Maya,

9

a collie that his parents had bought him for his sixth birthday. They had been inseparable, spending all their time together until Finn went off to college. When his parents called to say that Maya had passed, he was heartbroken, as if part of himself was lost, too. Two years ago, he had saved up enough for Tipper, a young pup.

"You're not going to want this one, though," said the breeder. "Little guy doesn't even have all his legs."

"I'll take him," Finn had said, handing over nearly two months of salary that he had diligently saved.

Finn's calloused hands grabbed the bag of dog food and poured it into a bowl while Tipper bounced around on three legs before launching headfirst toward the food.

"Easy there, Tip, it's not going anywhere."

Finn looked around his small apartment. He had a tiny living room with a black couch where he and Tipper would watch TV together, a little coffee table, and a window at the far end that looked out at the other apartment buildings in District Seven. There was a dark stain creeping in from the ceiling of the kitchen that ran down part of the wall. No matter what Finn tried, he couldn't get rid of it and had accepted the fact that it was as much a part of the apartment as everything else—much in the same way that Styre was a permanent part of the world.

Next to the kitchen was a small room that he had transformed into a workshop. As Tipper ate, he grabbed a beer from the fridge, walked into the workshop, and flicked on the light. The table was covered in an assortment of mechanical parts, wires, and tools. Partially assembled in the middle of the table was the makings of a canine leg. Finn had been working for months to build a mechanical back left leg for Tipper, which would operate, flex, and move in conjunction with the other three, but transitioning from blueprint to reality was proving difficult. Supplies were hard to get, and Finn didn't have some of the tools required. A small tablet lay next to the leg, and he touched it to turn it on.

He had been working to program the device to operate as a normal leg, but it never seemed to work in harmony with the others. He remembered the first time he attached it to Tipper and turned it on. The initial diagnostics were okay, and standing still, it worked great, but as soon as Tipper tried to walk, the mechanical leg began to move independently of the others, almost in a spasm, knocking Tipper over as he barked in surprise.

Finn sat down at the table and picked up the leg. One way or another, he was determined to finish what he had started, but he knew that he'd need a handheld laser cutter if he were to fix what he had identified as the problem. Necessity often outweighed availability these days.

The sound of metal on wood echoed in Finn's workshop until Tipper appeared at the door, nudging his bowl across the entryway. He laid his chin on the threshold and made a sound as he looked up at Finn.

Finn laughed, "You've had enough for tonight, Tip. Let's go out for a bit."

He got out of his chair and scratched Tip's head. They went downstairs, enjoying the cool, still night air while Tipper did his business, and then returned to the comfort of Finn's apartment. After putting the bowl back in the kitchen, he and Tip headed for the couch, both sitting in their usual positions—Finn in the middle and Tip stretched out next to him. They had a comfortable life together, both giving each other something they could not give themselves. For Finn, it was a purpose. Looking after another living being, knowing that Tip relied on him, was a reason to continue. Finn had never thought about suicide, but he often questioned what he was doing and for what greater purpose. *Survival*, he thought, *I'm just surviving.*

He pointed at the TV, and the screen turned on, casually motioning with his right hand to change the channel. As he flipped through the channels, he thought about the actors pretending to be other people, wondering if they were fulfilled. He wondered if they had found purpose through their work, or like him, if their job was just a means to an end.

He was often surprised that society had overcome the chaos first caused by Styre. Once infected, the symptoms came quickly. It started with profuse sweating, a high fever, and then blisters on the skin. After that, the blisters would seep pus, and then the body began to dry itself out as if all the moisture were slowly evaporating. As such, organ failure was the final stage before death. The entire process took two days. People started dropping like flies, with millions dying in the first month. When Styre hit in 2062, it spread through touch, lingered on surfaces, and traveled through the air. It was the deadliest virus the world had ever seen.

Over the past nine years, governments had worked tirelessly to develop a cure, but to no avail. The closest they had come was what the world was still using nearly a decade later, a suppression treatment that had to be injected daily. Before that, the world had panicked, and those who weren't self-isolating out of fear of catching the virus had turned to looting and violence for resources. The electrical grid had shut down, public transportation came to a halt, and governments around the world struggled to maintain order. And then the treatment was announced; as if out of nowhere, a breakthrough had been found. Suddenly, humans had a way to carry on—though the virus still lurked. The global infection rate hit 100%, but with the treatments, life slowly returned to some semblance of what it had been before.

Finn thought about when he learned his parents had died. It was his first year out of college; he was twenty-two years old and busy looking for a job in the city. He had been watching the news, unaware of the catastrophic implications this "unknown" virus carried. He had spoken with his parents, and although they weren't worried, something inside Finn told him that this was more serious than the news portrayed it to be. He decided the best course of action would be to leave the city and get away from people as soon as possible. His parents agreed that he could stay at their cabin outside of the city, but they were staying put. "New

York has been my home for over twenty-five years. If I'm going to die, I'm going to die in my home," his father had said, refusing to call the city by its new name. He was a good man with a unique set of values that both supported and destroyed him.

Having spent weeks at the cabin, tinkering with mechanical gadgets and keeping an eye on the news, and not having been able to reach his parents in over a week, that's when he saw it. The daily death toll for Central—as well as the nation—was broadcast each day, along with the days' recent victims of the Styre virus. July 5th, 2062, Elliot Brantley and Tara Brantley. His heart sank. A week later, his parents' lawyer called and informed him that he needed to come back to the city to deal with family affairs.

As he collected his things and drove back, his mind and the roads were empty. The grass along the highway was overgrown, and the city he used to call home was almost unrecognizable. Garbage had piled up, windows on some of the shops were broken, and there was no power. He saw some people on the streets, but most were holed up indoors or presumably dead.

He met with the lawyer, nodded his head at the condolences he was given, signed some papers, and was given a check for five thousand Units. Digital currency had replaced cash over a decade ago, and the world now operated on the Unit standard. His parents had been in debt, so most of the family assets, including the cabin, had been sold, with the proceeds going to the bank. A lifetime of memories and laughs, and five thousand Units were all that he had to remember his parents by. His lawyer recommended he find a Dose Depot to collect his allotted treatments before it was too late.

Thirty small, blue liquid capsules were all he was given. One month. Along with having to pay one hundred Units for the injection gun. The government had announced that all citizens would receive one month's worth of treatments before requiring them to find a job, or other means, to continue receiving treatments.

During that month, Finn had come to terms with living in a new reality, one in which survival trumped dreams, and Conserta had been the answer.

While scratching Tip's head, he looked down at the coffee table and saw one blue capsule and the injection gun. His last dose before he would receive ten more tomorrow. He had always planned to save the extra three doses a week, but finances were tight, and he had sold them to make ends meet.

"Let's go, Tip," Finn said. "Time for bed."

As Tipper got off the couch and curled up on his bed by the window, Finn lay on top of his grey sheets and stared at the ceiling, wondering if anything would ever interrupt the monotonous routine that had consumed his life. The things he had once dreamed of doing, or achieving, were now nothing more than scant ideas that would never come to fruition. He had been angry, at first, knowing that he would never achieve them, but that anger had turned into a numbness that now consumed him.

Tomorrow is another day, he thought, *and with that comes endless possibilities*, recalling what his father had always told him as a child. As Finn closed his eyes, he thought about the next day, not expecting anything to be different, but hoping for something more.

Chapter 2

The next morning began the same as all the others before it. Though the day was different, the routine was the same. The alarm went off at 3:30 a.m., the lights turned on, and Finn opened his eyes to stare at the ceiling before getting out of bed and heading into the kitchen. He poured himself a cup of coffee, put food in Tip's bowl while the dog did his early morning stretch on the couch, and then headed back into his bedroom to put on his blue Conserta coveralls.

As he had done each morning before heading off for the tram, he walked over to his coffee table, inserted the blue dose into the injector, and placed it against the upper part of his inside forearm. Another day, he thought as he pulled the trigger, and he watched the glass vial empty into his bloodstream.

"You be good," he said to Tip, whose face was buried in his bowl of dog food. On his way out the door, he caught a reflection of himself in the mirror, and the man he saw was no longer someone he recognized. His blue eyes that were once bright and full of curiosity had seemed to fade, and his once dirty-blond hair had turned almost brown, the same color as the stubble on his face. He had a strong jawline, and his cheekbones were now more pronounced since high-protein food had become a luxury he couldn't regularly afford. He thought of himself as handsome, at least that's what his mother had always told him, but as his father would retort, "Handsome can't put food on the table."

Ever the pragmatist, thought Finn, as he closed the door behind him and headed for the Conserta tram.

As usual, he waited beside the mag-lev rails and nodded in silence at the other men from Sector Three. A distant whir signaled that the tram was approaching, and as it pulled into the station, Finn noticed something that stood out against the white carriage. A spray-painted black stencil of a hand making a gun symbol with pointer and middle finger together and the thumb extended, pointed upward. Finn stared at it before the doors opened, and he took a seat.

"You saw it, too then, eh?" said Corbin, who sat next to him.

"Been seeing it more and more lately. I heard it belonged to some rebel group, but it's hard to know for sure with mixed messages on the news. Do you know what it means?"

"It's a sign of hope," said Corbin. "Whatever it is, and whoever it belongs to, sometimes the question is more important than the answer."

Finn paused for a moment, reflecting on all the times his mother had talked to him about hope before saying, "Maybe you're right. Perhaps the world will be better someday. But it's not really my concern. I'm not in a position to do anything about it."

"You aren't until you are," said Corbin.

The remainder of the ride was spent in silence, with Finn thinking about what his friend had said. Thinking about his life, he didn't expect there ever to be an opportunity for him to do anything different from what he was doing now, and even less so, do anything to make a positive impact on humanity. Existential questions swirled in his head until his thoughts were interrupted by the automatic voice telling the workers to depart the tram.

In the equipment room, Finn saw Wes gathering his tools and walked over to him.

"So, the other day, you asked if I needed something."

"What'll it be?" replied Wes with a grin.

"I need a handheld laser cutter. Do you think you can manage that?"

"I work in Sector Four," he said with a wink. "We've got all the good stuff up there. Shouldn't be a problem. I can have it by the end of the day. I'll meet you at the Conserta Dose Depot on the first floor. Payday today should be busy enough that I can get it to you without being noticed."

"I owe you," said Finn, patting Wes on the shoulder.

After the men had gathered their tools, filed into their appropriate elevators, and entered their designated workshops, the day began. Noises once again filled the massive warehouse of workshops that comprised Sector Three, and Corbin and Finn settled into their routine. Old robots, broken machinery, and outdated appliances were taken from a pile, moved to the table, fixed, and then shipped out, back into the world until they returned to Sector Three to be repaired again. An endless cycle, similar to taking doses, Finn had once thought.

"You ever think we're just like the junk that we fix?" asked Finn.

"Feeling philosophical today, are we?" Corbin asked with a smile. "I'll indulge you. Go on."

"We," said Finn, picking up a mechanical arm with only two fingers still intact, "are the same as all this broken stuff. The doses keep us from falling into permanent disarray, just like we do with this junk."

"Bit of a bleak outlook. You've got to start living your life, my friend, and not looking at it as survival. Surviving is easy, it's the living part that takes practice. Plus, you've got Tipper to look after."

"A dog isn't exactly the same as a family."

"Maybe so, but he's all you've got, so make the most of it. Plus, it's payday. Are we still on for that drink after work?"

"You better believe it."

"Good, because I've already let the wife know I'll be out tonight," said Corbin with a chuckle. "I'll catch up with you after work."

"Perfect," said Finn, as he slipped his welding helmet over his head and focused his attention on the mechanical arm.

As the day progressed, Finn kept looking at the digital clock on the wall, hoping, as he did each day, that time would go faster.

The crowd of protestors focused on the woman standing on the steps of BioDose, one of the leading manufacturers of the Styre treatments. Her long brown hair was pulled tight into a ponytail and her tan skin glowed in the sunlight. The unzipped black leather jacket showed a shirt underneath with the same stencil from the tram—a hand making a gun pointed upward.

"We demand a new government, one in which the people of this country are treated as equal! A government that distributes doses equally and fairly! A government that doesn't enslave its people just so they can survive! Survival is no longer an option—we must live!"

The crowd erupted with cheers. Many carried signs with the same symbol as on the shirt of Alayna Ramos. Now thirty-one years old, Alayna had been a voice against the government since the start of the post-Styre policies and regulations. Her ambition and understanding of the people she was fighting for had led her to become a symbol against the regime she was protesting.

"The people of this country will no longer stand for the inequality President Burke spews forth in his policies. Enough of the platitudes, the empty promise of a cure, and enough of the elite stockpiling doses while we live week to week. We all have the right to life, we shouldn't have to break our backs to have it!"

Again, the crowd cheered. Consisting mostly of laborers, blue-collar workers, and people who did what they had to do just to get a daily dose, people around the world, and especially in Central, were becoming more vocal about how governments had responded to the Styre outbreak.

"You call this the 'new normal'? Are we any better off than we were pre-Styre?"

"NO!" the crowd yelled back.

"Is it fair that we have to live day to day in hopes of a better tomorrow?"

"NO!"

"The time for change is now! I no longer worry about humanity; I fight for it. So, make noise, let your voice be heard, and together we can create change."

With her right hand, Alayna made a gun with her first two fingers and thumb and stretched it up into the air. The crowd did the same, and at that moment, Alayna knew that everything she had worked so hard for was no longer just her fight, but now belonged to the people she was fighting for.

Finn looked up at the digital clock just as it turned five, and the red lights flashed, signaling that the workday was over.

"Another day, another dose," said Corbin, putting away his tools and looking over at his workmate.

"Another dose, another day," said Finn, begrudgingly.

Corbin laughed, "Come on, man, cheer up. Let's go get paid."

The men in Sector Three filed into the elevators, all of them eager to collect their pay and supply of doses. Most jobs gave people a form with their allotted treatments that they would need to take to a Dose Depot to collect, but since Conserta employed thousands of people, the company had its own in-house Dose Depot, and today, that's where most people were headed.

After putting his tools back in the equipment room, Finn walked through the dimly lit corridors of Conserta to the Dose Depot. Men in different colored jumpsuits soon filled the halls. Finn wondered what it would be like to have a job that provided more than ten doses a week. He dreamed about the security that would provide, both physically and mentally.

With a job like that, he thought, *I could stockpile doses and retire early.*

No more blue jumpsuits, no more early morning tram rides, and no more time wasted doing something he didn't aspire to do.

The large neon sign of the Dose Depot flashed in the distance, and lines started forming. From behind, Finn felt a hand on his shoulder and knew from the meaty weight that it was Wes.

"Took a while, but I found what you were looking for."

As hundreds of men queued in front of the dispensary, Wes pulled a small cylindrical tube from his pocket and held it in his palm.

"You think this will work?" he asked.

"It's perfect," said Finn, taking the laser cutter and stealthily placing it in his pocket. "I can't thank you enough. I'll have it back to you as soon as I can."

"No rush," said Wes. "Sector Four won't realize it's missing, and even if they do, they can afford to replace it."

"Thank you. Oh, I didn't have a chance to ask earlier, but Corbin and I are grabbing a drink after we get through this line. You in?"

"Always," smiled Wes.

The crowd of men in colored work suits slowly moved forward, each man first approaching a window to swipe his wrist, which would electronically deposit their paychecks into their account, and then moving to the Dose Depot for treatments. Despite the setbacks in society caused by Styre, Finn had always wondered if there was a more efficient way to get the doses. Apparently, waiting in line was the most efficient method the government had been able to conceive.

When it was his turn, Finn approached the first window, placed his wrist on a glass panel, and a message on the window flashed, confirming that his weekly Units had been deposited into his account. He didn't have to look at it to know how much it was. His salary hadn't changed during the five years he had been working in Sector Three. Enough to survive, but never enough to live the life he had once dreamed about. Before he turned to go to the window at the Dose Depot, the payroll manager handed him a folded piece of paper.

"What's this?"

"Not for me to know. Please move along."

Before he had a chance to open it, the men behind him pushed forward, and he moved to the window at the Dose Depot.

"Wrist, please," said the attendant. Finn placed his wrist over the glass panel on the edge, and his information flashed onto the window.

"Ten doses for Brantley. Confirmed."

The attendant swiped his hand, and Finn's data disappeared. Next to the glass panel, ten blue vials popped up from the ledge's small holes, and

Finn grabbed them, placing them into his pocket. *Ten more days*, Finn thought, *it's always just ten more days*. He walked out into the main concourse of Conserta and opened the piece of paper the attendant had handed him.

"Finn Brantley: Please go to Sector Three head office immediately. "

In all his years at Conserta, he had only been to the head office once, on his first day. He thought about what they could want to talk to him about. He thought about the illegal laser cutter he had in his pocket, but there was no way they knew about that.

"Are you ready to go?" asked Corbin, who had just finished collecting his pay and doses.

Finn showed him the note and asked, "What do you think this is about?"

"No idea. But if the head office is asking for you, you don't really have any choice but to go."

"Wes is coming tonight as well. Go meet up with him first. I'll see what this is all about and I'll meet up with you guys after. Where'd you want to go tonight?"

"The usual?"

"Archer's it is. I'll see you soon."

"Good luck up there."

Finn walked over to the elevators in the main concourse and pressed the button for the seventeenth floor. His uneasiness grew but at least now it was justified. As the doors closed, he thought about the first time he had been in the Sector Three head office: the unwelcome fluorescent lights, the unnecessarily wide-open floor plan, and the big black desk that the Sector Three Overseer sat behind. He hadn't enjoyed his first visit here, and Finn wasn't expecting this time to be any better.

The doors opened, and light flooded into the dark elevator. The secretary looked up at him and said, "Finn Brantley. Please go in. The Overseer is expecting you."

She motioned to two large, black doors, and Finn walked across the large reception room and opened one of the doors. The anxiety inside him was palpable. His heart seemed to be beating like a giant drum and his palm was sweaty as he pulled open the door.

The room was sizable, with no windows, no plants, and no artwork. A large black desk was positioned at the end of the room, behind which sat a middle-aged man with broad shoulders, short black hair tinged with gray, and a disproportionately large belly compared to his skinny legs. He had a black mustache and wore black-framed glasses that sat at a tilt on his misshapen head. Corbin had once commented that the Overseer looked like something he'd draw with his left hand.

"Mr. Brantley, please, have a seat," he said, extending his thick hand toward the single black chair in front of the desk.

Finn sat down, and as expected, the chair was uncomfortable. He stared across at the man in front of him, who to this day, he wasn't sure what he was called, or if he even had a name. Everyone in Sector Three just referred to him as the Overseer. Despite not having seen this man in over nine years, he looked just the same as when he had met him on his first day.

"Any problems during your shift today?" the man asked.

"Same as usual," Finn said, not sure where the conversation was headed.

"Let me get right down to business," he said. "Sector Three, and Conserta as a whole, no longer requires your services."

Finn felt his throat go dry as he asked, "Am I being transferred?"

"No, Mr. Brantley. We are letting you go."

"On what grounds?"

"As per your Conserta contract signed on November 7, 2062, we are not required to state the reason. Simply put, as of today, you are no longer a Conserta employee."

"You can't do this," said Finn.

"Often, what can and should happen varies greatly from what does. And to your point, we can do this. I assume you've already collected your Units and doses for last week's work?"

"I have."

"Terrific. Conserta would like to thank you for your many years of hard work and wish you the best in whatever it is you do next," he said in an impatient, matter-of-fact tone.

"And what am I supposed to do after my ten doses are gone?"

"That," said the man, his thick jaw protruding from the rest of his face, "is entirely up to you. Today is today; tomorrow is tomorrow. Conserta has fulfilled all its contractual obligations to you. If there are no more questions, I have a lot of work to do. Thank you again, Mr. Brantley." The man stood up and motioned toward the door.

In merely five minutes, Finn's world had been turned upside down. As he walked out the door and back inside the elevator, his mind raced with thoughts. Staring at the wall, Finn began to wonder if this was the end. Would he be able to find another job? Was this the final nail in the coffin? What would he do with Tipper? Would anyone show up to his funeral? He'd been in precarious situations before, having to scrape for doses, but now, he had ten days left to live and wasn't sure if there would be any more after that.

Once out of the elevator, Finn got into a tram leading into the city and stared through the window at the rainy world outside. Neon signs flashed by as the raindrops battered the glass. Finn sat in silence, his thoughts nothing more than noise inside his head, like the faint buzz of a fly. After the tram pulled into his station, Finn exited the train and left the platform, making his way through the city to District 1 to meet his friends. The streets were filled with food stalls, people walking hurriedly to get home and out of the rain, away from the smell of desperation. Living in such a perpetual state of unknown, Finn no longer recognized the beauty around him.

He grabbed the handle of a large black door with a neon sign above it that read Archer's and opened it. There was a faint buzz of conversation while music played in the background. Waitresses in black dresses moved about the place, dropping off drinks and tending to the guests. At a booth

23

in the back of the bar, he saw Wes and Corbin in their blue suits and walked over to them.

"Hey, look who made it!" said Wes, taking a drink of his beer. Finn sat down and nodded.

"What'd head office want?" Corbin asked. Wes looked over to Finn, waiting for his response.

"I got fired."

"You what?" Corbin asked. "Fired? Like, for good?"

"Yep."

"Why?"

"The Overseer didn't say. Just said that my services were no longer required."

"That fat fucker, I never liked him," said Corbin. "He looks like God spilled a person."

Finn cracked a smile, and Wes caught the eye of the waitress, holding up three fingers, signaling for another round. "That's just like Conserta. Use us for what they need and then toss us out, like unwanted junk. How many doses you got saved up?"

"None," said Finn. "I've got ten from this past week, but over the years, I've had to sell any extra to pay for food, buy parts, fix up the place. You know how it is."

"Ten days," said Corbin, almost to himself. "Seems like the only choice you've got is to find another job or die."

Choice, Finn thought, *is a luxury reserved for those who can afford it.*

"Maybe it's fate," said Finn. "Maybe my life is supposed to end in ten days."

"Fate is a word used by weak-willed people," said Wes. "I'll be having none of that kind of talk at the table." He looked across at Finn. "Giving up is not even worth considering. You got fired, fine. Now, you've got to think about what you're going to do next."

"I'm with Wes on this," said Corbin. "You're young, you've got a lot of life to live."

Finn took a drink of his beer and thought about what his friends had said. For him, the gravity of the situation currently exceeded his ability to deal with it. The stability to maintain his life had been pulled out from under him, and now, sitting with his two friends, he felt more lost than he had in a long time.

"I suppose it's back to the grind of finding a new job," said Finn. "Not much else I can do at this point."

"Well," said Wes, with a smile, "you could always start working the streets. Plenty of ladies need a strong young man like you."

"Can you imagine?" laughed Corbin. "Out there with all the other dose doxies, just hoping someone wants to give you a ride for a dose or two. That'd be a sight."

Finn smiled and raised his glass. "To new beginnings, and hopefully more than the ten in my pocket." The three of them clinked their beers and drank in silence as the music in the bar filled the void. The neon lights from the signs above the bar reflected off the glass table, and for a moment, Finn felt he was exactly where he wanted to be. As the night wore on, they continued to drink, sharing stories from their time at Conserta, reminiscing about life pre-Styre, and theorizing about what the future held.

"There's got to be a cure," said Corbin, who now, after several beers, was at the point of indulging in conspiracy theories.

"If there were, they would have found it and started to produce it by now," said Wes.

"Ah, but that's my point. Maybe they don't want us to have it."

"Who exactly is 'they'?" asked Finn.

"The elites. The government," said Corbin, and in a hushed tone, added, "the Illuminati."

"Get out of here," laughed Wes. "The treatments are the best we've got. And everyone, including the president, has to take them."

"Have you ever seen Burke inject himself?" asked Corbin.

"Well, I've never seen him brush his teeth, but I assume he does."

"I'm telling you, the treatments are bullshit. There's something more out there. What do all men with power want?"

The others waited, knowing Corbin would soon answer his own question.

"More power. It's a tale as old as time. There's something weird going on, and you guys know exactly what I'm talking about."

Finn and Wes laughed. "May be time to get you back to your wife," said Finn. As the three men drank together, Finn thought about what Corbin had said—*there's something more out there*. He thought about what that something would be, or if it even existed at all.

As they continued to drink and laugh, Wes finished his beer and then placed his hand on Finn's shoulder. "You have to believe that things will work out. I know it's tough right now, but optimism is a strategy for making a better future. Unless you believe that the future can be better, you're unlikely to step up and take responsibility for making it so."

Finn took in the words, the ideas of fate and controlling one's destiny swirling around his brain. He knew Wes was right, that ultimately it was up to him how his life turned out, but with the soft numbing feeling of alcohol, any thoughts about manifesting a better future seemed like something that would have to wait until tomorrow.

After another beer, and Finn's thoughts drifted to Tipper alone at home, the trio decided to call it a night. They swiped their wrists on a glass panel on the table, paying their tabs, and helped Corbin out of the booth. Outside, the rain continued to fall on the dark streets, and Finn hailed a taxi for Corbin.

Once inside, Corbin rolled down the window and, through slurred words, looked at Finn and said, "You drown not by falling into the river, but by staying submerged in it."

"Another horoscope?"

"Paulo Coelho. Read a book, Finn," said Corbin with a smile. The window rolled up, and the taxi sped off into the night, the rain continuing to fall on those still left on the street.

Wes pulled out a cigarette and started to smoke. "Think I'm going to walk home, I'm not too far."

"I'll probably head for the tram."

Wes put a hand on Finn's shoulder and said, "Look, today was rough. There's no denying that. But things don't get easier or harder, they just are. Start looking for a new job. I'll put out some feelers and see what I can find. Things will be okay."

"I appreciate that," said Finn. "I'll see you," he paused for a moment before adding, "when I see you."

Wes nodded, pulled up the collar of his jacket over his work suit, and walked off into the night, plumes of smoke mixing with the falling rain.

Finn was alone. The rain hitting the street echoed in his ears. The nearest tram station was about a kilometer away, and Finn headed in that direction. The night was quiet, and those still out seemed to move with a purpose. No one lingered, nobody chatted with one another; everyone was moving. The neon signs of bars and shops illuminated the streets and the late-night food vendors selling hot noodles with plant-based meat.

As Finn walked, he thought about the conversation with the Overseer. In less time than it had taken him to apply for the job, he had lost it. The ease with which it happened seemed almost unnatural. He continued to walk, the rain falling off his black jacket when out of the corner of his eye, he saw a group of people about a block away. The bright blue neon sign of a Dose Depot lit up the street, and as Finn stopped to watch, he heard shouting. He slowly started walking toward the commotion, and suddenly, someone from the group threw a brick through the window of the Dose Depot. The sound of breaking glass mixed with the cheers from the mob.

As if fueled from the thrown brick, the group moved forward and started pushing their way into the Depot. Finn watched as men with steel pipes hit the door and broke the other remaining windows. The Dose

Depot's neon blue sign started flashing red, and a siren drowned out the yells from those breaking in.

Finn had seen riots at a Dose Depot before on the news, but this was the first one he had witnessed in person. He knew they had fail-safes in place to lock down the doses in case of a breach, but that didn't seem to stop those desperate enough to face legal ramifications if it meant the possibility of prolonging their lives.

A drone above with a spotlight shined down on the Depot and the mob, a voice on their intercom saying: "Cease and desist. Police are on their way. Any further action will result in the use of force."

Finn continued to watch. He knew he should leave, but the alcohol had numbed his mind, and he couldn't help but stare as the mob attempted to break open the sealed vaults of the Dose Depot.

"This is your final warning," the booming voice rang out through the streets. The spotlight cut through the rain, illuminating the Depot and those now inside. A crack rang out, and a flurry of rubber balls shot out from the drone, immediately felling those they contacted. Finn could hear a police siren echoing through the streets a few blocks away. He took one last look at the scene at the Depot and decided it was best not to be in the vicinity when the police arrived.

Finn walked through the empty streets, the rain now seeping through his jacket. Once at the tram station, he took the short ride back to District Seven and entered his building. The security guard was asleep, and as he waited for the elevator, he ran his hand through his wet, brown hair.

Inside the elevator, the hologram on the door continued to run government propaganda, saying: "Doses: the viable solution for today's world." He wasn't sure what caused him to do it, but without thinking, he punched through the hologram, his fist meeting the steel door. His mind was in a daze from his time at the bar, but he knew he'd feel the pain in his hand tomorrow.

After he entered his apartment, he took the elevator downstairs, allowed Tipper to relieve himself, then went back upstairs, fed Tipper, took off his rain-drenched clothes, placed his remaining ten doses on the coffee table next to the injector, and got into bed. He thought about finding a new job. He thought of other ways to prolong his life. Finn still wasn't sure why he wanted to live. Perhaps it was just ingrained in humans to fight for survival. Now, the problem wasn't so much why, but how. He closed his eyes. The sound of the rain pattering against the window, along with the alcohol in his body, lulled him to sleep, allowing the worries of today to be dealt with tomorrow.

A Viral State

Chapter 3

The rain had stopped, but gray clouds still lingered outside as the pale morning light reached into Finn's bedroom. He cracked an eye and felt a slight throbbing in his head. For him, a hangover was a familiar, albeit unwelcome, old friend. Finn looked at the hologram clock—nine a.m. No matter how badly he wanted to, he could never sleep in after a night of drinking.

He threw off the blankets and lay in bed for a moment, staring at the ceiling, lost in the empty thoughts in his head. Finn swung his legs off the bed, allowing his feet to feel the cool concrete floor. After throwing on shorts and a shirt, he walked into the kitchen, poured Tip a bowl of food, and himself a bowl of cereal. They ate in silence, with Tip focused on his food and Finn staring at the ten blue doses on the coffee table.

"What to do?" asked Finn out loud, with Tip momentarily looking up at him before returning to the bowl.

After they had finished eating, he sat on the couch and lined up the doses in a row. He grabbed one, put it in the injector, placed it against his arm, and squeezed the trigger. The blue liquid shot into his body, and for at least one more day, he was guaranteed life.

He thought about what his friends had suggested, finding a new job, and sighed at the daunting task. Having not had to worry about employment or doses for nine years, the thought of starting somewhere new and going through the rigmarole of applications and interviews was something he dreaded. He wasn't even sure if it was possible within ten days, certainly not with big corporations, but he knew of some smaller companies and shops that might be worth checking out.

Finn flipped his wrist to turn on the TV and, after a moment, switched it off. He was in no mood for whatever specious comments the government was eager to deliver to the masses.

"Let's go, Tip. Time for some fresh air." He got off the couch, put an electronic tracking collar around Tipper's neck, laced up his running shoes, and turned to look at Tipper.

The black dog hobbled over, and Finn strapped him into a harness with a wheel that he had built. It wasn't pretty, but with the mechanical leg still not ready, it was enough to provide Tipper with the mobility that all dogs crave. Once Tipper had given him a bark of approval, they left the apartment and headed out into the city.

Finn needed time to think, process his situation, and devise a plan. Time wasn't on his side, but he had to come at this logically and strategically if a solution were to be found. Outside of his building and below the gray sky, Finn quickly stretched and started to jog down the street, with Tip running by his side. The wind felt cool against his face, and the rhythmic pounding of his feet against the road seemed to drown the throbbing in his head.

Finn thought about the little savings he had stashed away, somewhere close to one thousand Units. Yesterday's pay from Conserta had already been allocated for food and rent for the next month. He knew of people on the street who sold doses, but never having been that desperate, he had no idea what small fortune they might cost. Dose depots were also out of the question without a digital prescription from the job he no longer had. If worse came to worst, at least street doses were an option, and he filed that idea in the back of his mind.

As he ran, he thought about how the city had changed. Small stores that he had once loved to shop in as a kid had closed after Styre, no longer able to sustain themselves, as the products they sold weren't necessary for survival. The butcher shop he had always gone to with his father on Sundays had also closed. Small shops such as these had either been replaced by huge conglomerates, like Conserta or replaced with shops that sold necessary goods.

His wrist pulsated, signaling that he had just finished five kilometers. He slowed down to a walk and looked down at Tip, always eager for a run, but grateful for the break. There were a few people out on the streets, but on an overcast day before lunch, most people were at work.

Finn leaned down to pet Tip and said, "Come on, time to head home." The two of them made their way back from where they had come, taking in the surroundings that had seemed to blur together while on their run.

Tech stores, groceries, spare parts stores, bodegas, and Dose Depots populated the ground level of downtown Central. There were a few restaurants that still operated, but since it was cheaper, most people these days cooked. The skyscrapers that towered over the city still housed the offices of corporations and the millions of people that worked to keep them going. Finn wondered how many weekly doses a government official or corporate employee received, but since those numbers were never disclosed, he was likely to never know.

He stopped in a small corner store to buy vegetables and tofu for lunch, and a dog treat for Tip. On his way out, he heard someone yell, "Finn!"

He turned to look and yelled back, "Josta!" A skinny man with curly brown hair and a blue shirt ran toward him, a black backpack bouncing on his shoulders.

"Finn, my man, I had a feeling I'd see you today. I woke up, you know, and I just had this feeling I'd run into you. And now, here you are!"

"Crazy how that works," laughed Finn. He had met Josta Almeda at university over a decade ago, who then had been an aspiring chemist. Nowadays, Finn wasn't exactly sure what Josta did, but knew he always had his hand in one thing or another.

"What's new with you, man? It's been a few weeks. Glad to see you out of that blue work suit for a change."

"It's a permanent change, unfortunately."

"Conserta let you go, huh? Let me guess, no explanation?"

"None."

"Those corporations are shady like that. How many days you got?"

"Ten, counting today."

"That's rough. Hey, I'm working on something big at the moment, let me buy you a drink this week. We'll talk."

"Sure thing. I'll give you a call."

"No leg yet," asked Josta, nodding toward Tip.

"It's a work in progress."

"Always is," laughed Josta. "I've got to run. It's always good to see you, my friend. Don't let Conserta get you down."

"You're on."

The two gave each other a quick hug and Josta bent down to pet Tip, then they went their separate ways.

As Finn and Tip walked home, he noticed several shops with signs in the window that read, "Not hiring. Don't ask." He had never planned to look for a job in a small street store, but if they weren't hiring, it didn't inspire hope that anyone was.

After he got back to his apartment, he poured a bowl of water for Tip and sat on the couch, staring at the nine remaining blue doses on the table. With no job prospects, little money, and no real assets, Finn didn't think things were going to work out, but he also didn't want to let them go.

———————

The week wore on, with each day bringing more certainty that Finn's existence would come to an end. Each day a blue dose was injected, leaving fewer days to be lived. He had made calls to companies, applied for jobs online, and asked his friends to help. The answer was always a resounding no.

"Sorry, Finn," said Corbin, who had called three days after their night out. "I've asked everyone I know—no one needs an engineer. I even tried to find some manual labor jobs for you, but no one is hiring."

There were three doses left. He knew that after they were gone, the symptoms would start, and he'd be dead within two days. There was no point in trying to go to a hospital. At first, ICUs were bombarded with patients, but after a month, hospitals began to turn away Styre patients, telling them to make their peace and die at home.

Finn wondered what it would be like, to suffer alone in his apartment, with only Tip there, uncertain of what was happening, but left alone once Styre had run its course. He wondered who would miss him, and more importantly, he felt an emptiness inside, knowing that his impact on this world had been nonexistent. He had worked for years to maintain his life but never did anything to better society or to move the human race forward. He had inspired no one and never had the chance to create any lasting legacy. He thought about what his father had said when he had asked him about death: "No one's ever really gone, our memories live on in the minds of others." Finn wondered how long his memory would continue to live on this Earth. Likely not more than a few years, he thought.

After another day of job applications, phone calls, and thoughts of dying, Finn remembered the laser cutter that Wes had given him, got up from the couch, and turned on the light in his workshop. Tip's mechanical leg stared back at him, reminding him of his failure to help the one being in his life who had always been there for him.

He sat down at the table, turned on the glass display, and picked up the laser cutter. The night sky was clear, and the stars and moon shone through the window. He began to work, meticulously moving wires, and using the laser cutter to make the precise cuts he hadn't been able to before. The power supply for the leg was fashioned out of an old drill battery from work, though he had worked to isolate the condensed particles and transfer them into a smaller container, about the size of a watch battery. Based on his calculations, the ever-moving particles would supply power to the leg for at least the next fifty years, which for Tipper, was more than enough time. The minutes turned into hours, and the moon moved across the sky as Finn worked. His workspace was cluttered with spare parts, particle condensers, wires, blueprints, a small tablet containing the coding for the leg, and various tools he had collected over the years.

Finn moved the welding shield up onto his forehead and looked down at the leg. He placed it on the glass panel, picked up the tablet, and checked the code one last time before uploading the algorithm he had painstakingly worked on.

When it finished, he picked up the leg and held it, the early morning sun shone through the window and reflected off the black metal. He placed it back on the table and decided to get some rest before seeing if his hard work had paid off.

His bed was comforting, and he let his thoughts fade away as sleep took over. After what seemed to be only a few minutes, he woke up to Tip licking his face. The sun was now overhead, and he realized he had slept far longer than he had anticipated.

Finn yawned and then went into his workshop, brushed aside the bric-a-brac strewn across the table, and grabbed the leg.

"Come on, Tip. Time to make you whole."

Sitting on the couch, Finn carefully attached the leg to the small nub of what remained of Tipper's missing leg. A look of curiosity and apprehension appeared on the dog's face, and Finn said, "Don't worry, boy. I got it this time."

With Tipper standing upright on the ground, Finn bent down and switched the leg on. After a moment, the leg began to flex a little, matching the other legs. Tipper slowly began to walk, and the mechanical leg moved in sync with the others. Growing more used to the metal leg, Tipper walked faster and jumped, the leg functioning just as a real leg would. He started to bark and ran over to Finn, licking his face.

Finn couldn't help but smile. For the first time in a long time, he felt proud of himself. In the grand scheme of things, a mechanical leg for a dog wasn't a game-changer, but for Tipper, it was.

As Tipper continued to try out his leg, Finn loaded one of the doses into the gun and placed it against his arm. Twenty-four more hours, he thought. The remaining two doses lay on the table, a reminder that his life was coming to a close. As he continued to think about what he would do with his remaining seventy-two hours, his wrist flashed, alerting him of an incoming call. He twisted his wrist outward, and Josta's voice came in through the TV speakers.

"Finn! Sorry, it's taken me so long to call; got caught up with work. What are you up to?"

"Just took my daily dose."

"How many you have left?"

"I've got today, and then two more doses."

"Don't worry; things will be alright. Do you have plans tonight?"

"Nope."

"Terrific. Let's grab a drink. You remember that place downtown, next to my workshop?"

"How could I forget?"

"True, we've had some nights there, eh? How does nine sound?"

"I'll see you then."

Finn turned his wrist inward, and the call ended. He laid back against the couch, watching the sun shine through the clouds, bathing the city in its warmth. With no other plans until the evening, he decided the most productive thing he could do was go for a run. The job hunt had proved to be a frivolous pursuit, and if he stayed inside all day, he was sure the thoughts of dying would drive him insane.

He laced up his shoes, threw on a shirt, and whistled as Tipper came running in from the living room.

"Let's see how you do on the street," he said, scratching Tipper behind his ears.

The afternoon was still. Finn hadn't been outside on a weekday afternoon since he started at Conserta. Sundays were his only days off, and those were usually spent inside, tinkering with small projects, or catching up on sleep.

The run was quiet now that the wheel no longer clicked against the ground. Tipper had grown accustomed to the mechanical leg quickly as if it had been there all along.

The rest of the afternoon was spent watching TV and cleaning up the apartment, during which Finn found himself wondering why he even bothered since he would be gone in a matter of days. Despite the thoughts, the routine helped calm his mind.

Around eight o'clock that evening, he took the tram to District Two, on the edge of downtown, and found a quiet noodle shop about a block from the bar. There, he treated himself to Japanese ramen with bamboo and pork. It cost significantly more than the vegetarian options, but Finn had decided that he would enjoy his last few meals on Earth.

Using chopsticks, he carefully picked up one of the crispy pieces of pork and put it in his mouth, savoring the flavor. The texture and taste of the fried meat brought back memories of his childhood. Growing up, meat had been part of his daily diet, and he never thought twice about the taste. As a child, eating meat was as normal as going to school. Now, livestock required far more resources and manpower than vegetables and grains, making meat a luxury item. He took a drink of beer and stared out the restaurant's large window, the neon lights of the shops opposite him reflected in the glass. He flicked his wrist and the time displayed on the window: 8:30.

He took the time to enjoy his meal, allowing himself to think of it as an experience rather than a necessary habit to fuel his body. A few minutes before nine, he got up from his seat and walked over to the counter to pay. After placing his wrist on the glass panel to pay, he looked past the waiter and saw a small piece of paper on a wall in the back—a black stencil of a hand in the shape of a gun pointed upward. He looked back at the waiter who caught his eye and said, "A necessary end comes when it is most needed."

Finn held his gaze, and before he had a chance to say anything, the waiter walked off to deal with the other customers. He took one last look at the piece of paper and then walked out of the restaurant.

The streets were dark, but the bar was just around the corner—The Drink Depot. Not a very clever name, but it was discreet and always had just enough patrons to not feel like you were alone. Finn pushed open the door and looked around for Josta, though not sure why, as Josta was notoriously late. His tardiness and his tenacity for his work, as far as Finn was concerned, were his defining characteristics.

A few men were sitting at the bar, and several of the tables had people sitting together, talking in hushed tones. The melodic, rhythmic sounds of synthwave added to the ambiance, and Finn walked to an empty table next to the wall. Before he had taken off his jacket, a bot hovered over.

Finn said, "Two beers," and the robot glided back to the bar.

Finn never understood the animosity toward automation. For him, robots were an inevitable part of the technological revolution, and although he felt for those who lost their jobs, the robots were what had kept him employed. Hover bots used in the hospitality industry were among the first to be used commercially, and over the years, Finn had repaired hundreds of them, usually those that had been damaged in bars. Drunks often seemed to think that basic norms of human behavior don't apply toward automated pieces of metal.

The bot moved silently back toward the table, setting down two glasses of beer and moving away just as quickly as it had arrived.

Finn took a sip and sat for a moment thinking about the drawing of the fist he'd seen at the restaurant. It seemed to be appearing more often than before. Maybe it had always been there, and Finn just wasn't paying attention. He glanced at the large glass screen above the bar, watching political pundits justify the government's actions. It seemed the news was the only thing on TV these days. Movies and TV shows were still made, but people were now more focused on survival. Most people living day to

39

day had little time to waste enjoying fictitious dialogue about fictitious events.

The bar door opened, and Josta walked in, wearing a black peacoat with a messenger bag slung across his chest.

After Josta sat down, Finn flicked his wrist to check the time, and Josta said, "Don't even bother checking, you know me; I know I'm late, but late or not, I'm here now."

The two men clinked their glasses together and took a sip of beer.

"How's it been? Not so good, I suppose," said Josta.

"It's been a weird week. I thought I'd have enough time to find another job, but no one is hiring. I guess in a weird way, I've come to terms with the fact that my life is about to end."

Josta smiled and quietly said, "Maybe it doesn't have to."

"Feeling generous? Are you going to make a dose donation to the 'Save Finn Fund'?"

"Something better," Josta said, sliding the strap off his chest and unzipping his bag. He looked around before pulling out a glass pad and placing it on the table.

"I've been working on something for a while now. I'm not saying I have it, but I'm close."

He placed his wrist on the piece of glass, and it turned on, revealing a series of equations, chemical mixtures, and the blueprints of a machine. Finn looked at it, then looked up at Josta.

"Give it to me straight; you know I never understood these things."

"I'm reverse-engineering the treatments."

"That's it? That's the big news? Josta, amigo, loads of people have been trying to reverse-engineer the doses for years now, and no one has even come close."

"They don't have this," he said with a smile as he touched his temple.

"So, you've figured it out?"

Josta looked down at the tablet and then back up at Finn. "Not yet. It's complicated. But I'm close. I still need more time to break down the chemical composition. Even after that, there's still the matter of producing it. My workshop doesn't have nearly the advanced technology that the government uses to make the doses, and even then, I'm not exactly sure what I'd need. Here's a rough idea of what I'm working on," he said, tapping the blueprint of a machine on the tablet.

"A few engineer friends and I have been working to build it, but you know how hard it can be to find parts these days."

"And here I was, thinking you'd found a way to give me more than forty-eight hours of life."

"Amigo, if I could, I would. Maybe in a few months or so, but two days? Impossible."

Finn looked over Josta's shoulder and looked at the TV, reporting on another protest that had taken place earlier that day. He tapped his wrist to the table, and the audio from the TV started playing from a speaker next to their beers. Josta turned to look at the TV as well.

"Earlier this afternoon, around one thousand protesters took part in a demonstration outside a government building, led by Alayna Ramos, one of the de facto leaders of the recent protests."

The TV switched to a shot of Alayna, wearing a shirt with the gun stencil, speaking in front of the protesters.

"The actions of this government, along with others around the planet, have ineffaceably changed our world for the worse. How many of us live in fear of not living to see another day? How long have we waited on the empty promises of a cure? No longer will we accept this system that keeps us enslaved to the government. Today marks a new chapter in our history. We demand fair and equal distribution of treatments and an answer to why, after almost a decade, we have yet to see any progress on a cure. Today, our voices will be heard! We will forever be remembered as the match that lit the flame of a revolution to create a better and more just world, both for us and future generations."

Alayna made a gun with her fingers and raised it into the air. The camera panned out and showed hundreds of other protesters doing the same.

Josta turned around and said, "She's got grit. I like that."

"Do you think it will amount to anything?"

"Not likely, but hey, something must be done, not only for us but for what's left of the world as we know it. But who am I to say? We're both trying to do something that may or may not amount to anything, but at least we're going for it."

"Cheers to that, and cheers to Ramos," said Finn, clinking glasses with Josta.

As they sat together, Josta continued to talk about his work with the doses, most of which was too technically complicated for Finn to understand. Still, he enjoyed the fervent way Josta talked about his work. Although he wouldn't live long enough to see the fruits of his friend's labor, he felt hope that others would.

After twenty minutes of lengthy explanations, Finn said, "Searching for something we know doesn't exist might give you purpose, but it's ultimately a futile pursuit."

"It is until it isn't," replied Josta with a smile. "Sometimes, humans will have to overcome the impossible."

Finn admired his optimism, something he wished he had more of given his current situation, but he doubted a more positive outlook would really change much.

Finn looked down at the schematics and chemical molecules on the tablet before Josta laughed and said, "If you keep thinking about it, you're going to confuse yourself more than you already are."

"You picked a strange time to give up your cushy lab job. What are you even doing for doses these days?"

"We live in strange times," said Josta. "For doses, what can I say? A little of this, a little of that."

"So, you're making and selling designer drugs."

"If the rich elites want to pay me in doses so they can feel something they don't normally feel, who am I to say no? It's a seller's market."

Finn smiled. Josta had been a brilliant chemistry student at university but was often accused, though never convicted, of stealing chemicals from the school's lab to mix up his concoctions in his dorm. People had paid him cash then, but these days, a dose had more value.

Finn glanced up at an analog clock on the wall, a relic, and saw that it was just past midnight. He now had a little less than forty-eight hours before Styre would run its course, and he would be gone from this Earth.

The two men continued to drink, with Finn still failing to understand the intricacies of Josta's explanations, but engaged, nonetheless. The night wore on, and beers were consumed until Finn decided that waking up hungover with such little life to live wasn't the best way to spend his time. Outside the bar, standing on the dark street, Finn said, "I'm sorry I won't be able to see if you crack the code or not."

"Just a matter of time. I'm sorry things didn't work out sooner. You know if I had any extra doses to spare, you'd be the first to get them."

"I appreciate that, Josta."

"Look, we've been friends for a long time, so I won't sugarcoat it. I'm not going to mourn your passing; I'm going to revel in the fact that we have shared over a decade of friendship, not something many people these days can say. When we're born, we're all diagnosed with the same condition: eventual death. That's to be expected. One day, my time will come as well. I wish there were more I could do for you, but I promise you this: I will continue my work, so others won't meet the same fate."

"You're a good friend, Josta. We've had some good times over the years, haven't we?"

"We most certainly have, my friend."

The two men hugged, and Finn took one last look at his friend before they turned and walked in opposite directions. Walking under the cloudy dark sky, Finn thought about his life and everything it had amounted to during his thirty-one years. Compared to the average life expectancy of sixty, factoring in Styre, he had come up short. As he continued to walk, still reflecting on the past, he wondered what he would have done differently if he had the chance. He thought about Josta and their time at college, and the woman on TV, protesting. He thought about what the waiter had said to him at the restaurant and wondered if he would live long enough to understand what he had meant. Finn kept walking, letting his mind wander as the dark clouds bellowed out with thunder, signaling that tomorrow would be another day of rain.

Chapter 4

Alayna sat at her kitchen table and stared at the rain. Despite the weather, the protest scheduled for this afternoon would still be held. Weather doesn't stand in the way of progress, she thought to herself as she pulled her dark brown hair up into a messy bun and flipped her wrist to unmute the TV. President Burke was speaking from the capital building and despite Alayna's personal resentment toward the man, she was always interested in hearing what new drivel the government had come up with.

"Over the years, scientists around the country have worked diligently toward finding a cure for Styre. Today, I am proud to announce that we are one step closer to achieving that goal."

Alayna scoffed and then took a sip of coffee. Burke and his cronies were always "one step closer" but never once was there any clarification on what exactly that step was.

"The past decade has reshaped who we as a people are, and our perceptions of how a society should be structured and governed."

He was right about that, thought Alayna.

Nobody except the elite were happy with how things had been handled since Styre hit. The government had mandated a state of emergency and overhauled the constitution, enabling Burke to remain in power for as long as he saw fit. Legally, no one was really sure how it was done, but the excuse had been that stable leadership requires a consistent presence in order to achieve positive results. Alayna, along with many others, believed it to be nothing more than an excuse to maintain power, but there was little they could do to stop it since voting was no longer permitted or, as Burke had said, "necessary."

"As always, our government is making every effort to find a cure while drafting policies that will directly benefit the people. Your confidence and belief in what we can accomplish together are appreciated." The news channel switched back to a panel of reporters who began to talk about the hard work and numerous accomplishments made by the government, and Alayna flipped her wrist, turning off the TV.

She had always wondered how people could have created a system that became bigger than itself and allowed people like Burke to consolidate power so quickly. Conversely, if such a system could be created, it could be destroyed, and through peaceful demonstrations and activism, that's what she intended to do. Like many in District Eight, Alayna had grown up poor. Her parents worked dead-end jobs to provide a better life for her and her sister but always took time to talk to them about the importance of standing up for their values.

"All good things require hard work, dedication, and the willingness to sacrifice," her father had said. "Standing up for what you believe is one of the hardest things to do, but ultimately the right thing."

The words still echoed in her head despite his passing when she was seventeen. His cancer had finally caught up with him, and despite the availability of treatments, he didn't have enough money to afford them. With little money for school, Alayna and her sister had decided to join the Army. There were no wars to be fought, but the military provided free meals and a small salary that both she and her sister, Maria, were able to stash away. They stayed in the Army for eight years, with Alayna becoming a medic and her sister a mechanic. In the last few years of their service, the military also provided a steady supply of doses and for the most part, Alayna was satisfied. They had been stationed in several posts abroad, including in South Korea and Turkey, which for Alayna, had felt more like an adventure than actual work. Despite the world initially falling apart when Styre hit, the Ramos sisters had each other, and the government took care of its soldiers. At twenty-five, Alayna was happy. Joining the Army wasn't something she had planned, but it provided her with a life that otherwise would have been unattainable on her own. In 2067, everything changed. The government announced cuts to its military budget, something no one had ever expected. The initial budget cuts were felt by personnel, with millions of people being let go. Alayna and Maria returned home to Central, both alone, after losing their mother to Styre a few years prior. With no further assistance from the Army, Alayna was hired by a small local hospital to work as a nurse as Maria continued to look for work. Times were tough, and Maria's extra doses from the Army started to dwindle until there were none left. As symptoms kicked in, and Maria died in the hospital while Alayna held her in her arms, unable to do anything but try and make her passing as comfortable as possible.

Having lost both her mother and sister to Styre and her father to a treatable, yet costly disease, Alayna was now alone in the world. She had a stable job that provided her with doses, but deep inside, she felt there was something that needed to be done about the system that had allowed her family to die.

During her first year at the hospital, at twenty-six, she had met other nurses who were part of a protest group that testified before Congress, arguing that doses dependent on work were indeed not a "viable" way to deal with Styre. A few years after the treatments were created, the death toll had risen to almost the death rate during the virus' first month. The statistics were readily available, but the system remained the same. Alayna had joined the cause, uniting people from all walks of life around the city to protest against the government. Things had started small, with protests, marches, and sit-ins at government facilities. Over the years, more people had started to join, and now three years later, Alayna found herself leading the fight, or as some referred to it, the resistance.

She glanced down at her left wrist and looked at the tattoo of the finger gun pointed toward her palm. For her, the symbol represented more than an attempt to change the system; it represented hope. And so long as there was hope, she would continue to fight for what she believed in.

As Alayna sat in her quiet apartment, listening to the rain lightly tap against the window, her wrist buzzed, and she swiped left to connect the call.

"Weather's a bit shit today," said Sam Platt.

"Never stopped us before."

"True. Things are all set. We're looking at around ten thousand for this afternoon. We'll march from District Two into the downtown area, and you're set for your speech at the BioDose HQ."

"Perfect," said Alayna. She had met Sam during her first protest with the nurses. A young man with bright green eyes who had become not only one of the primary coordinators of the movement but also her friend. Together, they had organized marches and testified before Congress, though to no avail, and now, with Alayna serving as the voice of the people, Sam was her right-hand man.

"I'll see you this afternoon then."

"Sure thing," said Sam. "And Alayna, be safe out there today. The bigger we get, so too does the target on our backs."

"You watch my back, and I'll watch yours."

Always," said Sam. Alayna twitched her wrist and ended the call. She thought about the position she now found herself in, unsure of how it came to be. She'd always had a sense of adventure and a fighting spirit, and she deeply cared for people, one of the qualities that made her a favorite among the hospital staff. She could have easily lived a content life, working as a nurse and perhaps one day starting a family and living a quiet life up until she died. Plenty of people lived that life, but Alayna always felt like if she had the opportunity to do something, to make a difference, it was up to her to seize it.

She also understood the risks involved. The government had created a system in which it was the primary controller. BioDose was a government-backed facility that was solely responsible for manufacturing the treatments that had become an integral and vital part of society. Although companies had some discretion as to how many doses were allocated to which job positions, the government had created a list and capped the amount per role, ultimately responsible for deeming which jobs were more important to society. Anything that remotely challenged this system would be dealt with in a capacity that was less than favorable for the challengers.

After the government's implementation of the dose system, there had been those who had openly spoken out against it, attempting to rally the masses, but those voices were quickly silenced. They had either disappeared or were involved in questionable deaths. As the number of protesters grew, it was harder for the government to make thousands of people disappear, but Alayna knew all too well that if you take out the commander, the unorganized troops were easier to pick off.

There had been some close calls over the years, with police detaining her, probing into her past and throwing around allegations that she was working for a terror organization intent on destroying the government. Baseless, of course, and Alayna continued to fight for what she believed in. This afternoon's protest would be no different.

Around 2:30 p.m., Alayna put on a hat, a pair of sunglasses, a black jacket with the collar pulled tight around her neck, and took the tram to District 2 to meet up with Sam. He was wearing a dark green jacket, black pants, and had an umbrella due to the slight drizzle. Protesters were starting to gather with signs and others with megaphones.

"Incognito, huh?" said Sam after the tram doors had opened.

"Price you pay to lead a revolution," she said with a smile as she took off her sunglasses.

"Can you believe how far we've come?" Sam asked, scanning the growing crowd outside the tram station.

"If you commit to the process, results take care of themselves."

The noise from the crowd started to grow, and at three o'clock, Alayna grabbed a megaphone and turned to address the crowd.

"Today is a milestone for those of us who believe in the right to life. Each and every one of you is here today because you believe. You believe in a better world. One in which our government looks after us, instead of keeping us under their thumb."

The crowd cheered. "Today, we will march through District Two, toward the steps of the BioDose HQ. Our actions today mark a new chapter for our cause."

She looked down at Sam for a moment, smiled, and then turned to face the crowd. "Long live the revolution!"

The crowd cheered; the voices of thousands of people amplified by the skyscrapers. Alayna not only heard them, she felt them; she was one of them. Her work as a nurse, both in the Army and at the hospital, was fulfilling, but nothing gave her the rush of leading ten thousand people in a cause worth fighting for.

The march began, and despite the rain, there was a sense of optimism and purpose that flowed through the crowd. People shouted, others marched in silence, but they all stood together with the same goal. News reporters were both among the crowd and on the sidelines, capturing every moment and broadcasting to all the major TV networks. The crowd had not even made it a block before police drones flew overhead, scanning the crowd for any malicious activity. At the front, Alayna saw tactical units lining the streets, but so far, there didn't appear to be any hindrance to the march. Sam had diligently filed the proper paperwork, and so long as things didn't turn violent, they were permitted to protest peacefully.

As the rain continued to come down, the protesters made their way into District Two. The monolithic government buildings seemed to loom over the streets, serving as a reminder that the government was omnipresent, forever looking down on those it controlled. Alayna had never understood the need for such colossal buildings, and with the thousands of protesters behind her, she felt a sense of security.

Police, both robotic and human, were stationed on each of the building's steps, silently holding their assault rifles at the ready.

"More than last time," said Sam, nodding toward the police.

"Maybe they're finally taking us seriously," said Alayna.

"I don't know whether to be proud or scared."

"Some things need to be done despite the consequences."

"Depends on the consequence," said Sam with a smile.

The protesters filled the streets of District Two, the dark clothes of the masses contrasting with the marble white government buildings. Shouting voices echoed through the otherwise empty streets while the riot police watched in silence. The drones continued to hover above the crowd, their silent blades battling against the rain. People in lofty apartments had draped flags outside of their window with the gun stencil and others shouted their support down to those on the streets.

About a block ahead, Alayna could see the bright blue light of the BioDose HQ. Beyond the steps were sharpshooters, their rifles pointed at the crowd. On the street in front of the building, she saw a line of riot police holding electrified riot shields. She had encountered one a few years ago, and after the officer hit her with it, fifty thousand volts shot through her body, rendering her immobile on the street until Sam had quickly come to pull her to safety. Each protest had the potential to escalate, and with today's numbers, she was hoping for the best but was prepared for the worst, likely the same thought process as the police.

The crowd moved through the streets like epoxy slowly spreading over a table, covering every inch of space. The BioDose sign was now directly in front of the crowd, and Alayna stood face to face with the riot police, the faint blue of electricity coursing through their shields. She couldn't see their faces behind the black visors, but she knew they would not hesitate to use force.

With the steps to BioDose blocked off, Sam unfolded a small ladder, and Alayna climbed up, grabbing hold of a streetlight with one arm and holding the megaphone with the other. Thousands of people in the street waited in anticipation.

"Since President Burke took office over a decade ago, inequality in this country has grown. Styre is not his fault, but the blame for his disastrous response is entirely his. Essentially, what we have here is a complete and utter failure to do the right thing."

The crowd cheered, with people holding up signs and shouting cheers of support.

"Mistakes were made, and those with loose morals were allowed to take advantage of the situation. This country, and this city, should no longer have to suffer at the hands of this Administration. This is our time! This is our revolution! And we will no longer remain silent!" Thousands of voices erupted at once, the noise reverberating off the marble buildings.

From her elevated position on the streetlight, Alayna looked out over the masses and felt the energy and pain from those in the crowd. Each and every one of them was fighting for their life, slaving away to perpetuate it. Then, as if in slow motion, Alayna saw what she had feared would happen. From the left fringe of the crowd, flying over the protesters' heads toward the line of riot police, the flame of a Molotov cocktail cut through the rain-filled sky and exploded against one of the shields, spreading liquid fire across several of the officers. The drones quickly flew overhead, and a shot rang out against the streetlight, narrowly missing Alayna's head. Sam grabbed her hand and pulled her down as the crowd started to throw more objects toward the police. Bricks, rocks, soup cans, and other projectiles were hurled toward the police, many hitting the shields, some finding the soft flesh of the riot police.

The drones began targeting protesters, shooting tasers into the crowd to quell the violence. "Non-compliance will result in lethal action," the drones' automated voice projected from high above. But the message was either lost in the downpour of rain or ignored, as the protesters brandished their homemade weapons and pushed their way toward the line of police, eager to break through the ranks and push on to the steps of BioDose. The police raised their shields and were forming a tighter line, the electricity coursing through them shining blue. The sharpshooters behind them were picking off protesters, some shooting the Molotovs in their hands before they had a chance to throw them.

"We have to get you out of here," said Sam, holding onto Alayna's arm. "Shit is about to pop off." Alayna nodded. Time for her seemed to move in slow motion—the shouts of the protesters mixed with the sound of electrified batons cracking against skulls. People were falling left and right, but the crowd continued to surge forward. She felt Sam grab her hand and pull her into the crowd, trying to move against the protesters pushing toward the front. Alayna did her best to keep her head down as taser bullets flew into the crowd, bringing down protesters around her.

"Disperse, or you will be fired upon," the drones said.

"Little late for that," shouted Sam, turning around to smile at Alayna.

The riot police at the front line were now slamming their shields into any protester that dared to cross the two meters that separated them, the electricity rendering their bodies temporarily paralyzed on the ground. Objects from the crowd continued to be hurled at the police, and taser bullets from the drones flew from above. From behind the crowd, a line of heavily armored vehicles approached, both Sam and Alayna heard them before they caught sight of them. Four SWAT officers hung off both sides of each vehicle; their weapons focused on the crowd.

"We've got to find another way," said Sam. He pulled Alayna to the left and spotted an empty side street. The crowd wasn't as dense now that people had begun to scatter, but a few thousand remained, keeping the riot police busy at the front.

The two made their way through the crowd, keeping their heads down as tasers flew through the rain until they found their intended target. Protesters fell around Alayna as she and Sam ran toward the street. Out of the corner of his eye, he saw a SWAT officer running toward them.

"Go," said Sam. "I'll be right behind you." He pushed Alayna toward the side street, and she began to run, unsure of where she was going, but knowing that anywhere was better than what the initially peaceful protest had turned into.

Sam watched as she ran down the street, turned to face the officer who was aiming his gun at Alayna's back and ran into him, knocking the officer over with his shoulder. He stared down at the large man in black SWAT gear before looking up for a split second. At that moment, he saw the flash from the end of a gun, and then everything went black.

The streets were chaos. People were shouting, bullets were flying, and the rain continued to pour. The city was rife with both sides fighting for what they believed in — one, a revolution, the other, to maintain order.

Alayna heard the shot and turned back, watching as blood streaked down Sam's face from the bullet hole in his head, and his body collapsed to the ground. She turned and kept running, tears running down her face that mixed with the rain. At the end of the street, she turned right and continued to run. Through the rain, she saw a drone fly toward her and descend until it was directly in front of her. Alayna froze in her tracks. She took a step backward, and before she could move any further, a voice shouted, "Take one more step, and you'll end up like your friend. Slowly turn around."

As she did, she came face to face with a riot officer; her face reflected back at her in the officer's black visor.

"You move, and that drone will make sure it's the last step you ever take. Wrist, now."

Alayna slowly held out her left wrist, and the officer tapped it with his hand. Although she couldn't see it, she knew her profile had been pulled up on the visor's screen.

"Alayna Ramos. Confirmed," he said. "Arrange transport immediately." The officer kept his hand on his holstered weapon and continued to look at Alayna from behind the dark visor.

"You can't do this," said Alayna. "I've done nothing wrong. I am a free citizen exercising my right to peaceful assembly. Am I being arrested?" The rain continued to fall, and the officer didn't say another word. In the distance, Alayna heard a vehicle accelerating through the streets, and at that moment, she knew her time was over. She had become the face of the movement, and over the past few months, she had been expecting this to happen. She hadn't been sure when, or how, but ultimately, she knew her time had come.

The sound of the engine grew louder until a black armored vehicle pulled up in front of them, and the rear doors were flung open.

"Hands in front," said the officer. As Alayna held them together, he pulled out a thin black rod and tapped it against her wrists. At once, the metal snaked its way around both of her wrists and then seamlessly melted into itself, forming a kind of infinity loop tight around her hands. She could see a faint hue of blue pulsating from the metal, and as she tried to pull her hands apart, twenty thousand volts of electricity shot into her body.

The officer grabbed her by the arm and threw her into the back of the truck.

"Where are you taking me?" she said in a faint voice as the doors slammed, leaving her alone in the back of the dark vehicle. Her body felt weak, as if the stun gun had penetrated her soul and zapped whatever life was left within her. With no windows, the only thing Alayna could focus on was the sound of the rain hitting the metal. She slumped in the seat, unable to stand or hold herself upright. As the vehicle accelerated, the momentum slammed Alayna into the door, bruising her shoulder.

She tried to calm her mind, knowing that now, things were out of her control. Handcuffed in the dark, unsure of where she was being taken, she could only focus on her breathing. She slowly inhaled, holding the air in her lungs. She had planned for this. There were contingencies in place in case she ever disappeared. Sam had made sure of that. She exhaled. Sam was dead, now nothing more than a bloody body in the street. She tried not to think about it, knowing she needed to stay focused. She inhaled again. Alayna thought about what the officer had said - "Confirmed." She was a target on someone's list. She exhaled. They would either execute her or lock her up. They likely needed information. She would survive.

She inhaled.

Prison would require sentencing, lawyers, and a judicial hearing. Too much work.

She exhaled.

If whoever had captured her didn't want her dead, and didn't want her incarceration to be public, there was only one place she could be headed.

Alayna continued to breathe, allowing her heart rate to slow down and focus on things from a rational and objective perspective. Her time in the Army had given her more than just a few free flights to new countries. It had trained her to be logical and calm in times of distress.

The truck flew through the empty streets, and thunder bellowed as the rain fell upon Central. Despite knowing where she was being taken, there was nothing Alayna could do now except wait and continue to breathe.

Chapter 5

Finn sat on the sofa, staring at the last remaining blue dose on the coffee table. He had been staring at it for over an hour, watching the way the light reflected through the glass capsule. Ever since Styre came into this world, the doses had become his reason for being. And now, on his last day, he wondered what he would do. There were so many things that he hadn't accomplished, and many more he wished he had done differently. The time Finn had spent on Earth was irretrievably lost, now nothing more than a memory that would soon be gone forever.

Finn had gone to sleep the night before, knowing that there was only one dose left but trying not to think about it. He had slept through the night and woken up, tried to recall his dream but realized there hadn't been one. He didn't dream these days, not since his reality had become a nightmare. Facing the finality of his life, unexpectedly, had allowed him to sleep better than before.

He wasn't angry, nor disappointed. It was easy to hate the situation he was in, but Finn believed that emotion was a waste of mind-space. There was nothing more he could do, and as best as he could, he had or at least was trying to accept his fate. He grabbed the injector, loaded in the dose, and held it against his arm. He looked out the window, taking in the warmth of the sun, and squeezed the trigger. Twenty-four hours, he thought, better make them count. Ever since the Overseer had fired him, Finn had thought about what he would do with his remaining days. His parents were dead, his friends were trapped in an endless cycle of work, and he hadn't had a romantic relationship for a few years. Finn looked over at Tipper, who was lying on the couch next to him.

"Just you and me, buddy. We can either stay in or go out. What do you think?" Tipper's ears perked up, and he jumped off the couch, wagging his tail.

"Out it is."

Finn went into his bedroom to get dressed, and he and Tipper left the apartment for what he expected to be their final outing. Outside, the sun was shining, and people strolled down the street, taking in the sunshine that had disappeared during yesterday's rainstorm.

As they walked, Finn thought about what would happen over the next few days. He knew the Styre symptoms would set in during the afternoon without the dose, and there was no point in going to the hospital. Forty-eight hours after that, he would be dead, another victim of the Styre virus. The digital implant in his wrist would send a signal to the central database that he had passed, and his belongings would be sold or destroyed, and his apartment cleared out to make room for the next tenant. The only thing Finn had thought about was what to do with Tipper. He was pretty sure dogs couldn't become wards of the state, and there was no way he was going to leave him on the street. He made a mental note to ask Josta later if he would be willing to take him after he had passed.

After not being able to find work, Finn had thought about ways to slow down or perhaps delay the symptoms. He'd known other people who had died from Styre, and despite alternatives to try to delay the inevitable symptoms, nothing had worked. Praying to a higher power, home remedies, odd concoctions of this or that, people had tried everything. The only solution was the treatments. Maybe Corbin was right, he thought. After over a decade of reliance on treatments, and no new advances or breakthroughs, or even a more sustainable treatment than once per day, maybe there was something more going on. Finn, however, realized he didn't have the time to spend thinking about things that, in 48 hours, would no longer matter.

Despite the nice weather and leisurely walk he was having with Tipper, Finn felt restless. He supposed it was only natural to look back on one's life when the impending end of it was coming soon, but he hoped to enjoy his last few days of life. He thought about his family and his job, and his life pre-Styre. His initial thought had been the cliché "those were simpler times," but the more he thought about it, things now were as simple as they could get: work to get your doses, take one daily, or die. He thought about his apartment and all the things he had furnished it with over the years. For some reason, he thought about the mismatched plates in his kitchen cabinet. In all his time on Earth, he never thought about what color plates he should buy. Too late for conformity, he thought.

He looked down at Tipper, tongue out and head held high, not a care in the world. Finn thought about what it would be like to be a dog, a thought he was sure he shared with just about every man in the world, who, at some point, had mentioned it to a friend in casual conversation. For the time being, the only thing he and Tipper shared was their general lack of purpose. They both existed in this world, not contributing anything and while not making the world a worse place, not doing anything to make it better.

Finn passed by a butcher and stopped outside the entrance. Tipper looked up at the meats on display, salivating just as much as Finn was.

"Let's live a little," he said, looking down at Tipper.

Finn entered, and ten minutes later, he walked out, holding a large bag.

"Seems silly for a dead man to have money in the bank," he said to Tipper. Finn knew he couldn't understand, but Tipper looked at the bag, and his eyes widened, understanding that tonight, they were in for a feast.

As they walked home, Finn thought about his plan for the day. With his final dose coursing through his system, this was his last day to fully enjoy life. Once the symptoms set in, he would be mostly bedridden and miserable until finally, his heart would beat for the last time. He'd thought about what he should do and realized that he was most happy spending time with his dog. And that was precisely what he had planned.

After arriving back at his apartment, Finn placed the bag of assorted meat on the counter, which had cost him close to a month's salary, and opened a drawer in the kitchen, pulling out a bottle of Macallan single malt scotch whiskey. His father had given it to him at his graduation, telling him, "There are moments in life when a man will need a drink. And at those moments, you're going to want the good stuff."

Tipper was lying on the couch; his eyes eagerly fixated on the bag while Finn poured himself a glass of scotch and took a sip. He flicked his wrist and said, "Play music." The rhythmic beat of an old Bob Dylan song filled the apartment, and at that moment, with the sun setting, a drink in hand, and his best friend with him, Finn wasn't sure he could have asked for a better last day on Earth.

He reached into the bag and started unwrapping the brown freezer paper, laying out the sausages, T-bone steak, pork ribs, and brisket. He placed a cast iron pan on the burner and started cutting sage and garlic, both of which had cost him more than what he would otherwise have spent in two weeks. Tipper continued to watch from the couch as Finn cooked, knowing full well that dinner would be ready in good time.

After the pan was hot, Finn placed in the T-bone, adding a sizeable portion of butter and the herbs and garlic. He took another drink of his scotch and thought of his father. Finn didn't believe in a higher power and had never ascribed to any religious doctrine, but somewhere in the back of his mind, he hoped he would see his father again. In what capacity, he wasn't sure, but he supposed the mystery of it all was what kept people going. The idea that his life was going to end lurked in the back of his mind, like an ever-present weight pressing against his brain, a constant reminder that it was there. He was trying to suppress the feeling with expensive meat and alcohol, an idea he was sure his dad would have given a nod of approval.

Finn flipped the steak and flicked his wrist and said, "Josta." After a moment, his friend answered.

"No invite to the end of Finn's life party?"

"Seemed too somber. Just with Tipper. Bought enough meat to feed a small army. I'll give you all the extras and first dibs on anything in my place if you look after Tipper when I'm gone."

"Finn, I'm not going to go ransack through your place while you suffer through Styre in bed until your final breath. That's dark, bro. I'll take the meat, no point letting it go to waste. And, of course, I'll look after Tipper. I've got a perfect spot for him at my place. It would be my honor."

"I know it's last minute, but I really appreciate it. I just couldn't imagine leaving him alone."

"Not a problem. Do you want me to come over tomorrow morning or what?"

"That'd be best. I expect symptoms to kick in by early afternoon. So, any time before then would be good."

"Look, Finn, if there were anything I could do to help…"

"I understand. It's just part of life. People die from Styre every day. Just this time, you know one of them."

Josta didn't say anything for a moment and said, "I'll see you tomorrow, Finn."

Finn looked over at Tipper and said, "You better enjoy tonight. Not sure Josta is exactly living the life of luxury that you've come to expect." He continued to cook, letting the T-bone rest while cooking sausages and some of the other meats. Finn sliced a few pieces of French bread and threw together a quick salad with the remaining vegetables in his fridge before placing everything together on the table. He hadn't had a proper sit-down meal with food on separate plates in years. With his work schedule and scarcity of funds, it was either vegetarian street noodles or vegetarian stir fry with what he could find, and afford, at the corner store by his building.

After he finished cooking and everything was on the table, he put together a sizeable portion of meat in Tipper's bowl and placed it on the floor. The dog jumped off the couch, and Finn sat down for what would likely be their last meal together.

He started with the T-bone, a cut of meat he had had a few times when he had lived with his parents, but not since Styre started. The first bite exploded with flavor in his mouth, and he closed his eyes, remembering how his father had barbecued on hot summer nights. They would sit down together for dinner and talk about their days. Connection was something Finn didn't have a lot of these days, and the opportunity to create any was gone.

Tipper hadn't looked up from his bowl since Finn had placed it on the floor and was happy he had been able to treat him to something more than dog food. For whatever reason, whether it was his upbringing or just life experience, Finn believed that feeling like he deserved something was a dangerous mindset to have, but tonight, on the eve of his last few days on Earth, he felt like he deserved to have a nice meal. Over the past few days, after each dose injection, he had wondered if he felt he deserved to live. Life was something that no one asked for, but once they had it, it was theirs to do with as they pleased. The dose system, however, seemed to put an asterisk next to that phrase. Finn thought BioDose should replace their slogan with "Life: yours to live unless you can't get doses, and then you die because ensuring the citizens of Central have a basic right to life is not an ideal we subscribe to."

The music continued to play, and Finn sat back in his chair, having eaten more than he had in a long time. The feeling of a full stomach with a glass of scotch in hand had given him a sense of contentment, compared to the usual feeling of complacency that filled his days.

Tipper looked up from his empty bowl, having licked it clean, and Finn smiled. He would miss their time together, the long walks filled with insouciant silence and the understanding that they were both giving the other something that they couldn't give themselves.

"I'll miss you, Tip," said Finn, rubbing his dog behind his ears. Tipper closed his eyes, and they both allowed themselves to enjoy the moment. Finn stared out the window and pushed the thoughts of tomorrow out of his mind. He was here now. Alive. Which was more than he could say for the millions of people who had already succumbed to Styre. Ultimately, he knew that his life would end one way or another, whether it was Styre that got him or natural causes, but he hadn't expected it to be so soon. He wondered if dying was perhaps a better alternative compared to another decade at Conserta, doing a job he didn't enjoy and surviving. Thirty-one years on this Earth, that was all fate had allotted him.

After dinner and several drinks, Finn cleaned up and walked over to the window. Tipper looked up at him from his cozy position on the sofa, as content as a dog could be. He glanced at the clock on the wall - two minutes to midnight. Today's dose would carry through until the morning, and then he was on his own, which for Finn, meant death. He had wanted to be mad, to yell and scream about the injustice of the dose system, to blame the government, to blame anyone for the state he now found himself in. His recalcitrant behavior as a child had landed him in plenty of hot water, both at home and at school. Still, now, he knew any aggression toward any one person or authority would be trivial. He had made the choices that had led up to this moment, and it was he alone who was responsible for not having enough doses. He learned long ago that not everything is worth fighting for, and even now, despite what choices he made, it was too late.

Perhaps he shouldn't have bought Tipper; maybe he would have been able to save more. Or maybe he should have studied something more worthwhile at university. Or he could have worked harder to find someone to marry, someone who could support him. The thoughts, along with the comfortable numbness brought on by the alcohol, swirled in his head as he looked out over District Seven, the dim lights softly illuminating the old apartment buildings.

He looked over at Tipper, who was now softly snoring on the couch and decided that he should do the same since there was nothing more to be done. He turned off the living room lights, walked into his bedroom, and lay on his bed, looking up at the ceiling. The silence of the city filled the room as he wondered how quickly the symptoms would set in. Josta would be over some time in the morning, and that would be the last time he would see both Tipper and his friend.

Dying alone wasn't something he had ever expected. Somehow the scenes from movies of dying in a hospital bed surrounded by loved ones had obfuscated his idea of death.

In actuality, he thought, *most people die alone.*

Car accidents, suicides, a wrong step while hiking, and now, Styre. As hospitals turned symptomatic Styre patients away, most people died alone at home. Sure, they might have their kids there, or a significant other, but by the time Styre started to guide you toward death's door, most people were so unaware of where they are or what was going on, they might as well be alone. Finn had thought about suicide, about making one last decision that was solely his before he left this Earth but believed that if there existed even the remote possibility of an afterlife, it would be better to let nature run its course.

Finn closed his eyes and sleep came. His apartment was quiet, as were the streets, as if providing some kind of calm before the storm that awaited him tomorrow. A storm that he would struggle against, but ultimately succumb to.

———————

He had woken up early to catch one last look at the sunrise while he drank his coffee. Despite the lack of distinctive or even beautiful architecture in District Seven, Finn liked how the sun seemed to bathe the buildings in its yellow glow. He slowly drank his coffee and did his best not to think about what awaited him in the afternoon once his body didn't have the usual blue dose coursing through its system. Tipper was half awake, lazily lounging on the couch, contentedly unaware that today would be different than all the others before.

Almost an hour later, around 9:00 a.m., Josta called. "I'm on my way over. Need anything?"

"All good. I'll see you soon."

Finn tidied up the apartment, but there wasn't a lot to be done. He typically cleaned up after each task, and the sparse furnishings he had accumulated over the years didn't need much attention. About an hour later, there was a knock on his door.

"Come on in, Josta," he said, hugging his friend in the doorway.

Tipper jumped off the couch and ran over to Josta, his tail eagerly wagging as he tried to jump on him.

"Good to know you two get on so well," said Finn, laughing.

"He's basically family," said Josta, petting Tipper. "Aren't you, buddy?"

"Look, I appreciate you taking care of him. I have some tools in my shop that you can have and anything else you might need. No point in keeping them here just to have them seized and sold by the government after I pass."

"It's a weird thought, but I can't argue with the logic. Let's see what you've got."

They walked into the shop, and Finn flicked on the light. Josta looked around and started picking up various tools, examining them as if he were a jeweler looking at a diamond someone had just brought in.

"No way," he said, picking up the small laser cutter. "Where'd you manage to get one of these?"

"Compliments of Concerta. Think of it as a retirement present that they didn't know they gave me."

"This could come in handy with some things I'm working on."

"All yours. Anything you need, Josta, just take it. Better off with you than sold off somewhere."

"You have a bag?"

Finn laughed, "I'll see what I can find." A few minutes later, he returned with an old duffel bag, and Josta started putting tools and scrap electronic parts into it. He had almost cleared out everything in the workshop when Finn asked, "You good on clothes?"

"Finn, I love you, brother, but there's no way I'm taking your clothes. I have standards, a certain je ne sais quoi that I just don't think your clothes would help bring out."

They both laughed and then headed into the living room, both taking a seat on the couch. Finn poured both of them a cup of coffee and sat in silence for a moment.

"When do you think symptoms will kick in?"

"Probably in the afternoon. Can't say for certain, it's not a situation I've been in before. But without the dose this morning, I'm certain they'll start today."

"You want me to stick around or...?"

"I think it's better if I'm alone for this. Plus, there's not a whole lot you can do. Just take care of Tipper for me."

"You know I will, Finn."

They got up from the couch, hugged each other, and Finn bent down to pet Tipper.

"You be good, Tip. I'll miss you more than you could possibly comprehend," he said, kissing Tipper on the head. "His leg shouldn't have any problems. And I've put his bowl and blanket in the bag already," he said, handing the bag to his friend.

"I'm just a phone call away," said Josta. "Anything, just call."

"Thanks, Josta. You've done more for me over the years than I could ever repay you for. It's weird to think that this is my reality."

"Reality seldom coincides with the way we envision it."

"Too true. I'll see you, Josta," he said, while handing him a bag of the leftover meat as Tipper followed him out. The door closed, and Finn was alone. It was still morning, just one hour past his usual injection time. So far, so good, he thought. He took a seat on the sofa and thought about what he should do. He wasn't hungry, his place was clean, he had no one to talk to, and he would be dead within the next 48 hours.

He turned on his TV. Finn had some books in his bedroom that he'd been wanting to finish, but with such limited time, thought that starting something and dying without knowing how it ended would be worse than never even starting.

Time flew by, with Finn watching TV, cooking lunch, doing the dishes despite wondering why he even bothered, and heading back to the couch to relax. He would have preferred to be in his workshop, doing something with his hands, but Josta had taken all his tools, and since he had finished Tipper's leg, he hadn't found the time to start on anything new.

He kept checking the clock on the wall, and placing the back of his hand on his forehead, checking for any sweat, the first Styre symptom. He'd seen it happen to people in public, with profuse sweat dripping down their faces and soaking their clothes. Nobody was at risk since everyone was already infected, but it made people think twice about any life changes that might disrupt their dose supply. Finn had thought about going out to shop or eat today, but after seeing people's symptoms show in public and feeling a bit nauseous afterward, he thought it best to prevent others from feeling the same. So, he stayed at home, watching TV while he waited to die.

Finn felt his stomach grumble, and he looked up at the clock – 6 p.m. He checked his forehead, no sweat. He placed his wrist against the coffee table and said, "temp," and 36.5C flashed. It had been more than 24 hours since his last dose, but everything so far seemed normal. He shrugged it off. Having already accepted the inevitability of Styre, he was certain the symptoms would come today, and at the latest, in the early hours of tomorrow morning. He looked at the coffee table and said "messages" and saw he had one from Josta, a pic of him and Tipper in his shop, with Tipper's tongue sticking out and Josta giving a thumbs up.

He swiped his hand, and the picture disappeared. Finn sat back against the couch and looked out the window, wishing there was sun outside but saw nothing but dark clouds. He wondered if, and for Finn, it was a big if, there was an afterlife and what would be like. There were so many possibilities. He didn't like the classic Heaven and Hell scenario because it didn't seem like there was any middle ground. Finn hadn't done anything extraordinarily good, but neither extraordinarily bad, and in the biblical afterlife situation, he wondered where that would leave him. He closed his eyes and thought about a situation similar to that of a ghost, where he would be free to roam around the city and check up on the people he cared about. For a time, it seemed like a nice idea. But in 100 years, stuck watching people he didn't know and not being able to interact with the changing city would drive him crazy. He returned to his initial idea that when you die, you're dead. That's it. Whether or not the soul existed and where that soul went once his material body died was of little importance to him.

His idea of death left little to the imagination. It was the most logical argument, especially since it didn't include ideas of theoretical places that were impossible to prove or disprove. For Finn, it was a comforting feeling believing that his death would be final and absolute. It was part of his inveterate nature to believe in pragmatic ideas rather than ones that inspired hope. Thoughts of death and the afterlife fired through his brain like hawkers at a street market, each one pining for his attention. Finn lay down on the couch and succumbed to the infinite ideas of the fate he would soon meet.

Hours later, Finn opened his eyes. His apartment was dark except for the faint light being emitted from his TV. He checked the clock, 5:00 a.m. He put his hand to his forehead, and it felt dry. He sat up and placed his wrist on the coffee table and said, "stats." The glass screen gave him a readout of his body temperature, heart rate, weight, oxygen levels, and other personal info. All readings were normal. Finn took a big breath. He was sure that by now, Styre would have kicked in. It was almost 48 hours since his last dose, and he felt fine.

He flicked his wrist and said, "Josta." After more than a few rings, his friend picked up.

"Finn, what's up, man? I usually don't answer the phone this early. Everything okay?"

"Everything is okay, Josta. That's the problem."

"What do you mean?"

"It's been exactly 44 hours since my last dose, and I have no symptoms."

There was a pause on the other end of the phone. "What are you saying, Finn?"

"I don't know exactly."

"I think I have an idea. If I'm right, which I expect I am, you need to get over here as soon as possible."

"What are you talking about?"

"Finn, now is not the time for questions. Grab whatever you need and meet me at my place. There's work to be done."

A Viral State

Chapter 6

The room was dark when Alayna woke. Silence accompanied the lack of light. The back of her head was throbbing. As she sat up, she tried to bring her right hand up to brush back her hair and was unable to lift it more than a few centimeters from the black marble slab's surface where she had been laying just a few moments before. The metal handcuffs that had previously secured both of her wrists were now only around one and programmed to stray no more than a couple of centimeters from the slab. Alayna looked down at her other hand, and while there was no metal cuff on it, she saw a white bandage over her wrist. As she moved it, pain shot up her arm.

The last thing she remembered was the sound of the bridge unfolding to allow passage for the military vehicle carrying her onto Manhattan Island, now unofficially referred to as *The 212*. The booming sound of metal scraping against metal as the bridge extended from the mainland out toward the island had penetrated through the sound of rain and the van she had been forced into. She had never seen the bridge unfold in real life, nor did she know too much about *The 212* other than the rumors, but she knew that when her time came, it would be the first and last place she would ever see.

Alayna did her best to try and piece together a timeline. She had likely taken a blunt object to the back of the head, and with the current pain and throbbing she was experiencing, she couldn't have been unconscious for more than a few hours. She guessed she had arrived late yesterday evening, and was knocked out, so it was likely early morning or afternoon. As she looked around the room for any discerning details, a row of halogen lights flicked on, and Alayna caught her reflection in the giant one-way mirror across from her. The layout was slightly different from those in police precincts, but she knew an interrogation room when she saw one.

Like clockwork, a door opened, and a man and a woman entered, both wearing dark suits. They sat down across from Alayna, and the man placed his wrist on the table, pulling up Alayna's file.

"Ms. Ramos," said the woman. "I assume you know where you are?"

"Officially? No. But it's what's left of Lower Manhattan, *The 212.*"

"Correct," said the man.

"Aren't you supposed to introduce yourselves and tell me what I'm being charged with?"

"If we were the police, we would do exactly that," said the woman. "However, circumstances such as this don't require us to do either. You can probably guess why you've found yourself here, but there's no legal charge officially."

"You can't legally do this then," said Alayna, attempting to move her hand but feeling the invisible magnets keep her wrist at bay.

"And yet, here you are," said the man. "Look, there's not a whole lot of time for what we can or can't do. It's done. For clarity, let me explain a few things. Your friend, Mr. Platt, is dead. As for you, Alayna Ramos no longer exists. Your nanobots, along with the biometric data they contained, including your financial data, have been removed, as have all links to the outside world, including your bank account, employment at Hospital Three, medical records, social media presence, and any trace that Alayna Ramos ever existed. You are, Ms. Ramos, essentially no more."

"What the fuck are you talking about? You can't do this! This violates every ethical and legal principle that this country was founded on!"

"I don't need you to talk. Just listen," said the woman. "You will remain at *The 212* until you die or you are needed in some capacity. Whilst here, you will receive weekly rations as well as one dose a day provided by the government so long as you abide by our rules, which are quite simple. You will make no attempt to leave, you will not kill anyone, and you must not attempt to communicate with the outside world in any capacity. Besides that, you are free to do as you please."

"And what about my life out there?"

"As far as the public is concerned, you disappeared yesterday during the protest. You are a fugitive of the state," the man said.

"That's bullshit," said Alayna, staring at the man in the black suit. She could feel the rage beginning to build inside her. Everything that she was and would have been had been stripped away. Every accomplishment, relationship, opportunity, and possibility were now gone, taken by whoever had given the order to do so.

"Human beings were built with a design flaw," said the woman. "We believe what we feel, rather than what is." The woman checked her watch and nodded at the man.

"You will be taken to processing, and after that, you will be taken to the central admin building. You will not see us again. Any other questions you may have should be directed toward the other residents."

The man and the woman stood up and walked out of the room. A million questions were running through Alayna's head, but before she had time to process any of them, the lights turned blue, and she felt a tug at her wrist. The metal handcuffs were following an invisible magnet that was moving toward the door. She stood up, with her hand being pulled along a few centimeters from the wall. As the door opened, the cuffs continued to move down the hallway, with Alayna slowly walking with her wrist a few centimeters from the wall. The hallway was concrete, with no markings or attributes except for the lights above spaced a meter apart.

As the cuffs guided her down several hallways and around numerous corners, she encountered no people or machinery. In a moment of anger at the situation she now found herself, she stopped walked and jerked back against the cuff. The magnetism grew stronger, and she could feel the invisible force tight against her wrist, eventually causing her to lose footing before she continued walking. Finally, she stood before a large black door. It opened, and she entered. The room was white, and the floor was illuminated. Alayna felt like she was standing in a sterilized operating room.

"Remove your clothes," an automated voice said.

"Fuck you," said Alayna. Immediately, a charge of electricity shot through her body from the metal cuff around her wrist, and the voice repeated its order. Alayna took off her shirt and pants, both of which had splatters of blood on them. Once naked, the voice said, "Please walk toward the illuminated area."

A section of the floor turned blue, and Alayna walked over. Warm water poured from the ceiling, and although she tried to move out of the way, she found that she was unable to step outside of the blue area.

A panel of the room opened, and a robotic arm extended a towel. "Proceed to the next area." Now covered, Alayna walked to the next blue area. "Wrist," said the voice. Alayna held out her wrist and from the wall extended an injector gun that positioned itself against her wrist. She noticed the blue dose capsule in the chamber and watched as it was injected.

"Please get dressed," said the voice. Alayna walked over to the last blue area, and another panel opened. A shelf extended, and on it were a pair of socks, underwear and bra, and a pair of dark gray pants and a sweater. She put on the clothes and put her hair up into a ponytail. Before she had time to take in her surroundings, a door on the far side of the room opened, letting in the first natural light she had seen since being put into the back of the military vehicle.

"Please exit the processing facility," the voice said, and she felt the metal cuff pull at her wrist as it invisibly guided her down a small hallway until she was standing in a room with nothing but a dark circle on the ground. The cuff stopped in the middle and Alayna looked around, with nothing but the halogen lights illuminating the otherwise empty room. The black cuff opened up and silently moved back into the hallway as the door behind her slid shut. She stood there for a moment, staring at the concrete walls, when a large disc in the ceiling began to move. Just then the first natural light she had seen since entering the facility hit her face. As Alayna closed her eyes and felt the warmth of the sun, the small platform on which she stood began to extend upwards until it was flush with the ceiling. Alayna was now standing on a concrete platform overlooking what was left of Manhattan.

From where she stood, the first thing she noticed was the large black wall that towered over her and extended around the perimeter of the island until it blended into the horizon. From what she had heard about this place, she knew the wall was meant to keep people in, not out. Standing underneath the wall, the sheer scale of it dominated every other feeling within her. Although completely vertical, Alayna felt like it was hanging over her and that at any moment, it would come crashing down on top of her. She watched as the wall mapped the curvature of the island and saw that it had no ramparts, no stairs, no turrets, no openings; it was only a wall.

She turned around and began to recognize her surroundings, or what was left of them. Just over the wall, she could make out the top of the Brooklyn bridge and then looked back toward the city. Manhattan Island looked different than it had before Styre. The grass was overgrown, and some buildings were covered in ivy and moss, while others, such as the AIG headquarters building, were nothing more than a pile of rubble. Alayna thought back to scenes from post-apocalyptic movies and wondered what had happened here.

Step after step, she walked toward the downtown area, unsure of where she was heading but certain that staying close to the now-closed processing facility would be a waste of time. She continued to take in the vaguely familiar surroundings, having wondered about this place ever since it was taken over and officially labeled "government property" over a decade ago. The wall had been built and those living in Central had asked no questions, afraid of what might happen if they did. Rumors filled the streets with what *The 212* had been or would be turned into, with each person convinced that their idea was right. Alayna believed it to be a government black site for covert military operations, but now she realized it was nothing more than a prison for those the government viewed as a threat to its existence. As she continued to walk, she saw a digital hologram overlaid on what was once a street sign. It read, "26 Wall St - Sanctuary." She looked up at the nearest street sign - she was just a few blocks away.

Against her better judgment and military training, she decided to head to where the sign had indicated. She was out of her element, both physically and mentally, and she figured whoever had put up the hologram had intended it for those arriving from the processing facility.

The streets were quiet. Birds flew overhead, and long grass and plants were slowly taking over the abandoned buildings, free to explore now that humans were no longer imposing their will for a clean-cut landscape. Some of the windows had been smashed, while other buildings were completely intact. Alayna felt like she was in some other world. The city's once burgeoning financial district and playground for the elite was now all gone. Reduced to a containment area for those forcibly removed from society.

Compared to the downtown area of District Two, where she had marched just yesterday, with its clean and orderly buildings, she was overwhelmed but also comforted by the disorder of *The 212*. It seemed that besides the addition of the large black wall surrounding *The 212*, the mechanized bridge system, and the gutted buildings, the government hadn't done much else. Instead, nature had taken over, and despite the chaotic look of what had once been a sprawling metropolis area, Alayna felt at ease here.

Walking in the middle of the street, with the sun high overhead, Alayna spotted a person's outline about a block away. She squinted her eyes to get a better look and saw that the person was waving. She bent down to pick up a brick from the street, hoping she wouldn't need to use it, but prepared to if need be, and walked toward what she could now make out was a man. As she got closer, she saw that he had gray hair and brown circular glasses. She guessed he was around 60 or so. Now, standing about a meter apart, the man looked at her face and then down at the brick in her hand.

"Planning on using that?" he asked with a smile.

"Only if I need to," she replied, gripping the brick tighter.

The man laughed, his green eyes sparkling in the sun. He brushed back his shaggy gray hair and motioned for her to follow.

"You can leave the brick," he said. "We're on the same team." He was wearing the same dark gray sweater with his sleeves pushed up, although his was more worn.

Alayna relaxed her grip on the brick and let it fall to the ground. It had made her feel more secure, but she still knew that if push came to shove, the old man wouldn't be too difficult to deal with.

"I'm Magnus. Been here for a few years. Got tossed in here for trying to rob a Dose Depot."

"Not regular jail? No due process?"

"Been to jail. And let me tell you, serving my sentence was a lot easier than being thrown in here knowing this is where I'll die. I guess after eight attempted robberies, jail wasn't going to cut it. So here I am. You got a name?"

"Alayna Ramos."

Magnus paused for a moment and looked at her, tapping his finger against his head.

"I've heard that name before. Give me a minute, it will come to me." Alayna looked at him until he said, "You're that protester! We've heard about you in here. Somewhat of a celebrity, I might add. We don't get a lot of news from the outside in here, but you've been all over the radio due to your, as they like to say, 'provocative antics.'"

"That's me - the provocateur."

Magnus laughed. "Well, I can't say I'm happy to finally see you in person, not in here at least, but the others will be honored to meet you, especially Kalum."

"And he is…?"

"You know, now that you ask, I'm not sure he has an official title. He helps us maintain a sense of purpose and keeps us together. It was savage in here for a while, everyone fighting to survive. When Kalum got here, he united us, in a way. Been peaceful ever since."

Alayna worked to process all the new information while they walked. They were now in the downtown area, and the sun sparkled off the now vacant office buildings that stretched high into the sky. The world inside the walls provided Alayna with an unexpected companionship, despite knowing she would be locked in here forever. Birds flew overhead, and the occasional cat skirted across the street. But aside from walking with Magnus, everything else seemed to stand still.

"Just over here," said Magnus, pointing toward the Federal Hall building that was now just pillars covered with ivy. "Think of it as a home base. Lots of options around here, but without working elevators, seemed a bit too much effort to take up residence anywhere else."

Alayna nodded. Caught up in her new surroundings and with a man she wasn't sure she could trust, she felt it was better to stay quiet until she had a better grasp on things. Before they entered the building, she turned to look at the city from the top of the steps. In the distance, she could see the towering black wall past the still streets.

"You'll have plenty of time to take in the view later," said Magnus, motioning for her to go inside.

Compared to the silence of the streets that led them there, a faint buzz of noise echoed through the spacious foyer. Thick bundles of cables ran across the floor, and some ran the length of the walls, snaking into various rooms. A large cluster of lights hung from the ceiling, illuminating the area in front of her. Alayna had visited the building pre-Styre when it was clean and orderly. Now, however, it looked like a small army had taken it over. Several large TV screens were mounted to the walls; some had maps, while others contained calculations and numbers that meant nothing to Alayna.

"Quite a sight, isn't it?"

"What is this place?"

"It's been called a lot of things over the years, but most people just refer to it as 'The Base.' Come on, let's get you squared away."

They walked up the stairs and through several hallways until they reached a large office with the door removed. Magnus stepped through and said, "Got another one, sir."

Alayna stepped into the room and, standing over a large table in the room, made eye contact with a tall man who looked to be in his 40s. His jet-black hair was tied into a bun on the back of his head, and he wore a loose-fitting white linen shirt that accented his tan skin.

"Come on in," he said. "Can I get you anything? I know processing can be somewhat of an unusual experience."

"I could use a drink," said Alayna.

The man laughed, the skin tightening around his eyes and high cheekbones, highlighting his distinct Japanese features. "Have two, it's past noon," he said, pouring three glasses of vodka.

The three of them threw back the shot as the man poured another.

"Introductions then. I'm Kalum Sakara. Arrived here a few years ago. 'Sedition' was the formal charge. Served in the 2nd Marine Raider Battalion and had the bright idea that with enough people on board, we could come back and overthrow Burke. I still don't know for sure, but I suspect there was a mole who brought our little operation to our commander, and I was tossed in here. No honorable discharge, no court proceedings, the same as everyone else in here."

"How is that legal?"

"It's not a question of legality. The better question is, 'what can we do about it?' and the answer to that is nothing. And you are?"

"Alayna Ramos."

"The protester," he said, looking over at Magnus. "We've been following the revolution, only through the news on the radio. The last protest had how many? Less than a thousand? And you were, as they put it, 'the ringleader'?"

"Don't believe everything you hear on the news," said Alayna. "I'm forever hearing stories concerning myself and my 'seditious' ways. They control the narrative just as they control us with the doses," said Alayna.

"I prefer to think of myself for as an activist. And we had around ten thousand. Things got out of hand pretty quickly. Heavily armed police showed up, and that's when I was taken. They were using live rounds. They killed my friend."

"I'm sorry for your loss," said Kalum. "It's a feeling many of us in here understand."

"Has anyone ever made it out?" she asked.

"Permanently? No. Bridges are the only official way in or out, and they're controlled from the mainland. There have been attempts to scale the wall, but it's made of a military-grade concrete polymer that sends out non-lethal charges of electricity to any living organism that touches it. The polymer project was scrapped as there were no external enemies left to fight, but Burke found uses for the foundry and kept pumping out this shit to build this monstrosity of a wall. Burke had all the subway entrances blown up. We've managed to tunnel our way through the debris, but there's still a way to go before we reach the city. A painstaking process, let me tell you."

Alayna tossed back the second shot. The finality of the situation was starting to set in.

Kalum motioned for them to take a seat on the couches next to the table.

"Look, this place is, for lack of a better term, fucked up. They've got us locked in here against our will, and the only guarantee that we'll live to see tomorrow are the daily doses delivered by drones. Even if you were to escape with no money, trying to find another dose within 24 hours is almost impossible."

"But why even bother keeping us alive?"

"Good question," said Magnus. "We're pawns in a chess match. Kalum was right - no one has managed to leave here, except when they're needed. Occasionally, people are taken when they serve a purpose. When Burke needs a victory, people are pulled out of here, and the government makes a big display about capturing them and restoring order. Until that time comes, we're locked in here."

"Other drones come once a week to drop off food," said Kalum. "Mainly rice, beans, and a few fresh vegetables. No meat, so don't get your hopes up. We're not exactly a high priority for the government. Things were pretty rudimentary at the start. We had to cook over open flames since the power was cut, but now we've got a fully operational kitchen thanks to the wall."

"What did they do to my wrist?"

Both Magnus and Kalum looked at the gauze bandage on her arm. "You've been removed from the system, as I'm sure they explained," said Kalum. "All digital traces of you have been wiped, and the nanobots in your wrist were surgically removed. My guess is that any news of your disappearance will be tied to the recent protest, and you'll likely be labeled as 'at large' by the government."

"That's what I was told," said Alayna. "It's fucked up," she continued, unsure of how better to articulate her feelings.

"It is," said Kalum. "And believe me, we understand how you feel better than anyone else will."

"How many people are here?"

"Around a hundred. People get taken occasionally, but new ones such as yourself arrive pretty regularly as well."

"I just can't..." said Alayna, trailing off as she looked out the window at the quiet streets below.

"It's hard to fathom, I know," said Kalum. "But despite what you think, this is your new reality. And as such, you might as well get the lay of the land."

He directed her attention back to the table and pressed a button on the side. A digital map of *The 212* appeared, with a large red line indicating the perimeter of the wall.

"Besides the limitations of the wall, we're free to go anywhere we like, which is essentially all of former Lower Manhattan all the way to Fulton street. Federal Hall, here," he said, zooming in on the map, "is our main base of operations. There's no WiFi, and we haven't been able to establish a hard line to the net, but we've managed to siphon off electricity from the wall, which, believe me, was no easy task. The Base is where we have meetings and figure out our day-to-day operations. You were brought in across the Brooklyn Bridge since the processing facility is underneath what used to be Pier 17. Further south," he continued, moving the map with his hand, "is our lab, which you'll recognize as the former Hamilton Customs House."

"Ironic that the government is locking us up against our will and without due process just a few blocks from the former UN headquarters."

"That fact wasn't lost on me either," said Kalum with a smile.

"Tell me about the lab. What's it for?"

Kalum looked over at Magnus and then back at Alayna. "Getting out is our top priority. We can't cause real change from in here. But without a steady supply of doses, we won't last more than 24 hours in the city. The lab was set up to, hopefully, re-create the doses or figure out something similar to keep Styre at bay. So far, we've had no luck, but with not a whole lot else to do, it's worth pursuing."

"Does the government know that you've basically set up a rebel camp and are attempting to escape?"

"I think they might have some idea of what's going on. They took a lot of precautionary measures, such as blocking the subways, taking away all the guns, blowing up the Manhattan bridge, and gutting anything that might help us, such as electronics, computers, blueprints, and things like that. But trying to sweep over 20 city blocks is no easy task. We've managed to scavenge and find things we need but so long as no one leaves here against the government's will, and we don't kill each other, they're happy to have us where they want us."

"We can't do much without more doses," added Magnus. "They are our only real shot at making sure we not only get out but stay out."

"People have been trying to make their own doses for years, and no one is any closer than the government is to finding a cure."

"My mother once told me that it's the thought that counts. And on many occasions, she was right. In this case, it's the action that counts, not the thought. I'll pursue a possibility rather than accept defeat any day."

"I admire your resolve," Alayna said. "What's this other building?" pointing at a large area of light on the map.

"That's 71 Broadway, the main area of residence for most people here."

Alayna laughed, "Living a life of luxury, I see."

"Just because we're locked in here doesn't mean we can't afford ourselves a certain level of comfort. Plus, it's one of just a few buildings that we've linked to the power supply. It's also just a few blocks from the Wall Street subway station - which we've tunneled into. It made it a lot easier to work in an area with a lot of people coming and going. Drones fly over every now and then, so we have to keep our 'seditious' activity as hidden as possible."

"Clever," said Alayna, looking from Kalum back at the map. Despite her current circumstances, she was impressed with everything they had accomplished.

"We have to keep windows covered at night to keep the light out, but besides that, it has everything one might need," continued Kalum. "You're free to live where you like, but there are rooms available there if you're interested."

"That's very kind of you," said Alayna. "I've always wanted to go inside."

"Well, now you can live in it," said Magnus with a smile.

"That's basically it," said Kalum. "Beyond the wall on Fulton, life is normal. Tourists come and visit Times Square, visit Central Park, and dine out on the upper east side."

"But how do they justify it?"

"You've watched the news," said Kalum. "It's a military supply base, which explains the walls and secrecy surrounding it. Plus, it's hard to get the truth out without any telecommunications."

Alayna looked from the map to the window, taking in the view that contrasted against the large black wall in the distance.

"These are the three buildings with power and our main hold-ups. We have scavenging teams that go out daily for supplies, a team of engineers working to further the tunnel, and another team working to establish comms between us and the outside. Right now, we've only been able to intercept radio, but the team says they're close to getting a transmission line established."

"And what role am I to play in all of this?"

"Right now, I'd advise you to take it easy. I appreciate your enthusiasm, but processing can take a toll, both physically and mentally. Magnus will help get you set up in the Gehry and after that, take a few days to yourself. Familiarize yourself with the area and feel free to visit the lab. It's quite impressive what we've managed to build with so few resources. I'm always here if you need to talk. Give yourself a week, and then we can discuss where you think you might be most valuable."

They rose from their seats, and Kalum extended his hand, "Welcome to *The 212*."

"Thank you," she said, shaking his hand.

"If you like, I can take you to the Gehry to get you settled. Dinner is in a few hours, so you'll have some time to relax, go for a walk, and meet your neighbors," said Magnus.

"I'd appreciate that," said Alayna.

After they left Central and walked through the streets, she saw the Gehry building, the prominent building she had often seen in pictures and even a few times in person. Now, standing before the entrance, Alayna felt a feeling similar to when she had first joined the army. The feeling that her life and her place in the world were controlled by something greater, and no matter what choices she made, there would always be an opposite counterforce pushing back. She let the feeling wash over her, opened the door, and walked into her new home, one that would be hers for the foreseeable future.

Chapter 7

"You've lost me," said Finn, looking first at the digital schematics of a large machine and then over to the machine itself.

"Aren't you an engineer?"

"This is infinitely more complicated than anything I was ever taught or have worked on."

"Fair," said Josta. "But this is our only chance. And now that you may be immune, we have an actual shot at reproducing a dose."

"We don't know that I'm immune," said Finn.

"My friend, it's been 72 hours since you've had a dose, and you have no symptoms. Every second that goes by and you remain healthy, my theory gets stronger."

Finn looked at his friend and then down at Tipper. Josta was right. There were several explanations for why he hadn't gotten sick yet, but the idea that he was immune was the most logical. It had never occurred to him that he was immune primarily because the government never tested for it. Society was structured around the idea that everyone was infected, and doses were taken daily so long as you had them. It had never occurred to Finn to skip a dose, nor had he ever dared to. Now, standing in Josta's workshop in the basement of an autobody shop, he knew his life had irreversibly changed.

After he had arrived at the workshop, Josta had talked at length about creating a dose from Finn's blood, the more technical aspects of which had gone over his head. The main idea had stuck: it was possible.

"Wouldn't it just be easier to buy one?" Finn had asked.

"Oh sure, Finn. Let's just walk over to the local chemical warehouse and tell them we'd like to buy a hematology analyzer as well as a plasma therapy accelerator because we're trying to make doses, which might I remind you, is illegal."

"You think we can manage to build what we need ourselves?"

"We sure as hell are going to try, now come over here and look at this section again," said Josta, pointing at an area of the schematic.

"This is going to take forever," said Finn.

"Then we better get started. And Finn, we're going to see this through. My dad always told me that you better finish what you start because if you don't, someone smarter and more motivated than you will. This is our chance to shine, and I'm not going to let that opportunity pass."

The two men continued to talk, tinker, and solder circuit boards for the next few hours as Tipper laid on the couch against the far wall. Josta had paid the mechanic upstairs cash for the workshop several years ago and was happy to have a place of his own, one in which he could work on projects with a certain sense of privacy. It was a large space with several tables, all of which had parts strewn across their tops. Several machines on tables were situated against the back wall with various tools and computer parts next to them. Large glass screens revealed indecipherable data and calculations, and an assortment of glass vials, tubes, and beakers covered what little workspace was left. Because the shop didn't have any windows, it was lit with, what Finn had thought, an unnecessarily large amount of halogen lights.

After several hours of work, Josta opened a fridge and grabbed two beers.

"This is going to change everything," he said, opening his beer and taking a sip.

"What exactly is the plan?"

"There are many routes we can take, but first and foremost, we need to check if we can actually make a dose from your blood. If we can, the next step will be to scale up production. Even if we manage 10-20 doses per day, that's still more money than you would have made in six months at Conserta."

"You think it will work?" asked Finn, looking at the assortment of unfinished machines on the tables.

"You need the money, and I need doses. It has to work."

"And you can sell the doses?"

"That's like asking if I can give away money. Finn, doses are the hottest commodity on the market. Out there is a marketplace where entropy reigns supreme, and we're the only ones with a sure thing. Supply and demand, my friend, therein lies the value."

Finn took a drink and thought about the situation. He looked over at Tipper and then back at Josta, grateful to still be alive and in the company of those he cared about, but unsure about the realization that he was immune. His life, for the first time in a long time, now had meaning. He knew he would need to keep quiet as Josta had assured him that the government wouldn't be too thrilled if they found someone who wasn't reliant on the system they had created. Finn had agreed. He had thought about trying to create a dose from his blood, but without a background in chemistry, he wasn't sure it was entirely possible.

"It's absolutely possible," Josta had said. "And that's exactly what we have to do."

"It's a risk," Finn had argued. "What if we get caught? Or what if it doesn't work? Or what if it hurts someone?"

"That is a risk worth taking," Josta had replied, steadfast in his belief in the project they had agreed to take on. "For too long, we, as a society, have been forced to work and forced to live day to day, wondering if we'll run out of doses and our life will end. We now have an opportunity to disrupt the system, to literally give people life."

Finn had never thought of himself as particularly generous or thought that his life could significantly impact someone else's. He was humble and hardworking, and although thoughts of doing something greater or more meaningful often ran through his head, he always found justifications to continue down the path he had found himself on.

"Know your place," his father had often said to him. Now, in light of his immunity and the possibility to do something with it, he knew his place in the world had changed.

As Finn and Josta drank their beers, they discussed the work that still needed to be done. Josta discussed the big picture while Finn focused on the step-by-step process.

"A few more days, and I reckon we'll be good to go," Josta said.

"If we're lucky," said Finn. "Plus, we're going to need a test subject."

"I'll do it."

"But what if it doesn't work?"

"Then I'll take my dose. The first few symptoms aren't so bad. I've missed a day every now and then over the years. I'll survive."

Aghast, Finn stared at Josta.

"Oh, leave it, Finn," he said when he saw him about to speak. "We can't exactly ask someone to inject an experimental dose and not have the word get out. It's better this way."

"There's something about your stubbornness that I admire," said Finn with a smile.

"Going on as I am the only thing I've got. Right, we should turn in for the night. We've got a lot of work to do over the next few days. Plus, there's a lot of parts I still need to go out and find. For tonight, I've got a spare cot in the back you can use, and I'll take the couch. Tipper," he said, looking over at the dog sprawled across the couch, "I'll make you a spot on the floor."

The two men finished their beers and turned off the lights in the workshop. The room was dark, and although Finn wished he could have looked out a window to see the stars and moon, he was thankful to simply be alive. The last 24 hours had been a whirlwind of emotions and revelations. Over the last decade, he couldn't recall hearing of anyone ever being immune. Part of him was still in a state of disbelief: him, a lowly Conserta worker who had recently been fired. Someone who had never amounted to anything and yet within him, his blood contained what he hoped would indelibly change the world. Thinking about the work that remained, and the possibility that it might not even work at all, was an ambitious thought to have, but it gave him hope. Hope that his life would be worth something, after all. He thought about the schematics he and Josta had drawn up, and as he went over tomorrow's to-do list in his mind, he finally succumbed to the fatigue of the day.

———————

Finn had been hard at work since waking up. He and Josta had a cup of coffee, fed Tipper, and then focused their attention on the machines that, along with Finn's blood, they hoped would be able to produce an efficacious dose. Around noon, when Finn's stomach had started to grumble, and Josta had excitedly declared that the liquid chromatography-mass spectrometry machine was almost complete, they both decided to take a break.

"You go out and grab us some lunch," said Josta, setting down a small hammer. "I'll go see if I can scrounge up an ionization probe and a pressurized pump system to finish up the LCMS. When I get back, we'll finish up the interface because, without it, the LC and MS devices are fundamentally incompatible."

"I don't know what I'm supposed to do with that information."

"I need more parts to make the devices work."

"Got it," said Finn with a smile. "It'll be nice to get out of here and get some sun. I don't know how you can stay down here for days on end."

"You get used to it," said Josta as he placed a keycard against a pad and the large freight elevator doors opened. After the lift opened on the main floor, they were greeted by a man in gray overalls with grease stains. "What're you boys working on down there? It's been non-stop racket since yesterday."

"Oh, you know, this and that," said Josta as they exited the shop.

The sun crept through the clouds, and Finn tilted his head to the sky, stretching his arms and letting the sun fall on his face with Tipper doing the same. He looked at Josta and asked, "Is he someone we should worry about?"

"Dave? No, he's not a problem. A little too inquisitive for my liking, but I've never had any problems. Pay him no mind. You get some lunch for us. I'm good for anything. Meanwhile, I'll go visit my dealer and see if I can get the parts we need."

"You've got a parts dealer?"

"I'm not exactly looking for spare wires and junk metal. So yes, I've got a parts dealer."

Finn laughed at the thought of a clandestine exchange of laboratory equipment parts in a dark alley and said, "Meet back here in an hour, work for you?"

"Perfect."

They headed off in separate directions, with Finn taking his time as he and Tipper strolled down the street, something he once thought he would never be able to do again. He walked down streets that he knew and passed by buildings that he recognized, but something had changed. Only a few days ago, he had come to terms with his death and, as much as a person can, had accepted it. And now what? Did he have a new lease on life? A new purpose? Finn wondered if people actually change or if they find and accept the opportunity to manifest another side of their character. Was that what was happening to him now? He continued to ponder the central quandaries of his life before arriving at a vegetarian Mexican restaurant.

Sitting at a table close to the window, he ordered two burritos, one cauliflower, and the other eggplant, and focused his attention on the TV in the corner while he waited. Most of the news was typical, with people in fancy clothes praising the government's recent crackdown on the violent protest that had taken place a few days ago. A large picture of a woman with dark hair in a black jacket appeared onscreen.

"The central leader of the radical protesters has gone missing," the newscaster said. "After a speech filled with seditious and provocative ideas, Alayna Ramos, the de facto conspirator, and perpetrator of the violence we saw earlier, has gone missing. Police are still tracking her whereabouts but have yet to apprehend Ms. Ramos for her illegal acts against the government. If anyone has any information, please call the number below."

Finn thought for a moment about where he had seen the woman, with her soft yet fierce brown eyes and high cheekbones. Suddenly, he thought back to the bar with Josta a few weeks ago and remembered seeing her on the news speaking so passionately about the injustices surrounding BioDose. He shook his head and sighed. Finn had been around long enough to know that if the news was reporting someone missing, it was because those who funded the news were the ones responsible.

Now working with Josta on something highly illegal, he wondered if he, too, would one day end up on the news as a "missing person," but what scared him more was if anyone would care.

The waiter set a brown paper bag with his food on the table, and Finn left. After he untied Tipper from the street sign outside, they set off for the workshop. Twenty minutes later, he was the first to arrive. He and Tipper stood outside the autobody shop listening to the cacophonous sounds of metal being cut, hammers pounding, and drills whirring away on a stubborn bolt. Josta had taken the elevator keycard with him, so Finn waited outside, happy to have a chance to soak in some sun before going back underground. Across the street, he noticed a large black building that looked to be abandoned. Several of the windows were broken, and graffiti covered the entire wall of the first floor. Among the various colors and tags, he saw a large stencil of a hand-shaped gun pointed toward the sky.

The words of the waiter a few weeks ago echoed in his head, *a necessary end to things comes when it is most needed.* He wondered if he was now part of the necessary end. Before he had a chance to think any further, Josta yelled his name.

"Christmas came early," he said, holding a large bag in one hand and a briefcase in the other.

"You got the parts?"

93

"You better believe it," said Josta with a smile. "Negotiations took longer than expected, but we, my friend, are ready."

"Let's get to it," said Finn, as they headed into the shop and took the elevator downstairs.

They ate quickly as both men were eager to get to work. The possibility that creating a dose was just on the horizon, both excited and scared Finn, but he was determined to press forward. After Josta laid out all the recently acquired parts and after the tasks for the remaining machines were divided between them, they got to work.

Finn had always liked engineering. He enjoyed the mental balancing act of maintaining the big picture idea while focusing on how each individual part would play a role in achieving it. Parts were put into place, circuit boards were installed, and wires were soldered. The men worked diligently and quietly, with Josta occasionally breaking the silence to ask Finn for a tool or tell him to shift a part a few centimeters higher. After several hours, all the parts had been installed.

Josta looked over at Finn, "Moment of truth," he said, flipping a switch. The screens on all of the machines flickered on, accompanied by the internal fans' gentle hum. Both of them smiled.

"There's still a lot to do," said Finn. "Plus, there's still the question of efficacy."

"Don't ruin the moment," said Josta, placing his hand on Finn's shoulder.

Josta flipped the switch, turning the machines off, and they both sat on stools across from each other at the table.

"What's the next step?"

"Make the dose," said Josta, knowing this wasn't the answer Finn was looking for.

"I mean…"

"I know what you mean," he responded with a laugh. "First, we're going to need blood. A lot of it - at least a few liters. After that, the rest is on me. The general idea behind extracting a treatment from immune blood is simple enough, but simple isn't the same as easy."

"You have my complete faith," said Finn. "Let's start tomorrow, I'm drained."

"You and me both, my friend."

Various vials of acidity regulators, neomycin, aluminum salts, and chemicals that had been found in the city covered the tables while the faint hum of the machines filled the workshop. Finn had filled several bags of blood after waking up, and Josta had gotten everything else in place - which Finn had described as "organized chaos." At some point in the morning, Josta had donned a white lab coat, which Finn had thought was unnecessary, but Josta had reminded him that "he was a chemist, after all."

Sitting at the table and looking at the LCMS screen, Josta was simultaneously scribbling numbers on a piece of paper. Finn watched the way he worked and was fascinated by his precise movements. Everything he did seemed to have been meticulously planned and thought out beforehand. Chemicals were mixed in test tubes, blood was dropped onto microscope slides, and Erlenmeyer flasks were connected to an intricate system of other assorted lab equipment.

"Is it going to work?" asked Finn.

Josta swiveled his chair around and shoved his goggles onto his forehead. "This isn't as easy as swirling around a couple of chemicals. Plus, let me remind you that this has never been done outside of BioDose, which has millions of dollars of funding and state of the art equipment. We aren't exactly working with top-rate stuff here. I mean, my lab isn't what you'd call 'up to code.'"

"Life isn't always up to code," said Finn. "Plus, we do have a top-rate chemist."

"You're goddamn right we do," said Josta as he lowered the goggles and turned back to his workstation.

After another hour or so, Finn watched as the beakers' contents were heated and changed color. At the end of the table, a small vial began to fill with a blue liquid. When it was full, Josta put in a stopper and held it up under the light.

Both of them stared at it before Josta said, "Finn Brantley, we have a dose."

"You're confident enough that it will work that you're willing to inject it into your body?"

"I've run the calculations, my measurements were correct, and you're definitely immune, so based on all that, I'm willing to take my chances. But remember, the best bets are still just guesses."

"Tomorrow morning, then?"

"Let's give it a shot."

"Punny," said Finn with a smirk.

The rest of the day was anxiously relaxing. Both Finn and Josta knew the next morning could potentially be one of the most important moments of their lives, but there was nothing to do but wait. They felt no sense of relief, nor victory, only a sense of unwarranted optimism. Finn had proposed getting a bottle of champagne to celebrate, but Josta had said, "People who stop to smell the roses lose sight of the mansion at the end of the garden. Let's wait until we're sure this works." The evening was spent talking about production plans if the dose worked, but both knew that conversation was speculative at best. They went out for dinner, had a drink back at the workshop, and retired early to bed, eager for the morning to come.

"You're sure about this?"

"Finn, I've told you a thousand times, this is the only way," said Josta, holding the injector gun against his forearm. "Wondering if I'll survive is about as useful as wishing upon a star. Trust me. Trust the science." The vial of blue liquid shined in the light, the fruit of both of their labors but also Josta's potential downfall. It was 9 a.m., but Josta had already been up for hours, double-checking his equations to give him peace of mind before the mixture of chemicals entered his body.

"Here goes nothing," he said, squeezing the trigger as they both watched the vial drain as the dose entered Josta's bloodstream. For a moment, neither of them said anything. Josta set the injector on the table, and they both looked at each other.

"How will we know if it works?" asked Finn.

"That's easy," laughed Josta. "If I don't start sweating and break out in blisters, we've got ourselves a winner. If I do, however, start to show symptoms, I want you to run to that cabinet and inject me with a real dose."

"And so, we wait," said Finn.

The day was relatively quiet. Josta poured over schematics for what he'd need to build to ramp up production. Finn had found an old book about ancient architecture that he was trying to read, but he found that rather than absorbing the words, they were only there to drown out the thoughts and questions he had had since arriving. Books had long since ceased to be something he enjoyed, but he didn't not enjoy them, either.

Every hour, Josta would record his vitals and then look over at Finn and give him a thumbs up. After several hours, everything still seemed normal. Quietly, internally, both of them grew more optimistic. Dinner was eaten with a passive hopefulness that both didn't overtly express but could sense in one another.

"This could change everything," said Josta laying on the couch. It had been over 12 hours since he'd taken the dose. Tomorrow, they would know for sure whether it had been a true success or not.

"Let's hope so," said Finn, turning off the light and heading into his room for the night.

The concrete felt cold against his feet as he walked into the main room of the lab. Josta was sitting at one of the tables, hunched over a screen.

"Good morning," said Finn.

Josta spun around, "My friend, it is more than just a good morning. It is a fantastic morning, one that will be remembered throughout history."

A smile began to creep over Finn's face. "You're telling me…"

"It works!" shouted Josta before Finn could finish his sentence.

"My vitals are stable. I've got no symptoms, and as far as I can tell, so far, no side effects. We did it."

"You did it," said Finn. "I just helped."

"Do you know what this means?" asked Josta excitedly. "For us? For society? For the world? This is going to set us free!"

Finn took a seat on the couch. A rush of emotions swept over him. It had never occurred to him that one day, he would have the opportunity to change the world, to cause a paradigm shift within society, and now, sitting in Josta's underground workshop, that's precisely what had happened.

"We have to make more," said Finn, unable to articulate the rush of feelings he was having.

"You're goddamn right we do," said Josta, grabbing a small screen from the table and turning it to face Finn. "And this is exactly how we're going to do it. Based on the amount of plasma I extracted from your blood and the serum in which it needs to be mixed, I estimate we can make around twenty individual doses a day. After a week or so, then it's time to figure out distribution. I've got a few friends who can help get these out on the street, but the real problem will be trying to increase production. Twenty a day is an okay number, but if we want to bring about real change, that number has to exponentially increase."

"Let's focus on the task at hand," said Finn, feeling his heartbeat from within his chest.

"Once we get a hundred doses, we'll sell them and make sure everything is okay before we start trying to become the next BioDose."

"You get some coffee, wash up, and let's get to work. It's time to change the world."

Finn watched as Josta carefully placed the hundred doses into a backpack. The past week had been grueling work, both meticulously measuring, processing, mixing, and packaging the blue doses that looked identical to the ones manufactured by BioDose. Josta had worked with one of his friends to create the same vial with the same BioDose etching at a price that Josta had only described as "fucking insane, but necessary." Josta had injected one of the homemade doses every day for the past week and was confident that it was working.

They had agreed to sell the doses under the condition that no one discovered they had been manufactured outside of BioDose. The last thing they needed was an investigation as neither wanted to spend the rest of their life in prison.

"Time to make some money," said Josta, slinging the backpack around his shoulders as they both entered the elevator. "I've already given my friend a heads up that we'll be meeting him tonight." Tipper looked up at Finn as the elevator doors closed, and all three remained silent, listening to the winches grind as the lift carried them up.

The garage was dark when the doors opened. The moon cast long white stripes of light across the half-assembled carburetors and hulls of semi-repaired trucks as Josta and Finn both let their eyes adjust to the darkness.

"Let's go," said Josta quietly, making their way toward the door at the far end of the shop. Finn wasn't used to such a quiet garage. Each time he had been there, noises had filled the air, and men walked around, each focused on fixing the cars and other machines. Now, it was still, as if something lay in the shadows, expecting their arrival.

Finn followed behind Josta, headed toward the moon that shone through the glass door, with Tipper by his side. Tipper suddenly stopped. Finn had just a second to notice the snarl coming from his dog before a light turned on. Facing them was Dave, still in his dirty gray overalls, as well as three other men in matching clothes.

"Where you boys headed at this time of night?" he asked. Tipper let out a low growl.

"Thought we'd take a stroll and enjoy the cool air," said Josta, placing a hand on one of the backpack's shoulder straps. "Too much time spent in the shop isn't good for the soul."

"What's in the bag?" asked Dave, his eyes glancing down at Tipper before shifting back to Josta.

"Frankly, that's none of your business, Dave. If you and your friends would kindly move, we've got places to be."

"Gimme the bag," said Dave, his tone now aggressive. "I know what you've been doing in that little shop of yours. That bag is full of doses." Finn took a breath to try and calm his heart rate, which he could hear in the now still garage.

Dave reached into his back pocket and pulled out a Beretta M9, holding it by his side. Finn hadn't seen a real gun in ages. Guns had been outlawed for public use, and though police still used them, each bullet and gun were equipped with nanobots that transmitted data back to the precinct to track each bullet that was fired, who it was fired at, the location and time that the trigger was pulled, and the result of the shot. Guns like Dave's, however, were relics and still used standard bullets, which were untraceable.

"I'm going to ask again," said Dave, his voice now a low growl. "Give me the bag or face the consequences."

"Oh, consequences? Like what?" asked Josta.

"Why don't you fuck around and find out?"

"You know what," said Josta, "I just might."

Finn wasn't sure exactly what had happened, but he was suddenly blinded by a bright light, and an arm pulled him to the side. He crashed onto the floor and heard men shouting. Several shots rang through the garage. Finn put his hands over his ears to stop the ringing. Time seemed to slow down. Through the chaos, he heard Tipper barking and then the sound of a man crashing to the ground. Once his eyes re-adjusted to the darkness, he saw that Josta was next to him, both hiding behind a large SUV. The moonlight passed through one of the vehicle's windows, illuminating a pool of dark crimson blood.

"Josta!" he yelled. "Are you okay?"

"They got me good," he said, through shallow breaths. His hand was pressed against his stomach, stained in blood.

"That condensed phosphorous grenade sure fucked them up, though," he said, trying his best to smile. "Take it," he continued, trying to loosen one of the straps from his shoulder.

"You're going to be okay," said Finn.

"Listen," said Josta, blood now seeping through his teeth. "Take the doses. I'm well past saving. Get out of here while you can," he said, handing him the small black backpack.

A stray bullet had hit the engine of one of the cars, and smoke was now filling the dark garage.

"We have to stay the course, Josta. I'm not going to just…"

"Go," said Josta, looking into Finn's gray-blue eyes. "You have to. I've run my course. Find Demetri. He'll help you with the doses." Finn watched as Josta's blood-soaked hands reached into his pocket and handed him a small piece of paper with a number scrawled in black ink.

Finn looked down at Josta's abdomen, now covered in blood

"Go, goddammit!" he shouted. Finn clutched the backpack and shuffled toward the end of the car. He took one last look at Josta, who nodded at him before closing his eyes. Finn peeked his head over the car and couldn't see anything except for the fire that was growing by the second.

He looked down at Tipper and said, "Let's go," while making a break for the door. Shots rang out, but Finn was solely focused on getting out of the garage. He heard shouts from the men but kept his head low and continued to race for the exit. He didn't even bother stopping to open the door, and the force from his shoulder broke through the glass, sending small shards flying everywhere. He saw Tipper jump through the frame, avoiding the glass on the ground, and they took off down the street. Finn jerked his head around for a moment and saw the flames licking at the sides of the shop. He looked ahead of him into the night, his hand clutched tightly around the black bag and ran without thinking, with no regard for anything except placing one foot in front of the other.

He heard the deafening sound of an explosion and stopped for a moment to see a large fireball race into the air. At that moment, he knew that the garage, and Josta, were now nothing more than memories that existed in the minds of those who knew them. In the distance, he saw the distinct red lights of police drones. He looked down at Tipper and then back at the road, knowing that now was not the time to mourn the loss of his friend. Now, he knew he needed to find somewhere safe, not only for himself but for the 100 doses that he hoped held the key to unlocking society from the tight grip of those in control.

Chapter 8

Standing outside the burned building, residual smoke still coming up from the crumbling walls, Nolan Parker looked up at the drones hovering overhead. The explosion had triggered the city's warning system, and police drones had arrived a few minutes later. Now, at 5:00 a.m. with the sun hiding just below the horizon, after the area had been sealed off and fire investigators had combed through the wreckage, Nolan had been called. As an official government special agent, it was his job to deal with matters that directly affected the stability of the Burke Administration. Ordinarily, a fire wouldn't have resulted in his phone ringing so early in the morning, but it was what police had found in the basement that had warranted the call.

The elevator shaft was still working. The smell of charred metal filled the air, even seeping through the gas mask Nolan was wearing. He'd given the order to clear out while he went to work. The elevator doors shut, and the winch groaned as the metal cables lowered him into the space below the autobody shop. Once the doors opened, he took off the gas mask and looked at the workshop. Chemicals of varying colors sat on tables in oddly shaped glass beakers, and vials and an array of machines were situated on the back wall. He shook his wrists, and a thin film covered his hands, masking his fingerprints the way a glove would have back in the day.

His eyes quickly scanned the room, taking in what he saw as his brain processed the information the way a computer might. He was meticulous, and despite the highly complex nature of his job, he always maintained an objective and pragmatic approach to his work. He'd seen dose labs like this before, but nothing quite as technologically advanced. He knew that whoever was working on this knew what they were doing. Walking over to one of the tables, he picked up the largest piece of what looked like a shattered BioDose vial and examined the etching on the outside. To the untrained eye, it would pass as official, but Nolan knew it was a fake. However, the question was whether the remaining few drops of blue liquid inside was efficacious, faulty, or deadly, like so many others had been.

From inside his black suit, he pulled out a small device the size of a pen and clicked it. A bright green light began to scan the room as he slowly rotated in a circle, making sure the light touched every inch of the underground shop. He didn't have a lot of time now but would be able to analyze the holographic rendering later. Once the scan had finished, he walked over toward the machines at the back table and picked up an assortment of vials and put them in a plastic bag. He'd send them to BioDose HQ later for testing.

Throughout his life, Nolan had worked for various government departments, though he no longer felt like the bright-eyed young political science graduate who had ambitions to make his mark on society. These days, his role was to maintain the status quo, which meant making sure that any insurrection or acts to challenge the Burke Administration were quelled before they became something bigger. His wife, Lara, had suggested he find a different line of work, something that inspired the passion he had once felt, but at forty-three years old and with Styre ever-present, it would be challenging to switch, primarily since his position provided him with the finances and resources to support both his wife and their young daughter, Abbie.

He looked around the room one last time before heading back to the elevator. The gray concrete walls and the metal tables unscathed from the fire above contrasted with the blackened elevator where he now stood. The doors closed, and the winch once again let out a groan as it carried Nolan up.

Police and firefighters were still combing through what remained of the garage. Several bodies were lined up in body bags, their charred faces visible through the translucent plastic at the top. Standing over one of the bags, Nolan paused for a moment and wondered who the man was.

His thoughts were interrupted by a young officer who said, "Mr. Parker, we got the footage you asked about." Nolan walked over and looked at a glass tablet that the man was holding. The video was from a drone and showed a man in his mid-thirties running away from the garage with a black backpack. By his side was a dog with what appeared to be a metal leg.

"Anything else?" Nolan asked.

"No, sir. Drones arrived after the explosion, and scans of the man didn't show any illegal

weapons, so they didn't pursue."

"Face ID?"

"Too far away, sir."

"Who are you?" asked Nolan quietly, watching the footage of the man. Gut instinct told him that whatever was inside of the backpack was what had set everything into motion, and why there were now five bodies in bags lying on the pavement.

"That will be all," said Nolan. The officer walked off, and Nolan stood still for a moment. He wasn't particularly fond of his job, but he was exceptionally good at it. Ever since he was young, he excelled at solving puzzles and finding answers where others had failed. He was quick to understand patterns and throughout his life, he had been pushed toward being a statistician or working on Wall Street, but for him, politics had always been his favorite sort of puzzle to solve. The actors were always different, and the stage was ever-changing, a complex system of infinite factors that affected the fate of billions. The Burke Administration had quickly understood the value of his skill set and, over the past several years, he had become the go-to for dealing with situations that required answers without anyone asking questions.

He flicked his wrist, and a moment later said, "We need a disposal team. Large basement, several unidentified chemicals. One suspect is on the run. No, sir, it won't be a problem. I'll take care of it. Understood. At once, sir." The call ended, and Nolan signaled the lead fire investigator over to him.

"What do you make of this?" asked Nolan.

"Fire wasn't intentional. Based on the bullet holes and the amount of gas and combustibles in the garage, I reckon a bullet punctured one of the car engines. It was only a matter of time before the whole place went 'boom.'"

"Has anyone taken the elevator downstairs?"

"Just you, sir. We were on strict orders to only deal with the garage."

"When you're finished, clear your team out of here," said Nolan.

"Yes, sir," said the man.

"Detective," shouted Nolan at a man in a dark suit across the garage.

"Fucking mess," said the man, looking at the charred walls and chunks of charred metal that lay scattered across the floor.

"Drone surveillance caught a man running from here after the explosion. Anything you can tell me about him?"

"Right now, not much. We ran analytics but no positive facial ID. Based on the footage, the suspect is a male, early thirties, with light brown hair, about 185 centimeters, and was carrying a black backpack. Contents unknown. One odd thing was the dog. It looked like a Labrador, but not conclusive. Don't see many of those these days, do you?"

"Especially not ones with a functioning prosthetic," said Nolan. "I want a full report of all dogs purchased in the last ten years, as well as any parts purchased that are related to a mechanical canine leg. Send them to me when you're finished."

"Anything else, sir?"

"That will be all," said Nolan, watching as the man walked off. Despite the early hours, Nolan felt energized by the case. For him, it wasn't the accomplishment of something that held value, but rather the pursuit. He lived for the pursuit.

Nolan walked outside the garage and toward his car. His work here was done. The police and firefighters would clear out soon, and the disposal team would arrive later to take care of the basement. News crews would also show up, but by that time, there would be nothing more to report than an accidental explosion at an autobody shop. He'd make sure to get a script to the network that they knew to follow. The unknown suspect with the dog was not something that needed to be made public, nor was the underground dose lab. There was still more work to be done, and the citizens of Central were on a need-to-know basis, and right now, they would know only what he allowed them to.

"And why are you telling me about an explosion at a small autobody shop?" asked President Burke, clearly irritated by Nolan's report.

"The focus is on the lab, sir. In the basement. There's also a suspect on the run with what I believe to be a large number of manufactured doses."

"And why does this concern me, Parker? I pay you to handle these kinds of things. You know full well what would happen if the public got wind of a homemade dose that actually worked. BioDose would become obsolete, and we'd have chaos on our hands. I don't care about the report. I only care that you handle the situation in any way you see fit, so long as it's handled."

"Yes, sir."

"You know what's at stake, don't you Parker?"

"I do, sir."

"Then I don't need to remind you of its importance. Come back to me when it's dealt with."

Nolan nodded and then walked out of the president's office, hearing the doors shut by the two guards stationed outside. He had a healthy amount of fear and respect for the president. Not so much for him as a person, but for what he had been able to accomplish. He walked down the hallway, listening to the murmur of voices coming from each room, a constant flurry of activity, all of which he knew was important, though the nature of what exactly went on in those rooms remained a mystery to him. Tasks were given to him by the president's chief of staff, and he was told to make frequent reports on the progress and when the job was finished, though President Burke had made it abundantly clear that the latter was all that mattered. He walked down two flights of stairs until he was on the main floor and headed into the East Wing of the Central Government Building, walking down a series of hallways until he entered his office.

The room, like all the others, was white, with simple black furnishings. On Nolan's desk was a picture of his wife and daughter, and on the wall hung his Medal of Honor from when he served as special ops after college. Nolan wasn't sentimental, but he thought it was important to have at least some tangible representation of both his past and future. The medal, for him, was nothing more than unnecessary pomp and circumstance for doing something he had been trained to do. After several members of his team had been kidnapped in the New South Pacific, he had made his way through the enemy compound, taking out those he needed in order to rescue his squad. His commander had recommended him for the medal. On the day of the ceremony, Nolan donned his military uniform and accepted it, albeit somewhat reluctantly.

"It's a great honor," the president had said. "Men like you make this nation great."

"Thank you, sir," he had managed to say as the medal was clasped around his neck. Photos were taken, and hands were shaken, though Nolan had only been counting down the minutes until he could return home and take off his uniform. Despite having served for nearly a decade, after his stint in Asia, and the atrocities he had experienced, he was ready for something different. He wanted to serve his country in a way that didn't involve bullets and bloodshed. After entering the political sphere and making his way through the ranks, his background as a military veteran had come back to the forefront. Though his current title sounded more prestigious, he was still at the core, a soldier. The only difference was he now carried out his duties in a suit instead of combat gear.

He tapped his wrist on his desk, and two lights blinked on the perimeter. He waved his hand, and a list of names appeared as a voice started to speak:

"Mr. Parker, here is the list of those who purchased dogs in Central in the last decade. Around a hundred or so. I cross-referenced the list with those who legally purchased a robotic actuator, a rare part typically only used for robotic prosthetics. List narrowed to around fifteen names. Let me know if you need anything else."

The recording stopped, and Nolan scanned the list of names. Nothing immediately jumped out to him, but he knew that one of them was the man with the backpack, and he was going to sniff him out.

Before he had the chance to open the police investigation file from the garage, his door opened, and in walked a man in a black suit with short hair.

"Hard at work, are we Parker?"

"Just the usual," he said.

"What have we got?"

"You know I can't discuss ongoing matters, Bryant."

The man cracked a smile and said, "Always a stickler for the rules, Parker. We're on the same team, you know. I'd be happy to lend a hand. Wouldn't want another repeat of what happened in 2067."

Nolan continued to look at Bryant, thinking back to the mission he'd been assigned a few years prior after police had been unable to locate and deal with a rebel group aiming to bomb the BioDose headquarters. He had gone in alone and handled the situation, leaving a wake of fifteen bloody bodies, resulting in no further intel. Nolan had considered the mission a success, as President Burke had only been concerned with "dealing with it," but some special field agents, along with others in his department, had criticized his approach and taken to calling him "the butcher." However, Nolan had always thought the nickname lacked the eloquence with which he had taken out his targets.

"I'll be fine," he said unflinchingly.

"Maybe try and keep this one alive," said Bryant, laughing as he closed the door to Nolan's office behind him.

Taking a life wasn't new for Nolan. During his three years as special ops, killing had become second nature to him, like brushing his teeth - a necessary action to achieve a desired outcome. Those he served with, both abroad and now back in Central, said he was highly effective but ice cold. A few years before his father died, Nolan had been sitting with him in the hospital, listening to the dull beep of the machines in the stillness of the room. His father had lowered his oxygen mask and said, "It takes a certain kind of man to do what you've done, and I often wonder if I'm to blame for the way you turned out." Nolan had remained quiet. He had always understood his father's rebuke and disappointment in the type of work he had chosen to undertake but had never tried to justify it. Then, as always, Nolan had quietly nodded without saying a word and watched as his father took his last breath, the machines sounding out a steady beep. Now, sitting at his desk, he thought about those words again before pushing them out of his mind. He wasn't one to dwell on the past, not when there was work to be done, but he allowed himself, just for a moment, to feel the guilt that comes from a father's disappointment.

The file on the bodies didn't tell him much more than he had discovered himself in the garage. The forensic pathologist had written a detailed report and identified the bodies, though one stood out from the others. Five mechanics, most with a history of aggravated assault and minor theft, but the other, with a background in chemistry, had caught his eye. Josta Almeda, thirty-three years old, with an advanced degree in chemistry. He'd been arrested before for production of an illegal substance, and though his employment status had read "unemployed," Nolan knew he had been working on something big in the workshop's basement.

"Known associates," he said, and the screen flashed back with "unknown." Nolan hadn't expected much but had always found it easier to cast a wide net and slowly tighten it until his target was trapped.

He pressed a digital button on his glass desk, and a message appeared: "In progress." He had little patience for the lab's testing procedure, which often took longer than desired, but he had time to wait. Based on the test results, he knew this case would quickly become a priority if the dose proved effective, but for now, his job was to track down the man and get as much information out of him as he could. Despite Burke's clear directive to "handle the case," he still wasn't sure what to do after he had interrogated the man. He was authorized to use force, and if need be, kill, but depending on the dose analysis, it was probable that Nolan would be required to take the man to *The 212*. He'd have to wait for further instructions.

Over the years, he'd put countless individuals into *The 212*, separating them from society because the government deemed them a threat. He knew that some were taken out and used for propaganda purposes, and although personally, he didn't see the point, he continued to follow his orders.

He pulled up the list of the fifteen names the detective had compiled and looked over it. A few had prior convictions, but nothing serious. He could personally investigate each name, traversing the city like some salesman going door to door, but he knew there was a more efficient way to go about it.

The street cams and daily drone sweeps near the garage didn't prove fruitful either. There had been so much traffic over the past week that it was impossible to sort through each person. Further, Nolan had no idea when the man had arrived at the garage. For all he knew, he could have been living in the basement for months. He sat back in his chair and took a breath. He felt awake and alert, the same feeling he had when he had tracked down targets with his squad in the recently formed New South Pacific. No matter the circumstances or the individual he was required to track down, there was always a rush as if all his senses were heightened and being pushed to their limits as his brain worked out solutions to the task at hand. No matter the situation, he was glad he never ended up in a mindless desk job like most.

He flicked his wrist, and the drone footage of the man running away from the explosion appeared.

"Who are you?" asked Nolan quietly. He moved his wrist again, and a hologram of the basement appeared. He looked at the light shining up from his desk, carefully searching for clues he might have missed. The gears in his brain went to work, analyzing the information he had and ruling out possibilities of what remained unknown. He moved his fingers, and the hologram zoomed in to one of the tables, scattered with equipment and various vials. He closed his eyes and after a minute, opened them, clear about what needed to be done.

He flicked his wrist and, after a moment, said, "Get me a list of people recently laid off, fired, or resigned from Conserta." Nolan looked back at the hologram and smiled. Sitting on the table was a laser cutter with the distinct etching of the Conserta logo, a unique item that could only have been obtained, illegally of course, from the robotics repair company.

"See you soon," he said to the image of the man with his dog, before swiping his wrist, clearing his desk of the images.

A hologram of a man in his mid-thirties with brown hair and pale blue eyes stared back at Nolan. To the right of the image showed the name Finn Brantley along with his personal information - single, both parents deceased, fired from Conserta a few weeks ago, and currently unemployed. He looked at the weekly salary Finn had been earning from Conserta and understood why he had gotten involved with making black market doses. Without a weekly supply of doses, Finn's life would soon be over. The same question he'd been asking himself for the past week began to resurface. How was Finn able to survive after being fired a month ago? Did he have a stockpile of doses? The raid on his apartment hadn't revealed anything except empty dose cartridges and a few household items scattered across the floor. The place looked as if someone had ransacked it in a rush and had no intention of returning. So how was Finn still alive? Nolan was still waiting on a report from the lab concerning the doses from the basement. Even though he wasn't one to rush to judgment, he had a feeling this case would soon become a top priority.

Nolan didn't believe that the government had created a fair system, but so long as he was employed and his family was taken care of, he didn't question it, at least, never openly. A small part of him hoped that Finn had managed to create a functioning dose, that the lab's analysis would prove that two men had managed to do what it had taken the government months to figure out. Nolan had always believed in the capacity of mankind's potential, and though the homemade dose would never be accessible to society, the fact that it had been done gave him hope in his convictions. Ironic, he thought, that despite these beliefs, he was the one responsible for shutting them down, to destroy what had, even for a moment, inspired him.

The paperwork from Conserta had arrived a few days ago, with a list of thirty employees who had been fired or let go within the past month. Cross-referencing that list with those in Central who had purchased a dog in the last decade now left Nolan sitting face to face with a hologram of Finn Brantley, his target. Finn's home had been raided, and although Nolan had taken his time picking through what remained of the mostly empty apartment, nothing substantial had turned up. Despite a lack of evidence to lead him in the next direction, Nolan had felt a sense of excitement. The hunt was afoot, and Nolan had no intention of letting his prey escape, allowing his belief to solidify into an inexorable fact.

Nolan continued to pour over Finn's details and profile, looking for clues he might have missed. However, he knew that a man on the run was likely to make a mistake, and when it happened, Nolan knew he would have him. Finn's data and facial ID had been uploaded to drones and street cameras across the city, and with Nolan chasing him down, it was only a matter of time.

He turned his attention toward the photo of his wife and daughter, smiling as he thought about them. Despite the nature of his work, he firmly believed that the ends justify the means, and he would continue to do whatever was necessary to support his family. He looked back at Finn's hologram and quietly said, "It's not long now, Mr. Brantley," before swiping his wrist, watching the image disappear and closing his eyes, knowing that all he needed to do was bide his time until his target slipped up.

Chapter 9

The hotel wasn't particularly clean, nor was it filthy. It was the perfect instance of mediocrity; a place Finn had thought fitting as a reflection of his own life. Sitting on the bed, he looked at the backpack he had taken from his apartment, filled with a few clothes, his small stash of cash and some things for Tipper. He realized that when he had taken his last look at the place he had called home for the past several years, there had been no feelings of loss or regret.

He'd never imagined himself as a fugitive, but now, he was living like one. Finn knew that any digital transaction would be flagged, so he'd found a small hotel in a quiet alley with a blue neon sign and had paid for two weeks in cash, throwing in extra to allow Tipper to stay there as well. The room was on the third floor and had a single bed, a small mirror, and a window that overlooked the dark alley outside. The single light in the room emitted a dull glow, and although he could have afforded nicer accommodations, he didn't know how long he would need to stretch his cash.

The past two days, he'd stayed in his room, thinking over everything that had happened, still in a state of shock from what had taken place at the garage. Josta was gone. He reached into his pocket and pulled out the piece of paper his friend had given him, now stiff with dried blood, and stared at the number. Though wary, Finn knew if Josta trusted someone, then he could too. The black backpack full of doses was stashed under the bed, though it remained at the forefront of his thoughts.

Tipper was lying on the floor and occasionally looked up at Finn, as if hopeful that they would be returning home soon. Finn took a deep breath and allowed himself to feel the pain of losing Josta. For years, Josta had always been there when he needed him. They had talked and laughed and shared moments, and most importantly, Josta had been the friend that walked in when the rest of the world walked out. He felt angry that the world had taken such a brilliant mind, and that Josta would never see the world that he had been working to change. Finn, however, took solace in the fact that Josta knew he had successfully created a Styre dose, something that no other person outside of the government had been able to do. Despite his fears and the risk involved, Finn knew he owed it to Josta to ensure the doses got where they needed to go.

Reaching under the bed, he grabbed the backpack and pulled out a small disposable phone, which had been harder to acquire than he had planned. He held it, feeling the cold metal against his palm, and thought about the age in which devices like this had been commonplace. For Finn, it was like holding a relic from a museum. With the paper in hand, he dialed the number and listened to the distinct ring, something he'd only heard in movies about the past.

The line connected but remained quiet.

"Demetri?" asked Finn.

"Who's calling?"

"A friend of Josta's. I've got something, and he told me to get it to you."

"Where's Josta?"

"He's dead," said Finn.

The line was quiet for a moment until the voice said, "Tonight. 9:00 p.m. Brooklyn Public Library."

Finn thought for a moment and then said, "That building has been closed for years."

"Be there," said the voice, and then the line disconnected.

Finn looked at the clock on the wall, 4:00 p.m. His heart was racing as he thought about meeting the unknown man named Demetri at a location that the government had shut down. No one, including Finn, was quite sure why the public library had been closed, except for the government's announcement that "funds have been allocated to more beneficial programs for society."

He had gone out and bought dog food and water for Tipper in case something unexpected happened, and he was gone for longer than anticipated. Despite the uncertainty of the situation, he knew there was no choice but to wait it through and endure. As Finn sat in his hotel room and the sun began to fade, he let the quiet wash over him. Life is strange, he thought. Just a few weeks ago, he had been ready to die, a man who had lost his job and sat in his apartment counting down the hours until his inevitable death. Telling himself that this was his fate, that destiny had spoken, and it was his time. And now, sitting in a small hotel room with a bag of efficacious doses that he and his now-deceased friend had somehow managed to create, and with the knowledge that he, and only he, was immune to Styre, his destiny had changed.

The room was dark when Finn filled up a bowl of food for Tipper and kissed him on his head before grabbing the backpack and closing the door behind him. He knew it would be foolish to take the subway and instead walked through the tenuous areas of the alley toward the street to hail a cab. Despite the proliferation of digital payments, there were still those who accepted cash as it was still useful for purchases that one wouldn't want logged into the system, and taxi drivers were among that group.

"Brooklyn Public Library, Central branch," said Finn, getting into the back of the cab.

"It's closed," said the driver, not turning to look at him.

"Just take me there."

"You got it." The car pulled into traffic as Finn watched the street flights flicker by as if fighting to stay lit against the long, ugly night sky, the blackness thick like paint. With summer having ended, the nights were getting darker earlier, and Finn could feel a faint chill through his jacket. His heart was beating faster than normal, and he clenched and stretched his fingers to try and relax. He looked over at the backpack on the seat next to him and silently wished that everything would work out tonight.

When the car reached Union Street, it pulled over to a curb, and Finn paid in cash. He exited the cab and walked toward what was left of the library. A few people were on the streets, but it was relatively quiet. Finn looked up at the library's large curving facade with its large black door and looming pillars on both sides. The large rectangular windows on either side were black, and ivy had started to wind its way up the structure. Now, the building served as nothing more than a relic of what the world had been when it had enough resources to allow the public access to reading materials.

He checked his watch, 8:57 p.m. The backpack weighed heavily on his shoulders as he stood by the entrance, unsure of what to expect. Finn noticed a security camera on one of the streetlights and turned his back just as a man walked by and said, "follow me" without stopping.

Finn didn't reply but turned and followed the man who was walking at a leisurely but intentional pace toward the back of the building, staying a few feet behind. The man turned the corner and then grabbed Finn, pushing him toward the door.

"You're Josta's friend," he said, asserting the fact rather than asking the question.

"Yes."

"Let's go," said the man, inserting a key into a nondescript door and opening it, entering first with Finn following behind.

They walked through the dark library, the rows of books illuminated by nothing more than the moonlight that shone through the windows. It was quiet as if all sound had been eliminated along with the library's closure. Finn watched as the dust from where he walked was kicked up into the air, seemingly suspended in beams of light.

With no other words spoken since entering the building, they reached the fiction section, and Finn saw two men sitting at a table with a small lamp in the middle.

"Sit," said the man, taking the seat next to him.

"I'm looking for Demetri," said Finn, scanning the faces of the two men.

"Pleased to make your acquaintance," said one of the men, extending his hand. As Finn reached to shake it, he noticed a tattoo on the man's inner wrist, the same graffiti drawing of a hand shaped like a gun that he'd noticed spray-painted around the city.

"A necessary end to things comes when it is most needed," said Demetri with a smile, catching Finn's glance. "Sorry for the secrecy," he continued. "Can't be too careful these days. I'm sorry to hear about Josta. He and I did a lot of work together over the years. Good man."

"He was," said Finn.

"You mentioned you had something?"

Finn placed the backpack on the table and pushed it toward Demetri. Slowly, he unzipped it and reached inside, pulling out one of the dose vials and holding it close to the light; everyone focused on the blue liquid inside.

"Is this what I think it is?" he asked, not taking his eyes off the dose.

"It is. Josta had been working for a while to develop a Styre dose, and he called me because he needed some help."

"Does it work?" asked one of the other men at the table.

"Josta had been taking it for about a week, and he showed no symptoms. Long term, I have no idea, but based on the data we collected and monitoring Josta's health over the week, it seems to be effective."

"And how many are in here?"

"Around a hundred. We had plans to ramp up production, but as we were leaving his shop, we got ambushed by the garage workers upstairs. There were guns, the kind from before, and Josta got shot. I rushed out of there, and then there was an explosion. No one made it out alive."

The table was quiet for a moment; each man's face illuminated by the dim light before Demetri spoke.

"How did you manage to make the dose?"

Finn didn't answer for a moment, taking the time to think about his answer before finally deciding to be honest.

"I'm immune."

Demetri, along with the two other men, stared back at him in disbelief.

"To Styre?" asked one of the men.

Finn gave him an odd look. "Yes."

"There's no way," said Demetri. "No one has been immune in the last decade."

"There's a first time for everything," said Finn.

"We have to make more," said Demetri. "One hundred is a good start, but if you're willing, this is our chance to bring balance back to the system, to take the fight into our own hands."

"If you've got a team, I'd be happy to help," said Finn, not sure what other choices he had.

"For now, we'll run some tests on the doses, but if your claims are true, you've done something incredibly valuable for society." Demetri reached under the table and slid a small messenger bag over to him. "For your troubles."

Finn opened it and saw stacks of cash inside.

"That's just the start. Josta was a businessman, and these doses are a lot more valuable than anything else he's sold me over the years."

"I can't accept this," said Finn, despite knowing that he needed the money.

"A person can't be truly selfless and survive," said Demetri. "Take it. Spend it. Live a little. We'll be in touch with how to proceed next. And believe me when I say that this is going to change everything."

Finn looked at the bag and then back at Demetri. Before any of the men stood up, one of their heads hit the table, and dark crimson blood began pooling around it.

"Go!" shouted Demetri, and Finn and the two other men leapt out of their chairs and hid behind bookshelves. One of the men peeked his head over the shelf to get a view of where the shot had come from, and a hissing bullet pierced through his forehead, knocking him back.

"Get to the exit," said Demetri, who was holding onto his gun. He held it up over the shelf and fired several rounds, the sound reverberating throughout the abandoned library.

Before Finn had a chance to move, he heard the same hiss and watched as the last of Demetri's men was knocked backward, the same splatter of blood on his head distinct from the light.

Finn heard footsteps across the marble lobby but dared not look over the bookshelf, unsure of who had followed them into the library but certain it wasn't worth finding out. Demetri, filled with the same fear, held his gun up and fired blindly from his position. In that same instant, Finn watched as Demetri's hand exploded, followed by a yell of pain, listening as his gun clattered to the floor. Before Demetri could let out another scream, a gloved hand holding a gun appeared from above the shelf and left a clean hole through Demetri's head, ending the screams, the library now as quiet as it had been before they entered.

"Mr. Brantley," the man said, more of a statement than a question.

Finn looked up at the man. He was tall and had broad shoulders, but despite the muscles, Finn knew he was agile, like a swimmer who could bench twice his body weight. He had short brown hair, and given what had just happened, Finn knew the man had training. Looking down past the man's black suit, he saw the gun in his left hand and remained sitting with his back against the bookshelf. The bellicosity with which the man had intervened in his rendezvous with Demetri made it difficult to respond, but he managed a quiet, "Yes."

"On your feet." As soon as Finn stood, the man grabbed his hands and forced them behind his back, placing electro-cuffs around his wrists. Finn could feel the faint heat from the metal and knew better than to exert any force against them.

As the man picked up the two black bags, one with doses and the other with money, he turned and said, "You've been busy."

"Who are you?" asked Finn.

"Parker."

"Am I being arrested?"

"You'll wish you had been," said the man, grabbing him by his elbow and walking through the library's central area. Before Finn had a chance to respond, the man flicked his wrist and said, "Clean-up crew. Brooklyn Public Library. Three bodies."

Without looking at Finn as they kept walking, Parker asked, "How'd you do it?"

"Sorry, what?"

"The doses. How'd you do it?"

The adrenaline pumping through Finn's body, along with the fear and uncertainty he now felt, made it difficult to elicit a response. He was still unsure of who this man was or how he had known there were doses in the black bag but knew better than to tell him the truth.

"I was working with a chemist."

"Mr. Almeda," said Parker. "Recently deceased."

Finn felt his face get hot and clenched his fists, feeling the warmth of the electricity coursing through the metal around his wrists.

"We ran our own tests on the dose, and although we haven't pinpointed exactly how you and Mr. Almeda managed to do what no one in the past decade has been able to do, you no longer have to worry about them."

"Where are you taking me?"

"*The 212*. You got lazy, Mr. Brantley. Security footage tagged your facial ID outside the library. You should have stayed where you were. But no, you got lofty ambitions and decided to fuck around and play God."

Finn had heard about *The 212* before, a walled area of what had formerly been known as Lower Manhattan, but with all the various rumors, no one knew for sure.

"What about my rights?" asked Finn as Parker pushed him through the door through which he had entered.

"Don't worry about those, Mr. Brantley. You won't need them where you're going."

The air outside was cool and crisp, redolent of his childhood spent outside with his parents after dinner, laughing and talking as the city transitioned from summer to fall. He knew, however, that although the weather was the same, tonight would be much different than any he had experienced before.

As they approached a black SUV, Parker flicked his wrist, and one of the doors opened. He pushed Finn inside, and with another flick of his wrist, the door closed. Everything he had worked for, that Josta had sacrificed his life for, was gone. Finn felt ashamed for allowing himself to believe that he might be someone he knew he wasn't. He had tried, for a moment, to help the greater good, to be the person he had always thought himself to be, and had failed.

"You're part of the problem, you know that?" said Finn as Parker started the car. "I was trying to help people." He could feel the anger swelling within him, could feel it rising in his chest. "You go around killing people that don't fit into the bullshit narrative you're helping perpetuate. You... you titanic, fucking asshole."

"I respect the sincerity of your beliefs," said Parker in a flat voice. "However, those beliefs have landed you in this situation, so perhaps it's best to rethink them while you still have what little life you do."

The remainder of the drive was quiet. The rear windows had turned black, and Parker had put up the middle window, sealing Finn in darkness as the car moved through Brooklyn. He knew the location of *The 212* and was aware that there were only two bridges leading into it, though he had never seen one operate before. Despite the fact that one of the bridges would be expanding for him, he was still likely never to see one operate.

As the car weaved in and out of traffic, the quiet hum of the motor the only sound that Finn heard, he thought of his life, now essentially under the control of the government, and wondered if he would have been better off dead. If he hadn't been immune, Josta would still be alive, and he wouldn't be trapped in the back of an SUV headed for a secret government black site. Finn thought back to his time at Conserta and now, given his current circumstances, wondered if his life had been as bad as he had once believed it to be. His thoughts were interrupted by the sound of metal scraping against metal, and he knew the bridge from the mainland was slowly extending out to *The 212*, piece by piece, slowly stretching itself across the East River. When the final section was in place, a loud set of beeps and large metal barriers lowered themselves into the ground, allowing Parker's car to cross. Finn could feel the small bumps as they crossed over each section of the bridge, and eventually, the car slowed.

He heard the ignition cut off, and Parker's door open and slam closed before his own opened. Parker grabbed him by the elbow and moved him out of the car. They were standing in front of the massive black wall, and Finn had to strain his neck up just to see where the edge of the black wall met the chilled, flat black night sky.

"You're headed to processing."

"My dog," said Finn, now thinking about Tipper locked inside his hotel room.

"You've got bigger things to worry about, Mr. Brantley," said Parker, pulling him toward a large concrete building next to the wall.

Parker placed his wrist against a panel on the outside of the building, and a door slid open, with Parker pushing Finn in and then following behind him. The lights overhead slowly turned on, revealing a small room with nothing more than a glass display on one of the walls, a small concrete bench, and another door on the opposite wall.

"Sit," said Parker as he approached the glass panel and tapped his wrist against it. The display illuminated, and Parker moved his fingers across the screen, moving digital bits of information while Finn sat on the cold concrete bench, the cuffs securing themselves to the magnets inside.

"What is this place?" asked Finn.

"Processing," said Parker without looking up from the screen.

"There has to be something else," said Finn. "Somewhere else you can take me. What about the police? Or jail? Or my right to an attorney?"

Parker paused for a moment and then looked over to Finn. "Look, I have a job to do. You knew that making doses is illegal, and you went ahead and did it anyway. You broke the law, and due to the sensitive nature of the crime you committed, you are being put into *The 212*. You will be put through processing, and after that, you will spend the rest of your life beyond these walls until you die, or the government deems you necessary. Now put away that petulant look before you hurt someone with it."

"This isn't how it was supposed to go," said Finn quietly to himself, not realizing he had spoken the words aloud.

"Life only begins when we accept our fate," said Parker, watching the screen go blank and then turning toward Finn. He flicked his wrist, and the cuffs released themselves from the bench, allowing Finn to stand, and Parker motioned him toward the door.

"Through the doors, Mr. Brantley."

Finn looked at him with rage seething behind his eyes while feeling a growing hopelessness within him. Parker had been right - he had engaged in an illegal act which had resulted in the end of what he would have referred to as a normal life. The door at the far end of the room opened, and Finn slowly walked toward it, unsure what lay beyond it but certain that this would be the last time he would ever set foot beyond the looming walls outside. He thought of Josta and the doses they had risked so much to create, now sitting in Parker's car. He thought of Tipper, alone in the hotel room, and he thought of the life he had had before. Fate, or whatever people called it, had brought him to this moment. There was a faint light coming from the room beyond the door, and as Finn passed through the doorway, the steel door slid closed behind him, tangibly letting him know that his life now belonged to *The 212*.

A Viral State

Chapter 10

Standing atop the concrete platform that had brought him up from the processing facility, Finn looked at the buildings, many covered in ivy while others looked as if they had been transplanted from a war zone. The air around him was still, and there was a silence that wasn't so much soundless as it was familiar. He turned around to look at the giant black wall behind him and watched as it stretched around the end of Lower Manhattan, like a massive snake that had coiled itself around its prey, unable and unwilling to let it go from its snare. He turned back around and started to walk to the city, unsure of what else to do.

The sun was out, almost high above in the sky, and although Finn didn't know what time it was, he knew he had been in Processing for hours. The men in the suits and relentless questions had worn him down, but he had managed to keep the fact that he was immune to himself. He didn't want to end up strapped to some table in the basement of BioDose, an experimental guinea pig, for whatever tests they would inevitably want to run on him. And so, despite the questions, the injection, and his fatigue and hunger, he had answered everything but kept silent about the one thing he still had in this world.

Finn passed by what had once been small shops and bustling office buildings, and although they were still here, they were nothing more than reminders of a society that was unlikely ever to exist again. For years, he, along with everyone else he knew, had wondered what Lower Manhattan had been transformed into, and now inside, he was disappointed to learn that it was nothing more than a prison. As he walked through the streets, he thought once again about Josta and Tipper, helpless to have done or do anything to alleviate either of their lives. As he continued to walk, he heard a voice shout out, "Afternoon, friend."

He turned toward the voice and saw a short man in the distance, his body a silhouette against the sun. Though hesitant to approach him, he knew there wasn't much to lose after what he had recently gone through, nor was there another option.

The man walked toward him, Finn saw his gray hair and short gray beard.

"Afternoon," said Finn. The man extended his hand and said, "I'm Magnus."

"Finn."

"Processing can be quite the ordeal. If you follow me, I'll take you into town and get you settled."

"Who are you? And how did you know I'd be arriving?"

"I work for Kalum, our sort of de facto leader here in *The 212*. We hooked up a sensor close to the platform where you came out. When it moves, it can only mean one thing - a new arrival. I know you have a lot of questions, that's understandable. But right now, let's get you some lunch, and Kalum can explain everything."

Finn nodded and followed as the old man turned a corner and headed north.

"You been here long?" asked Finn.

"Few years. Not so bad considering my age, but it isn't exactly how I had planned to spend my retirement."

Again, Finn nodded, unsure of what to say. Walking through the quiet streets with a stranger, empty buildings towering over him on both sides, he felt both overwhelmed and confused. Though the agents in Processing had explained to him what *The 212* was, they hadn't fully conveyed what had happened to this place and the state that it was in.

"It's surreal," said Finn quietly, taking in the vacant streets littered with garbage that he once remembered as lively and full of energy. Like many who lived in New York City pre-Styre, he'd visited Lower Manhattan many times, meeting friends for lunch, going to museums, and now, it was almost unrecognizable.

"Just a little further," said Magnus. "I think you might recognize our main base."

Turning the corner, Finn saw Federal Hall, its long pillars covered in ivy. Although it had a similar look to the surrounding buildings due to the years of neglect, it looked more welcoming, almost as if it had somehow survived whatever had happened to Lower Manhattan.

"You work here?"

"Most of us," said Magnus, walking up the steps with Finn. "It's one of just a few buildings that we've managed to get power to, so the day-to-day stuff is handled here. We've got a small infirmary in the basement, and we store supplies in the vaults. Come on; I'd like to introduce you to Kalum."

Finn was taking in his surroundings, trying to understand exactly what this place was and what role he was going to play in it. Once through the doors, the main hall was alive with the sound of people walking around and talking amongst themselves at tables that held various electronic equipment.

"This way," said Magnus with a smile. "Pretty crazy what we've managed to accomplish, eh?"

"I didn't know what to expect," said Finn, who was still having a difficult time finding the right words to convey his sense of curiosity and desire to understand. For the time being, Finn thought that perhaps some things aren't meant to be understood.

Magnus knocked on a door, and a voice inside said, "Come in."

"New arrival, sir. Mr. Finn Brantley."

"Welcome," said Kalum, walking over from a table and shaking his hand. "I'm Kalum Sakara; I see you've already met Magnus."

"Nice to meet you," said Finn. "Yes, he was very helpful."

"I'd also like to introduce you to Alayna Ramos." Kalum swept his hand back toward the table.

Finn saw a woman look up from the table, her brown eyes meeting his, and he paused for a moment trying to recall where he had seen her before. There was something about her that was so familiar, and as she shook his hand, it came to him.

"I know you," he said. "I've seen you on the news. At the protests. I thought you were a fugitive on the run."

"Don't believe everything you see on TV," said Alayna with a smile.

"Alayna got here a few weeks ago and has adjusted quickly. It can be a strange experience, being separated from everything that had once so clearly defined your life, but we do what we can here. There's obviously a lot to cover, but before we begin, can I get you anything?"

"I don't want to impose, but I'm starving," said Finn. "I can't even remember the last time I ate."

"Of course. Please, have a seat," said Kalum. "Magnus, can you run down to the kitchen and see if they can get something for Mr. Brantley?"

Finn sat down opposite Kalum and Alayna, and although unsure of where to start, just started to talk.

"I'm Finn, from New York, or Central, or whatever they want to call it these days, both my parents died from Styre. I studied engineering in college, and when Styre hit, I was forced to find a job and consequently worked at Conserta for close to a decade after I graduated. I was recently fired, and a few weeks later, here I am."

"What were you arrested for?" Alayna asked.

Finn paused. The agents who had processed him knew he had been manufacturing doses but weren't privy to how he and Josta had managed to successfully do so. In their minds, it was pure dumb luck that, but he thought sooner or later, someone would figure it out. Finn, despite agreeing with them on the luck, knew that his immunity, depending on who knew, would either be an asset or a detriment both to himself and society as a whole. Sitting in a strange building, with people who he had only just met, far away from what little life he had lived only a few days ago, he knew he had nothing more to lose.

"My friend and I made a batch of doses," said Finn.

Kalum looked at him questioningly, trying to process exactly how an engineer had gotten involved with complex chemistry, but continued to listen intently.

"We weren't sure they would work, but Josta, my friend, injected himself with them for a week, and he showed no symptoms."

"That's incredible," said Alayna. "Forgive me for asking, but how exactly did you manage to achieve that?"

Finn looked across the table, both at Alayna and then over to Kalum. The fear he had felt in Processing had mellowed into something else: a contentment, a stillness. Quietly, he said, "I'm immune."

"How do we know what you're saying is true," said Kalum.

"I wouldn't be in here otherwise."

"He's got a point," said Alayna. "Plus, if he's sure he's immune, we'll soon find out tomorrow if he skips his dose and the symptoms don't set in."

Kalum looked back at Finn. "How?"

"There's not much to be said about how this came to be. Ever since I was 17, I took my daily dose, just like everyone else. I missed a day every now and then, but I always just assumed the symptoms took longer for my body, and I never went more than two days without a dose. After I was fired, I scrambled to get more doses, but ultimately, I had to come to terms with the fact that I would die, just like my parents. But after two days, and then three, nothing happened. I felt fine. I called Josta, explained to him what had happened, and we got to work making a dose."

Kalum and Alayna sat in silence, showing a mix of both disbelief and curiosity as they listened to Finn recount the details of what had occurred in the final days before his arrival.

"I'm sorry for your loss," said Kalum after Finn had finished. "Sadly, I know exactly how you feel. Just like everyone else in here, we've all lost someone, and that pain is what keeps us going. It's easy to be angry, but it's not hatred that keeps us going. It's hope. And that, Mr. Brantley, is exactly what you have just given us."

Finn looked over to Alayna, who had a smile on her face. Her brown eyes staring back at his.

"You know what this means, right?" she said. "We can rewrite history. Think of the possibilities. We can make doses, maybe even a cure. We can bring BioDose to its knees. There will be a revolution!"

"One step at a time," said Kalum with a laugh. "It's true; this is an incredible opportunity. But we'll need to run tests, take samples, and then we can get to work."

"You have a lab here?"

"Not sanctioned, of course, but we've managed to set up a working lab over at the Alexander Hamilton U.S. Custom House and for the past few years, we've also been working to make a dose, although unlike you, haven't been able to produce anything substantial. Who knew the only thing we were missing was someone immune."

"I'm happy to help in any way I can," said Finn.

Magnus entered the room and set a plate down with a vegetable-filled pita and a beer.

"Best we could do," said Magnus.

"It's perfect," said Finn, taking a big bite and then twisting off the bottle cap.

"I understand that there will be a period of adjustment, but if you don't mind, we could use your expertise with our tunnel project," said Kalum.

"Certainly," said Finn, following Kalum over to the table with the pita in hand.

"Over the past year, we've been working to tunnel through Wall Street Station to Clark Street Station. The government imploded all the subway entrances and rerouted the tracks outside of *The 212*, but the tunnels are still intact. However, we've run into a bit of trouble trying to tunnel through the debris.

Finn looked at the glass panel with blueprints of the Subway system and watched as Kalum traced the planned route with his finger.

"It's complicated," said Finn, taking another bite of his food. "There's a lot of factors to take into account. Machinery, manpower, the tunnel's structural integrity, and of course, where to drill once we come out the other side. Can't exactly pop up in the middle of Times Square unannounced."

Finn continued to look at the detailed blueprint and said, "If you can give me the details of what you have to work with, I should have a workable solution in a few days. It's nice to work on something other than fixing junk robots."

"I can imagine," said Kalum. "Take your time. That seems to be the only resource we aren't running short of these days."

Kalum picked up the glass tablet and handed it to Finn. "For now, why don't you go with Alayna, and she'll get you set up over at 71 Broadway. There's plenty of rooms available. I imagine it's an upgrade over wherever you were staying out there."

"My tiny apartment didn't exactly set the standard too high," laughed Finn. He took a sip of his beer and looked over to Alayna who looked back at him with a small smile that had a warmth to it he hadn't experienced in years. There was something undefinable about how, amidst moments of chaos and confusion, there always seemed to be a glimmer of hope. Finn smiled back at her and set down his beer. He picked up the glass tablet Kalum had given him and followed Alayna out of the room.

"Quite the operation you've got going on here," said Finn.

"I've only been here a few weeks, but I'm still impressed. Never underestimate the will of people who have something worth fighting for."

"And you? What are you fighting for?"

Alayna stopped walking and turned to Finn, looking into his blue eyes. "I'm fighting for everyone out there that has lost a loved one to Styre. I'm fighting for my sister, my mother, and perhaps one day, my child. The world's a fucked-up place, and I owe it to those who don't have a voice to do something about it. Plus, it beats sitting around here all day doing nothing."

"I've always thought about my life," said Finn. "Wondering where it would take me, what I would be doing, and the type of person I would be. For a long time, my life seemed like something that was inevitable, like a narrative I was unable to change. But now, I don't know, things are different. Life perpetuates that which we don't expect, and I certainly never expected to end up here, but in a weird way, I'm glad I did."

Alayna smiled at him. "Me too."

After leaving Broadway, they walked through the streets while Alayna explained everything she had been told less than a month ago. Finn was quiet, trying to mentally sort through the details of what she was saying while taking in his surroundings. He felt like a tourist exploring a foreign country. He had known *The 212* existed despite not knowing what it was being used for, and he had been here pre-Styre, but now, it was unlike anything he had ever seen.

"Why not just put us in prison?" he finally asked.

"I've been asking myself the same question. From what I've gathered, it mostly comes down to a lack of resources, manpower, and the necessity to create a narrative. Prisons have public records; *The 212* doesn't. I'm sure right now, there's a picture of you plastered all over the news blaming you for the explosion at the garage and the deaths of everyone involved. I doubt they'll talk about the dose lab in the basement, and they definitely won't let the public know you successfully created a dose. Wouldn't want to give the people hope."

"God forbid," laughed Finn.

"By spinning that narrative about you, the government can look like the hero for capturing you in the future, while instilling fear in the public. It's the same reason Burke's Administration hasn't managed to find a cure, or at least a better alternative than a daily dose. Even more so, that's why BioDose is the only company permitted to manufacture doses. It's all about creating a dependency to establish control and maintain power. A power that can corrupt even the most ideal versions of ourselves."

"It's crazy that we let it get to this point," said Finn.

"You know what would be even crazier? Changing it."

"Doesn't seem like there's a lot we can do from in here."

"It's our only choice," said Alayna. "Plus, despite your best efforts, you got caught out there, and that didn't help anyone. At least in here, despite the drone surveillance and the lack of resources, there are no police, and we don't have to worry about doses. Which I guess for you isn't much of a benefit," she said with a laugh.

Finn smiled as they walked through the streets. It was a strange sensation, the idea of a place not only changing physically but also its purpose. There were no longer people walking freely down these streets, and restaurants and cafes that once served the public were now empty storefronts, the windows collecting dust. The strangest thing for Finn was the quiet. With no cars, no people, and a lack of electricity, he felt like he had stepped into some otherworldly void, and he was the sole inhabitant.

"You get used to it," said Alayna. "You're thinking about the quiet, right?"

"How did you know?"

"We all do. Beyond these walls is the world we knew and the things we had grown accustomed to. Perhaps things we had even taken for granted. But in here, the feeling of not having those things gets amplified. It's New York City. The noise is the first thing people notice, and once it's gone, it's the first thing you miss." Alayna grabbed his hand and said, "You're going to be okay. I'm not saying it won't be hard, but we're fighting for something we believe in, and you're a key part of that now. Once we adapt, then we can overcome."

Alayna let go of his hand and then pointed at a large building and said, "Home, sweet home."

Finn looked up at the large apartment building with the number 71 engraved on a sheet of metal over the entrance. Though the architecture would be what many called old-fashioned, Finn felt it still had the classic New York City mood and, compared to his old apartment, this was definitely an upgrade.

"As Kalum said, this is one of just several buildings that have power, but during the night, we try to keep it down to a minimum. The floor-to-ceiling windows are suitable for natural light, but keep them covered at night. We aren't exactly paying for the electricity."

"It's pretty incredible what they've been able to accomplish given the circumstances," said Finn, following Alayna into the building.

"I haven't been here long, but Kalum said it was pretty bad at the start. And although we are locked up here against our will and kept alive only for the government to use us later, somehow there seems to be a collective idea that surviving isn't enough. We've got to fight and try to make a difference any way we can."

"Do you miss it out there?"

"Yes and no. My family is gone, the soldiers I served with either died or moved back home after they came back, and I didn't have a husband or even a boyfriend for that matter. I was so caught up in my work at the hospital, and any free time I had was spent organizing and planning the protests. I forgot what a social life was."

"I understand the feeling," said Finn. "I was working ten-hour days at Conserta and spent most of my time after work tinkering around in my shop or hanging out with my dog."

"What was his name?"

"Well, I like to think that he's still alive. His name is Tipper. I left him at the hotel when I went to bring the doses to the Demetri guy I was telling you about. I can't do much about it here, but he's got plenty of food and water. Despite the freedom we might have beyond those walls, and on a rare day, the chance to eat meat, I'm going to miss him the most."

"I'm so sorry. That's horrible." Alayna placed her hand on his arm and said, "We're going to get out of here. At the very least, we'll die trying."

Alayna opened the door to the stairwell and they both entered.

At that moment, Alayna thought of her friend, Sam, and vividly thought back to that rainy afternoon, watching as an officer killed him in cold blood. She remembered how his body had fallen to the ground, his life taken solely for fighting for something he believed in. She could feel her face flush as she looked at Finn, trying to suppress the emotions she still felt when thinking about that cold day a few weeks ago. She had meant what she said and knew that if her life must be sacrificed to liberate *The 212*, as well as, potentially the world, then she wouldn't have died in vain. She wasn't the type of girl to so easily let things go, and the anger she felt toward the government was the fuel that kept her going.

"Let me show you to your room," she said, breaking away from her thoughts.

They walked up several flights of stairs, and she opened the door to one of the rooms. It was furnished, but only with the essentials. The walls were white, and the furniture was gray. Despite the lack of color and other amenities that might make it feel more like a home, Finn smiled.

"It's perfect."

"Most of us live here. There are a few who live in other buildings, but without power, I'm not sure what the draw is."

"Are you here?"

"Yep, floor below."

Finn looked around the room and then said, "Moving in will be easy."

Alayna laughed. "If you want to spruce it up a bit, you can scavenge around in some supermarkets or shops, but the government went through and wiped out most of the stores. Most places have already been picked through, but I know a few spots. I can show you later if you want."

"Looking forward to it."

"Anyway, I'll let you rest. Processing can be rough. We'll have dinner back at the Main Base in a few hours, sort of a communal thing we do each night. Also, there are a few clothes in the closet. Some people like the gray pants and sweaters, but personally, I don't see the appeal."

"Thanks," said Finn as Alayna closed the door behind her. He sat on the bed and looked out the large window, able to see part of the black wall tower over some of the dilapidated buildings. No one could disagree that the wall had become a permanent physical attribute of Lower Manhattan, an inviolable and immovable force above all others. Though Alayna and Kalum had assured him that he would get used to things inside *The 212*, he wasn't sure he'd ever feel comfortable with the wall serving as an ever-present reminder of his captivity. He took a deep breath and slowly let it out, working to calm his mind and focus on things that were in his control. He grabbed the glass display Kalum had given him and looked over the plans, now complete with the data points he had asked for. It had been a while since Finn had done any work related to engineering, but with a project that could potentially liberate him from the confines of the wall, he was eager to get started.

The dining area wasn't intended to be as such, but like many places in *The 212*, it had been adapted to the needs of its residents. The Federal Hall building's basement had been cleared out and filled with several long wooden tables and benches. Some of the vaults had been converted into kitchens, with several gas grills and the smell of cooked vegetables and spices filling the air. People were filing into the makeshift dining room, holding their bowls and eating utensils. Although there were no windows, several lights were on, and lamps were placed in corners to add ambiance. Chefs from the kitchen brought out large pots and bowls of food, placing them on each table as people began to sit down and talk. The room filled with a dull roar, and as Finn descended the steps, he saw Alayna give him a wave, and he walked over.

"Charcoal suits you," she said, smiling as she nodded toward his sweater.

"It was either this or a blue dress."

"We never quite know who is going to come in through processing, so each room has an assortment of clothes. We can swap out the dresses for more suitable attire. That is unless you want them."

"A swap sounds great," said Finn with a smile.

Magnus sat down beside Alayna and slid over a black metal bowl and fork to Finn. "Thought you could use these. Sure beats eating off the table," he said with a wink.

"Thank you."

A loud voice from the head of the table echoed throughout the room, one that was both deep and naturally commanding, and the chatter quickly subsided.

"First, I'd like to congratulate everyone on the extraordinary progress we've made over the past few months. It hasn't been easy, but I'd like to take a moment to acknowledge everyone's hard work.

"Second, we have a new addition to *The 212* - Mr. Finn Brantley."

The hundred or so people clapped while some whistled, which certainly hadn't been the reaction Finn was expecting.

"He's an engineer," continued Kalum, and someone from the back of the room shouted, "Finally!"

"Yes, finally. I wasn't joking when I said we could use your expertise," said Kalum, now looking right at Finn.

"But perhaps more importantly, Mr. Brantley is…" he looked over to Finn, who nodded his head. "…immune to Styre."

The room grew quiet.

"How immune?" said a small man from one of the tables, pulling his glasses over his eyes to look first at Finn and then back to Kalum.

"Immunity doesn't have degrees. You either are, or you aren't. He's been off doses for weeks and hasn't died yet."

People around the tables began to talk, the dull roar beginning to fill the room again.

"What's this mean?" shouted someone else.

"We'll coordinate with Dr. Merric to run some tests, but the top priority is manufacturing doses, so we have a chance to survive out there once, and if, the tunnel project is successful, which Finn will also be working on."

A young girl with sandy-blonde hair sitting next to Dr. Merric raised her hand, forming her fingers into a gun, and slowly, the chatter died down until the entire room had their hands in the same position, all pointed toward the ceiling. Kalum was the last to raise his hand, and after a moment, smiled and shouted, "Let's eat!"

It had been a long time since Finn had been a part of a community. He had had friends at Conserta, but not since college had he been involved with a group of people working to fulfill similar goals and with the same baseline ideology. He spooned a heaping portion of minestrone over the rice in his bowl and began to eat, letting the slightly spicy bite take over his senses. The room went quiet for him, and he looked across the table at Alayna, who was talking to Magnus. For just a moment, she caught his eye, smiled, and then focused her attention back on her conversation.

Though perhaps too soon to call this place home, and despite the circumstances, Finn felt a calming sense of contentment. He once again thought of the man in the restaurant and the words he had spoken: A necessary end to things comes when it is most needed. Though true, for Finn, this was just the beginning.

Chapter 11

Nolan Parker hated going to the hospital, especially this hospital. Its stark white walls, and ultra-minimalist aesthetic always seemed to make him feel cold and unwelcome. He hadn't been happy about admitting his daughter here, but it was the best hospital in Central, and since the government was paying for it, he had little choice. For months he had been coming here, and each time he silently cursed the machines neatly organized in the room, their beeps and digital readouts a constant reminder that his daughter was unable to live without them. The machines were keeping her alive, but also preventing her from living a normal life. The irony wasn't lost on Nolan.

He had brought a book with him, one of Abbie's favorites: Redwall. She'd giggled at the idea of animals talking to one another, and every time he had stopped, she'd begged him to continue. He missed the days when they could visit a park, and he and his wife would watch as she chased the ducks around. It had been months since she'd been able to get out of bed, and although he had asked time and time again, the doctors never had good news.

"We need more time," they'd say before walking out of the room. "Patience, Mr. Parker. We're doing everything we can." He hated doctors. Lara, his wife, would always place her hand on his shoulder before he could snap at the doctors in their white jackets, never offering anything more than empty platitudes.

Abbie was quiet today, her eyes closed, and light-brown hair softly splayed across the white pillow. Nolan wasn't sure if she could hear him, but he opened the book to where they had left off and began to read, the soft hum of the machines ever-present in the background.

With all that was happening, Nolan didn't have much time off work, but when he did, he spent it with Abbie. Despite his persistent questions and, at times, threats, the doctors had no idea what was wrong with her, except that the Styre virus wasn't remaining suppressed as it had in every other person younger than 17. A few months ago, she had come down with sweats and constant headaches, and her temperature varied to extremes frequently throughout the day. She complained about headaches, and despite their best efforts, the symptoms persisted.

Abbie was soon admitted to the hospital, and though tests hadn't come back with anything conclusive, the doctors had agreed that Styre was ravaging her body, though it showed no signs of being lethal at this point. Both Nolan and Lara had agreed that despite losing a daughter, death might be better than the torture Abbie was experiencing from constant pain.

As such, she was often sedated, hoping that sleep and painkillers would be able to give her at least some solace. Nolan looked up from the book and watched Abbie's chest slowly rise and fall. No nine-year-old should have to go through this, and he felt angry that it was his daughter, the one-in-a-billion anomaly that Styre had chosen to inflict its pain upon. Abbie's immune system was stable, her blood results were normal, and throughout the hundreds of needles and tests and nanobots that had coursed through her body, the only conclusion was that she needed time or a cure. Abbie still received her daily Styre dose, but the symptoms remained, though, over the past few months, she still managed to evade death.

Nolan spent the rest of the afternoon reading, and when Lara brought him dinner around 5:00 p.m., he ate slowly, out of necessity rather than a desire to eat. The surroundings and mood always seemed to curb his appetite.

"They'll figure something out," said Lara, looking over at her husband. "This is the best hospital in the country."

"I'm running out of patience," said Nolan quietly.

"Focus on what you can control. She needs you to be strong for her. When do you have to go back to the office?"

"Soon. I have a briefing with Burke in an hour."

"She'll have appreciated you coming," Lara said, leaning over to kiss her husband's cheek. "Abbie always loves when you read to her."

Nolan looked back at his daughter lying in bed and handed the book to Lara.

"I better get going. I'll be home later."

"I love you," said Lara.

"Always," said Nolan, getting up to kiss his wife and then walking out of the room. The hospital hallway looked like everything else, stark white with glass panels to the right of each door displaying each patient's vitals and other necessary information. He buttoned up his suit jacket and briskly walked into the main hallway and exited, not bothering to acknowledge the nurses at their desks.

Outside, he took a breath of the cool autumn air, something he felt the hospital lacked, and got into his car. Despite most government officials having drivers, Nolan had always preferred to drive himself for two main reasons. First, he didn't trust other people and sitting in the back of a car with someone else at the helm made him feel vulnerable. His time in the military had taught him to trust the other soldiers in his unit and often rely on them, but in the real world, he was all he had. And second, he liked the feeling of being in control. The offensive intractability of life had an unexpected way of causing chaos. Despite the insignificance of being the one to control a moving piece of metal, it gave Nolan a sense of security.

The streets weren't busy as most people were at work at this hour, and Nolan took his time as he drove toward Central HQ. Pre-Styre, the White House in Washington, D.C., had been regarded as a symbol of power and strength, but the Burke Administration had abandoned it in favor of "a new start" after the government's move to New York. Pulling up to the outer gates of the new "White House," Nolan looked up at the monolithic building with its large glass and concrete façade. It towered over the other smaller federal buildings surrounding it, with Burke residing in the penthouse at the top and smaller Administration offices on the other hundred floors below. Though he never thought of himself as someone interested in architecture, he often wondered if this building was an improvement over the former White House or a gaudy representation of the government's newfound powers. Regardless, this is where he worked, and once inside, the building's design didn't matter anyway.

With the concrete barrier in front of him still raised, he waited while a neon green light swept over the car, and the two guards kept their guns at the ready position. Once the light stopped, a mechanical arm extended from a wall, and Nolan rolled down his window. He placed his wrist on the small piece of glass, and it turned green before retreating into the wall. The barrier slowly began to lower, and one of the guards waved him through. In his rearview mirror, he watched as the giant concrete barrier rose back up from the ground as he proceeded down the road. Gun turrets were placed within small concrete domes every 50 meters on both sides of the road, where trees likely would have been if not for the security requirements of Central's HQ.

Once inside the underground carpark, he headed for the elevator, which once again required him to place his wrist against a glass panel. Though Nolan had never thought about the injected nanobots as intrusive, he still felt uneasy having them inside him. They were necessary to live in today's society as they contained one's biometric ID and data that were used in all aspects of life, but Nolan hadn't seen anything wrong with the old system. He often thought societies rolled out new initiatives and systems to declare progress just for progress' sake, despite life not necessitating such a change.

The elevator opened, and after Nolan entered, the doors closed. There was only one place this elevator would take him - the security entrance for all personnel. The doors opened to two armed guards as Nolan walked over to a small white circle on the ground and stood atop it. A green beam of light shone down from the ceiling, and an automated voice said, "Modified Glock 19, assigned to Nolan Parker, Special Agent. Entry authorized."

The green light disappeared, and Nolan walked over to another set of elevators. The guards never offered any greetings, leaving Nolan nothing to reciprocate. Inside the elevator, he pressed the 100th-floor button with more force than necessary and stared straight ahead as the doors closed. The umbrage he felt going through the countless security measures was not nearly comparable to how he felt speaking with President Burke, where he was now headed.

Over the past several years, he had reported directly to the president. His assignments came from other departments, often solely in the form of a file with a name and some background information, and Burke had started to take a personal interest in his work. Though not abnormal, it now meant that Nolan had to have more face time with the president than was desired. He was a tough man, and Nolan respected Burke for his achievements, though he had little to say about how such achievements had been reached. Burke was ruthless, and anyone who knew him outside of his public persona felt the same.

The elevator opened, and he walked down a hallway, glancing out the large glass window that extended the length of the hall. A guard was stationed by a door at the end, and Nolan placed his wrist against a glass panel, and it turned green. The door slid open, and Nolan entered.

The room was spacious, much larger than was needed for one man to govern, but like most things at HQ, appearances were everything. Unlike other places in the building, this one had marble flooring and a large portrait of Burke on the room's far side. Blue curtains hung on both sides of the windows, the same blue that had bled into all things pro-government. Soldiers and police officers all wore a blue band on their arms. Government buildings, however small, all featured the same blue, either in a piece of the exterior design or blue banners that draped over the entrances.

"Parker," said Burke, walking over to him from the other side of the room.

"Mr. President," said Nolan.

Leon Burke was tall with broad shoulders and a thick neck. Nolan had never seen him in anything but a dark suit but could easily imagine him as a rugby player in a former life. Although he didn't know exactly how old he was, his hair had gone white, but Burke kept it short, and though not as fit as he once was, he still had an imposing frame.

"What's the situation with Brantley?"

"I took him to *The 212*. His nanobots were removed, and he was processed."

"And the doses?"

"I took them to BioDose HQ for testing, but preliminary results show that they are effective."

"How did he manage to make them?"

"We're not quite sure yet, sir. He was working with a chemist, Josta Almeda, who died in an explosion at a mechanic shop."

Burke sat down in a large leather chair and poured himself a glass of bourbon.

"How did this happen?"

Nolan wasn't sure how to respond since he wasn't sure himself. "Perhaps it was inevitable, sir."

"I don't have time for bullshit, Parker," Burke said sternly. "You either know, or you don't."

"I don't know, sir."

"If you can't provide more actionable intel, then what use are you to me?"

"Sir, if I may. What exactly is your interest in Mr. Brantley? He's just one of many to try and make doses. And although his were effective, they didn't reach the populace, and he has been wiped from every database and put into *The 212*."

"Do you know what would happen if people found out that someone other than BioDose could make doses?"

"I imagine there would be chaos, sir."

"You're goddamn right there would be. I got to where I am now because I handled things and shut them down before they became problems. We need to find out how Mr. Brantley managed to make a dose when so many others failed."

"Yes, sir," said Nolan. As he turned to head toward the door, Burke said, "There's something else."

Nolan turned around and faced Burke, who was sitting behind his large desk and gripping his glass with his meaty hands.

"For some time now, the doses have been an effective way to ward off Styre. Though not a permanent solution, they've served their purpose. Do you think a cure would be helpful or hurtful to society?"

"I think the future of our planet demands a cure. It would restore order."

"Order is maintained because I allow it!" said Burke. "What good would a cure actually bring? Do you remember a world where disobedience ran rampant? Where nations fought wars over resources? Do you want to return to that?"

"Of course not, sir. It's just my daughter, Abbie. I hope we find a cure, for her sake."

"There comes a time when every man must accept the fate of those he loves. Perhaps Darwin was right - Styre is just weeding out the weak," said Burke, finishing off his bourbon. "And besides Parker, not everyone you lose is a loss."

Nolan clenched his fist, and he could feel his face getting hot. He wanted to grab Burke's head and slam it into the table. He wanted to watch as the blood dripped onto the white marble floor, knowing that he would never have to hear Burke speak another vitriolic word ever again. Instead, he remained silent, staring at the man in front of him.

Burke poured himself another glass and said, "Surviving is a choice. You and Lara are both healthy, and the doses seem to be working for both of you. I'm sure your daughter is just going through a phase."

"It's been months, sir," said Nolan, actively trying to keep the tone of his voice level.

"My mother used to say that things get broken. It's an inevitability of life. And sometimes they get repaired. But regardless, you realize that no matter what gets damaged, there's always an opportunity to start anew. Uncomfortable decisions are often the ones that require the most immediate action."

"I'm not sure I follow."

"Maybe it's time to pull the plug. Try for another kid. Who knows what the world will be like by that time? Perhaps we might even have a cure. That'd be something, eh?"

Nolan had nothing to say. There was nothing he could say. Burke was anathema to him, the only singular person in his life whom he had ever harbored such strong feelings against. He had served in the military, dealt with arrogant special forces soldiers, boisterous and insulting drill sergeants, and crazy fanatics intent on ending his life solely because he was "the enemy," but the way Burke spoke and thought often pushed Nolan to his tipping point. Burke had crossed a line, but Nolan was in no position to point that out nor argue with his superior. He needed this job, for Abbie's sake, and despite his current feelings, all he could muster was "Yes, sir."

He could feel the pressure on his palm from the force of his fingers and said, "If that will be all, sir…"

"Find out how Brantley made the doses. And Parker, don't fuck around with this. Sooner started, sooner finished."

"Yes, sir," said Nolan, turning around and walking out of the president's office. He felt the anger seething within him. As the door shut behind him and he walked away, his black dress shoes clicked against the hallway's marble floor. The sun was setting, and Nolan looked out the large window, watching as orange and yellow hues reflected off the glass of the buildings below. He saw the hospital where Abbie and Lara were and the old library where he had captured Finn. At this height, one hundred stories above the streets below, it was easy to lose focus of people as individuals and think of them as nothing more than numbers, pieces in the ever-changing landscape that forms a society. Burke had lost his focus a long time ago, and although Nolan believed this, the words never left his mouth.

The other people he worked with in his department, though cooperative when information or help was needed, were too clever to be trusted. Everyone who worked in Burke's Administration was either looking to maintain their position or move up. Information, both useful or detrimental, was the primary factor in one's ascension or downfall. Any admittance of one's negative opinion of Burke would surely make the rounds, and Nolan would find himself out of a job and worse, possibly dead or sent to *The 212*.

Before heading home, he thought it would be wise to check in with the laboratory in person. He exited the main building and headed for a spherical white building a couple of hundred meters away. It was here that the first Styre dose had been discovered. Though the BioDose HQ was located outside the main government compound, the initial laboratory had been preserved and still served as a place to conduct confidential experiments. As Nolan walked toward the building, he thought about how much money had been poured into this place and now, after all these years, wondered if that money would have been better spent improving the lives of the citizens of Central instead of funding a lost cause. Several years ago, he had hoped that they would find a cure. That it was right around the corner, and soon, Styre would be over, and the world could return to normal.

Then Abbie got sick, and months passed as Nolan still hoped for a cure, but over time, that hope faded like the color on a worn shirt. These days, he didn't have time to indulge in hope. He focused solely on what he could control and worked hard to ensure his daughter was comfortable before, like Burke had said, she would inevitably cease to exist. He pushed the thought out of his mind as he scanned his wrist on a glass panel that one of the laboratory guards held out. It flashed green, and the large glass door opened.

Despite advances in technology, laboratories hadn't changed too drastically. Nolan was standing in a large room with various lab equipment on the tables and large screens filled with incomprehensible equations and data. Two long hallways extended off the main area, and Nolan chose the one to the left, walking past several chemists in white coats without acknowledging them. He'd been in the building several times, and there was only one person he was here to see. His shoes clacked against the concrete floor, and he glanced up at the camera at the end of the hallway. Despite the usefulness the city's ubiquitous cameras gave Nolan, he didn't like being on the receiving end of them. He lowered his head and continued until he reached a door with a glass sign that said, "Dr. Thorin," and knocked. There was no response. Nolan knocked again and looked in the direction where he had come and saw no one. He grabbed the handle, and to his surprise, the door opened.

Nolan entered and closed the door behind him. The room had a bookshelf on the wall with a desk in front of it, a small couch, and a table with a coffee machine. Covering the desk's glass overlay was an assortment of different colored files and paper. Nolan walked over and sifted through the papers, casually glancing at their titles, and moving them around as if he were rifling through a magazine to see if it were worth reading. He picked up a blue folder, opened it up, and began to read. From what he understood, it looked like an update to a clinical trial, though with the amount of medical jargon, it was hard to be sure. But one thing stood out - the constant use of the term "SC-17."

Continuing to read through the file, he took a seat on the sofa. The room was quiet, and with no windows, the only light came from the single bulb hanging from the ceiling. Without knowing what SC-17 was, Nolan wasn't exactly sure what information he was absorbing. Still, he had a feeling it was important, especially since the doctor hadn't shared this information with him when he asked for an update last week.

The door opened, and without looking up, Nolan said, "We need to talk, Dr. Thorin."

"Mr. Parker," said the man in a startled voice. He adjusted his black glasses and closed the door, staring at Nolan sitting on the couch. "I wasn't expecting you this afternoon."

"Thought I'd see how you were doing on the analysis of the confiscated doses I dropped off last week."

Dr. Thorin looked at the blue folder in Nolan's hand and then said, "Still working on it, sir. We should have an answer for you in a week or so."

Nolan nodded and then looked up at the doctor. He was older than Nolan and shorter, and his hair was beginning to gray. They had worked together on a few projects, as much as Nolan dropping things off for analysis, and the doctor giving him a report could be classified as working together.

"This is an interesting report," said Nolan, tapping the blue folder as he stood up. "Seems you neglected to tell me about it during our last meeting."

Dr. Thorin shifted a little and again adjusted his glasses. "I'm sorry, sir. You don't have the clearance," he said quietly.

"Excuse me?" said Nolan, stepping toward him. "I have top-level security clearance. Anything that goes on in here, I'm permitted to know about."

Dr. Thorin looked down at the ground and then back up at Nolan. "Not everything, Mr. Parker."

"Sit down," said Nolan, motioning to the chair behind the desk. Dr. Thorin slowly walked over to it, but stood standing. Without a word, Nolan moved toward the doctor and grabbed him by his throat, pressing him up against the wall.

"Do you know how easy it would be for me to crush your windpipe right now? Just a few more pounds of pressure and your life would cease to exist. You're going to tell me what this report is about, or you're going to have more problems than breaking protocol."

"You don't have the authority," said Dr. Thorin, struggling to breathe.

"You can't begin to fathom the power that comes with my role."

The doctor shifted his eyes away from Nolan's and looked at his wrist.

"You flick that wrist to make a call, and I'll end your life before you get one word out."

The doctor tried to take a breathe and managed to said, "Let me see it." Nolan relaxed his grip, and the doctor sank into the chair, his face red and body weak from the lack of oxygen. Nolan handed over the folder, and the doctor opened it.

"Ah, the SC-17 report. What do you know about it already?"

"If I knew something, I wouldn't be here asking you."

"I can't speak of what you're asking," he said quietly.

Nolan raised the gun and pointed it directly at the doctor's head. "If you don't tell me, you'll never speak again, nor will your wife."

The doctor was silent for a moment as he stared down the barrel of the gun and then said, "Where do I even begin? A few years ago, my team was tasked with finding a cure for Styre. We spent years trying to find a formula. We finally got to a point where testing could take place on humans, and the testing was, well, let's just say it didn't produce the results we expected."

"What happened?"

"That batch, SC-14, worked for a while. Subjects didn't show any symptoms for a few days, and no doses were required. But on day 4, they were all dead."

"Who ordered you to undertake this project?"

"We both know the answer to that," said Dr. Thorin.

"Burke."

The doctor nodded. "Since then, we've worked on some new iterations, SC-15, SC-16, and finally SC-17."

"And what does this report tell you?"

"It's effective."

Nolan stared at the doctor, trying to process what the man in the white lab coat was saying. "A cure?"

"Essentially, yes."

Nolan felt like he had been punched in the stomach.

"Why hasn't this been in the news?"

"The project was classified as top-secret from the get-go. Only me, two of my team members, and President Burke know about it."

"I assume you used test subjects for the SC-17 efficacy trial?"

"Yes. Five people. They were kept off the grid, and the serum proved effective. They went for two months without a dose and showed no symptoms."

"What happened to them?"

"They were disposed of."

"Excuse me?"

"One day, they weren't in their quarters. There was a memo from Burke telling us not to worry about them, but we haven't seen them since."

"And what about SC-17? Are you putting it into mass production?"

"We haven't been given any orders to do so."

Nolan stared across the desk at the doctor. He took a deep breath to calm the confusion and rage that was boiling inside him.

"Where is it?"

"Where is what?"

"The cure. Where is it being kept?"

"I don't know, sir. After the trial proved successful, we were told to wipe all data and destroy all evidence of ever having worked on the project. Well, almost all of the evidence. A few months ago, I arrived at the lab, and everything was gone, as were the few vials of SC-17 we had. I haven't seen my colleagues who worked on the project with me since then either."

"Where are they?"

"Do you know the expression 'three may keep a secret if two of them are dead'? Well, it seems I'm the third person."

"Why are you alive then if Burke also knows about it?"

"I suppose it was smart to keep at least someone alive who was capable of making the serum again if need be. When it comes to my life, I didn't think it wise to question why I still had it. I only spoke with Burke directly a few times, but he made it clear that this was a classified project, and the fact that I'm now telling you has put both me and my family at risk. You can't say anything, sir. If Burke finds out..."

"He won't," Nolan interrupted. "Do you have any more SC-17 in this facility?"

"As I said, all samples are gone. Even if I wanted to, which I very much do, try and recreate SC-17, it would be impossible. Security has tightened up here, all our work is observed, and all chemicals we use are signed and accounted for. There's nothing going on here that Burke doesn't know about. I'm sorry, Mr. Parker. It's out of my control now."

"How could you have let this happen?"

"If I had known better, we wouldn't be in this situation, now, would we?" Dr. Thorin shot back.

Nolan sat back in his chair. He felt like his reality was beginning to crumble. For years, the world had suffered from Styre, its impact affecting every aspect of life. And now, with his daughter in the hospital, all he could do was stare at the blue folder on the table and wonder what Burke was planning to do with SC-17 since Nolan knew from the conversation in Burke's office, he wasn't planning on sharing the cure with the world.

"You're not going to tell anyone we had this conversation. Besides the fact that President Burke is ethically destitute, he's still in charge, and neither you nor I are in a position, currently, to challenge such power."

The doctor nodded as Nolan continued.

"I want to be informed, off the record, of any information that comes through here about SC-17, even if it isn't substantiated by evidence. Do you understand?"

"Yes, sir."

"And you're going to keep quiet because I guarantee if Burke finds out that anyone besides the two of you know about the cure, he will erase your bloodline from this Earth after he tortures both you and wife. Believe me, that man is capable of far worse than anything I could do to you."

The doctor nodded as Nolan stood up from the chair and walked toward the door. He opened it and, before leaving, said, "Don't worry, Dr. Thorin, I won't let Burke get away with this."

The doctor stared up at Nolan before he finally said, "Hope is a mistake."

"Believe me, I understand that sentiment far more than I wished I did. But this is too important."

Nolan walked out of the room and closed the door behind him while tucking his gun into the holster under his suit jacket. He knew Dr. Thorin would keep his mouth shut for the same reason he continued to work for Burke - the fear of losing the ability to provide for one's family. As he walked down the white corridor, he felt both anxious and angry at the thought of Burke ordering the scientists to work on a cure without letting the public know. And worse, it was successful and kept under wraps. It was easy to understand why Burke had made such a decision, but morally, it crossed every line. It came as little surprise to Nolan, yet the anger within him still grew. Nolan knew he would have to be smart about how he approached this, as he didn't want to end up like the other two scientists that Dr. Thorin had previously worked with.

Despite the risks involved, something inside Nolan told him he had to pursue this. Not just for the sake of his daughter, but for the greater good, something Burke had always talked about when assigning him targets. But it wasn't until this moment that Nolan realized that if he did indeed want to do something to help the greater good, then this was it, finding and making the cure available to the world.

He left the lab and headed to his car. He thought about his next plan of action but knew he needed time to think about everything he had just heard. Confronting Burke directly would be a mistake, as he would likely deny that SC-17 existed, and Dr. Thorin would likely disappear. But doing nothing would prolong the pain Abbie was in. Nolan drove out of Central HQ and watched in his rearview mirror as the giant concrete barrier slid back into place. He wasn't in a rush to deal with the recent news, but the sooner he acted, the sooner his daughter might have a chance at living a normal life.

Chapter 12

"How you doing back there?" yelled Dr. Merric, his voice echoing throughout the makeshift laboratory in the Customs House.

"Almost done!" shouted Finn as Alayna pulled out the needle and held up the plastic bag now full of Finn's blood.

"I think this should do it," she said, putting a band-aid over the small drop of blood on Finn's forearm. Finn smiled as he stood up from the stool, and they walked into the hallway. Over the past few weeks, he, along with the team of chemists, or rather, anyone who had any relevant experience in chemistry, had been working on re-creating the doses that he and Josta had managed to make over a month ago. Aiden Merric, the head of the project, had grilled him about formulas, chemicals that had been used and the exact measurements of each, equipment that had been used, an endless onslaught of questions that Finn didn't have all the answers to.

"I was a glorified assistant!" he had finally shouted, exasperated after hours of what he felt was a well-intentioned interrogation.

"Josta did most of it, I just supplied the blood and helped engineer the machines, which I have already described in detail. You're the chemist, you figure it out!" He had apologized later, both Dr. Merric and Finn realizing it was, as Josta had once said, "Not as simple as swirling a bunch of chemicals around."

"You think we've got a shot this time?" Finn asked Alayna.

"I don't see why not. Each time is a new opportunity for success."

"You sound like one of those motivational posters in an elementary school," said Finn.

"Doesn't mean I'm wrong," said Alayna. "Besides, we've got the best blood on the market. Sooner or later, either by accident or not, we're going to crack this."

They turned a corner and entered a large room filled with an assortment of electronics and glass vials. When Kalum had first brought him here, Finn had wondered how they managed to get any work done amidst the piles of various scrap parts and beakers that seemed to be piled in no apparent order. Finn quickly realized he had been wrong about Josta's laboratory and that this ramshackle operation was clearly much worse. Though given the circumstances, he wasn't about to make his opinion public.

"You never know what you might need," said Dr. Merric, seeming to understand the look on Finn's face.

"I'm pretty sure hoarders say the same thing," Finn had said, and they both laughed.

Alayna walked over to the far side of the room and placed the bag of blood on a table, while Finn walked over to a table to his left and spoke with one of the engineers responsible for repairing a centrifuge.

"How goes the beast?" asked Finn, using the nickname they had given the machine due to its complexity and unwillingness to function if even only the slightest element were off.

"I designed robotic vacuums before I got in here," said Darin Ward, without looking up, intent on his work. He was a young man in his late twenties, and though not prominently muscular, he had the sinewy build of a kickboxer. His jet-black hair hung loose over his brow and a black sweater covered his tan skin. After a moment, he set down the glass panel with the schematics they had drawn up. "This is way more complex than anything I've ever worked on."

"If I remember correctly, you figured out a way to build explosive drones and programmed routes for them to fly autonomously into US military factories, which is why you're now in here helping me with this," said Finn.

"Well, yes, that too. Thanks for reminding me. But this machine requires precision. And parts. Parts we don't have."

"Salvage what you can, and we'll make do. A team is out right now scavenging for everything we included on the list. But without the glass components, this machine is a make or break for moving forward with the doses."

"Understood," said Darin. Finn patted him on the shoulder as he walked over to where Alayna had dropped off the blood.

"Piper, bring me the smallest screwdriver you can find," said Aiden Merric. After a moment, she showed up and handed her father the tiny tool. He took it from her slender hand, made a few adjustments to a small machine on the table, and then said, "This should just about do it." As the lead on the dose project, he had been in charge of delegating the responsibilities and overseeing the plans. A difficult task for anyone, but even more so with limited resources and manpower. He was a tall man and skinny, like many people in *The 212*, but he had a quiet confidence about him that gave Finn hope. However, he was very brisk and concise when he spoke, as if any superfluous words were a waste of his time. He straightened his black-framed glasses and then scratched his greying beard as he looked down at his desk.

"We've been working to separate the plasma from the blood, and once the Ultra-Performance Liquid Chromatography is up and running, we can get a full analysis of the blood plasma. We've been trying to breakdown the doses from BioDose for over a year now but haven't been sure what we're looking for. If we can replicate what you and Mr. Almeda did, I think we've got a real shot."

"That's terrific news," said Alayna with a smile. Finn also smiled. The past few weeks had been excruciatingly slow. His apartment was comfortable, and he enjoyed the communal dinners, but he was anxious to do something, to contribute, to see the results of his labor. Making the dose was the top priority, and with the schematics they had drawn up for the centrifuge and UPLC, and his blood, the idea of making a functional dose was on the horizon. For now, finding the parts for the UPLC had been a continual and slow process as many required components couldn't be forged; they had to be found. After the sweep to clear out *The 212*, not a lot was left.

He thought about Tipper, alone in that hotel room, wondering if someone had found him and if he was safe. He thought about Wes and Corbin back at Conserta and who was now living in his apartment. Wondered if they had a family or perhaps small children to fill the rooms with sounds of laughter that he had never known while there.

His thoughts were interrupted by someone shouting "Finn!" from the doorway. He turned and saw Kalum in a yellow hardhat and a red flannel shirt. Finn waved and turned to Alayna, "Looks like I'm being summoned."

"Go," she said with a smile. "I'll finish up here."

Finn walked over to Kalum, who said, "We've hit a roadblock. You're needed in the tunnel." Finn nodded, and the two of them briskly walked out of the lab and headed for Wall Street Station.

"What's the status?" asked Finn.

"We've been clearing out the rubble for weeks now, as discussed, but we think the explosives that Burke used have weakened the supportive concrete structure. Some of the diggers spotted a big crack running along the ceiling, and there have been sounds echoing down there, almost like something straining under an immense amount of weight."

"Are they still down there?"

"Everyone's been cleared out."

"If it's beyond salvaging, is there another tunnel we can start working on?"

"There are lots," said Kalum. "But starting fresh will set us back months. It's better if we can isolate the problem, deal with it, and forge ahead."

Finn nodded. They walked quickly to the station. Due to the drones that occasionally swept over the city, the station was kept looking much like it did before they had started tunneling through the debris. Rocks and other waste were collected in bags and then quickly hurried over to the lobby of the abandoned Trump building across the street. The only opening was a small hole that was kept covered with a large truck tire.

The men nodded at Finn, and one of them handed him a hard hat. Finn pushed back the tire and made his way into the tunnel. It was small, much smaller than he would have liked as he felt the concrete press against his shoulders as he shimmied into the station. He turned on the light on the hardhat and continued his descent. He finally reached a small ladder and dropped into the open area, dust flying up as his feet hit the floor. The chamber that the workers had made was an impressive feat given the lack of tools and experience. The area was the former Wall Street station platform, and underneath the grit, Finn saw the cracked white marble of what had once been a bustling transportation hub. Finn looked over to the right and saw a stack of broken concrete and rubble where the track would have been. He raised his head and followed the light until he saw the problem.

The men had been working to clear out the rubble, aiming to use the subway tunnel under the East River to reach Clark Street station in downtown Brooklyn. Kalum had shown him the plans, and although the distance was a little under two kilometers, it was the amount of digging Finn knew would prove to be the biggest obstacle. However, Finn was staring at a large crack in the concrete ceiling and knew that the digging was now the least of their worries.

The dust began to settle while Finn pulled out a small glass tablet and aimed it at the crack. He started to move in a circle, holding the screen at the ceiling, aiming to digitally map it out so he could have time later to work out the math and find a solution. He heard a groaning sound, and he stopped moving. Down in the cold, dark station, Finn listened to the sound echoing throughout the platform. The stability and integrity of the station had always been a point of concern, especially after the explosives had been detonated, and Finn knew that if he didn't figure this out, lives would be lost, and *The 212* would never have a chance to get off the island.

He finished mapping the area, took one last look at the massive crack, and then yelled, "Coming up!"

Finn started to climb the ladder and then pulled himself up through the hole, moving slowly to not disrupt the already fragile environment. Once back on solid ground, Finn dusted himself off and took off the hard hat.

"It's not great," he said. I have a digital rendering of the environment and the crack, so give me some time while I work out if it's feasible to continue or not."

"We're depending on you," said Kalum.

"No pressure, right?" said Finn with a smile.

Finn shook hands with a few of the workers and headed to Federal Hall where Kalum had given him an office. It wasn't much, a small desk and a window overlooking the financial district, but for Finn, it was everything. He had found a large metal table and moved it against the wall on the right side of the room. Throughout his ventures in the city looking for supplies needed for the lab equipment, he had also been working to collect various tools and scrap pieces for his own make-shift workshop. Unlike working to make Tipper's leg, he didn't have a personal project in mind but wanted to be ready if something came up.

He opened the door to the room and set the glass tablet on his desk. He pressed a button, and a bright blue hologram of the platform projected up into the air. Finn pressed another button, and a series of red lines with figures imposed themselves on the perimeter of the room, giving him the height, width, and total area of the space in which the men had been working. He then zoomed onto the crack in the ceiling and did the same. Once the red results were displayed, Finn sighed. The crack wasn't deep enough to cause permanent damage, but due to the thickness of concrete separating the platform from the surface, it would have to be dealt with before work could proceed.

There was a knock at the door, and Finn said, "Come in!"

"Just thought I'd see how you were doing," said Alayna. "You gave a lot of blood today, so I brought you a cookie."

"What am I? Five?"

162

"As a certified nurse who also served as a field medic in the army, I have deemed this cookie a necessary part of your recovery," she said, placing it on his desk.

Finn smiled at her. Despite their different duties in *The 212*, he found himself spending more time with her than he had expected. His days were split between working with the other engineers at the lab trying to build the centrifuge and other machines, while also overseeing the tunnel construction. Alayna worked to keep the medical bay stocked and functioning and also spent some time in the lab due to her background in medicine.

"Thank you," he said, taking a bite. Finn took a moment to savor the sugar, letting it tingle on his tongue before swallowing. Sugar was rare in *The 212*, and although the government dropped off supplies every week, sweets of any kind were never on the list.

"It's incredible," she said, pointing at the hologram.

"Also potentially deadly," said Finn. "The crack is stable for now, but if they keep clearing out the space, they're bound to dislodge whatever is currently stopping the crack from spreading."

"How does one fix a crack?"

"To tell you the truth, I'm not sure," said Finn. "Unfortunately, my university did not offer Crack Filling 101."

"You could brace it," said Alayna.

"True, and I thought of that, but the combined weight of the ceiling is likely more than anything we could construct to hold it. At this point, I don't think it's possible."

"That may be," said Alayna, "but it's necessary."

"I appreciate the optimism, but sometimes what you want and what you're capable of are two entirely different things. Believing otherwise is a mistake."

"And sometimes, the mistake is not having a belief in the first place. Trust me, it's a stronger factor than most consider it to be."

"Always a rebuttal," laughed Finn. "Anyone ever tell you that you're impossible to argue with?"

"Only my mother," said Alayna with a smile.

"How's the lab?" asked Finn, changing the subject.

"Dr. Merric is happy with the blood we dropped off today. They're working on separating the plasma and, more importantly, waiting on the UPLC."

"Don't remind me," said Finn. "You know, out there, before all this, I wished I had had a purpose, something to strive for. And now that I do, I forgot how much work having a purpose actually entails."

"Having a purpose comes at a cost. But what we're working on is indefinably vital for the continuation of our species," said Alayna.

"You sound like a speechwriter," laughed Finn. "You're right, though. Burke doesn't seem any closer to finding a cure, and I have a curious sense that he's not too intent on doing so. Seems cliché that a group of rebels with limited resources would be the ones to finally crack it."

"Our circumstances have nothing to do with it. We have you," she said, her brown eyes catching the light from the window. Finn stared at her, knowing that she, too, had placed her faith in not only his blood but his abilities to execute the projects that would allow a dose to be made. Though the pressure was tangible, Finn felt more motivated than he had in years. It was as if something inside of him had finally woke him up and roused him from the fugue he had been living in for the past few years. He now understood what needed to be done, and more importantly, had chosen to undertake these things with his own free will. He wasn't working to develop a dose because he was required to do so, but because he could.

"In the meantime, I've figured out what to do with this crack."

"Can you plug it?"

"It's not a leak in a hose," said Finn. "It's a massive crack with over 100 tons of pressure pushing down on it from above. Can't exactly just tape over it."

"What if you filled it?"

"What could we possibly…" Finn began before looking back down at the hologram. The crack was large and, based on the schematics, deep, but that could prove an advantage.

"We're going to need epoxy," said Finn. "A lot of it." He did some math on a piece of paper next to him and said, "About 30 liters worth."

"If it's out there, we'll find it," said Alayna.

Finn wrote down the type of epoxy he would need, along with a few other items.

"Give this to the salvage team. I'll go meet with Kalum and give him the news."

"You're smarter than you look," said Alayna with a smile before leaving the room. Finn sat at the desk and continued to stare at the crack. He was glad to be working, to feel useful and needed, feelings that he had been lacking during his time at Conserta. There, he was nothing more than a worker needed to help the monolith company continue to churn out a profit. Here, among the exiled, there was a sense of community and an unspoken bond between the residents of *The 212*. Though from different backgrounds and placed here for various reasons, everyone was fighting for the same goal - a better life beyond the wall.

———————

Work on the tunnel had been on standby for a week as scavenger crews scoured the city for the type and amount of epoxy Finn had requested. Now, a crew of 6 stood on the platform staring up at the crack, with buckets of epoxy next to them.

"You think it'll work?" asked one of the men.

"It better."

Two ladders were put in place, and two men scaled them while the others passed up the buckets. A pump had been fastened with a nozzle,

165

and though this wasn't exactly up to code, Finn had resolved that this was the only way to do it. First, a thick sheet of metal was fastened over the crack, secured with bolts drilled into the concrete. A small hole had been cut out, and the idea was to pump in as much epoxy as possible and then plug the hole.

"This how you usually do it?" asked one of them.

"No. But despite the current situation, I'd say we're making the best of it."

The man nodded as if Finn's answer had sufficed.

Once the metal sheet was secured, one of the men on the ladders inserted the nozzle into the hole and pulled a makeshift lever on top of the bucket, allowing both compounds of the epoxy to mix together. He then turned a knob on the hose, and the liquid started to pump into the crack, with the men below watching as the epoxy level of the bucket slowly lowered.

"Almost there!" yelled Finn. It was dark on the platform, but with the battery-powered lights that had been set up, and careful not to kick up any dust, it was a passable work site.

Once the epoxy had been emptied into the crack, the man pulled out the tube while another man simultaneously shoved a cone-shaped piece of plastic into the hole and hit it with a hammer. The men on the platform waited in silence as if all waiting for the plug to come loose and the epoxy to come pouring out, but it never did.

Finn took a breath and, with a smile, said, "Boys, I think we did it." The rest of the crew smiled and, one by one, exited the platform. After Kalum was briefed on the surface, he put his hand on Finn's shoulder and said, "Your talents were wasted at Conserta. You're a hell of an engineer, Finn. Don't ever let yourself get fooled into believing you're something other than what you know to be true." Finn shook his hand. "Give it a few days, and we'll see if it holds."

"I'm sure it will," said Kalum.

Finn turned back to look at the hole amid the pile of rocks covering the once-bustling Wall Street subway station entrance. Two men moved the tire back into place, and Finn took a deep breath of the crisp air. The past week had been hectic with the amount of work needed to complete the project. Even with Styre, completing a project like this would have taken a few hours on the outside. But in *The 212*, everything took longer. Supplies needed to be foraged for, and despite that challenge, the tools were even harder to come across. The drill had been found in the closet of an apartment building by chance, and the large piece of metal had been cut from the bathroom door of a restaurant that had decided on an industrial look, using heavy sheet metal throughout.

The pump had been fashioned from a grime-encrusted beer keg and pressurizing the barrel with epoxy had been simple enough. All in all, the project had gone smoothly, Finn had thought, considering all the factors. The true test would be when they got back to work in a few days, continuing to clear out the rubble and large blocks of shattered concrete until a passage under the East River was possible.

As Finn walked back to the apartment building with Kalum and Piper, he saw Dr. Merric running toward him from about a block away, his perpetually clean white overcoat trailing in the wind behind him.

Taking a few breaths and stretching his back, he finally managed to say, "Finn, you have to come to the lab. Now. Kalum, you too. You'll want to see this."

"See what?" asked Kalum.

"I think we did it," said Dr. Merric with a huge smile creeping over his face.

"Really?" asked Piper, her young face beaming up at her father with a look of both hope and pride.

"Well, at least everything is in place. We got the parts for the UPLC, and as far as we can tell, it's working. We did a few test runs on it with your blood, and despite a few odd noises, there doesn't seem to be any irregularities in the data."

167

He looked over at Finn. "We're about to start on the first dose, and considering that it's your blood that we're using, I thought you should be there."

"It'd be an honor," said Finn. He knew about the noises Dr. Merric was talking about. For whatever reason, no matter what parts he used or different ways he and the other engineer had tried, it occasionally made a clicking noise, like someone dropping a plastic spoon on the table. The machine had come together quicker than he had thought, as the scavenger crews had found everything on the list, as well as an assortment of spare parts in case the originals didn't work. Despite having written "functional UPLC or centrifuge" at the top of the list, Finn knew that finding one would be a longshot.

Though having announced the machine as complete, Finn had been called away to work on the tunnel and was grateful that Dr. Merric had invited him back to the lab to witness, at least for everyone else, something that no one had ever done before. Finn thought about what Alayna had told him a few days ago, that belief was an important factor, and now, he knew she was right.

"If I'm being honest, when you told me you were working on a dose, as well as tunneling through the exploded subway, I didn't think either could be done. There was just so much…"

"Work?" said Kalum, finishing his sentence. "You're right. There was and will continue to be. I knew it would be challenging, and I knew you might feel overwhelmed, especially not having had time to adjust to *The 212* before being asked to help on the two most important projects we are undertaking. But I think you realized the same thing we all came to: It's not who you trust, but in what. If you believe in the cause, we're the ones to help make it happen."

"Though I understand your perspective," said Dr. Merric. "If I may be so direct in pointing out that science and rigorous work made this happen. Belief will only get you so far."

"Ever the pragmatist," said Finn. The three walked through the quiet streets and finally entered the lab. There was a quiet feeling of optimism in the air as people rushed about, some carrying glass tablets while others had small vials of various liquids.

"We're all set up," said Dr. Merric, taking a seat at one of the tables. "You ready?"

"No time like the present," said Finn. The doctor took one of the vials of blood and placed it in the UPLC. The machine whirred to life, along with the clicking noise, but after a while, the screen flickered and showed the data. Dr. Merric took the blood and grabbed several other vials of liquid and moved toward a larger machine. In separate slots, he placed each vial, and the liquid slowly began to empty. Finn presumed one of the vials was the plasma that had been separated from his blood but was unsure what the others contained. With his lack of knowledge concerning chemistry and how exactly a dose would be made, he didn't ask.

The room fell silent as everyone held their breath watching the orange liquid began to drip into an empty vial. The room was silent, and each drip seemed to signify that hope was on the horizon. After what seemed like an eternity, the liquid stopped dripping, and Dr. Merric put a rubber top over the vial and removed it from the machine. He held it up to the light and quietly said, "I think we've done it."

The room erupted into applause and cheers, with the undertones of a silent sigh of relief. For weeks, the team had worked to build the equipment, prepare the serum, separate the plasma, and meticulously go over formulas to create a single dose.

Once the room had quieted down, Dr. Merric turned to Kalum and said, "It's a risk," to which Kalum replied, "one worth taking." Dr. Merric loaded the dose vial into an injector gun and placed it against Kalum's wrist. He then pulled the trigger, and the room watched as the orange liquid entered Kalum's bloodstream.

"Don't take your dose tomorrow morning. We'll keep you under close observation to check for symptoms and any potential side effects, but we've gone over the numbers and triple checked the formula. I'm confident this will work."

"I wouldn't have volunteered if I didn't believe in you," said Kalum. "We'll continue work on the tunnel, and after a week of these doses, if they prove effective, we'll scale up our operations and start stockpiling," said Kalum.

"If you don't mind," said Dr. Merric, "I'd like to show you two something I've been working on." He led them over to a desk in the corner while the rest of the team talked excitedly about what had just happened. He tapped on the glass screen, and a complex formula appeared, along with several molecular structures.

"It's all theoretical at this point, of course," he began slowly. "But what you're looking at is, potentially, a cure."

Finn and Kalum stared at the digital rendering.

"Like everyone else, we'd floated the idea during dinner conversations but no matter what sequence or combination we tried, nothing seemed like a viable option. Until him," Merric said, pointing at Finn. "Your blood, and whatever is in it that makes you immune, was, for lack of a better analogy, the key to unlocking the code."

"Can you do it?" Kalum asked.

"Theoretically, yes. It's possible."

"There's no time to waste," said Kalum.

"I don't mean to sound negative," said Finn. "But wouldn't our time and resources be better spent stockpiling doses instead of working on something that we don't even know will work."

Dr. Merric smiled and then said, "It only has to work once."

"If you think it's possible, I say we go for it," said Kalum. "A cure would change everything. Get the team to start producing more of the dose and set up another team to start working on a cure. Finn and I will continue to work on the tunnel." Kalum extended his hand to the doctor and said, "Incredible work."

"It really is quite something to see the human mind create a tangible result from just an idea."

"Never underestimate the survival instincts of those with something worth fighting for," said Kalum. "Let's get cleaned up and ready for dinner. We've got some exciting news to share with everyone."

They said goodbye to Dr. Merric and left the lab, standing for a moment outside to watch the sunset over *The 212*. Neither said a word to the other, but both knew what the other was thinking. For the first time in a long time, they both had hope. Hope that a future existed outside these walls, a future that was worth fighting for.

Chapter 13

The days had been long and often monotonous, but progress had been made. The indefatigable efforts of everyone in *The 212* had made sure of it. Over the past month, Dr. Merric and his team had managed to produce close to 300 doses. The week after Kalum had been injected with the first batch of trial doses, he had been closely observed, poked, and prodded, but no symptoms arose, and despite the constant attention and questions from the medical team, there were no other side effects. Production had been ramped up, and the team had scoured the city for empty dose vials that could be sterilized and reused.

Despite Finn's lack of energy from the large amount of blood he had given over the past few weeks and his itinerant schedule between the lab and the tunnel site, he was in good spirits. Hope has a funny way of doing that to a person.

Finn had woken up early that morning intent on checking out the tunnel. The crack hadn't expanded, much to everyone's relief, and work had resumed. The Trump building's lobby was now full of rocks, bags of dirt, and chunks of concrete as the workers continued to dig out the subway's platform. Based on blueprints he had found of the city's subway network, Clark Street station was about a two-kilometer walk, but he had yet to find a way up through the station.

"What if we get there and it's imploded like this one?" he had asked Kalum.

"It's likely," he said. "Whether it's imploded, locked, or gated off, we won't be using the main entrance anyway. Clark Street is on the other side of the wall, and there are service doors and corridors that branch off from the metro's tunnel. We'll be able to use one of those, though finding one will be a process of trial and error. First, we've got to make it through the debris."

"We're close," Finn had said. "A few more days and we'll have it."

Today was a few more days later, and it was with high hopes that Finn had gotten dressed, had his breakfast, and met up with Alayna after she had taken her daily dose. He had gotten used to the sudden buzz of the drone as it flew into the city, and a metal cable dropped off a Styrofoam box with the allotted number of doses for those in *The 212*, though Finn's were now being added to the stockpile at the lab.

"Big day," said Alayna. "I hear we might be expecting a breakthrough, literally."

"That's the plan," said Finn. "Though, nothing here is guaranteed except for…"

"The wall," she finished with a laugh.

"I hate it when you finish my…"

"Sentences?"

Finn groaned and then smiled. There was something about Alayna that made him feel comfortable. She was assertive when she needed to be, like when she was taking his blood, but also calm and comforting. She had talked about what had happened to her family, and Finn had shared what had happened with his. Both of them were alone in the world, isolated together behind a black wall, and the government was intent on keeping them there. Though often busy with their individual projects, they had grown closer, finding time to spend together in the evenings and now walking together every morning to Federal Hall.

"Once you're through the rubble, you figure out how you're going to get out?"

"Kalum and I are working on it. We've got the blueprints, and we have some options, but we won't know the state of the station until we get over there."

"I want to go." Before Finn had a chance to interject, she continued, "I've got people who need the dose; people I care about. Plus, there are a few personal items I've been meaning to pick up."

"It's not going to be a shopping trip," said Finn. "Besides, how exactly do you intend to buy things without the nanobots?"

Alayna instinctively reached down to touch the small scar on her wrist and said, "Cash is king. Besides, what I'm after can only be bought with cash."

"What's on the list?"

"Painkillers, antibiotics, various medical tools, and a gun."

"What do you need a gun for in here?"

"It's for out there. If we get through the tunnel and find a way out, I imagine we'll be making several trips, each bringing with it more risk. If we get caught, they're going to kill us. And I refuse to go down without a fight."

Despite the danger involved, Finn felt the same way. It was extremely risky to try and leave *The 212*, and since they were already here, if they were identified and caught, Finn knew they would be executed.

They turned a corner, and the tall walls of the lab building were illuminated in the early morning sun, like a giant golden blanket bathed in sunlight. In that moment, Finn cleared his mind to intentionally take stock of the moment and recognize the beauty before him. He had started doing this a few weeks ago when he felt himself getting caught up in his work and realized his life had fallen back into the same routine as Conserta - monotonous repetition. Though the work needed to be done, and he was the man to do it, he had started to appreciate moments that moved him or caught his eye, much the same way a piece of art does. Sometimes, Finn wasn't sure what exactly it was about a moment that caused him to pause, but he paused and allowed himself to mentally be in that moment, taking in his surroundings and acknowledging its beauty.

Sometimes it was a meal or a conversation with Alayna, and now, it was the way the sun was shining on the former customs building.

"Busy day for you?" he asked, turning his attention back to Alayna.

"Helping Dr. Merric package the doses. Kalum will be stopping by later, and we'll go over the distribution plan."

"I still can't believe they put his daughter in here. How old is she? Like fifteen or something?"

"Piper? She's almost seventeen. Youngest ever 212 resident. She was with her dad when they discovered him attempting to make doses on the outside. Figured it was just easier to send both of them here. Plus, since she's underage, she doesn't need the doses yet."

"At least they get to be together," said Finn. "But I couldn't imagine spending my youth trapped inside here. Brutal."

"Brutal regardless of age," said Alayna. "What did Kalum say about the first run?"

"We'll start with friends and family, but Kalum has made it clear that there needs to be no contact, which was a hard pill to swallow, but it's the logical approach. If they can track where the doses come from, we'll be shut down immediately."

"You mean murdered."

"Exactly. The safest way to get the doses to the people we care about is to do it anonymously. Once production increases, we'll be working on a more streamlined distribution plan, one that both decreases our time spent out there and minimizes the number of people we come into contact with."

"Good luck, Alayna," he said.

"You too. My plan is nothing unless that tunnel works," she said with a smile.

"I better get on it then," he said, watching her walk toward the lab, her brown hair shining in the light of the sun. Finn walked slowly toward the tunnel, pulling his jacket a little tighter to fend off the wind while feeling the faint rays of light bring warmth to his face. He was glad the tunnel project was close to being done, especially with the days getting shorter and the weather growing colder; it would have been brutal to get anything done.

Finn turned a corner and saw part of the black wall in the distance, a constant reminder that this place, despite the community and common goals, was not his home but a prison. He had never liked the feeling of being confined, but in the last few years, he had grown accustomed to the stifling presence of small spaces. His apartment, the tram, the small workshop at Conserta, everywhere had felt like a box keeping him in. And now, walking on the empty streets full of abandoned buildings, he knew that he was still in a box, though perhaps one larger than he was used to.

The tunnel was the way out. The only way out, though not a permanent solution. Without nanobots and the ubiquitous presence of facial scanners around the city, he, like everyone else in *The 212*, knew the tunnel would not be a one-way trip. Eventually, they would have to return despite the desire to stay.

"Finn!" yelled a man from the lobby of the Trump building. Finn walked toward him and said hello. Enzo Foster was the second lead on the project when Finn had been called away. He was a large man who looked like he would have been a Viking in his past life. He had thick, broad shoulders and a large beard. Standing amidst a pile of rubble and bags of rocks covering the lobby floor, Enzo smiled.

"We should be breaking through any time now."

"Are you sure?" asked Finn.

"There's about half a meter left at the weakest point. I've had the team put the braces and stabilizers in place. Once we're through, we should have access to the main tunnel. From what we know about the bombings, they only targeted the entrances; everything else should still be intact."

"How many are down there now?"

"Four-man crew. Working with hand tools to minimize the chance of it caving in."

"Good work, Enzo, Mind if I hop on down there?"

"Your operation. Go for it."

Finn nodded and then slowly climbed into the hole, letting his feet find the ladder and then climbing down onto the platform. Two men continued to hammer at the concrete while the two others turned toward Finn.

"Almost there," shouted one of them. Finn looked toward where the two men were digging and saw them working feverishly to break through the remaining rubble. He then glanced up at the large piece of metal they had used to cover the crack in the ceiling and breathed a silent sigh of relief that it had held.

He walked over closer to where the two men were digging and watched as bits of concrete were chipped away while the other man scooped it into a large bag behind him.

"How much longer you think?" asked Finn, who got his answer straight away as the air in the platform suddenly became cooler. The worker set down his pickaxe, turned around, and said, "We're through."

The men hugged each other and then ran over to give Finn a hug as well. Though unexpected, Finn felt the men's relief as much as he felt it himself. The tunnel project had been a longshot and not without its challenges, but now, looking at the small hole formed amid the debris, it had all been worth it.

"When do you think we'll be ready to go through?"

"Another hour or so. We'll widen the hole and need time to brace it, but the hard part is over."

"I'll go inform the others. Good work, fellas. Given the circumstances, you did a hell of a job."

The men smiled and said goodbye as Finn climbed back up the ladder and walked over to Enzo.

"They've done it."

"They're through?" Enzo asked excitedly.

Finn nodded, smiling. "They'll need some time to widen the hole and get everything ready, but yes, they've managed to break through."

"Incredible," said the man, looking at the subway entrance.

"I'll go speak with Kalum and figure out the next step. Just make sure everything is safe for when we go through."

Enzo nodded, and Finn walked toward the HQ building, proud of what he and his team had accomplished but still remembering that there was much to be done.

———————

"Three teams of two. I'll lead one while Alayna and Finn will head the other two," said Kalum. The candles and small lights illuminated the large hall where they had all finished dinner. All 100+ residents of *The 212* sat quietly and listened as Kalum spoke.

"We have just over 300 doses to give out. 150 will be dropped off at Central Hospital, another 100 will be given to the Warehouse, the main base of operations for the resistance group, and the remaining doses will be used to trade for things we need."

"What about our families?" asked someone in the crowd.

"Right now, we need to keep a low profile. Once we get more doses and establish a safe route, we can help our loved ones. Any other questions?" The residents of *The 212* remained quiet. It was a risky operation, and though beneficial, both for *The 212* and those they would be helping, everyone understood the risks.

"We'll need three volunteers," said Kalum. "I understand what I'm asking. There is a chance that some of us won't come back, but this can't be done without your support."

A young man at one of the tables raised his hand. Kalum silently nodded and moved his attention toward the other two hands that slowly went up. After three hands were raised, Kalum said, "Thank you. Those who have volunteered stay here. Everyone else, enjoy your night."

People got up from the tables and hugged those who were staying behind. Once the room had cleared out, Kalum sat down at one of the tables with the three volunteers, as well as Finn and Alayna.

"Finn and I have run the route. It's about 2 kilometers from Clark Street station and, as expected, has been locked. We did, however, find a service route that has a door in a back alley. It was locked, but we managed to pick it. All three teams will leave from there and then split off into our respected groups. Each person will have a backpack with 50 doses."

"We're just going to take boxes of doses and drop them off at the door?" asked a young man.

"At the hospital, yes," said Kalum. "I'll be meeting with one of the leaders of the resistance, and Alayna has some contacts to meet for trade." He looked over at Alayna and said, "Nothing except what's on the list."

"Understood," she replied.

"What about the cameras?" asked another of the volunteers.

"Cameras are an inevitable part of the world Burke has built. We'll have hats, but the best advice I can give is to keep a low profile. Mission time is one hour from when we leave the service exit. If you get split up, or something happens to one of you, the other should head back to the exit immediately, no questions asked."

"When do we leave?" asked Finn.

"First thing in the morning, before dawn, around 5:00 a.m. That will give us enough time to avoid the crowds and be back before sunup. Any questions?"

The table remained silent. Everyone understood what was on the line - the paucity of hope that their mission would succeed kept their fear at bay.

"Tomorrow morning will irrevocably change the paradigm," said Kalum quietly. Alayna and the others nodded.

"On that note, get some rest, and I'll see you at Wall Street station at 4:30 a.m."

Everyone from the table got up without saying a word, each thinking about the task that lay before them.

———

The sky was dark and cold as Finn and Alayna walked silently toward Wall Street station. It had been a restless night, and Finn was awake before his alarm went off. Dressed in black pants and a matching jacket, he pulled his baseball hat down to cover his face and walked through the quiet streets. The others were already there at the station, and Kalum handed each person a small black backpack.

"You have your routes. Stick to the plan. One hour. That's it. In and out."

The others nodded quietly. Though nervous, Finn knew what was expected of him and focused on the task at hand.

"Let's go," said Kalum as he moved the tire, and one by one, they descended onto the platform below. The tunnel leading into the subway system had been widened and braced, though only big enough for one person to enter at a time. Once through, Finn stopped for a second to take in the expansive tunnel before him. He had run the route with Kalum several times while searching for a usable entrance tunnel, but he was still in awe that they had been able to break through. He also wondered why the tunnel hadn't been completely destroyed and was thankful that only the entrances had been targeted.

Each person flicked on a flashlight and began to jog through the tunnel, the soft padding of their footsteps reverberating off the concrete walls. Finn ran through the route in his mind. Alayna had described the hospital to him, and though he wished she were coming with him, only she was able to meet up with her contacts to make the trades. He was headed for what had formerly been called the Brooklyn Hospital Center, just a few blocks from Clark Street station. For whatever reason, it had been renamed "Hospital Four," and his objective was to drop off the doses at the nurses' entrance. Kalum had made it clear that he and the other volunteer assigned to the hospital were not to make contact with anyone so as not to raise any questions. Alayna had the idea to place the two backpacks near a door on the building's side solely used by the nurses.

"They'll know what to do," she had said.

The group continued to move through the tunnel, no one saying a word, each of them filling the silence with their own random thoughts. Near the end were four doors, two on each side and Kalum motioned for them to go toward the ones on the left. They hoisted themselves up onto the concrete side, and Kalum opened the door. Moving past a network of pipes and electrical wire, they came to a set of stairs, and once up, there was another door.

"This is it," said Kalum. "It's 5 a.m. now. I'll see you back here at 6. Good luck." He slowly opened the door and went outside, the morning cold flowing through the open door. Kalum and another man went first, walking through the alley and turning left, disappearing into the shadows of the city. Alayna and the female volunteer went next, Alayna turning around to smile at Finn before heading out.

"Ready?" asked Finn, looking at Darin.

"As I'll ever be," he said. They crossed the threshold, listening to the door close behind them, and then walked down the alley. The morning was still, with only the occasional car passing by. The streetlights were still on as Finn and Darin turned right and headed toward the hospital. Finn pulled his hat down over his forehead and kept his head down. The winter winds blew, and the chill set their teeth on edge.

They walked at a brisk pace, but not awkward enough to draw attention to themselves. Finn had memorized the route, which was just a little over a kilometer, and though he didn't expect any trouble, he could still feel his heart racing. Darin didn't say anything, and Finn returned the silence as they walked through the quiet streets of Central, the stillness reminiscent of that inside *The 212*.

It had been a little over a month since Finn had been taken to *The 212*, and though he missed the idea of freedom that came with not being inside, he was grateful to be somewhere that valued him, somewhere that gave him a purpose. He thought of Tipper, and while he had verbally agreed to the plan Kalum had laid out, Finn had something else in mind.

"We have to make a stop after the hospital," said Finn.

"We're on a schedule," said Darin, not looking over to Finn.

"It's my dog. I have to find him."

"There's a time to leave things behind."

"Not Tipper."

Darin was quiet for a moment before finally saying, "One stop. If he's not there, we're going directly back to the station."

Finn nodded as they kept walking to the hospital. In the distance, Finn could see the black of the night beginning to fade as light began to fill the horizon, like ink being dropped into a cup of water. A few blocks away, Finn could see the tall brick floors of Hospital Four, and the two men quickened their pace.

Alayna had described the entrance and was adamant they couldn't miss it. About a block away, Finn could see the hospital's entrance, with the occasional doctor in red scrubs walking through the door with a coffee in hand.

"On the left," said Finn. Darin nodded.

The men walked slowly across the street, walked to the left of the entrance, and made a right. The main building was large and entirely made of brick and to their left was a smaller brick building, some type of special ward, as Alayna had described. About 50 meters in front of them, Finn saw the white door.

"Just set the backpacks outside of the door. Someone will pick them up."

They walked toward the door and paused for a moment before gently placing the two black backpacks on the ground. Just before they had a chance to walk away, the door opened, and a nurse in a white outfit stood at the threshold, looking at both men in black clothing.

Finn felt like his heart was about to jump out of his chest. He froze, unable to think or say anything, only able to look back at the nurse with her hair done up in a bun.

"We're..." Finn started to say before the nurse interrupted him.

"It's cold. You'd best be getting back to wherever you came from," she said, bending down to pick up the two backpacks. Finn and Darin turned to walk away and made their way back toward the hospital's entrance.

"Where's your dog?" Darin asked.

"At a hotel just south of here. I don't know if he's still there, or if he's even still alive, but it's the only place I know where to look. It's close to the library."

"That's at least five blocks from here," said Darin, looking down at his watch.

"We have time," said Finn. "Please." The young man nodded and then said, "Let's go."

They headed south with their backs to the hospital, walking quickly as Finn glanced up at the sky and saw the yellow light mixing with the dark on the horizon. He knew he was taking a risk, and ultimately one that might prove futile. It had been over a month since he had last been at the hotel, and who knows what might have happened to Tipper. For all Finn knew, he could be dead. But despite the possibilities, he had to at least check.

The streets seemed to fly by in a flurry of gray concrete as Finn and Darin walked toward the hotel. Once in the alley, Finn told Darin to stay put as he walked toward the hotel he had checked into just a month prior.

An old man at the counter lifted his head and looked up at Finn without saying a word.

"Sorry to bother, but I was here a month ago, and I left a dog in my room."

The man didn't say anything as he slowly looked Finn up and down before finally catching his gaze.

"I might know something about a dog," he said through yellow teeth. "What's it worth to you?"

"It's my dog," said Finn.

"And you left it here for over a month. It seems to me that a dog like that can be sold for a pretty price."

Finn had expected this. Survival in Central had led to a decline in acts of kindness and had forged a quid pro quo mentality, anything that might help someone survive. He slowly reached into his pocket and pulled out five doses, and set them on the counter, the blue liquid refracting on the counter from the light.

"This should suffice."

The man didn't say anything. With a grizzled hand, he scooped the doses off the counter and put them in his pocket.

"Back exit," he said.

Finn walked through the hotel and out the door at the back, entering another alley. He saw nothing except a few garbage cans and trash bags.

"Tipper," he said, though not too loudly. From a distance, he heard a small bark, and he headed toward the sound. Tied with a chain to a metal ladder mounted to the wall, he saw Tipper, though hardly recognized him. He had lost significant weight, and patches of his fur were gone.

"Good to see you, Tip. Let's go."

Finn ran over to him and unclipped the chain from around his neck. He picked him up and then walked toward the main street and over to the adjacent alley where Darin was waiting.

"We've got to go." Finn looked down to check his watch. It was 5:45. The sun was beginning to creep over the horizon and people were starting to fill the street.

Finn set Tipper down, and they walked quickly back toward the hospital and then a few blocks east to the subway. They kept their heads down, careful to avoid looking up at the facial scanners that had become a ubiquitous part of the city. Tipper was limping, and Finn could see it was difficult for him to keep up. His mechanical leg hadn't been properly looked after, and he suspected that some parts had begun to rust. Though functional, its condition was starting to worsen.

The trio moved through the streets, blending in with the others on their early morning commute. The city was beginning to come to life, and Finn knew it was vital they make it back before the drone did one of its passes over *The 212*. He looked at the watchtower in the distance positioned high up on the wall and continued moving. Though he never saw anyone in it, he was sure someone was always watching. They quickened their pace, and Finn saw the alley where they had come up ahead.

"Come on, Tip," he said encouragingly.

They made their way into the alley and saw the others standing outside the door. It was a few minutes past 6, but they had made it.

Kalum looked down at the dog and then back up at Finn. Before he had a chance to say anything, Finn said, "I had to."

"We'll discuss it later," he said. "Time to go."

Alayna looked at Tipper and then up at Finn, "Cute dog," she said with a wink before picking up a large backpack and heading into the service entrance. The others followed, with Finn and Tipper taking up the rear.

Finn placed a large piece of metal across the door, securing it in place, and walked down the steps into the subway tunnel.

He caught up with Alayna and said, "Find what you're looking for?"

"And then some," she said. "How'd you find him?"

"Hotel owner had him chained up out back. Think he was trying to sell him."

"And he just gave him back to you?"

"For the low price of five doses."

"Sounds like a deal," she said.

Finn laughed. The lights illuminated the dark tunnel as they walked the two kilometers back to *The 212*. As far as Finn knew, everything had gone smoothly, which was more than anyone had expected. Anxiety and fear were part of the imperfect reality of being human, but so too were hope and determination. The six of them, with Tipper at the rear, made their way to the only place they could call home. A desolate and isolated existence for those the government had intended to use for its own political purposes. But despite the circumstances, they thrived. They came together, formed a community, and were now working toward a common goal. The first part of which had been achieved in the early hours of a cold November morning.

Chapter 14

Nolan stared at the file on his desk. It had been a few weeks since he had learned from Dr. Thorin that a cure existed, and he had spent that time thinking of what to do. The information could have catastrophic consequences if not used correctly. The worst of which would not only be his death but that of his family as well. It was clear why Burke hadn't made it public - control; the only thing Burke cared about. The president, Nolan concluded, not for the first time in his life, was nothing more than a power-hungry man intent on serving his own interests.

He thought about all the sacrifices people had made and the relentless effort to secure their daily dose. Many had died in that pursuit, and others continued to live a life centered only around surviving for one more day. As far as Nolan could tell, it had been at least a year since the cure had been developed, and Burke was keeping it for himself. He looked at Abbie's picture on his desk and then turned his head to look out the window. It was a quiet evening on a cold December morning, and the sky looked as if it were about to snow. The colorful fall leaves had long since passed, and though it was now winter, Nolan was nowhere closer to figuring out what to do with the information in the blue folder that now sat on his desk like a paperweight. He glanced at his closed door before grabbing the folder and placing it into file drawer below his desk. Once closed, he tapped his wrist against the cold steel drawer and a red light indicated that it was locked.

He kept it from his wife, as he knew that the fewer people with knowledge of the matter, the safer they would all be. Nolan knew what she would say: "You need to make this public! The people deserve to know!" She was a woman of ideals, one who believed in the greater good, and Nolan wondered if he too held the same ideals or if they had dissipated with time amidst the work he now did. Burke liked to use that phrase too, "the greater good," but Nolan reminded himself that Hitler had once used that expression as well. The words weren't as important as the perspective and intention behind how they were used and by whom.

Nolan presumed that leaking the news to the public wouldn't amount to much, as Burke's disinformation machine would quell the story as soon as it had begun, and innocent people would be permanently silenced. Doing nothing was equally worse. He leaned back in his chair and looked at the naked tree branches standing still among a gray sky, the sun not visible but it's light still present as if fighting against the encroaching night.

He had been busy over the past few weeks, handling an increasing number of "tasks" that he had been assigned. The resistance group was growing, despite one of its most prominent leaders being taken to *The 212.* Burke had described it as the most dangerous threat to his Administration, at which point Nolan had clenched his jaw and did his best not to lash out at the egotistical and morally bankrupt leader whose sole focus was on his continuation of power. He wondered if Burke had taken the cure. That would certainly explain why he wasn't focused on Styre, and though he did see his secretary drop off Burke's daily dose, Nolan was skeptical of whether it was actually being injected or not.

There was a knock at his door, and Nolan said, "Come in." He looked up and saw a tall man in a tight-fitting suit. Nolan didn't know much about him, except that he worked in internal affairs. He always seemed to be in on everyone else's business, a perfidious trait Nolan didn't take kindly to. Nolan couldn't remember his name, only that he went by Reeves and Nolan wondered why he was now standing in his doorway.

"Parker, I thought you would have gone home by now."

"Just finishing up," he said in a hushed tone. Reeves stood in front of his desk, looking at him with his little beady eyes as if searching for an answer.

"What can I do for you?" he asked.

"I was hoping for some more information on a person of interest," he said, placing a red file folder on Nolan's desk.

Nolan looked at it and then back up at Reeves.

"Well, go on, open it."

He slowly flipped the file open and saw a picture and details of Finn Brantley. He looked back up at Reeves and asked, "What about him?"

"We understand he was processed into *The 212* about a month ago and we're just following up that everything went according to the standard process."

"Is there any reason you suspect it didn't'?" asked Nolan, feeling a pit of anger starting to grow inside him.

"No, no, of course not, Parker. Just standard procedure. I was hoping you could run me through what happened after you first made contact."

"It's all in my report," said Nolan. "Which is here in the file."

"It would help if I heard it from you," said Reeves.

Nolan liked Reeves no more than he liked visiting his daughter in the hospital. Both got under his skin, like a faint buzz that won't go away.

He watched as Reeves took a seat and stared at Nolan as if he were about to regale him with tales from the war.

Nolan began, starting with the moment he had received Finn's file and his plan to track him.

"Why was he off-grid?" Reeves asked.

"You'd have to ask him," said Nolan. "My best guess is because he illegally created a dose."

"An efficacious one," added Reeves

"Yes."

Reeves was intelligent, and he made no attempt at hiding it. Not enough to be overbearing but more than enough to be annoying.

"Why do you think he was able to do so when no one was able?"

"Are you asking me to speculate?"

"If you would."

"Because he, along with his associate, Mr. Almeda, figured out the precise chemical compounds and the order in which to combine them."

Reeves laughed. "Very precise, Parker. Please, continue."

Nolan then talked about the firefight at the library, the deaths of the other men, and how he had taken Finn into custody and then to *The 212* for processing.

"And nothing seemed abnormal about his behavior?"

"Nothing that stood out," said Nolan. "He wasn't injured, and *The 212* processing unit sent back a report that said everything was normal. The drones have also sent visual confirmation that he is still in *The 212*. What exactly is the point of this questioning?"

"As I said before, it's just routine. We're all very aware of your reputation, Parker, and just wanted to check that everything went like it was supposed to. What was it they call you?" asked Reeves, looking at Nolan with a glint in his eye. "The butcher, that's it," he said, answering his own question. "You seem to have a number of questions yourself, Parker. I'm curious what makes you so curious."

Nolan didn't respond. No matter what he did or how long it had been, his past seemed to cling to him like a scar. The room was still as both men looked across the desk at each other. The gray walls and minimal furniture seemed to compliment the hygienic quiet.

"Will that be all?" asked Nolan, eager for Reeves to leave.

"For now," he said, standing up. "We'll be following up with Mr. Brantley's processing as well as interviewing the processing unit at *The 212*. If any irregularities are found, I assure you, you'll be the first to know."

Before Reeves left, Nolan stood up and asked, "What's your aim here, Reeves?"

The man slowly turned around and adjusted the button on his dark suit.

"You can be one of two things to us, Parker: an asset or a hazard. I'm here to ensure you aren't the latter."

Nolan looked at the man and then said, "I didn't realize how much I don't like you until right at this moment."

"We'll be in touch, Parker," said the man, closing the door behind him, leaving Nolan alone in his office. Reeves' arrival was unexpected but gave Nolan pause for thought. He didn't understand why Internal Affairs was so interested in routine processing. Finn hadn't done anything worse than any of the other inmates in *The 212*, and he knew that Reeves' use of 'standard protocol' was an excuse, but an excuse for what? The last thing Nolan needed now was something else to look into, but he mentally added it to the list of things that required his attention.

He reached into a drawer, pulled out Finn's file, and looked over it, searching for any clues he might have missed. Nothing stood out to him, but he was sure there was something he was missing. Internal Affairs wouldn't check on things if they didn't have a good reason, and that was exactly what Nolan was intent on finding out. First, though, he needed to deal with Burke and the fact he was hiding the cure from the world. He put Finn's file back into the drawer and slid his finger over the glass screen to turn it off before leaving the quiet office and heading home.

With no immediate tasks to handle and in between his trips to the hospital and his office, Nolan had made a decision about Burke and the cure. He had gone over the scenarios, calculated the risk versus reward and ultimately decided it was best to passively bring it up, putting the ball in Burke's court. It was a risky move - letting Burke know that he knew about the cure, and although it also put Dr. Thorin's life at risk, Nolan could no longer stay silent.

Walking from the car park through the Central compound, Nolan pulled his black peacoat tighter against the cold winter winds. The sky was gray, and though it was still early afternoon, Nolan knew the sun would soon fade. Nolan had an intention but hadn't prepared anything specific to say. He would have asked his wife but had decided it'd be best to handle this himself.

Nolan had never considered himself a humanitarian, and although he was loyal and what some would consider a patriot, his ideals had shifted with age. Marrying Laura and having Abbie had solidified his belief that family came first, even at the expense of others. Though he hadn't been close to his family, starting his own had changed his perspective. Over the past few days, he had thought long and hard about what his values were, even going so far as to try and write them down on a piece of paper, but ending up with only "family," "trust," and "survival." He thought about the people in his life - his high school teacher who had spent hours with him after class helping him with physics - the military nurses who had bandaged his wounds - people who made sacrifices for others. He wondered if he were that kind of person and if he would be able to find out when his back was up against a wall.

The main building's large gray façade loomed before him, and he walked in, passing through the security clearance area and taking the elevator to the top floor. He knew Burke would be in his office, sitting at his large desk with his perpetual look of arrogance and power. Nolan made no attempt to speak with Burke more often than necessary, but this was an exception.

The elevator dinged, and the doors opened. He walked down the long hallway, this time without looking out the large windows, his gaze focused on the large black doors ahead. They opened, and he entered. Burke was sitting at his desk. "What do you want, Parker?" he asked, not looking up from the paper he was writing on.

Nolan entered the room, and the doors closed behind him. "I've been spending some time at the lab, sir. Trying to figure out how Finn Brantley managed to make the doses."

President Burke placed the pen on the desk, and looked up at Nolan, his piercing gray eyes glaring through Nolan's expressionless face.

"And?"

"There's nothing out of the ordinary about how he did it, sir. As far as we can tell, he just did it."

"Who is 'we'?"

"I met with Dr. Thorin. He's been updating me about the analysis they are conducting on the doses we confiscated."

"And neither of you found anything conclusive," he said rather than asked.

"No, sir."

"Well, keep after it, Parker. I pay you to find answers."

"Yes, sir."

Though Nolan knew that in Burke's mind, the conversation had finished, he stood there and waited for Burke to look back up at him. Time seemed to stand still until the large man finally said, "Was there something else, Parker?"

"As you know, sir, my daughter, Abbie, is sick. Her life, at least for the last few months, has been in a circular state of convalescence. Though the doctors have taken good care of her, they say there's nothing that can be done."

Burke didn't take his eyes off him while he waited for Nolan to get to the point.

"As such, sir, I'm asking for one of the cure doses. For Abbie."

The room remained quiet as Burke looked at Nolan, his face not giving away any information, but Nolan knew there were a series of questions running through his head. Burke pushed his chair back and rose. Nolan watched as Burke walked over to the window overlooking the city below. He stood there, his large body silhouetted against the cold gray sky outside.

Without turning around, Burke said, "Do you know what the difference between an outbreak and an epidemic is?" He paused for a moment, but Nolan knew he wasn't expecting an answer.

"It depends entirely on how the disease is sold to the public."

Nolan continued to stand where he was, keeping his eyes on Burke's back.

"The system we have created is working. You, me, the citizens of this country, we all have a role to play, and any disruption to the system would bring it crashing down."

Burke turned around and smiled but his eyes were still calculating the request.

"How you found out about the cure is irrelevant. Bold of you to bring this to my attention, but given the circumstances, I'm sure I would have done the same. Your request is simple enough, but ultimately, we must remember that progress comes at a price."

Nolan had expected Burke not to be direct, as was so often characteristic in the way he spoke.

"Sir, I understand your position. But given the severity with which my daughter is suffering, a cure is her only chance of survival." He paused for a moment before adding, "It's the right thing to do."

Burke immediately snapped back, "Some things are more important than the right thing. This is one such case."

Nolan could feel himself wanting to yell, to lash out, and physically hurt Burke, knowing full well that he could, but refrained and instead said, "So what's the result then? Keep it for yourself and keep everyone under your thumb? Millions of people out there are suffering. Is it just about maintaining your power?"

Burke smiled and said, "When, Mr. Parker, in history, has it ever been about anything different?"

He walked closer to Nolan and looked down at him, his voice had become soft and intense, "Your daughter is no concern of mine. She got sick, and nature should have to run its course. The integrity of our system will not be compromised based on what you believe to be 'the right thing.' I don't need to remind you that if any information related to a cure gets brought to my attention, your daughter will disappear along with the entire Parker family. You will be erased from this planet, as if you never existed. The only thing that stands between you and being dead is you."

Nolan could feel his face flushed and his muscles tight. The only thing he managed to say was, "Understood, sir."

Burke walked back over to his desk and picked up his book.

"It's best you remember your role, Parker. Entitlement isn't a quality I'm looking for in my agents."

"Yes, sir," Nolan said, watching as Burke picked up his book and continued to read. He turned around and walked through the door. The hallway seemed longer than usual as Nolan walked once again without looking out the windows on his right. His conversations with Burke were anathema to him - this one in particular. It had been a risk to bring up the cure, but he knew it was his only option to save Abbie, and now that Burke knew that he knew about the cure, he wondered if now he was in more danger than before.

He knew what Burke expected of him - to keep his mouth shut and be a good soldier, and they both knew that Abbie's life depended on him doing so. Nolan hadn't had much negotiating room to begin with, and now he had none. So, he would do what was expected of him, toe the line and fulfill his duties as a loyal agent to the Burke Administration. He got into the elevator at the end of the hallway and stared ahead at the doors to Burke's office as the elevator doors slowly closed.

Sundays were usually spent at the hospital, reading to Abbie and spending time with her, trying to comfort her despite the symptoms that had grown more severe over the past month. This Sunday, however, Nolan wasn't headed to the hospital. It was early morning, and snow was beginning to fall as he and Laura drove east, headed outside the city. Neither spoke to one another. After close to an hour, Nolan stopped the car, and he and Laura got out, letting the small white snowflakes fall onto their black coats. They walked over to a large tree and nodded at the priest before looking down at the small casket perched above the hole in the ground.

Abbie had passed away a few days ago, succumbing to Styre, in what the doctors had called "a rare occurrence." Nolan had pressed them about what had caused her death and they had replied, "At this point, we aren't certain. All signs point toward Styre, but there were complications that we were unable to identify the cause of." He had continued to press them for information, but they were of no use. Nolan knew that Abbie was indeed one of the rare children to experience Styre symptoms but couldn't help but wonder if her death had been precipitated by Burke. Was he capable of killing a child? And what would that even serve to prove? Nolan pushed those thoughts aside, resigned to the fact that Styre had run its course and, in the process, ended Abbie's life.

Nolan hadn't said anything while Laura had burst into tears, running over to Abbie and stroking her hair while the nurses unplugged her from the various machines. Something inside him had gone numb. He was isolated within himself, unable to allow himself to feel the pain of losing his daughter.

Nolan and Laura agreed that it would be a private service with just them and the priest they had hired, and the funeral arrangements had been made. Though not religious, Laura had insisted on having a priest to give the funeral a sense of closure that neither Nolan nor Laura felt they could express in their own words.

They listened as he recited passages and spoke about the beauty that children bring into the world. Laura bowed her head as tears flowed down her cheeks, and Nolan gripped her hand tighter. Snow fell on the small black casket, and after the priest finished, he walked away, giving the Parkers time to say their final goodbyes. Laura placed a wreath of white lilies on the casket and watched as it was lowered into the ground. From within his jacket, Nolan pulled out the copy of Redwall he had finished reading to Abbie in the hospital, the spine worn from use, and placed it on the casket as it continued to descend into the ground.

He swiped a tear away from his eye as he watched Laura turn and walk back toward the car. Nolan knew this was difficult for her, and it was the same for him. He had thought about the life Abbie would no longer have and the moments he would no longer share with her. He would never watch her graduate from high school, never meet her future partners, and never watch her blossom into the woman she would one day become. She was gone. Forever. The emotions, watching his little girl being lowered into the ground, swelled within him. Anger, loss, guilt, sadness, and a growing sense of injustice. He turned to look at the sky and watched as the snow danced above him and made its way onto his face. Nolan was angry. Angry that he hadn't been able to give Abbie what she so desperately needed and angry at Burke for denying his request.

The worst, for Nolan, was knowing that Abbie was innocent in all of this. It wasn't her fault her body had succumbed to the symptoms when so many others hadn't. She was an innocent victim of Burke's perpetual pursuit of power, and Nolan knew, looking down at Abbie's casket, now lightly covered in snow, that he would no longer allow Burke to hurt any more innocent people. He softly whispered "goodbye" and then walked back to the car to begin the quiet drive back to the city.

It had been a hard week. The funeral had been tough for both Nolan and Laura, though Nolan had continued with work, hiding the fact that he had just lost one of the most important people in his life. No one needed to know what had happened, as he was sure that Burke would find some way to exploit his loss, and Nolan needed to stay focused. Again, he had made plans and kept them from Laura. She was taking Abbie's loss hard, and Nolan didn't blame her. He missed her laugh and their talks, but she was grieving in her own way. She had started to have extreme bursts of energy, which she channeled into exercise, and then long bouts of sleep, sometimes spending almost the entire day in bed.

For Nolan, the loss of a child wasn't something he ever expected to experience. He had learned to compartmentalize pain, loss, and guilt from his time in the marines, but this was different. This was Abbie, and no matter how hard he tried, he couldn't stop thinking about her. For a brief moment, he tried to push those thoughts aside and focus on the task at hand.

197

Spread across his desk was a holographic map of *The 212* displayed over an older paper map of Lower Manhattan. Underneath the map, sticking out just a bit, was the red file containing Finn Brantley's information. He looked up at his door to make sure it was locked and then looked back down at the two maps. *The 212* had been designed from the ground up, and besides the Processing Center, the wall and guard towers were the only other infrastructure Burke's Administration had bothered to build. Nolan knew that his only chance to speak face to face with Finn would require him to go in alone and somehow bypass the processing center.

Nolan had wondered what to do about Burke the moment he had denied Abbie access to the cure, and most of his plans hadn't seemed to result in anything except his death. He had thought about shooting Burke, or perhaps planting an explosive in his office, but knew that what Burke had created was bigger now than simply one individual. Nolan needed to change the system, and the only way to do that required a disruptor. In a system that kept people reliant on the doses, the only option was to remove that necessity. And Finn Brantley was the only man so far to have figured out how to do that.

Nolan knew the guard towers did sweeps every few hours, and the drones usually only passed overhead during the day. At night, the processing facility would have minimal security, and Nolan knew how to override the door's passcodes. Despite all this, it was still a high-risk decision, and he sat back in his chair as he thought about what he was planning to undertake. And at what cost? Meeting with Finn wouldn't bring Abbie back, and it wouldn't help console his wife. But deep down, somewhere within him, he felt it was the right thing to do, a feeling that had been in constant conflict with his choices over the past few years.

The next two days passed as usual, with Nolan fulfilling his duties at work and coming home at night to spend time with Laura, often over a quiet dinner and then to bed early. On the third day, once Laura was asleep, Nolan got out of bed and changed into a black pair of pants and a matching jacket. In his closet, he dialed the security code for the safe and removed a black Beretta, a relic from the pre-Burke days that didn't have a digital imprint of his ID. He tucked it into his waist, grabbed a small black duffel bag from a shelf, and left the house.

The drive to *The 212* was quiet, the streetlights the only sign of life amidst the snow-covered ground. He drove to the bridge, showed his ID to the guard, and watched as the bridge unfolded from *The 212* until it stretched out toward the area formerly known as Brooklyn. The guard pressed a button, and the large concrete wall lowered. Nolan drove slowly, looking back at the guard whose back was toward him. He was glad he hadn't asked any questions, but they rarely did, as Nolan's security clearance provided him the privacy that he needed.

Once across the bridge, he parked his car and got out, looking at the large concrete building and the door leading into the processing facility. He walked around the back and found another door, it's bolts rusty from a lack of use. From the duffel bag, he removed a small crowbar and pried the door open. He entered and closed it behind him. He thought back to the map and knew he was in one of the service tunnels. Nolan clicked on a flashlight he had taken out of the bag and walked down the wet corridor, the pipes running across the wall like snakes.

He moved quickly, his feet splashing through puddles on the ground. At the end of the corridor, he turned left and moved through the darkness. After a few minutes, he faced a small metal ladder and followed it up to the ceiling, where he saw a manhole secured with two locks.

Climbing with one hand and holding the crowbar in the other, he balanced himself while he broke the two locks and used his shoulder to lift the metal cover. Once pushed to the side, he hoisted himself up and saw the large circular platform used by the processing facility to the left. He quickly moved the cover back into place and began to run into the city.

Though he had never been inside *The 212*, he had scanned the drone footage and figured out the general area where most of the people inside congregated. Finding Finn would be a challenge, but he hadn't come this far to give up. He ran toward Wall Street, the small duffel bag bounced on his back as the stars rifled through the inky black sky above. It was quiet, even more so than the drive over had been. The buildings stood like giant, abandoned relics.

Once at Wall Street, he stood on the street and scanned the area, looking for any sign of life. The buildings were dark, offering no confirmation that anyone was there. Out of the corner of his eye, to the left, he saw a faint glow of light from the upper story of one of the buildings, which he recognized as 71 Broadway. He smiled at the thought of those sentenced to life in *The 212* living in such luxury and silently headed toward the buildings. Besides the light from the window, the building appeared quiet and lifeless.

He grabbed the gun from his waist and repositioned the duffel before grabbing the handle of the door and moving inside. The lobby was quiet and dark, save for a faint light from the room on his right. He placed himself against the wall and looked around the corner. A woman was sitting on a sofa reading a book, a small lamp illuminating the otherwise empty room.

He entered the room, pointing the gun at the woman who didn't look up from her book.

"Don't make a sound," he said in a low voice. The woman looked up with wide eyes and slowly set the book down next to her.

"Stand up." The woman did so, and before she had a chance to say anything, Nolan said, "Finn Brantley. Take me to him."

He gestured to her to move toward the stairs with the gun, and she did so. Walking up the stairs, Nolan kept the gun at her back, and they moved up through the building at a steady pace until she stopped on the landing of the 4th floor.

"This is his floor," she said, looking first at the gun and then at Nolan. The stairway was dark, but Nolan thought she could probably make out some of the details of his face.

"Let's go," he said, nodding toward the door. The woman opened the door, and they both entered the hallway. It was dark, as the window at the end of the hall was covered with a dark curtain. The woman walked down the hallway until she stopped in front of a door and then looked at Nolan. He stood behind her as she knocked on the door. The hallway was quiet. The door opened, and from the small light in the room, Nolan looked at Finn Brantley.

Finn's eyes were big as he recognized Nolan, but before he had a chance to say anything, Nolan pushed the woman into the room and closed the door behind him. From the corner of the room, Tipper growled and stared at the intruder.

He lowered his gun and said, "I know this is a lot to process, but you're going to need to stay calm."

Finn and the woman stood in the room, with only a lamp illuminating their three faces, as Nolan took a seat in one of the chairs and gestured for the woman and Finn to do the same. "I'm here to help. We need to talk."

Chapter 15

The conversation was brief. Nolan explained his reasons to Finn and the woman, with both keeping a close eye on the gun Nolan had placed on his lap while they talked. Afterward, before saying anything himself, Finn had simply said, "There's someone you need to meet."

The woman returned to her room, and Nolan and Finn had walked through the dark streets in silence and entered the HQ building. Whether or not Nolan was impressed remained a mystery as he gave no indication of his thoughts on what he saw, nor did he ask about how they had managed to get electricity to power everything inside. Finn knocked on Kalum's door, and a groggy voice inside said, "I'm sleeping."

Finn opened the door and said, "Sir, you're going to want to hear this." Kalum rose from the couch in his office and turned on the light. Upon seeing Nolan, he reached under his desk and pulled out a gun, pointing it at Nolan, and said, "What the fuck is he doing here?" The anger in his voice was palpable. His hatred for men like Parker stemmed from his perennial loathing of government officials who selfishly served their own interests rather than those they were appointed to look out for.

Nolan held up his hands and said, "A necessary end to things comes when it is most needed." Kalum lowered his gun and motioned for the two men to sit. Kalum sat on the sofa and placed the gun to his left, keeping it within reach if need be.

"Impressive setup," said Nolan. "All things considered."

"That's none of your concern," said Kalum. "My concern is what you are doing here."

"I need your help."

"That's an unusual request from someone who put the majority of us in here."

"I'm out of options."

"What do you need?" asked Finn, his curiosity outweighing the anger he had initially felt upon seeing the man who had taken away what little semblance of a life he had had on the outside.

"The Burke Administration has been manufacturing cures. I don't have proof that they're effective, but I have no reason to doubt they are."

Before Kalum or Finn could say anything despite the clear astonishment on their faces, Nolan continued. "A week ago, my daughter died. Burke refused to give me the cure. And for a long time, I have disagreed with the methods Burke has been using to consolidate his power."

"Forgive me for interrupting," said Kalum. "I'm sorry about your daughter, but if you think we're going to believe you, a loyal thug to Burke, then you are wasting your time."

Finn kept silent, though he felt the same as Kalum. He knew that people could change, and alliances could shift, but something felt off about Nolan's explicitly direct message about changing teams.

"At my daughter's funeral, standing outside in the snow watching her being lowered into the ground, I felt something go cold in me - so I decided 'fuck it'. I don't expect you to believe me," he said. "But for what it's worth, maybe you can believe the facts." He reached into his bag and grabbed a blue file, while Kalum moved his hand closer to his gun. Nolan extended the file in his direction, and Kalum took it. He read through the document, and though not fully understanding the science behind what he was looking at, he knew enough to understand that what he was looking at was indeed about a cure.

"How long have you known?" he asked.

"A few weeks."

"And how much has been produced?"

"I don't know," he said. "It's a top-secret project, and I only discovered it by accident."

"Who knows?"

"Burke, a scientist at our lab, and me."

Kalum shifted his eyes back down to the file before handing it to Finn.

"And you're here for what? To compensate for all the wrong you've done? To feel better about locking up innocent people?"

"If you fight with monsters for too long, you become a monster. And I'm tired of being one. Besides my wife, the only other person I loved in this world has been taken from me. I'm in a position to do something, something radical, to permanently change the state of our world, and I need your help to do it."

"And you think we're just going to forgive you for what you've done and blindly trust that you're now acting in good faith?"

"Mistakes were made," said Nolan.

"Do you know why I hate that expression?" asked Kalum. "Because it avoids blame."

"Let's just all take a breath," said Finn, placing the file on the floor next to him. "What is it that you think we can do for you?"

"Based on our information, you were the only one to successfully create an effective dose," said Nolan, looking at Finn. "I want to help you create more."

"How much more?"

"Enough to stop being reliant on Burke and his government-funded BioDose."

Finn looked at Kalum before turning back to Nolan. "We don't need your help with that."

Nolan looked at the two men. "You've already started," said Nolan, stating a fact rather than looking to ask for their confirmation.

"That's right," said Kalum.

"How much have you produced?"

"Enough to cause a disruption."

"We need to get started on producing a cure."

"I don't understand exactly what you mean by 'we,'" said Finn. "You put us here, and we, as in, those of us locked inside, have been producing the doses. And if anyone is going to figure out how to make a cure besides Burke, it will be us. Besides trying to replace the guilt you feel, what can you bring to the table? I don't know you, but I know you aren't a scientist, and you aren't rich, and besides this file, which doesn't even outline the chemical properties of the cure, what do you think you can do for us?"

"I have access. And I'm the only person who can get in and out of *The 212* without being seen. Which means I can get you supplies and information, and if it works, help with distribution. At this point, what do you have to lose?"

Kalum quickly shot a glance at Finn before looking back at Nolan.

"Despite my lack of trust in you, in addition to my complete disregard for everything you stand for, it stands to reason that it would be beneficial to have you as an ally rather than a foe. At this point, we aren't inclined to disclose everything that we're working on, nor share with you the complete details of our dose production process. But if you want to be a part of this thing we're doing, we need a sign of good faith."

"Name it," said Nolan.

Kalum looked over at Finn and nodded.

"We're going to need more information regarding Burke's cure, as well as some parts for a machine that's necessary to start cure production."

"And guns," said Kalum.

Nolan nodded. He knew at this point it would be foolish to ask questions about their demands.

"Make a list, and I'll see what I can do."

"Do you think this will work?" asked Finn. "I mean, a rogue government agent, a merry band of insurrectionists, and a plan with a minimal chance of success - it all seems too cliché to actually work."

"The future demands otherwise," said Nolan. "Styre changed our world in unimaginable ways. And yet, we're still alive. Civilization might continue, but I believe it lost its way a long time ago. We have a chance to right the wrongs, our own as well as those of our government."

"Your optimism is appreciated," said Kalum. "However, for the time being, let's proceed under the assumption that you aren't going to fuck us over. Give us an hour to make a list, and we'll go from there."

"I can come back in a week," said Nolan.

"And what will you do in the meantime?" asked Finn. "Continue to lock up people for fighting for what they believe?"

"I'll bring you what you need," said Nolan, standing up. I'll wait in the lobby until the list is ready."

Kalum and Finn stood up as well and walked out of the room.

"I'll go find Dr. Merric," said Finn.

"I'll escort Mr. Parker downstairs," said Kalum. The men parted ways, and Finn headed upstairs to find the doctor who had a better idea of what parts were needed. At this point, creating a cure from inside *The 212* had been nothing more than a theoretical idea, but Finn had argued that it was better to get started on the machines they would need to make it a reality. With Nolan's promise to help them, though still unsure of his intentions, the cure might come sooner than he had imagined.

After close to fifteen minutes with Dr. Thorin, writing down everything that they hadn't been able to find or create themselves, Finn walked into the building's lobby and saw Nolan and Kalum both sitting quietly in chairs on other sides of the room. Finn walked over to Kalum and handed him the list, with Kalum nodding and then pulling out a pen and adding a few things. He stood and then handed the list to Nolan, who put it in his blazer pocket without looking at it.

"I'll get you what you need," he said. "If you don't mind, I have a wife I need to get back to. I'll be here next week. Same time. Try not to do anything stupid before then." He extended his hand first to Finn, who shook it and then over to Kalum, who paused for a brief moment and then shook his hand as well. Despite his size, Nolan moved quickly and intentionally, every movement was done in the most efficient way. He walked over to and out the door before either Finn or Kalum could say anything. They walked over and opened the door, looking out at nothing but the white snow on the ground and the blackness of the sky above, the wind the only response to the unspoken questions that both of the men shared.

Burke's rise to power hadn't been expected, nor was it a surprise. He had been a newly appointed president in Central and Styre hit in his first term. Swift and decisive, much like the virus itself, Burke had seemingly done what he could to prevent the spread, though his efforts were futile. By consolidating power, often with the overwhelming support of those in his party and amending the Constitution to grant him powers that he claimed were "instrumental in the fight against Styre," Burke amassed supreme control over a country that had once proclaimed to be democratic, even if just on paper.

The doses had been his doing, for which he had received international praise. They offered people a chance at a normal life. Still, much like everything else that people wanted, its distribution shifted into something more of a commodity than something the government felt responsible for providing. Proposals were put forward, and a system had been developed, one in which a person's contribution to society was evaluated, and a corresponding number of doses were allocated to them each week. The algorithm, or whatever it was in the system, calculated one's societal contribution. As expected, the only people to have problems with it were those only receiving daily doses. Burke and his fellow party members were constantly commending themselves on what a harmonious system it was and how it had saved society from ruin.

Despite the anger and cries for help from the public, no one had the capacity to do anything about it. Protests had ensued, and carried on to varying degrees throughout the years, but nothing had resulted in change. BioDose continued to manufacture the doses and the system continued to distribute them as it saw fit. People died, of course, but many continued to live under what had been deemed the new normal. Nolan, however, no longer saw himself as part of that equation. The path he had recently chosen to go down, was, he knew, a one-way road. He had told Laura about his visit to *The 212* and his agreement to help those inside, and she had simply said, "Abbie would be proud of you."

The last few days had been quiet. He had slowly acquired the items on the list, including the firearms, and was now on the last item. He looked down at the crumpled piece of paper sitting on his desk and looked at the final item scrawled in Kalum's handwriting - "BioDose scientist."

Initially, Nolan had thought it an odd request, to ask for a human being rather than something that could be stolen or simply acquired by taking it. But he understood the rationale. Creating a cure was by no means a small feat and given that those in *The 212* were trying to do so in less than ideal circumstances, he had begun to think about how exactly he could deliver the final item on the list.

Nolan turned around in his chair and looked at the snow-covered buildings outside until his eyes came to rest on the laboratory a few hundred meters away. He grabbed the piece of paper, put it in his pocket, and left the office.

Upon entering the laboratory and passing through security, he headed straight to Dr. Thorin's office, and when he got there, he opened the door without so much as a knock. Sitting at his desk, Dr. Thorin looked up at the imposing man in the doorway and didn't say a word as Nolan closed the door behind him.

"What have you done?" asked the doctor.

"I've created an opportunity," said Nolan. "Burke knows that I know about the cure. But what he doesn't know is that you were the one who told me about it. I'm sure you'd like to keep it that way."

"I don't want any part of this."

"You're already involved, doctor," said Nolan. "I have a way to ensure safety, though I admit, you probably aren't going to like it."

"What do you propose?"

"I've been in contact with those inside *The 212*. They have been manufacturing doses for a few weeks now and aim to produce a cure.

They need help. And since you were directly involved in helping create a cure for Burke, I can't think of anyone better suited to assist them."

"You're out of your goddamn mind if you think I'm going to go to *The 212* to help a bunch of criminals produce a cure."

"It wasn't a suggestion," said Nolan. "One word from me to Burke, and you and your entire family will disappear. Inside *The 212*, you will be safe and have the chance for your work to change the lives of billions of people around the world."

"And how exactly do you propose I get in there?"

"Don't worry about the logistics. I need you to be ready to go by tomorrow night."

"You expect me to just leave my family and my job and disappear?"

"Again, you don't have a choice. One way or another, you will be taken to *The 212* tomorrow evening. I'm giving you the opportunity to say your goodbyes."

"Why me?"

"It was you who left the file about the cure on your desk. If it weren't for you, I wouldn't be here. Additionally, it's only a matter of time before Burke kills you. You've already produced the cure. What more use to him are you?"

Nolan buttoned his jacket and turned toward the door. Dr. Thorin stood up and said, "How can you live with yourself?"

Without turning around, he said, "We all rationalize our actions in our own ways. I'll be in touch." Nolan opened the door and walked out, leaving Dr. Thorin alone in his office, staring at the door in front of him.

The sky was black, and small flakes of snow drifted onto the street as Nolan drove. Dr. Thorin had been where Nolan instructed him to wait but Nolan wasn't at all surprised that he had shown up. Under threat of death, for both him and his family, it wasn't a difficult choice to make. Now, driving through the quiet streets of Central, with Nolan at the wheel and the doctor hidden in his trunk, along with everything else that Kalum had asked for, he drove toward *The 212*. Just as he had a week ago, Nolan didn't expect any hiccups, and while not customary for him, he hoped there wouldn't be any either. He had thought about following through with Kalum's request for a scientist and once again found himself pondering the moral implications of doing so. However, similar to how Burke had preached the idea of serving the greater good, so too had Nolan justified his threat to coerce Dr. Thorin. Ultimately, ameliorating the situation in Central, as well as the world as a whole, was significantly more important than one man's personal desires.

The guard station before the bridge entrance came into view, and Nolan slowed the car. A young man dressed in an all-black military outfit came out from the post and tapped on the window. Nolan gave him his credentials and placed his wrist against the small glass tab the man extended.

"What's your business at the Processing Center?" asked the soldier.

Nolan slowly turned his head and locked eyes with him. "That's none of your business."

The man repositioned his weapon and said, "That's entirely my business. My duty is to safeguard this bridge and it's important to know the business of everyone who crosses it. Please step out of the car, Mr. Parker."

Nolan looked at the large concrete barrier in front of him and then exited the vehicle. Snow continued to fall, and small white flecks rested softly on Nolan's short hair as he stood a good head taller than the soldier.

"I'll need to see your authorization papers," said the man.

Nolan stepped toward him, causing the man to take a step back. "You must be new. Do you see this?" he asked, pulling a red card from his pocket. "Do you know what this is?"

"Yes, sir," he said. "I'm…"

"What's your name?"

"Robinson, sir."

"And what is the significance of this card?"

"Special agent, sir."

"And what does this card allow me to do?"

"No-question authorization, sir."

Nolan stepped even closer, putting his face close to the young soldier's. "If this happens again, I'll see to it that you never get another government-administered dose again."

"Understood, sir."

Nolan turned and got back into his car as the soldier ran into the building and initiated the bridge sequence. Once it was in place, the concrete barrier lowered, and Nolan drove forward, catching the soldier saluting him as he drove past. He'd been lucky that he hadn't needed to scan the card, as it would have triggered an alert that would be logged into his agency's database, and the last thing he needed was more questions from Reeves. He had seen him around the office over the past few weeks, so perhaps it was just a matter of time.

He drove across the bridge, feeling the slight bumps where the bridge sections came together, and once he was across, he parked the car on the side of the Processing Center and got out. He looked around and saw that the only tracks on the ground were those of his car. He walked to the trunk and opened it, first taking out two large black duffel bags and then saying, "Let's go, doctor."

Dr. Thorin crawled out of the trunk and picked up one of the bags Nolan had placed on the ground. Nolan grabbed the other one and then paused for a moment to look up at the massive black wall, seemingly suffocating the city in its grip, and then moved quickly toward the door. Nolan pulled it open, having broken the lock on his last visit, and they moved through the service tunnel without saying a word.

At the ladder, Nolan turned to Dr. Thorin and said, "Don't delude yourself into thinking this is anything other than what I told you it would be. You have a job to do. I expect you to help the others make a cure. Anything short of that will result in your wife's death. And believe me, that is not an empty threat. If I receive any reports about your non-compliance or find out that you are attempting to hinder their progress, I will end your wife's life faster than you can imagine. Do you understand?"

"I do," said Dr. Thorin.

The two men ascended the ladder, pushed aside the metal grate at the top, and moved into the city. The sky was dark as the night grew deeper, with only the soft crunch of snow beneath their feet disrupting the stillness around them. As they headed toward the HQ building, Dr. Thorin asked, "How long am I going to be in here?"

"As long as it takes," said Nolan. "If you create a cure, I guarantee I will get you out of here."

The large pillars of the Federal Hall building came into view as they headed toward the building. Kalum had told them to meet there instead of the Broadway building, and though Nolan didn't know what the building was used for, he gathered that it was likely their main base of operations. Inside the building, looking at all the tech equipment amidst the marble flooring and walls, Nolan's guess was confirmed. For a bunch of inmates locked up against their will, he was impressed by what they had managed to build.

From the shadows, Kalum said, "Follow me."

Dr. Thorin and Nolan moved through the dark, following Kalum's tall frame through several hallways until they came to a door, and Kalum opened it. Inside were Finn, Alayna, and a few other men, including Dr. Merric. Nolan and Dr. Thorin set the two large duffel bags onto a nearby table, and then Nolan looked at Kalum.

"This is Dr. Thorin. He is, or was, the lead scientist at Central's main government lab. He was the one to first make the cure."

"Can he be trusted?" asked Finn.

"We have an understanding," said Nolan. "He knows what's expected of him."

"Did you get everything else on the list?" Kalum asked.

Nolan went over to one of the bags and unzipped it, pulling apart both flaps to reveal everything inside. He then went over to the second bag and did the same.

Finn and Dr. Merric went over to the first bag and started pulling out various laboratory instruments, chemicals, and electronic gadgets and setting them on the table. Kalum reached into the second bag and pulled out a military-grade matte-black machine gun, turning it over in his hands and then checking the chamber.

He lowered the gun to his side and then said, "Thank you."

Nolan nodded. "It's a risk coming here to meet you. I'll only come here again once the cure has been made and we're ready for distribution."

Nolan reached into the bag and grabbed a small black walkie talkie. "It's a bit old but this is the most secure way to get ahold of me. The range is about 20 kilometers and drones shouldn't be able to pick up the frequency. Call me when you're ready."

The room was quiet as Dr. Thorin looked around, and the others in the room shifted their eyes between Nolan and Dr. Thorin.

"See it through, doctor," said Nolan.

"Yes, sir," he said.

Nolan shook Kalum's hand and before he turned to leave, said, "If, for whatever reason, something happens to me out there, Dr. Thorin is free to leave once the cure has been made. He has a wife."

Kalum nodded. Nolan opened the door leading outside and felt the cold chill of the wind hit his face. He looked up at the black sky and then looked around at the vacantly quiet buildings. The black wall could be seen towering over the skyline. Nolan descended the steps and made his way back to the tunnel. He had taken a risk, and one he wasn't sure would pay off. Dr. Thorin had made the cure once, but replicating it, especially with the limited facilities and experience of those inside *The 212* would prove to be an obstacle. Distribution was the other issue on Nolan's mind. They would never be able to produce the necessary amount, and even if they managed to create a substantial amount, who would get them? And what effect would that have on society?

The questions and doubts consumed Nolan's thoughts as he pulled his jacket tight and walked silently into the night, away from those confined inside and toward a life that would never be the same.

A Viral State

Chapter 16

Over a thousand doses had been produced and delivered from inside *The 212* since production had started. The trips were always a risk, and though Finn knew each one might be his last, he continued to make them. He had started this, and he was determined to finish it. The hospital was always one of their drop-off points, as well as Alayna's contact for trade, while others changed week to week. Sometimes doses were given to a resistance group with a more detailed list for distribution, and other times they went to factory workers or to the front steps of the few remaining NGOs in the city.

Finn had just returned from a distribution run and sweat glistened on his forehead as the sun rose blearily through the panes of early morning mist. He looked over at Alayna, who, as usual, carried a large duffel bag full of whatever she had traded the doses for.

"Please tell me you have something other than guns in there."

"As a matter of fact," she said with a smile, "I do." She pulled out a bottle of whiskey and a small black box the size of a small bowl and handed them to Finn.

He flipped the box around in his hands, and his eyes got wide. "How did you manage to get this?" he asked. "You have no idea how painstaking trying to build the machines in the lab has been without this." Finn continued to stare at the small 3D printer and looked up at Alayna.

"Don't play around with it. I was only able to get ahold of four alloy cartridges and two glass particle cartridges. You should be able to print everything you need, but once those cartridges are gone, it's of no use."

"I'm forever grateful," he said.

"I've got some stuff to drop off at the armory. I'll meet you over at the lab."

"See you soon," said Finn. He shifted the 3D printer under one of his arms and wiped his brow. The run had been smooth, and he had again gone to the hospital. Each time he dropped the bag off at the side entrance, he always expected to see the nurse from his first visit, but the door had always remained closed. He had once asked Alayna why they were giving doses to the hospital and how she could be sure that the doses were going to those who needed them, and she had simply said, "The doses are in safe hands. Trust me." For Finn, that was the only answer he had needed.

He walked toward the lab, with the sun now just over the horizon, casting its orange glow over the snow-covered city, its buildings still empty and lifeless. Finn thought about what he would do with the printer, and a long list of tools and pieces came to his mind. *The 212* had provided about one-third of what was needed, Alayna had traded for a few items, and Nolan had brought what Kalum asked for, but it wasn't enough. The 3D printer would be able to create the missing pieces, and Finn was excited at the thought of being one step closer to producing a cure.

Part of him had felt guilty that it was he who was immune, and not someone more deserving. Each morning he watched as everyone in *The 212* took their daily dose while his was placed with the others meant for distribution. Another part of him felt empowered by what he was doing. Finding out that he was immune had happened by mistake, an unfortunate series of events that, for anyone else, would have led to their death. But now, Finn was working to prevent others from meeting that fate.

He arrived at the lab, and when he opened the door, he found several people gathered around a large hologram of the Styre virus arguing in loud voices. He turned and saw Piper Merric and Magnus sitting in chairs at one of the tables a few meters away. She looked at Finn and held her hands up as if to say, "No clue." Finn smiled and then walked toward the group of men.

"I think if there's a way to screw this up, you'll find it," said Dr. Thorin, clearly agitated at the conversation he found himself in.

"That's rich coming from the man who didn't even actually make a real cure!" shouted Dr. Merric, holding a gun pointed at Dr. Thorin. "You lied to all of us and have jeopardized the entire operation."

"It was the only way," said Dr. Thorin. From the looks on their faces, Finn knew they had been arguing over the same thing for a while.

Finn made his way over to the group and set down the black box. "What's the problem?" he asked. "And put down the gun, there's no need for that." Dr. Merric ignored Finn and kept the gun on Dr. Thorin.

"The definition of a cure compared to how it functions is essentially a moot point," said Dr. Thorin, keeping an eye on the pistol pointed at his chest. "As I was explaining to Aiden, here, it's not as simple as killing the virus. Yes, it can be destroyed, but because it is so widespread, it has adapted, which makes the probability of a functioning cure unlikely. The doses have managed to prevent the onset of symptoms for a day, and the cure I made wasn't so much a cure as a permanent inhibitor of Styre symptoms."

"Then why call it a cure?"

"Because that's what the president asked for. And if it produces the same results as a cure, then he is none the wiser. Scientifically, Burke doesn't know the difference, I wasn't going to be the one to tell him I didn't deliver exactly what he wanted by quibbling over the definition of what a cure is. If you shoot me now, everything we've worked for will be lost."

Finn looked at Dr. Merric, who lowered the gun, still keeping a grip on it by his side.

"So, what are we aiming to do here then? Make a true cure to kill the virus and eradicate it from the human population, or make a super-dose like the one you created out there?"

"We have to consider what's in the best interests of the population. I'm confident I can produce the same variant of the cure I previously made, or as you call it, a super dose. However, as a scientist, I believe it's my fundamental duty to push forward the field I have chosen to work in. I say we try to find a cure, something that will eradicate Styre."

The others standing around the table were talking amongst themselves, and Finn moved toward them. "We move forward with finding a true cure. One month. That's all you have. If a cure isn't produced in that time, we work on creating the super dose as an alternative."

Dr. Merric turned to him and said, "Do you realize what you're asking? Years have been spent trying to find a cure, in facilities much better equipped than this place, with teams of scientists and chemists, and nothing more than a super dose was created. How do you expect us to possibly do that?"

"Big things have small beginnings," said Finn. "With Dr. Thorin's knowledge and expertise, as well as everyone else's, I'm confident in your ability to come through on this."

Dr. Merric rubbed his eyes and turned to Dr. Thorin, and said, "Logistically speaking, is it possible?"

He thought for a moment before answering and said, "Yes."

"Let's get to work then," said Dr. Merric, and the team moved to different tables to get started. Finn grabbed the 3D printer and moved it to a table where Darin was sitting.

"The final piece of the puzzle," he said, as he watched Darin's face light up when noticing the machine.

"Is this what I think it is?" he asked.

"Alayna traded for it on the run this morning." Finn placed the six small cartridges on the table and said, "This is all we have. Four alloys and two glass. We need to finish up the schematics and double-check the designs. We have no room for error."

Darin nodded. "What's the priority?"

"Glass for the sub-microliter injection system and the alloy needs to be used for the microprobe thermometers and ECG monitoring system."

"I'm on it," said Darin pulling out a glass tablet and opening up the designs they had been working on.

Finn turned around and looked at the people gathered at various tables, all bent over different machines, papers, or holograms, discussing what steps needed to be taken first. Everyone was working toward the same goal, each with their own personal reasons, but all with the same goal. People had loved ones they wanted to save, families to return to, or they simply felt it was the right thing to do. He turned to look at Piper, who was organizing various glass tubes with Magnus, helping in any way she could. Her bright red hair the only spot of color in a room of varying shades of gray. He had never known what it was like to have a child and imagined that Aiden would do whatever he needed to do to provide a safe and healthy future for his daughter.

Finn had no one in his life like that. Like him, Tipper was immune to Styre and wasn't at any risk, and although Finn was safe and had no real reason to be working on a cure, this was his opportunity to give back to the world. He knew he would never design a bridge that would be used by millions, or develop tools or create something of tangible value, but by helping to distribute doses to the public, and now attempt to make a cure, he knew his contribution to humanity would be unfathomably important, if successful, and he was determined to see it through.

Files with the names of insurrectionists and others deemed "a detriment to society" had been piling up on Nolan's desk faster than he could take care of them. Attacks on Dose Depots, protests, and violent threats to Burke had grown over the last three weeks. Nolan had been informed over the radio that Kalum and the others had distributed over 5,000 doses to the public and that more were on the way. The cure was still being worked on, with Kalum stating that "progress was being made." Though Nolan didn't ask how they had managed to find a way out, he wasn't entirely surprised that they had. Nor was he surprised by the growing hostility in Central. Nolan understood that the policies of the current

Administration were slowly strangling society and like anything not getting sufficient air, they would fight to survive.

Burke had been in a fouler mood than usual, and his orders to handle the growing unrest were shouted at Nolan and the other field agents. Though Burke seemed to inflate the idea that they were losing their grip on the city and generally overstating the seriousness of the situation, Nolan could feel the winds changing. People were angry, and rightfully so. He had lost a daughter and couldn't imagine how many others had lost loved ones to Styre through no fault of their own. It also didn't help that Burke had started to ration doses and decreased the amount being given out. Many with menial jobs had lost the security of at least one dose per day and now had to find one or two extra doses on their own per week just to survive.

The shift in policy had been blamed on a lack of necessary resources in dose production. Still, Nolan knew Burke was asserting his power so those more likely to revolt would focus on work instead of protesting. The allocation adjustment, however, was having the opposite effect.

Nolan looked at the files on his desk and saw that more than half had a "terminate on-site" order rather than a "212 processing." Burke was growing impatient with the unrest, and though not impossible to quell, Nolan knew he was looking for a permanent solution.

Laura was opening up more at home, smiling more often, and engaging in conversation, which was a relief for Nolan. Grief was difficult to deal with, and both were struggling, though it was getting easier day by day. Initially, he had felt it was unfair. Unfair that his beautiful little girl had died. Unfair that neither she nor her parents had gained any control over the situation, but Nolan quickly realized that unfair doesn't make it untrue. She was gone, and now he and Laura had to move on, each in their own way. Nolan was now working with *The 212*, and though he never showed it, he was nervous. Each time his door opened, he was prepared to be arrested, which in the grand scheme of things would be nothing more than a formality because, in the end, he knew he would be shot, as would Laura. Each visit with Burke caused his anxiety to increase, though neither of them mentioned the cure. Their first conversation about it had been their last, with the consequences for any further mention of it clearly laid out.

Nolan continued to do his job, numb to the fact that he was killing more people now than he had during his time in combat. For him, they were a sacrifice that allowed him to continue helping those in *The 212* create a cure. It would be a dark period of history, but if a cure were to be made and distributed, Nolan believed the ends justified the means. What exactly the ends were, however, was cause for speculation. There were a number of unknowns, such as if *The 212* would be able to make a cure, and even if they managed to get it out into society, they would never be able to manufacture enough for everyone. Even if a few people took it, what would that result in other than peace of mind for a limited few? Would it really change anything? Again, Nolan thought about two things that rarely, if ever, crossed his mind - hope and faith. Two words that didn't alleviate the anxiety and questions he had about his involvement but the only two things he had to rely on.

Now, he was holed up in his office, counting down the minutes until he met with Burke. He knew neither was looking forward to it, and it was very likely that Burke just needed someone to take his frustrations out on. Nolan knew the numbers, had read reports about the growing anti-government sentiment in the city, and it was no surprise that Burke wasn't happy about it. He looked at the glass clock on his desk and decided it was best not to be late. He headed out of his office, took the elevator, and passed through the security checkpoint before entering Burke's office.

The large man was standing when Nolan entered, and he whipped around as soon as the door had closed.

"What is happening out there, Parker? You are in charge of dealing with this sort of thing. Yet report after report keeps piling up on my desk. And can you guess what they each say?"

"I'm aware, sir."

"What are you doing about it?"

"My job, sir. There are millions of people in this city alone and only a handful of agents. Severe cases are being dealt with permanently, and those that prove potentially beneficial to your Administration are being processed in *The 212*. What else, exactly, would you like me to do, sir?"

Burke walked closer to him, and though his face didn't express it, Nolan could feel the rage emanating from the president.

"Don't you take that tone with me, Parker. You know goddamn well what I want done. If you and the other special agents don't handle this, I'll personally see to it that you are never employed anywhere ever again!"

Nolan took a breath and watched as Burke walked over to the window and looked at the city below. It looked peaceful from so high up, a sprawling city covered in snow full of ordinary people living and surviving. But down below, in the streets, they both knew something was brewing. The city's energy had shifted, and people were no longer afraid to express the discontent they had been feeling for so many years, fulminating against the government.

"Perhaps it's the recent change in the dose policy, sir. It seems to be having unintended consequences." Nolan knew he had crossed a line, but considering what he had recently gotten himself involved in, he figured pushing Burke was the least of his worries.

"And what would you know about government policy? You're nothing more than a glorified brute who is lucky to have found himself a job." He turned to face Nolan. "You have no idea what it takes to run a country, to set a plan in motion and see it through. One day, you, along with everyone else, will understand that the ends justify the means."

"And what exactly is the end?"

"It's not for you to understand, Parker."

He walked over to his desk and sat in his chair, placing his large hands on the desk.

"Don't forget that you and I are cut from the same cloth. We're both ruthless in our own right and willing to do whatever must be done to preserve that which we hold most sacred. Do your job, Parker. I expect results."

"Yes, sir," he said, turning to go. As he reached the door, Burke said, "Give your best to Laura for me. I hear losing a child is a painful experience."

Nolan stood in the doorway for a moment. He wanted to turn around and kill Burke with his bare hands, to watch the air slowly leave his giant body as Nolan watched his hands tighten around the president's fat neck. He wanted to feel the rush of adrenaline that comes from taking a life, to lose himself in that brief moment where one's life is in his hands before he extinguishes it.

Instead, he nodded without turning around and walked back toward the elevator, not hearing the door close behind him nor his footsteps across the white marble floor as he walked back to his office and slammed the door shut.

————————

Kalum had called the day after his meeting with Burke telling him that they were close, which Nolan hadn't clearly understood because when it comes to a cure, they either had it or they didn't. On top of that, Kalum had requested more weapons. Nolan was aware that once the cure was developed, there was no more need to stay in *The 212*, and if they were to survive outside the wall, they would need some sort of defense.

He had written down what Kalum had asked for and immediately realized it would be impossible to get everything. He had access to this bureau's armory, but all those weapons were programmed to operate only for those whose digital ID was connected to them, though he was sure he could get some photon-grenades and mini-EMP bombs since those were "open-source," a term used for weapons that operated without a digital ID.

Surprisingly, Kalum hadn't asked for any lab equipment nor chemicals, which he assumed meant they had everything they needed to create a cure. Nolan looked up from the list and wondered what the world would be like once the cure became ubiquitous. A world free from oppression, but not the same world it once had been. Styre had affected the very social fabric that wove through society. It had instilled fear and cultivated a survival instinct unparalleled to perhaps any time in history. Even with the knowledge that Styre had been eradicated, Nolan was keenly aware there was no going back to normal, whatever that meant. The obvious conclusion was that even with a cure, the world had been irrevocably changed and would once again be so post-cure, though Nolan wasn't sure he would be alive to see it.

He had seen Reeves only a handful of times since their meeting, and each time he had smiled politely, as colleagues do, though Nolan was unsure of what kind of smile it was. Nolan knew Reeves was up to something but didn't have the time to look into it further.

Nolan turned back to the list and made a mental note of where he would procure the weapons. He would visit the armory later today, and collect the spare weapons he kept at home, but knew there was one more stop he needed to make.

He flicked his wrist and waited for the line to connect. Once the line opened, Nolan said, "High Street Metro Station. 9:00 p.m. Autos, hands, kev. All OS. One hundred Ds," and then flicked his wrist to close the line.

Nolan sat back in his chair and closed his eyes, thinking about what he had gotten himself into, but knowing that regardless of the consequences, he would be on the right side of history. The day ended without any interruptions, and Nolan grabbed the black bag full of explosives he had picked up from the armory and drove home to collect the few guns he had. Laura was asleep on the couch, and he moved quickly to gather the weapons. He put them in the bag, kissed Laura's cheek, and then headed for the subway station.

Nolan left the duffel bag in the car and only grabbed a small backpack before he descended the stairs into the High Street station. It was quiet as he stood on the platform, as most people had already finished work and headed home. He looked ahead at the white tile and gray concrete and then checked his watch. From behind him, a man said, "Always early."

Nolan turned around and looked at his friend and said, "Been a long time, Scott. Thanks for coming."

"Not very often you get to catch up with an NSP buddy." He kicked a large black duffel bag with his foot and said, "Christmas came early."

Nolan handed him the backpack full of doses and said, "I can't thank you enough."

"No need to thank me. This never happened."

Nolan smiled.

"It's a fucked-up world out there," said Scott "Take care of yourself."

"I always do," said Nolan, reaching down to pick up the duffel bag. He and Scott shook hands and went their separate ways, with Nolan heading back up the stairs and his friend getting onto the approaching train.

Getting unverified weapons in Central was always a risk, and though Nolan had connections from his time in the military, there was always a chance that something could go wrong. He took a breath as he drove toward the bridge heading for *The 212*. The young recruit who Nolan had seen a few days ago was on duty, and said nothing as Nolan flashed his badge. The bridge began to unfold, and the young soldier saluted him as he drove over the icy river below.

Nolan grabbed both bags and carried them by his side as he entered the maintenance tunnel, moving slowly due to the weight. Once he reached the ladder, he placed the bags on the ground and climbed to the top, moving the metal grate ever so slightly. IT would allow Kalum to move it from above when he arrived. He descended the ladder and then pulled out the radio from his pocket.

"Sakura," he said. "Come in, over."

He waited for a moment, letting the static echo through the concrete tunnel until a familiar voice said.

"News? Over."

"Special delivery. The burrow entrance. Over."

Though the tunnel could have referred to any number of places, they had agreed to refer to the Processing Unit's maintenance tunnel by code.

"Much appreciated." The line filled with static for a few seconds before Kalum said, "Be careful out there. A war is coming. Over and out."

Nolan put the radio back in his pocket and moved back through the tunnel. He thought about what that word meant, war, and knew that Kalum was right. In one form or another, a war was indeed coming, and whether he liked it or not, he was a part of it.

As he drove back over the bridge, Nolan thought about how things would play out, and ultimately, what fate would have in store for him. Things had been put into motion, and now with momentum, there was no stopping them. *The 212* was armed, they were developing a cure, and the rising anti-government protests in Central were growing. Burke's tightened dose policy had fanned the flames of an already hostile city, and Nolan knew that Kalum was right. A war was coming.

Chapter 17

"I miss her," said Laura, sitting on the couch, drinking a cup of coffee.

"Me too," said Nolan. "Every day."

"Will it get easier?"

"No," he said. He had asked himself this question, wondering if the gut-wrenching pain he felt would ever subside, if the thoughts of Abbie would ever pass, and had concluded that they would remain with him for the rest of his life.

"We have each other. Whatever you need, Laura, I'm here."

She smiled and grabbed his hand. He squeezed it and then stood up, looking out at the snow through his living room window. It was a calm morning, and as Nolan watched the snow, he wondered how nice it would be to be so blissfully unaware of all the complexities it meant to be human. No pain, no loss, no risk. He bent down to kiss Laura on the cheek and then put on his black peacoat and headed out into the cold.

Nolan hadn't heard anything about his recent drop-off to *The 212* in the past two weeks, nor had he seen Reeves around the office, which he was grateful for. He also hadn't heard anything from Kalum but expected he and the others were focused on developing the cure. He again thought of Dr. Thorin, locked in *The 212*, away from his wife, but knew that sometimes bad things had to happen to good people to get them to do what he wanted.

As he drove to work, the city around him was quiet. It was early, and though a few people were out walking, Nolan was reminded of his life before Styre. He had met Laura a year after returning from the New South Pacific, just as he had begun working for the Burke Administration. She was an art dealer, and they had met at an NGO event. There was something so easy in the way she carried herself; the way she laughed and spoke came from a place of comfort with oneself, a trait that Nolan had continually struggled with. She knew who she was, and had accepted it, while Nolan continued the internal fight.

A year later, they were married, and soon after that, Laura was pregnant. Tears had streamed down his face when he had found out she was pregnant, a moment in his life he never thought he would get to experience. He was doing well at work at that time, and though at times, he wondered if he would forever remain a killer, the presence of Laura and his forthcoming child had kept those thoughts at bay.

The years had passed, and he was happy. Happier than he ever could have imagined. But life happens, and Abbie got sick, and months passed, and so did Abbie. Nolan had been whole, but now something was missing. A piece of him gone, a piece that was singularly unfillable. But he would persevere, as he knew he should. Much like the transition the world made with Styre, so too would Nolan continue to live with a perpetual feeling of loss.

The days continued to pass, and Nolan continued to work. Names on the files of his desk were soon marked with "deceased" or "processed." It was business as usual under the Burke Administration. He still hadn't heard anything from Kalum, nor news about any strange disturbances within *The 212*, which he both took as a good sign. For much of his life, Nolan had been the catalyst, the one to make things happen, and now, out of the driver's seat, he was anxious for something to happen. He waited for his radio to buzz, for a government report stating that the people of Central were rebelling en masse rather than in the isolated pockets they had seen so far. Or, less likely, that Burke had been killed. It was a long shot that the latter would ever happen, but Nolan was an optimist.

It was a Friday that Nolan arrived at his office and found Reeves sitting inside when he opened the door.

"Good morning, Parker," he said, seated in a chair wearing a black suit.

Nolan didn't say anything as he placed his briefcase on his desk and took a seat across from Reeves.

"No need to sit," he said. "We're headed somewhere else." Reeves stood up and motioned for Nolan to take off his jacket. "Big day ahead of us."

Nolan did as he was told, hanging his jacket on the coat rack in the corner and then grabbing his government-issued gun from a drawer in his desk.

"You won't be needing that," said Reeves, holding the office door open as Nolan placed the gun on the table, closed the desk drawer, and walked out into the hallway. He followed Reeves through the white hall, neither saying a word to each other. Reeves wasn't his superior, but Nolan knew that internal affairs had certain powers over special agents, and he knew he was to do as he was told. Any refusal to do so could be grounds for further investigation.

They moved through various hallways until Reeves tapped his wrist against a door, and it opened. He motioned for Nolan to step through, and they descended a flight of stairs into what looked like a government bunker. Reeves tapped against another small piece of glass, and another door opened. The halogen lights illuminated the cold, gray room. Inside was a table and two chairs. They stepped through, and Reeves motioned for Nolan to take a seat, with the sound of the door closing echoing throughout the empty space.

"I didn't even know this place existed," remarked Nolan.

"It doesn't," said Reeves.

Nolan looked around and saw a small camera mounted in the corner, and though he had never been in this room before, it was clear he was in an interrogation room. He suddenly had the cold realization that this might be his last moment on Earth. Reeves must have found something on him. Maybe the soldier at the bridge had reported him, or perhaps he had been followed. Or the armory could have put him on a watch list for his sign-out of the explosives. He had been careful, but knew that if someone were paying attention, there were always dots to connect.

Reeves placed a green file on the metal table and looked across at Nolan.

"You're highly qualified for your position. Ten years as a marine, five years abroad, and now four serving in the Burke Administration."

Nolan remained silent.

"Which makes me wonder why someone, who at least on paper is so devoted to their job, would commit treason."

Nolan stared at Reeves. Neither one of them had opened the file sitting on the table, but Nolan knew that whatever was in it was likely what had brought him to the interrogation room in the first place.

"I don't know what you're talking about," said Nolan.

"Typical," said Reeves. "You seem to have found yourself in a predicament from which there is no coming back. Though perhaps what changed was the death of your daughter, Abbie, right? The loss of a child can significantly impact what we believe to be right or wrong, just or unjust. Is that it, Parker?"

"Don't talk about my daughter," he said through a clenched jaw.

"I'm sorry to say, Parker, that generally speaking, you are no longer in control. You have lost the ability to dictate the terms of your own fate."

With one hand, Reeves flipped open the file on the table. The first page had a records log of Nolan's visits to *The 212*, with the ledger's entry and exit times to the right.

"Can you explain why you visited *The 212* so frequently, and often without a detainee?"

Nolan looked up from the file and said, "That's classified."

"Oh, don't worry about that, Parker. I have clearance."

"I had business at the processing facility," said Nolan.

"At these hours? It seems awfully late to be meeting with the staff there, especially alone. I'll accept your answer. However, I don't think you'll have such an easy time explaining this," he said, as he moved the records log and, with his long finger, moved a picture from the file over to Nolan's side of the table. It was a picture taken from a drone showing him walking through *The 212*. Though dark, and the person in the photo was wearing black, it was clearly Nolan.

"Are you aware of the law preventing any person other than those processed from entering *The 212*?"

Nolan didn't have time to respond before Reeves answered for him. "I'm sure you are. So, Parker, please, enlighten me about what exactly you were doing inside a restricted zone."

"What are you hoping to achieve here, Reeves?"

"There are rules to be followed and laws to be maintained. If a special agent is found in breach of protocol, or in your case, flaunts a blatant disregard for the rules, they need to be dealt with."

"What are you thinking? Few weeks paid leave?"

"I'm afraid the consequence will be something a little more permanent. Though before your departure, I'm interested in what exactly you were doing inside *The 212* and what was in the bag."

"If you think I'm going to answer your questions, I'd say you'd lost your mind if you had possessed one to begin with."

"Just remember, it's your actions that have resulted in an irrevocable consequence. You're responsible for what's about to happen."

Reeves flicked his wrist, and metal buckles on Nolan's chair flicked over one hand, but not before Nolan managed to move his left hand before the buckle strapped over it. Gripping the chair handle with his right hand secured against it, he stood up and swung the chair, turning in a circle and whipping it toward Reeves, who stepped back just in time. Both men now stood opposite each other with the metal table in the middle and Nolan still holding the metal chair in his hand. Nolan again swung the chair and Reeves sidestepped and then punched Nolan in the chest. He staggered back and then steadied himself, looking across at the man he intended to kill.

"This really is unnecessary," said Reeves.

"I'm going to bust you like a piñata," said Parker. He lunged forward and swept the chair like an uppercut, toward Reeves' face. It caught him under the jaw, and Reeves crumpled to the floor. As Nolan rushed toward him, Reeves lashed out with a foot to his knee. Pain lanced up and down his leg and Nolan struggled to keep his balance.

Reeves shot his foot out again, snapping Nolan's head to the side and splattering blood over the nearby concrete wall. Nolan shook his head, wiped his bleeding nose with his free hand, and then reared back with the chair. Before he could bring it crashing down onto Reeves, the door burst open, and Nolan found himself staring down the barrel of a large gun held by President Burke.

"Sit down," Burke said. "You too, Reeves. I thought you'd be able to handle this on your own."

Reeves stood up and rubbed his jaw where the chair had clipped him, leaning his back against the cold concrete wall as Burke pulled up a chair. He kept his gun pointed at Parker.

"You have served me well over the years," he said, his grey eyes focused on Parker. "But our time together has come to an end. Your recalcitrant attitude as of late is something that neither I nor my Administration will tolerate. Do you understand what I am talking about?"

"Yes," said Nolan. At this point, there was no denying that he had gone to *The 212* on several occasions, though he knew it was important not to disclose why.

"What was in the bag?" Burke asked.

"Go fuck yourself."

Burke nodded toward Reeves, who stood up and punched Nolan in the face and then stood back to watch the blood slowly drip from his nose.

"What are they up to?" asked Burke.

Nolan smiled and said, "You've lost, Burke. Your pathetic attempt to consolidate power is about to come to an end. And I'm happy to have been a part of it."

Burke smiled and then again nodded toward Reeves, who pummeled him with punches. Nolan's face had started to swell, and he knew it was only a matter of time until his vision would go, though he wondered if he would die before that happened. He had been tortured before in the New South Pacific, as the Chinese didn't take lightly to interference from the United Federation, and though not a pleasant experience, it was a familiar one. Nolan had also been on the opposite end of the chair, having used a variety of tools and methods to extract information from those he had shackled to a chair. He didn't particularly enjoy either side of an interrogation but knew his training would pay off to perhaps not survive the ordeal, but at least buy *The 212* some time.

After several hits from Reeves, Nolan looked at Burke and said, "You think the rest of us don't know how the world works. You seem to have tried to create a fantasy world where power is more important than the people you govern. It will fail, Leon, and we both know it. So why not try and do the right thing, for once. Then maybe, on a rare day, you just might be able to live with yourself."

There was a moment after he had finished speaking that no one in the room moved, with Burke and Reeves focused on Nolan and Nolan looking at Burke. That moment ended when Reeves' fist came crashing down on Parker's face.

It was inevitable. The clash of ideals had manifested itself into a fight that neither man would back down from. Reeves had done everything he could to extract from Nolan the information that Burke wouldn't, but Nolan had been through this in his training. No matter what Reeves did to him, he wouldn't break. The costs were too high, and though Reeves had pummeled Nolan's face, cut him, and waterboarded him, the government agent remained silent. Reeves was furious, with an intensity in his eyes that played out in the force with he struck Nolan, but still, he offered no information.

Blood dripped to the ground, pooling on the concrete floor below Nolan. His blazer had been taken off, and his arms had streaks of red lines from where they had been cut with a razor blade. Water dripped from his hair from the countless times Reeves had placed a rag over his face in his futile attempt to waterboard him. He now sat in the chair, slumped over but still alive. He thought of Laura and Abbie and those fighting for a better future in *The 212*. Nolan had never believed in an afterlife but knew that if one existed, his actions in the past few months would never make up for the atrocities he had committed. Though pain surged through his body, deep down, there was a feeling of accomplishment. A feeling that he had made a difference and that maybe, just maybe, future generations would be able to live a life free from the oppression that Burke had created.

"Sooner or later, he'll talk," said Reeves. He, too, had removed his jacket and stood over Nolan with his white collared shirt sleeves rolled up and speckled with blood.

Nolan sat up and felt the cool metal of the chair against his back. He lifted his head and looked at Burke and said, "I loathe you in ways that are unquantifiable." His comment was met with a swift blow to the temple from Reeves. His head snapped to the side and slumped down. Pain pulsated from the side of his head deep into his body.

Burke sat in a chair about a meter from Nolan. He knew he wasn't going to talk. Nolan was a trained soldier and had gone through rigorous training to become a special agent. He glanced at his watch. It was late, and the past few hours hadn't produced any substantial intel on Nolan's collusion with *The 212*.

"I was wrong about you, Parker. When we met, I thought you understood my vision. Understood what I was trying to create. A world that could live at peace with Styre but that could still press forward. To work, to achieve, and to prosper."

Nolan didn't say anything as blood continued to drip onto the floor. His white shirt was stained with sweat and blood. They both knew it was over and that in the end, Nolan wouldn't be walking out of this room alive.

"How fortunate we all were to live in the time of Burke," said Nolan, spitting on the ground in front of the large man.

Burke looked up at Reeves, who punched Nolan in the gut, causing him to reel over, gasping for air. Burke picked up the gun and pointed it at Nolan, waiting for him to catch his breath until he looked up and they locked eyes.

"Any last words, Parker?"

Nolan paused for a moment, looking at Burke's cold gray eyes. The barrel of the gun was pointed directly at his head. He took a breath and then sat upright. His body had become numb to the pain as if it had accepted the fact that it would only last a few moments longer.

"A necessary end to things comes when it is most needed," he said.

Burke smiled and then pulled the trigger, sending a smattering of brains and blood flying against the wall behind Parker. Burke placed the gun on the table and then stood up, looking first at Nolan's dead body and then over to Reeves.

"Clean this up. Erase his files — all of them. Take care of his wife. The last thing we need is a grieving widow going public about her husband's disappearance."

"Yes, sir," said Reeves.

Burke walked over to the door and turned around before opening it.

"And Reeves, figure out what's going on in *The 212* and shut it down—by any means necessary."

Reeves nodded and watched as Burke left the room. He stood alone in the large concrete room with Parker's lifeless body, immobilized in the metal chair. Blood covered the floor from the hole in Nolan's head as Reeves picked up his blazer and draped it over his bloody arm.

"So long, Parker," he said, walking over to the door and turning off the light before leaving the room.

A Viral State

Chapter 18

Dr. Merric and the others in the lab watched as Alayna was injected with what they hoped would prove to be an effective cure. Countless hours and days had been spent tweaking the formula until they had come up with what Dr. Thorin had claimed to be a workable cure. The room had been quiet when they asked for volunteers, with everyone knowing that there was immense risk involved with allowing a foreign chemical compound to be shot into their bloodstream. They had no time for a trial period and no lab animals to test first. Alayna had raised her hand, and no one had protested. "I'm sure," she had said when Dr. Merric had asked if she was certain about what she was volunteering for.

Dr. Thorin had placed the vial with a light orange-tinted liquid into the injector gun and placed it against Alayna's arm as the room watched in silence. He squeezed the trigger, and it was over. Alayna instinctively placed her hand over the spot of the injection, and Dr. Thorin said, "Now, we wait."

It was a tense few days as Alayna was closely monitored each morning, with her daily dose being added to the distribution pile. On day four, a blood sample was taken, and the team went to work analyzing it, looking to see whether they had replicated Dr. Thorin's permanent symptom suppressant or whether they had indeed created a functional cure.

After several hours, Dr. Merric lifted his head from a microscope and turned to Alayna. "It's still too early to say confidently, but as far as I can tell, it worked. Your blood contains none of the Styre viral pathogens, and all other tests have come back normal."

Alayna didn't respond. She looked down at her arm where she had received the injection and then back at the doctor. He walked over and placed his hand on her shoulder, "You just might be the first person to have ever been cured." She smiled and then started to laugh. The tension in the room seemed to slip away, and soon, people started clapping and then erupted in shouts and cheers. Creating the cure had been a grueling process, with many sleepless nights, and everyone felt a sense of relief, and more importantly, hope.

Dr. Thorin smiled. For him, creating the cure had been the means to an end, the only way for him to be reunited with his wife, and now, thanks to his hard work and Alayna's bravery, he could return to her.

From amongst the crowd, Kalum walked over to him and extended his hand. "Thank you," he said. "I know you didn't come here of your own accord, but what we've managed to do here is extraordinary."

"Thank you," Dr. Thorin said quietly.

"Give us a few days to produce more and keep an eye on Alayna. During our first distribution run, you can come with us and go back to your wife."

Dr. Thorin smiled and then turned back to the crowd, seeing the smiles and tears of joy rolling down the faces of some. It was a momentous occasion, to be sure; he just wished it wasn't under such circumstances. It was an extraordinary accomplishment, and Thorin was excited about the possibilities it would bring. Though deep down, there was a fear that he wouldn't live long enough to see what new world a Styre cure might shape.

True to his word, a few days later, Kalum came to Dr. Thorin's room and told him they would be leaving that evening. He said that Alayna's vitals had remained stable and based on preliminary bloodwork, the virus had been eradicated. Dr. Thorin nodded. He looked around the mostly empty room and knew that he would be leaving the same way he had come in—empty-handed. Unlike the others in here, his stay would not be a permanent one, and though he knew about their dose distribution runs, he wasn't sure if one day, they might not come back. Though he knew that freedom came at a price, a life on the outside spent in exile, banned from the system, would be no life at all, he thought. He lay back in his bed and began to count down the hours until his departure.

The lab had been in a state of controlled chaos over the past 72 hours, working to make and bottle as many doses of the cure as possible. Their efforts had resulted in just over 100 small glass bottles of the orange-hued liquid. The question on everyone's mind was who would get it. Some had argued in favor of families of those in *The 212*, while others had made the point that resistance groups on the outside should be the first. After much debate, a list was made containing a few select names, as well as a general list of the first recipients of the cure.

"It will take time," Dr. Merric had said when asked how long it would take to make more. "Even working at full capacity, we'll never be able to make a significant amount before we're found out."

"Make as much as you can," said Kalum. "Even one dose is significant for someone."

The usual distribution team gathered in the dining hall for one last meeting before they set off. Finn, the engineer Darin, Kalum, a few others, and Alayna, who, after much protest, had been allowed to go.

"Half will go to resistance fighters at the Warehouse. Finn and Darin, you'll take yours to Central Hospital, and the others will go to the families. I don't need to remind you that this is a critical moment for everyone out there who is fighting for a better future."

The others nodded. The appetite for a new country, for a new government, and a new life, unbound by the constraints and policies of the Burke Administration, was palpable. They each understood the importance and historic nature of what they were doing.

Finn looked over at Alayna and smiled. Though each distribution run was potentially his last, there was an energy about this run that was palpable. He held one of the small cure vials in his hand and felt an overwhelming feeling of accomplishment. They had managed to do something that, for years, many had believed to be impossible. Though the vial itself wasn't anything special, it represented the possibility for a better future for billions of people, and Finn was grateful he had had the opportunity to be a part of it. The pain and loss he had suffered

241

throughout his life could never be erased, but now, sitting at a table with the only people he now considered family, Finn felt a sense of purpose. He had set out to help the world if only in some small way, and in a few hours, he would do just that.

As they got up to leave, Kalum pulled Finn aside and said, "I've radioed Parker over the past few days. No response. Either something's happened to him, or he's turned on us. Maybe he's dead. Regardless, we've got to move things along faster than planned."

"Understood," said Finn, thinking about what could have happened to the government agent while trying to keep his focus on tomorrow's run.

The crew slept little that night, and Dr. Thorin, not at all. He would be joining Finn and Darin and then head off on his own once the cure had been dropped off. Finn had started looking forward to the distribution, if only for the change of scenery. Inside *The 212*, even with the drone presence and perpetually silent watchtowers, he had grown accustomed to the people, and his surroundings and the runs outside of the walls offered an opportunity to break up the routine, which he gladly welcomed.

The early morning came, and the three teams and Dr. Thorin huddled together on the subway platform. Kalum could tell that the doctor had been trying to work out how they had been getting out of *The 212*, and the look of surprise on his face seemed to have answered his question.

"Let's go," he said as they began the quiet 2-km jog toward Clark Street station. Nobody spoke, largely because there was nothing to say, but also because there was a rhythm to their process. The teams knew the fastest way to their targets, and besides Finn's unexpected change of course, to get Tipper almost a month ago, nothing else unexpected had happened.

Once at the utility door, the pairs broke up and headed to their respective destinations, with Dr. Thorin tagging along behind Finn and

Darin. After about five minutes, he began asking questions, to which Darin had responded with a cold look, and they moved on. It had just finished snowing, and their feet crunched through the soft layer of white powder overtop the compacted snow beneath. They moved slowly, but eventually, the hospital came into view, and they made their way to the side entrance. Finn slowly removed the backpack containing 30 cures and placed it on the doorstep.

Finn was never sure who exactly was getting the doses they delivered here and had the same curiosity concerning the cure, but regardless, he was happy he was helping at least one person. Knowing that kept his curiosity at bay. As they turned to go, the darkness of the early morning still hanging in the sky, Finn turned around and saw the door open. The black nurse stepped out into the snow, looked down at the backpack, and then up at Finn. She opened the bag and saw the orange liquid and looked up at him but remaining silent.

"It's a cure. It works."

She smiled, and then forming her hand into a gun, raised it into the sky. She held the pose for a moment and then grabbed the backpack and shut the door behind her. Finn smiled. He had felt the same sense of respect and admiration seeing Alayna do the same thing on TV, and though his first time seeing the hand-gun symbol had left him full of questions, he was now clear on what it stood for and represented. A defiant hope. One that required its believers to take a stand, to fight for their cause, and to never waiver in their belief that they could create a better world. Finn turned around and continued to walk with the two other men and noticed that Darin had slowed down.

Darin pulled out a small black gun from his tight winter jacket and pointed it directly at Dr. Thorin's head. Finn saw them outlined against the pale light of the early morning and paused before running through the snow over to them.

"Darin," he said. "What are you doing?"

"We can't trust him," he said, keeping the gun firmly centered on the doctor's head. Dr. Thorin had slowly raised both his hands and said, "I'm not going to tell a soul, I swear!"

"He's a loose end," said Darin. "He's not one of us."

"We had an agreement," said Finn, looking first at Darin and then over to the doctor. Though killing the doctor had never crossed his mind, Finn, at one point or another, had shared similar thoughts concerning the doctor's departure. Darin was right; there was nothing to stop Dr. Thorin from ratting them out once he was reunited with his wife. And it was likely that once he was IDed from the street cameras, he would be interrogated about his absence. Both men had their doubts about where the doctor's loyalties lay. The obvious conclusion was that Dr. Thorin would need to die to protect their plan, but Finn didn't want any more blood on his hands.

"It's the only choice," said Darin. "Our plan must succeed, at any cost." The intransigent look in his eyes told Finn that Darin had already made up his mind.

"We can't," said Finn. "This isn't who we are." From his pocket, Finn pulled out a piece of paper given to him by Kalum. He looked at Dr. Thorin and said, "Block 1, residence #4. Three-bedroom apartment. Your wife, Amy Thorin, 46 years old, often visits Trinity Park. You drive a gray electric Chevy and take 43rd street to work." He put the piece of paper back in his pocket.

"Do you understand what I'm saying?"

"I have nothing to gain by talking," said Dr. Thorin quietly. "I promise."

Darin lowered the gun and then put it back inside his jacket. "If he talks," he said, turning to Finn, "this is on you."

The wind blew and sent a flurry of snow across the ground as the three men stood outside the hospital.

"Go," said Finn. "But keep in mind, we're watching." The doctor nodded and then started to walk away, his shape slowly blending into the snow until he turned a corner and was gone from sight.

"We made the right decision," said Finn.

"Time will tell. Let's go."

The two men hurried back toward Clark Street station at a brisk pace. It was a cold morning, and the streets were still empty when they turned down the alley and waited outside the subway's utility door. Alayna and another woman came into view, and then a few minutes later, Kalum and his partner showed up.

They opened the door and started the walk back to *The 212*.

"Did you kill him?" asked Alayna after a moment.

Darin looked at Finn and then said, "Against my better judgment, we let him go."

"If we don't keep our word, we're no better than Burke," said Kalum. "Believe me; it was not an easy decision for me to make. But per the agreement, if he helped us make the cure, then he would be able to return to his life outside the wall."

"We need to move up the timeline," said Finn. "Dr. Thorin is a risk. If he talks, they'll obliterate us, and everything we worked for will be lost."

"We'll ramp up cure production, begin distributing it, and plan our escape."

No one else talked while they made their way through the dark tunnel back to the only place they called home. The decision to let Dr. Thorin go free had been agreed upon, and he was headed home to his life beyond the wall while the others headed back inside. It was easy to theorize about what the doctor would do and what potential consequences his choices might bring to *The 212*, but there was work to be done, and they all knew they needed to focus.

For some reason, Finn couldn't help but think of his mother. Ever the optimist, no matter the situation, she had always had a positive outlook. "My love," she would say. "Everything is as it should be." She died soon after stating that Styre wouldn't last long, and he wondered if his mother's fierce optimism had perhaps been her downfall. Walking through the dark tunnel now, believing that everything with Dr. Thorin would be okay, he wondered if perhaps it would be his downfall, too.

"You have to!" shouted Amy. She was in tears and had been so ever since her husband had walked through their door a few hours ago, covered in snow and looking like he hadn't slept in days.

"It's not that simple." The question of whether to get in touch with Burke and essentially spill the beans on what was happening in *The 212* was something Dr. Thorin had considered, but the recent threat from Finn was fresh in his mind. He hadn't planned on telling Amy about it for fear that might send her over the edge, but without doing so, he was in a losing argument.

"They kidnapped you!" she shouted. Her eyes were red, and she was squeezing her husband's hands as they sat on the couch as snow fell outside, covering the windows in white.

"Amy," he said quietly. "We made a cure."

"A what?" she asked. She wanted to say more but couldn't find the words.

"I was taken to *The 212* to produce a cure, and we did it. It works."

Amy stared at her husband and wiped away the tears with one of her hands. He knew what a whirlwind of emotions his wife must be feeling, the same anxiety, fear, and small sense of hope he had felt the day Parker had walked into his office and told him he would be going inside the wall.

"If I tell Burke that I made a cure, I'm as good as dead. But if I don't, they'll kill me for conspiring against the government."

"Honey, tomatoes don't grow so that they may be looked upon; they grow to be eaten. He'll be thrilled you managed to make a cure. They'll forgive you for perhaps making it for the wrong side, but if you tell Burke everything, you'll be a hero. You did it against your will, but you still did something that no one has ever been able to do. You have to talk to him. Please."

Thorin sighed. He had had this conversation in his mind a million times inside *The 212* and was still at a loss about what to do. He had been gone for a little over four days and knew that he was being looked for. He was a high-profile government employee, and since he, along with Burke, were the only people who knew about the long-term dose, he knew he couldn't stay hidden for long.

"I'll go this afternoon," he said. Amy smiled, her eyes still swollen from the tears.

Thorin tried to smile back, but was only able to manage slightly pursing his lips rather than giving her an actual smile. He knew what would happen if he went to see Burke but didn't see any way around it. Either way, his fate had been sealed the moment Parker had walked into his office. Though he hadn't thought it out at the time, he knew that whether or not he went to see Burke, his life was already over.

The afternoon saw him take a shower, have a small lunch, and put on a gray suit before hailing a taxi to Central HQ. He looked out the car window and saw the large black wall of *The 212* in the distance and thought about what his visit with Burke would mean for them. However, the thought didn't last long as his head was soon filled with the vision that Burke might actually forgive him if he told the president what was going on inside *The 212*. The drones clearly hadn't picked anything up, and he was the only person besides Parker with inside information. As he pulled up outside of the concrete walls of the HQ building, Dr. Thorin paid the cabbie and stood outside for a moment, looking up at the point where the gray concrete wall met with the gray sky overhead. He tapped his wrist onto a glass panel on the wall, and the soldier watched him as it turned green, and he passed through the entrance. Before Dr. Thorin had made it ten meters into the compound, two men in suits approached him, taking him by the arms, and started escorting him toward the main building. He didn't resist. He had expected something to happen once his ID triggered the system, and he walked with the men toward the large building in front of him.

During his time in the taxi, Dr. Thorin had convinced himself that by exposing the truth about the on-goings inside *The 212*, he would be hailed a hero, and his life would be saved, perhaps even Amy's too. The thought settled over him like a gentle cloud. Technically, he had done what he had under duress, and Burke would surely understand that he was in no position to negotiate with hostile forces. As the two men escorted him into the elevator, his sense of fear started to dissipate, and he went over what he would say to Burke in his head. He and the two men walked down the long hallway, the men now on either side of the doctor but no longer grabbing his arms. As they approached the door, the men stopped, and when the large door opened, Dr. Thorin was the only one to step in.

As usual, President Burke was sitting behind his large desk while the rest of the room remained empty. Dr. Thorin had always wondered why one man needed so much space but thought it wise never to voice that question.

"Seems you disappeared from us for a while," said Burke, focusing his large gray eyes on him.

"Yes, sir. I was taken."

"Taken by whom? And where?" asked Burke. He gestured toward the chair in front of his desk, and Dr. Thorin walked over to it slowly and sat down.

"Nolan Parker, sir. He told me I was needed in *The 212*, and he was the one who took me there. You can ask him yourself."

"That's no longer necessary, nor possible," said Burke with a look of boredom, as if he was annoyed, he had to explain what had happened over the last few days. "Continue," he said with a gesture of his finger.

"Once inside, they told me they wanted me to help them make a cure."

President Burke leaned forward. "I'm sorry, did you say cure?"

"Yes, sir."

"And did you?"

Dr. Thorin paused. He hadn't decided whether to tell Burke the entire truth until right at this moment. "Yes."

"The same as what you made for me?"

The doctor became agitated and squirmed a little in his chair before answering. "Not exactly."

President Burke stood up and walked behind his desk toward the window. "Please, elaborate."

"What I created for you is technically a cure, but it's more like a permanent suppressant. It's able to permanently prevent the Styre symptoms, but the virus is still in the body. Scientifically speaking, it's not a cure but produces the same effects. Inside *The 212*, we were able to create a functional cure, one that completely eradicates the virus."

"How?" asked Burke quietly, with his back turned to the doctor.

"It was a very rudimentary setup, but there are several brilliant individuals, um, locked up inside. But it was predominantly possible because one of them is immune."

Burke turned around and walked over to his desk, placed his hands on the hard wood and leveled his gaze even with Dr. Thorin's.

"Did you say immune?"

"Yes, sir. We analyzed his blood and tested it over and over again. He doesn't have Styre. Quite an anomaly, actually, if you think about it. We then extracted the plasma from his blood to create a serum, which was then turned into a cure. So far, only one person has been injected, a woman. And based on preliminary tests, it destroyed Styre, and she is holding steady."

"What is his name?"

"Whose name, sir?"

"The man who is immune," Burke growled.

"Finn Bridges, or Branson, or Br.."

"Brantley," Burke said. Dr. Thorin nodded, not bothering to ask how Burke knew his name.

"So, Parker took you into *The 212*, you helped them make a cure, and decided you would just come back to work and life would go on as normal?"

"I was planning to come to see you, sir. It's quite an achievement what we did in there. If you were to say, perhaps go into *The 212* and take it, BioDose could start reproducing it, and you would be hailed as a hero."

Burke lifted his hands off the desk and stood up, his frame casting a shadow over the sitting doctor.

"Why is it that everyone keeps failing to see the bigger picture?" asked Burke, primarily to himself, though the question had been directed at Dr. Thorin.

"Pardon?"

"Never mind. Listen, I'm glad you came to see me," said President Burke. "Your loyalty won't go unnoticed. Before you go, I'd like to introduce you to Mr. Reeves. He works with internal affairs and will help you write up a report for what Parker got you involved with. Just a few questions should be all – standard operating procedure for irregular situations that occur within my Administration."

Dr. Thorin nodded and turned around when he heard the door open. A tall man with thick brown hair swept across his head, entered, and smiled at Dr. Thorin.

"Please, this way," he said, gesturing for Dr. Thorin to leave the room.

"Thank you," he said to Burke. "I'm eternally grateful for your understanding."

"But of course," said Burke, forcing a small smile and then having it disappear from his face, once Dr. Thorin started to walk down the marble hallway followed by Reeves. The doctor hadn't gone more than two meters before Reeves pulled out a large gun, pointed it at the back of Dr. Thorin's head, and pulled the trigger. The doctor's frail body fell to the ground as flecks of blood spattered the large windows, contrasting with the white scenery outside. Reeves looked back to see President Burke nod from behind his desk, and then the doors closed. He had been in this line of work long enough to know that if he wasn't doing the killing, he would soon end up on the other side of it, much like what had happened to Parker. Reeves stared down at the body, unimpressed by how easily it could be destroyed. A small fragment of metal could end a life at a moment's notice, and there was nothing the doctor could have done to stop it. He was a liability, and per Burke's order, liabilities needed to be dealt with.

Reeves flicked his wrist and said, "Disposal unit. Top floor. One body," and then flicked his wrist to end the call. He stepped over the body and then paused for a moment to watch a drop of blood slowly slide down the glass window as snow fell outside and then continued to the elevator at the end of the hall without looking back.

A Viral State

Chapter 19

The streets were quiet as a group of hooded figures moved quietly through them, keeping close to the walls. Black hoods covered their heads, and masks kept their faces mostly hidden from the prying eyes of the drones overhead. A few streets ahead, they saw a large, armored van shine a large spotlight down the side street, and then it moved on. Waving his hand, the leader motioned for the group to move forward. The six people dressed in black moved quickly as if slicing through the cold winter night with a hot knife. A block later, they crouched against a wall, with the leader, a man with a thick beard, peering out from the wall to look at the building across the street.

"Everyone ready?" he asked. The others nodded.

"Let's go."

From their position, two moved forward and pulled out a small cylindrical device and pointed it at the large metal gate in front of the BioDose HQ. A blue beam shone from the device, and the gate's metal started to melt, creating a pool of liquid on the ground. Once through, they motioned for the others who ran to join them. Inside the large compound, the leader focused his assault rifle on one of the watchtowers, waiting for the guard to appear. Moments later, a man in full assault gear turned the corner, taking his time as he clutched his rifle in one hand and held the other on the railings of the tower. The man with the beard sighted the officer and then pulled the trigger. There was a soft spurt as the bullet passed through the silencer and the guard fell, blood bursting from where he had been shot in the neck.

The man lowered the gun and then, using his hand, motioned for the group to move forward. The main building of the BioDose HQ was several hundred meters beyond the gate, with a large concrete courtyard in front. The group crept forward, cast in the soft white glow of the lit BioDose sign high above. They crouched in front of the stairs, with one of the group's members pulling out several packs of C4 and other explosives from a bag and distributing them to the others.

"No hesitation," said the leader. As they stood up to climb the stairs, a drone flew overhead and paused over their position, shining a light from above. The man with the rifle spun around and shot at the drone, only managing to clip one of its rotors, causing it to veer left and crash into a nearby building. There was a small explosion, and the group waited as the noise reverberated through the quiet streets. Floodlights from the top of the BioDose building sprang on, illuminating the group as several heavily armed officers appeared at the top of the stairs.

"Drop your weapons," one of them shouted.

The group members froze for a moment before the bearded man raised his rifle and shot at one of the guards. A frenzy of bullets sprayed from the stairs, riddling the group as a flurry of blood splattered against the concrete floor and bodies clad in black dropped. As the guards continued to fire, a deafening sound ripped through the air as a bullet made contact with one of the bundles of explosives, knocking back the officers on the stairs and sending a huge plume of fire into the air. Several nearby drones flew in and circled overhead, waiting for the smoke to clear to assess the situation.

One of the guards stood up and looked down at the scene. Pieces of bloodied bodies were scattered around the courtyard, with a small hole ripped in the concrete along with a massive area of charred Earth. The fence was mangled with body parts and twisted like some grotesque art installation. Chunks of debris had flown up onto the stairs. Alarms were blaring from inside the main building, and there was now a cluster of drones overhead, all shining bright lights down onto the scene of the blast.

One of the guards flicked his wrist and said, "This is Captain Garza at BioDose HQ. We've just been attacked. Several high explosives. Casualties unknown. Tell someone to get ahold of President Burke immediately. He's going to want to know about this."

He moved his wrist to end the call and looked down at the plumes of smoke that were still rising in the sky. Drops of blood highlighted the white snow, turning a faint pink the further they were from the center of the blast. This hadn't been the first attack on BioDose HQ, and if there was one thing Garza knew, it wouldn't be the last.

There was a palpable tension in the air, something not seen by the eye but felt by all. The city was beginning to tip, and everyone knew it. Though unsure exactly how it would manifest or what inevitable consequences might result, it was clear that the city was about to break. The past week alone had seen over a dozen attacks on Dose Depots and increased protests in the streets. Windows of government buildings had been smashed by silent protestors clad in black hurling bricks, and cars with government license plates had been set on fire, burning quietly in the night until they finally exploded. No one had claimed responsibility for any of the attacks, but with each news story about the insurrection, Central citizens felt inspired to keep up the assault.

Never one to back down from a fight, nor wishing to relinquish any of the power he had worked so hard to consolidate, Burke responded in the only way he knew how - with force. Hundreds of riot police were dispatched throughout the city, and protestors unlucky enough to be caught in any act deemed hostile to the government were immediately detained. Security checkpoints were established for public buildings, and roadblocks were put into place around the city. Despite the amplified presence of officers and drones, an increasing amount of anti-government graffiti, many depicting the finger-gun pointed to the sky, started to appear on city streets, the sides of buildings, and on store-front windows. No matter how much Burke tried, the city was pushing for a revolution, one that was unlikely to be deterred.

Finn and the others in *The 212* had managed to make two more distribution runs, each delivering around a hundred cure doses. The notion of a cure for Styre was no longer a myth nor an impossibility, and people had started to take notice. On each run, Finn had seen more stencils of the resistance symbol, and though he still wasn't sure where it originated, it gave him hope. The people were no longer staying silent.

As per Burke's orders, the news had gone into overdrive, attempting to quell any idea that a cure existed and that the daily doses created by BioDose were the only safe and reliable way to continue living a harmonious and healthy life. Whatever stories of a cure had surfaced had been labeled as nothing more than a drug dealer peddling harmful chemicals that under no circumstances should be injected. The recent attacks on government buildings had been labeled an act of defiance by a terrorist faction, which the government and local authorities were diligently working to track down to ensure the safety of the city. People were encouraged to continue working and stay at home as much as they could.

The days were cold, and snow continued to fall as the city was now in the depths of winter. People went about their days, bundled in coats and scarves while keeping a watchful eye on the police who patrolled the city, ever mindful of the automatic weapons they kept a tight grip on. Drones flew over the city streets so often that people stopped talking about them. They had become part of the new normal and, with the increasing volatility of the city's inhabitants, had been expected. But despite everything, life went on, the same as it had once Burke had introduced his plan to fight Styre over a decade ago. People had always been flexible and adaptable, but in certain circumstances, there was an uncomfortableness that also arose. Much in the same way that although some can adapt to life in prison, there's always that feeling in the back of their mind reminding them that something is off.

Despite what the news had said about "fake cure doses," something was different this time. People all over the country were talking about "the orange," and no matter how hard the news cycle pushed to manipulate the story and beat the idea out of people's minds, it is often hard to kill the truth. Videos had surfaced of people online injecting themselves with the cure and livestreaming themselves in an isolated room for a week with nothing more than food and water. Though not substantial evidence that the cure worked, it had inspired hope, and perhaps even more so, anger. For years, the government had been adamant that a cure was impossible, despite their best efforts. And out of nowhere, a black-market cure shows up, which many claim to have come out of Central, with all evidence pointing to its efficacy. Though tightly controlled, conspiracy theories started showing up online, with videos denouncing the government as liars seen by millions before being scrubbed by authorities. Time, though, would be the ultimate test of whether the revolution would succeed or whether Burke's powerful government would push people back into submission.

Despite the giant wall and lack of connectivity, *The 212* knew a storm was brewing. The increased drone activity overhead had been the first indicator, and distribution runs brought an increased level of risk due to the sheer amount of police on the streets at all hours of the day. On several runs, Finn and Darin had been passed by blaring police cars, screaming past them in the early hours of the morning to deal with whatever act of protest the people of Central had chosen to partake in. A curfew was in effect, but it fell on deaf ears, as society had chosen to continue their fight against Burke's government, no matter the consequences.

"We have to continue," Kalum had said, addressing everyone at one of their group dinners. "The only way to create change is to keep getting the cure out."

"And what about us?" someone had asked from one of the tables.

"Our time will come," said Kalum. "For now, we need to focus on creating more cure doses and figure out our plan of attack. Once we leave here, permanently, it's not going to be a quiet fight. I've spoken with resistance groups on the outside, and they're getting ready for us. We'll have a place to stay, along with more weapons and provisions, but understand the seriousness of what I'm about to say: this will be the fight of your lives."

The room was quiet as candles flickered on each of the tables, softly illuminating the faces of everyone who had spent so much time locked behind a wall. Everyone knew what lay ahead, and though scared, were prepared to face it head-on.

"Where are we with production?" Kalum asked, looking toward Dr. Merric.

"With a fully staffed team and the remaining supplies, I'd say we can produce a thousand more vials, give or take, over the next few days."

"Keep up the good work," Kalum said, smiling at the doctor and then looking out to face the group. "We are about to embark on the greatest revolution this country has ever seen. Burke's time is over, and it's up to us to make it so."

The group cheered while some pounded the table to show their support. Their respect for Kalum was implacable, as he had always kept his promise to lead them into a better future. And here he stood before them again, promising not only them but people around the world a better future. Though the world might not know who Kalum Sakura is, in time, they would.

"The path we have chosen to embark on is one that will ultimately lead some of us to our death. But the path will have been blazed so those who come after us may walk safely and openly. Let us discover a world beyond fear," said Kalum, turning his head to glance at each and every person he had looked after over the past several years. It hadn't been easy, and for a time, he thought they would never make it, but they persevered, as he was hoping they would on this endeavor, too.

"A necessary end to things comes when it is most needed." No one spoke as each person in the room slowly started to raise their hands, their fingers pointed in the shape of a gun. Kalum did the same, and after a moment, he nodded and then lowered his hand.

"Get some rest. The real work begins tomorrow. To those of you I previously spoke with, please stay." People shuffled about as benches were moved and seats were cleared until only six people were left sitting together at one table.

Kalum took a seat and looked at Finn, Alayna, Dr. Merric, Magnus and his gray hair, Finn's lab assistant and distribution partner Darin, and finally, over to Enzo, the man built like a brick wall who had helped Finn orchestrate the tunnel through the blasted subway station.

"The logistics for what we're attempting are a nightmare," he said. "There's no way to sugarcoat this. As you're all aware, they've increased drone surveillance over *The 212*, even in the early hours. I don't think they know anything, but they certainly suspect us."

"How many days do you think we have until they come in here?" Alayna asked.

"Soon," said Kalum. "I've spoken to the resistance groups on our runs, and things are crazy out there. You've all seen the increased security in the city. It's due to the fact that society knows there's a cure. Reports are flooding in of protests all across the country. Burke has kicked his government machine into overdrive, and it's only a matter of time before he pushes too hard, and things burst."

"Do you have an exact time frame?" asked Finn.

"Three days. That will give us enough time to produce cure doses for everyone in *The 212*, as well as a significant amount to distribute once we leave here for good."

Everyone at the table nodded and looked around at each other. They had all dreamed of leaving *The 212*, and Kalum had finally made their dreams a reality. Though in three days, they wouldn't be returning to the lives they had so often reminisced about; they would be fighting to forge a better future.

"Dr. Merric, you and your staff focus on producing as many cures as possible. Finn, you and Enzo figure out how to get as many people down into the subway as fast as you can. Every person in here is getting out, and we can't spare any time, especially not with the increased surveillance. Alayna, take inventory of our weapons and distribute them to anyone who doesn't already have one."

"How long until they realized we escaped?" asked Darin.

"Not long," replied Kalum. "Once we start, we'll need to have everyone out of here within two hours. Once inside the city, we'll break off into four groups and head to four safehouses in the city that are expecting us. We'll take stock, get some rest, and then in a few days, once everything and everyone is ready, we'll launch our assault."

"What's going to be different this time?" asked Finn. Most people had asked the same question when Kalum had laid out the plans for an attack on BioDose and Central HQ. Many had watched failed attempts on the news, and several people inside *The 212* were there because they had taken part.

"To be frank – we've got power in numbers. The cure we've distributed has ignited an idea in society, and with the already growing anti-government sentiment, we'll have a turnout unlike any other throughout the city and potentially, around the country."

"And if it fails?" Enzo asked.

"Then we'll have died trying to make this world a better place. Look, I know what I'm asking is borderline insane. We're attempting something that has never been successful, and our opposition is better equipped and experienced. But what would you rather do? Spend another decade trapped in here only to die? What's ahead of us is daunting, I understand that, but I have hope. If you assume there is no hope, you guarantee there will be no hope."

The table was quiet as they took in Kalum's words.

"You all have your assignments. Two days. That's it. If you have any issues, come find me, but I expect you're all capable of handling what needs to be done. Let's see this through."

Kalum stood up, as did a few of the others, and walked out of the room, leaving only Finn and Alayna at the table, the soft candlelight casting a warm glow over their faces.

"You ready?" asked Alayna, putting her hand over Finn's.

"I will be," he said, looking into her brown eyes. "I have to be."

"I have faith in you."

Finn looked down at their hands and then back up to Alayna's face. "What if we do our best and the world still doesn't become better?"

"Don't forget that everyone who came before once had dreams and aspirations, too. We're fighting to ensure that the next generation of dreamers has the potential to achieve them, rather than solely living to survive. If Burke wins, and we all die, then I'll be satisfied knowing that at least we gave it a shot. I couldn't live with myself knowing we had the opportunity to do something, but instead, we stayed locked up in here and did nothing."

"Seems like just yesterday I arrived in here, unaware there was a microcosm of people planning to overthrow the government."

Alayna smiled. "Welcome to the resistance. It's crazy what we're doing, there's no doubt about that, but in times like these, I remember something my mother used to say, 'Look before you leap, so long as in the end, you leap.'"

"In a similar vein, my father used to say, 'Never start something you're not willing to finish.'"

"Seems like we both had parents that spent too much time reading motivational quotes."

Finn laughed and squeezed Alayna's hand. The room was quiet. Finn was happy to spend time alone with Alayna, as the past few weeks had seen them both surrounded by people, busy working to achieve their common goal.

"I suppose it's good to try and change the world. Even just a little bit."

"Be safe out there," she said.

Alayna moved her head closer and kissed him, feeling the softness of his lips on hers. She ran her fingers through the hair on the side of his head and said, "I always am." Finn smiled and kissed her again. He paused for a moment, wanting to tell her how he felt but before he could speak, she simply said, "I know." Alayna knew before he even opened his mouth; before he had even planned to tell her at all. They both stood up, blew out the candles, and walked out of the dark dining hall into the cold black night, both anxious for what was yet to come.

Chapter 20

Snow continued to fall on the city, blanketing it in white, seemingly as if to cover up the blood and tears that were being shed on its streets. Clashes between protestors and riot police occurred daily, mainly taking place in Central, but reports of protests in other major cities around the country had reached the public, igniting their fight further. Burke had initially appeared on TV, trying to appeal to people's sense of good and ask them to trust him and his Administration, though his appearances seemed only to have stoked the fire. Since then, he hadn't made any public appearances, hiding in the depths of Central HQ, doling out orders to his subordinates, and hoping the situation was dealt with as quickly as possible, by any means necessary. For Burke, the desire to do good often came after the desire to maintain one's social status.

In response to the recent attack on the BioDose HQ, a curfew was put in place. 10 p.m-6 a.m. Essential workers were still able to commute to work, but besides them, the streets were to remain empty, and anyone caught without a certifiable reason would immediately be treated as hostile and detained. Drones flew over the city streets at all hours, sometimes whooshing past in a rush to get somewhere and other times idling, keeping an eye on those below. For many, it was nothing short of a police state, and despite cracking down on hundreds of protestors, there seemed to be an increasing number of reports of violence and acts of treason.

For Finn and the others in *The 212*, their lives largely remained the same. Drone activity had been increased but hadn't resulted in any changes in their plans. Dr. Merric continued to work on creating vials of the cure, getting them packed away as soon as the cap had been placed on the small ampule, the orange-hued liquid shining in the sun beaming through the lab's windows. Kalum and his team had taken inventory of the guns, and though short of arming everyone in *The 212*, they had a sufficient number, and he was sure they'd be able to get more once they met up with their allies on the outside. He was still nervous. The mass exodus would require a significant amount of time, and that was something they couldn't afford to waste.

Getting up from his desk, he looked out the window of his office onto the empty snow-covered streets. The barren trees with their lifeless limbs stretched out toward the sky, with no signs of life to disturb the peaceful landscape. He breathed and closed his eyes, thinking of his childhood in Japan. He had grown up in a small prefecture outside of Tokyo and remembered a similar landscape in winter. Kalum had liked to wake up early on the weekends and go up to his roof, sitting there wrapped in a winter coat and hat, looking out over the buildings as the snow fell and people were still inside fast asleep. Much like what had happened to his prefecture after Styre hit, he knew peace wasn't sustainable.

People had raided the stores, burned buildings, and eventually, most people fled to other parts of the country. Kalum, however, had fled the country a few years before Styre. His father had been an executive with an American company, and with an apartment in New York that Kalum had often spent the summer in, his family had believed it best to make it their permanent residence. Japan had been ill-equipped to deal with Styre, and although unbeknownst to them, Kalum's father thought America would be the best place for his son to have a future. Kalum was 17 when he moved. After finishing high school, he had joined the military and moved his way up the ranks. Styre was an ever-present issue to deal with, but wars still needed to be fought, and it had provided him with a stable income and, more importantly, a steady supply of doses.

There were only a few other times in his life that he had felt true peace and calmness looking at the snow, watching as it quietly fell, wrapping its cold hands around whatever it touched. But it wouldn't last, as nothing usually does. His time in *The 212*, *The 212* itself, Styre, President Burke, none of them would exist a hundred years from now, and although the snow would fall again, it wouldn't be the same as it was now. It never was.

Finn had spent the evening going over blueprints for a proposed hydraulic lift down onto the subway platform. It was an ambitious plan for the two days they had left, but Enzo had vehemently said it could be done.

"There's just not enough time," said Finn. "The engineering required to pull that off is possible, just not in two days."

"We have to find a way to get people down there faster than one at a time," Enzo had said, looking back down at the blueprints.

"What about a slide?" asked Finn.

"Like a park slide?"

"Call it a chute if you prefer, or a slope, or an elevated ramp. It would be easy to fabricate, and then we just cut the tunnel a little wider to fit it in."

Enzo took one last look at the hydraulic lift blueprints, slowly moved them toward the edge of the table, and then looked back up at Finn. "A slide it is."

The plans were drawn up, opting for slightly curved pieces of sheet metal to be welded together, which would then be lowered into the tunnel, allowing faster entry onto the platform than if 100 people had to slowly climb down as they had been for the past few weeks. Finn had helped Enzo's team weld for a while before finally calling it a night.

"You get some sleep," said Enzo. "We'll finish the slide tonight, and you help us get it installed tomorrow."

"Thanks," said Finn. "You're a lifesaver."

"Quite literally," laughed Enzo.

Finn whistled, and Tipper jumped up from the corner where he was lying, and they left the former Trump lobby where the welders were going to work on the metal. They walked through the quiet streets back to Finn's apartment. He stopped to look up at the sky, letting the snow fall onto his face, with Tipper looking up at him. He closed his eyes and allowed himself a moment to clear his mind, which over the past few weeks, rarely occurred, if at all. The buzzing sound of a drone's rotors could be heard in the distance, and though Finn and Tipper both turned to look for it, they couldn't see anything past the blanket of white falling from the sky. They continued walking, with Finn thinking about how drastically his life had changed in just a few months and wondered whether it was for the best or not.

The realization that he was immune had come as a shock to him, as had his firing from Conserta, but maybe that was precisely what he had needed. His life was going nowhere, and deep down, he had known it. He could have easily spent the next thirty years working right up until the day of his inevitable death, and it was likely that a few years after that, someone would say his name for the last time. He had no family, no real friends, and no purpose, or at least no sense of purpose. But here, locked up for trying to help society, he was needed, and he was a contributor to something he believed in. It was highly risky, and the probability that it would end with his life intact wasn't very likely, but he had embraced it. For the first time in a long time, he was happy.

Finn unlocked his apartment door and walked in. He turned on the small space heater in the corner and hung up his jacket. Tipper walked over to the bed and jumped up, settling down in a comfortable position on the edge and watching as Finn shifted through an assortment of documents on his desk. The slide idea he had drawn up with Enzo wasn't an elegant solution, but it was the most efficient given their timeframe. After a while, he stood and looked outside the window, watching as the snow fell over a part of the city that at no point in his life did he ever think he would be. Lower Manhattan, the once burgeoning center of the world's greatest city, a former economic and cultural powerhouse, had been gutted and transformed into a prison, while the rest of the city had been stripped of everything that made it great in order to facilitate its transformation as the country's capital.

What a waste, Finn thought.

He took off his shoes and laid in bed, stroking Tipper's back as he closed his eyes. He was exhausted. The past few days had been strenuous, and there was a lot of work to be done in the next few days. Work that would allow everyone he had grown close to in the past few months to escape from a place that had been built to keep them in.

Escape is the wrong word, he thought.

They would be liberated, free to rejoin a society that they had just as much right to be a part of as anyone else. Finn continued to think about the future, letting the warmth of the heater seep into his body until, at last, he fell asleep.

Hours passed as Finn slept soundly, with Tipper resting peacefully next to him. The soft glow of the lamp in the corner cast its glow over the room, and the heater provided warmth against the cold winter weather outside.

Around 3 a.m., under cover of darkness and falling snow, a drone appeared. It hovered outside Finn's window for a while until a small laser quietly cut through the glass and flew into the room, sending the pane crashing silently to the ground below. It hovered over the bed for a moment before flying into the middle of the room. The drone was black and only emitted a soft buzz from its rotors. Though not as large as those used in the military, it was bigger than those used for surveillance. Welded to the front of the drone was a small barrel with an attached silencer fixed on Finn.

From a small lens, a life-size hologram of a man was projected. He was tall and wore a black suit, and though he was a projected image, he was incredibly life-like. He looked around the room for a moment, checking over the papers on the desk, and then turned his attention back to Finn.

"Mr. Brantley," he said. Finn slowly opened his eyes and began to make out the man standing at the end of his bed. Confused, he sat up in bed and reached for the gun in the drawer of his bedside table. Tipper also woke up and began to growl at the man, with the drone hovering behind him.

"I wouldn't do that if I were you," he said. Finn ignored him and opened up the drawer, reaching for the gun inside. The drone emitted a soft sputtering sound, and the bullet from the attached gun pierced through Finn's left hand. He yelled as blood began to pour over the ground, the pain searing through his body. He wrapped his hand in the white blanket, and Tipper began to bark, baring his teeth in anger.

"Keep it quiet, or I will," said the man. Finn looked at the projection and then, with his good hand, stroked Tipper's head until the dog stopped barking.

"Who are you?"

"You can call me Reeves. I work for the Administration."

"And what do you want with me?" asked Finn, looking down at him as the blood seeped through the blanket around his hand.

"You're the first person to be immune to Styre. I thought, now there's someone that's got to have an interesting story."

"I don't," said Finn flatly.

"Oh, that's not true, Mr. Brantley. As far as we're aware, you've been working to make a cure."

Finn kept his eyes focused on Reeves' face, watching it occasionally flicker as the projector moved to keep up with the man's movements.

"Dr. Thorin was kind enough to give us a detailed account of what was going on in here, so no need to confirm or deny what you've been up to."

"What did you expect?" asked Finn defiantly. "Did you think we were just going to surrender? Just sit back and do nothing?"

"The Administration expects the citizens of this country, including Central, to follow the laws of this great nation. You, Mr. Brantley, have broken several laws, some which put you inside here, and several while incarcerated. I am here, as you might have expected, to put an end to such behavior."

Finn knew his time was over. He had expected this day to come, and now, facing the projection of a man who would end his life, he felt a sense of fulfillment. He wasn't scared of dying, though he wished he could have lived long enough to see the results of everything that had already been set in motion. He looked over at Tipper and stroked his head. The life he had planned and the life he was living didn't align in the way he had thought, but he had found purpose. He had lost friends along the way and would likely lose many others in the days to come, but for Finn, there was nothing more he could do. His blood had been used to create a cure that would give people the opportunity to live a better life than those that had succumbed to Styre through no fault of their own. Opportunity and hope. Hope for a better world, free from the oppression of the Administration and free to explore a life worth living.

"You're too late," said Finn, looking up at Reeves. "Things are in motion that will permanently change the course of this world. Your efforts are futile. Killing me might give some solace to the Administration that you're maintaining the precious regime Burke has worked so hard to create, but you've already lost."

"You speak with the confidence of a man about to die, with nothing to lose," said Reeves. "Whatever is going on in here will be stopped. I'm afraid you've underestimated the reach and ability of this government."

Reeves nodded toward the window and Finn followed his gaze. A few blocks away, he saw the red lights of three drones overhead and watched as three missiles flew into the U.S. Customs building, sending a burst of flames into the sky. It was late, so Finn was confident no one was in there, but as he watched the flames climb higher into the sky, he suddenly felt an emptiness that everything they had been working on was lost.

"Looks like you won't be having a cure anytime soon, Mr. Brantley. And without you there to supply them with fresh samples of blood, it seems your rebellion has failed before it started."

Finn closed his eyes and thought about the fact that how you spend your days is how you spend your life. He recalled the past few days he had spent working to complete his projects with people he enjoyed being around and knew, that despite everything that had happened over the past few months, that he had lived a good life.

Finn opened his eyes and stared at Reeves, "A necessary end to things comes when it is most needed."

Reeves smiled and then said, "Goodbye, Mr. Brantley." The gun on the drone fired a single bullet that shot through Finn's head, knocking him back against the pillow as blood poured across the white linen. The hologram of Reeves flickered away as the drone projector shut off. The drone fixed the gun on Tipper, who was now barking loudly, but suddenly turned and flew out the window into the night, meeting up with the three drones outside and they silently flew off into the darkness.

Tipper began to whine, licking the blood from the bed and nudging Finn with his nose. Cold air and snow blew in from the open window, and Tipper began to bark again. A few minutes later, there was a knock at the door, and Tipper continued to bark. The door opened, and Alayna walked in, looking first to the open window and then over to the bed, seeing Finn's blood all over. She walked over to him and began to cry, grabbing his right hand and holding it while she sobbed in silence. Alayna reached up and closed his eyes with her fingers, wiping away the tears that were welling up. She took a moment to be there with him, to share time with the man she had grown close with over the past few months. But the moment didn't last long, and from her back pocket, she grabbed the small walkie-talkie and immediately called Kalum.

"Sakura, we have a problem. 71 Broadway. Finn's apartment. Over."

Static echoed in the room before Kalum responded. "Five minutes. Over."

Alayna took a seat in the desk chair and looked at the bed, wondering how anyone had been able to get inside *The 212* and let alone inside the building to kill Finn, and then escape without a trace. While she thought of how Finn had been killed, she also thought of their time together. Their talks in the dining hall, the intimate moments they shared when they finally had the chance to be alone together, and the discussions about right and wrong. She sat there with a heavy heart, thinking of the all the unsaid words but knowing they had both understood how the other felt. Alayna had suffered significant loss in her life, and though she was numb to this feeling, losing Finn still hurt. So much had been taken from her life, and even in somewhere like *The 212*, there was always still more to lose.

Kalum walked in the door, a little out of breath, looked at Alayna, and then saw Finn's dead body. He walked over to take a closer look.

"It was a drone," he said. "Looks like it had the gun mounted. Shot him first in the hand, probably to stop him from going for his gun," he continued, nodding at the half-open table drawer. "Shot him in the head and then flew out of here. See the bits of broken glass spilled on the window ledge and right below it? It was a forced entry."

"We have to get out of here," said Alayna. "Whatever safety we thought we had is now gone."

"I agree," said Kalum. "There was an also explosion at the lab. I sent a team over to assess the damage. We'll bury Finn, get everything finalized, and then leave tomorrow morning. In the meantime, go back and get some rest. I'll get a team up here to clean this up and get Finn ready for his burial tomorrow."

Alayna offered a small smile, and as she began to walk out of the room, Tipper whined and jumped off the bed, walking toward her and brushing up against her leg. The two walked out of the room and left Kalum alone.

It had been a few years since he had seen a dead body, and though he had grown accustomed to it, it was something he still preferred he didn't have to see. He had known that sooner or later, each person inside *The 212*, even himself, would face their day of reckoning but hadn't expected such a brazen attempt by the Administration to happen so soon.

Alayna was right, it was critical they leave, as any one of them was a potential target for another excepted attack.

Neither Kalum nor Alayna slept that night as they coordinated the final details before the departure. Enzo's team finished fabricating the slide and put it into place while it was still dark, sliding the large tire back over the cover until it was time to go.

The damage to the lab had been minimal, only destroying the outer wall and the majority of the lobby. The wall to the lab had been blown apart, but the fire had been put out and to everyone's relief, the cure vials were intact. After several members of *The 212* had gotten the fire under control and cleared away the debris, Dr. Merric and his team had worked to use the last of the serum from Finn's blood to make around 200 hundred more cures, adding to the 300 already packed up. Dr. Merric had paused in the doorway of the laboratory, looking at the place he had spent countless hours, many in frustration, until one man had entered his life and changed everything.

"Come on, dad," said Piper, placing her hand on his shoulder. "We've got to go."

"I'm going to miss this place," he said quietly, looking down at Piper. "Even if is one of the worst labs I have ever worked in," he added, nodding toward the charred white walls and chunks of concrete strewn about the floor.

"I know," she said with a smile as they both turned around, and the door to the lab closed behind them.

Alayna had coordinated with *The 212*'s small medical team and packed everything they could. They had accumulated a number of supplies over the years, and thankfully, hadn't needed to use many of them. But she knew that with what was on the horizon, medical supplies would be in great demand. Two large duffel bags had been filled with empty syringes, gauze, artificial skin, self-binding band-aids, an assortment of medication, and IV tubing. She and her team, like everyone else, had positioned themselves in one of the buildings facing the Wall

Street subway entrance, waiting for their turn to enter the platform and make their way into the city. The sky was dark, on the precipice of late night and early morning.

Kalum didn't like having to push up their departure but knew that it was no longer safe inside *The 212*, and he couldn't risk losing anyone else. He and those selected to be on his team had worked to burn important documents inside the Base and dismantle and destroy the electronic operations center they had built. Once they left *The 212*, it was certain that field agents and police would comb over this building, and the more time they bought themselves meant more time focused on toppling the Administration.

Once finished, Kalum also took a moment to internalize everything that had happened inside *The 212*. He had been in here longer than anyone and had seen the chaos turn into order and, finally, into a community. Kalum wasn't excited to leave, necessarily, as he had nothing to go back to on the outside. However, he was eager to be a part of a movement that intended to make real change, not only for those he cared about but also for change on a global level, something that, for Kalum, was difficult to comprehend but easy to visualize.

Standing in one of the dark lobbies of the buildings on Wall Street, he looked out the window and saw the large tire in front of the pile of rubble they had dug out. Although he hadn't seen it himself, Enzo had assured him that the slide would work. Kalum looked across the street at Alayna and pointed at her to go. She got her team ready, and they ran toward the subway, with two of them pushing the tire out of the way and then, one by one, slowly disappeared into the tunnel. Alayna tossed the duffel bag onto the slide and then slid down as well. Kalum waited until each team had successfully made it into the tunnel before he decided to head there as well. It was a quiet morning, and the air was still. He knew that at least above ground, he was the only person around for at least a few square kilometers. But below him, he knew that the people he had grown close with over the past few years were starting to make the trek to the city. Kalum turned to take one last look at the giant wall and the looming buildings covered in snow before jumping onto the slide and effortlessly gliding for a few seconds and reaching the platform. Looking up at the entrance, he paused for a second, thinking he had heard the faint sound of a drone but couldn't be sure. He lowered his gaze and watched as people lowered themselves off the platform and started walking through the tunnel. The work to get to this point had been grueling, and each team knew where they were headed in the city; it was still a risky operation.

Kalum turned to look back at the slide and motioned for Enzo to close the entrance. With no one left on the outside, the tire was no longer an option, so the engineering team had fashioned a cover out of metal and painted it gray. It was sitting on two wooden blocks placed into the rubble, and as Kalum watched Enzo pulled the rope, the blocks flew out of position, and the metal clang of the cover falling into place echoed throughout the platform. The floodlights on the platform were turned on, illuminating the chamber, and Kalum had to smile at Finn's ingenuity to build a slide. Despite its simplicity, Finn had been right that a slide was far more efficient than a ladder. Kalum tried not to dwell on the loss of his friend, knowing that now, he had more important things to deal with, and the time to grieve would come later.

"How are we doing on time?" Kalum asked, looking over at Darin.

"Two hours until daybreak. We should be okay."

Kalum nodded as he stepped off the tiled platform and onto the abandoned subway tracks, joining the others in the walk to the city. Though Kalum had made this journey several times before, during the distribution runs, it felt different this time as he knew there would be no returning. Despite the circumstances, *The 212* was the only place he could call home, and now, he found himself walking in a dark tunnel toward a city and a future full of unknowns. However, like everyone else in *The 212*, he was ready for a new future, even if he had to be the one to forge it himself.

Chapter 21

December 2071

The situation in Central had grown tense. Even the snow seemed to fall on the city more aggressively, as if to remind the citizens that perhaps there was no force stronger than mother nature. It had been three days since *The 212* had broken out, and their escape hadn't made the news, though no one had expected it to. Kalum and the others had holed up with other resistance groups in the city, sharing with them doses and cures in exchange for food, weapons, and a place to stay. Tomorrow had been decided as the day. There was nothing special about it, and the weather wouldn't be particularly good, but there wasn't any reason to wait any longer.

Security inside Central had increased, with drones now flying over the city and squads of police officers and special forces units continually sweeping the streets. Reports of arrests of rioters, insurrectionists, and other "bad actors" were broadcast to the masses, hoping to instill fear or discourage them from joining the growing rebellion. Still, to Burke's detriment, it had the opposite effect. People wanted retribution for the conditions they had been forced to live under for years, and now that a cure had been discovered, with no help from the government, all their anger was focused on Burke and the Administration.

Kalum had met with the other resistance leaders to discuss a plan of attack, and though none of them were entirely confident in it, they had no other options. Supplies were running low, and the cures that had been distributed weren't nearly enough for everyone involved. Tomorrow, everything would change, or those that believed in that change would die trying.

The sun was nowhere to be seen as snow fell on Central. A gray light filtering through the cloudy sky permeated the darkness as morning came. Across the city, thousands of people had woken up with only one thought:

take down the Administration. Plans had been discussed, and targets had been acquired. Killing Burke would be ideal, but if they managed to take down the systems he had built, his fall from power would be inevitable. The five main resistance groups in the city had been designated a color, and each group was responsible for a primary target.

Kalum, leading the blue team, placed a handgun into his coat and loaded a clip into his assault rifle as snow fell on his jacket from the open door of the warehouse.

"Let's go," he yelled to the close to 300 people behind him. They were focused on sealing in the police compound, or at least keeping them at bay while the other teams focused on their targets. The police HQ was several blocks from the warehouse and heavily fortified. They moved through the streets, their feet crunching under the snow, and as they did, more and more people joined them, coming out from their houses and apartment buildings, becoming one with the moving wave of resistance.

———

Alayna gripped her two handguns and moved quietly with the ten other people in her group. The yellow team was responsible for taking out the Administration's communications systems. Due to the large number of people in the yellow team, they split into smaller teams to cover more ground. Alayna was headed downtown and though usually unguarded, she knew the comms systems would be heavily defended once Burke knew what was taking place. Several of her team members carried backpacks with C4, mini-EMP grenades, and other explosives. Though a tactical operation, destroying the comms systems didn't require a lot of finesse and everyone knew that once they started, the only option was to keep pressing forward. Ahead, she saw their primary target – a large satellite dish on top of a concrete building with several armed guards posted outside. She turned to the others in her group.

"We'll take out the guards from here. Take the explosives to the east side. Once the charges are set, get out of there and meet us back here." The others nodded and then split from the group and headed down the street to secure their positions. Alayna grabbed one of the rifles and sighted the first guard in her scope. She didn't hesitate as she slowly exhaled and pulled the trigger, watching as blood splattered against the building's wall. Alayna quickly moved the gun and sighted the next guard, sending him to the ground before he had a chance to locate where the shot had come from.

———————

"This is about securing and commandeering, not destroying," said gray team's leader. He had reiterated this point several times to the 100 men assigned to him. This target, as everyone knew, was critical to the entire success of their operation, regardless of the risks involved. Hiding in a large underground parking garage two blocks from the BioDose HQ, the gray team was nervous.

"We blow the wall and that's it. I don't want to see any more explosives once we're inside. Take out the guards, and move in to secure the facility," the leader continued. "I want a team in place on the stairs to take out the drones because believe me, they are coming, and they will fuck you up if you let them. Any questions?"

"What do we do once it's secure?" asked Darin, who had been assigned to this group, along with Dr. Merric.

"We get to work. Keep the production lines going. It's an automated system, but we need to get the doses boxed up and ready to move. Are the vans in place?"

"Yes, sir," said a woman in the back.

"Once they're full, take them back to base and then come back for more."

The garage was quiet as the group listened to their leader. They all knew what was at stake, but had decided to forge ahead, no longer willing to live just to survive.

"Stay the course. Keep your head down. Make them pay. Let's go!"

There were no cheers or applause as they made their way out of their garage. Instead, each was focused on the task at hand and trying to prepare for the unexpected.

"Sir, it's happening," said a man in the suit. "Comms Tower 2 went offline a few minutes ago, and it looks like they're headed for the others. There's also been movement reported a block from BioDose HQ as well as a mob headed for the police HQ."

Burke continued to stare at the window and watch as plumes of smoke spiral into the snowy sky. It was clever to go after the comms system first, but ultimately it wouldn't matter. These were nothing more than criminals and ordinary people fighting for what they believed to be a better life but selfishly unwilling to accept the sacrifices that come with it.

"Call in special forces. I want air support and drones covering every inch of space above the city. No one gets in or out without my permission. Shoot to kill. We end this today. And take care of *The 212*."

His aide nodded and left the room, closing the door behind him. Burke continued to look out the window. He had expected an uprising at some point or another, though today's was much larger than he had anticipated. He wasn't worried; instead, he enjoyed the challenge to his authority as it allowed him to flex his power in ways that were otherwise looked down upon. Today, the insurrectionists would come to realize his authority and, in the end, would either bend or break to it.

Bullets whizzed overhead until either finding their mark or piercing through the buildings behind the blue team. Kalum and the others were crouched behind concrete dividers, holed up in buildings, and trying to avoid the mob of police officers trying to break through the police HQ entrance. The initial assault had caused every officer to gear up and head toward the gate, and now, Kalum and his team were doing their best to keep them in.

"We can't just wait here," said a man next to Kalum. He peeked his head up above the barrier, and a second later, he slumped down. A bullet had pierced through his skull, and blood mixed with the snow next to Kalum. He pulled out his walkie-talkie.

"This is Kalum with the blue team. We're pinned down outside of police HQ, but we're holding them. Whatever you need to do, do it now. We can't hold them much longer."

He put the walkie back in his jacket and grabbed a grenade from a bag on the ground. With his back against the barrier, he lobbed the grenade backward, waited for a moment, and then braced himself as it exploded, followed by splatters of blood and the screams of those who had been hit but survived. He had heard screams like that before and although Kalum didn't miss war, at least this time, he was fighting for a cause he believed in.

"Get rid of those drones!" shouted Alayna with her back pressed against an alley wall, the same as the others in her group. Taking out the first comms tower had been simple enough, but on route to their 2nd target, the drones had shown up and opened fire on them, taking out three members.

Peering around the corner, a young man with a long tubular gun pointed it toward the sky, waited for a moment, and then pulled the trigger. A giant mesh net made of metal filaments flew out from the end, expanded in midair, and then enveloped the drones, cutting out their power supply as soon as it came into contact with them and sent them crashing to the street below.

"Let's go," said Alayna, taking one last look up at the sky before leaving the refuge of the dark alley.

As they ran through the streets toward the second tower, she radioed Kalum.

"Comms Tower 2 is in sight. How much longer can you give us?"

The line echoed back static before Kalum responded. "Five minutes. Good luck."

In front of her, through the snow, she saw the large antennae tower on top of a large building.

"How are we going to get inside?" asked one of the members.

"Ask politely," said Alayna, cocking her handgun. "We've got five minutes before the police are all over us. Everyone clear about what to do?" The others nodded. "Let's get this done."

The red team had been in the tunnels under Central for over an hour now. They were dark, cold, and covered in a thin film of grime that, no matter how hard they tried, seemed to end up on their clothes anyway. Enzo held a paper map under his flashlight and then looked up, trying to assess which direction they should go. After a moment, he folded the paper and nodded toward the left tunnel. The group of six trudged through the shallow water and pressed forward.

Enzo had been assigned to the red team, or the demo crew as they called themselves because if he could fix a tunnel, he could easily destroy one. Packs of C4 and other explosives were loaded into each members' backpack, and though pressed for time, they were careful about how they proceeded.

Attacking Central HQ or any other prominent government buildings would be nearly impossible to do from ground level. A full-frontal assault would inevitably lead to mass casualties - something the resistance couldn't afford if they were to come out of this successfully. The demo crew had taken to the tunnels and were tasked with planting explosives under key targets. They had acknowledged the fact that by destroying the buildings, they would invariably be obliterating the transportation system and damaging key infrastructure. Still, the resistance leaders had agreed that it was worth it.

"We're about a block from the police HQ," said Enzo. "Get the charges ready."

The sound of a passing subway train echoed through the tunnel, but the group continued onward. Once at the site, Enzo pointed out the spots for the charges, and each member carefully placed them on the wall. The team stepped back a bit and shined their lights on the charges. Enzo looked at the placements and nodded.

He pulled out his radio and said, "Police HQ is locked and loaded. Blue team, now would be a good time to head downtown to rendezvous with the black team. We're about to blow the pigpen into oblivion."

The gray team leader looked up in shock as gun turrets materialized from the 3rd story concrete wall of the BioDose building.

"Cover!" he yelled through a volley of bullets as men and women around him began to fall. They had breached the wall and taken out the guards without so much as a hint of resistance, and although they had expected confrontation, the turrets hadn't been in the intel. They must have added them recently, he thought, but he focused his attention back on the mission.

"We have to push inside," he yelled to the others crouched behind the guard tower. "And at all costs, Dr. Merric needs to make it in alive." Aiden looked into the man's eyes and nodded. They all felt an unspoken fear mixed with a determination to succeed. For them, there was no other choice.

"Now!" he yelled as the hundred or so remaining fighters rushed across the courtyard and pushed up the steps. The turrets turned and opened fire, sending bloody bodies hurtling down the stairs. A few fired back up at the turrets, though to no noticeable effect. Once a few had reached the stairs, they dived forward, hoping to pass into the building and out of the sightline of the turrets outside. After Dr. Merric had jumped, he looked out of the doorway from where he sat and saw the bloody courtyard, a mix of bodies, weapons, and blood-stained snow.

He, along with several others, had made it inside BioDose HQ. They had achieved what many had thought impossible, though at a price that none of them would forget.

"Kalum made it out in time," said Magnus over the radio. "Looks like he and his team are headed to meet with the black team." He looked over at Piper Merric and smiled. In front of him was a holographic 3D projection of Central, with a number of colored dots moving between the projected light. Before they had left *The 212*, Magnus had suggested that a few people wear tracking devices so they could keep track of each other.

"And my dad?" asked Piper.

"From what I can tell, he made it into BioDose HQ. He's safe," he said, answering her implied question.

She smiled and looked at the hologram. "And what are these?" she asked, pointing to a group of green dots.

Magnus quickly grabbed the radio and spoke, "Alayna, you've got a swarm of drones headed your way. Whatever you're doing on the roof, get it done and get out of there."

"Copy that," she said. Magnus switched channels and said, "Enzo, come in."

"What's up?" came a gruff voice.

"It's not clear right now, but it looks like you aren't alone in the tunnels. We've got our own drones over the city mapping it out right now, and it looks like the thermal cameras have picked up activity other than yours down below."

"How many?" Enzo asked.

"Hard to tell." Magnus zoomed in on the area of the map. "Maybe a dozen or so. Get out of there while you can or lay low."

"I'll handle it. Thanks for the heads up. Over and out."

"The eye in the sky," said Piper, offering a small smile.

"Yes indeed," said Magnus. Though he had offered to grab a gun and fight, he knew that at his age, he wouldn't have been much help. Plus,

Aiden had asked him to look after Piper until this ended and, if need be, look after her in case he didn't make it out alive. Magnus knew that his role in all this was just as important as those on the frontline and intended to keep his promise to Dr. Merric. After leaving *The 212*, they had joined the purple team, focusing on supplies and reconnaissance. Though spread out across the city, Magnus and Piper had set up their base of operations in an abandoned bookstore on the tenth floor of a building downtown. They had a clear view of the city, and Piper walked over to the window and looked down at the snow-covered streets.

"Magnus, I think something's happening down there."

"I see it too," he said, staring at the hologram.

"Come see it for real."

Magnus walked over to the window and looked at the streets below. Amidst the towering government buildings and skyscrapers, thousands of protestors, rioters, resistance fighters, and other armed individuals were amassing on one side of the street while police units, special forces, and armored vehicles were establishing an opposing force directly opposite them, maybe 300 meters away.

"We have to get out of here," he said quietly. "The war is starting."

The drones flew over Central like falcons stalking their prey down below. Hundreds of them swarmed to locations where violence had been reported, sending a live-feed back to police and military units. This was the 2nd time the military had been called into the city. The first was when Styre had first hit, and it was the only way to stop the chaos. This time, Burke had insisted that the military was the only way to stop the uprising, and though several government officials questioned his call, no one said it out loud.

"This is drone swarm 3. It looks like they're in the tunnels," said an operator. "It appears they've blown the police HQ from underground. Casualties unknown. Rioters are moving downtown."

"Take them out," said Burke calmly, listening to the report. "I want no survivors."

There was a moment of silence over the radio before the operator said, "yes, sir."

He focused the group of drones on the small dark figures running from the police HQ and opened fire, sending a hailstorm of bullets upon them. Several dropped, and stains of red appeared on the snow. The figures scattered, some running into buildings, others turning their guns to the sky and firing, and others continuing to run down the street. The operator sent the drones lower and continued to fire upon the rebel fighters, killing anyone within distance. One of the drone feeds went black as a bullet from below destroyed it. The operator quickly tasked a second drone to target the man who had fired and ended his life with the press of a button.

The operator looked at his glass screen and saw a flashing red light. He pressed it and heard Burke's voice say, "Take out *The 212*. I want it eviscerated. We have no use for it now."

"Understood, sir." The operator grabbed a second glass tablet and tasked a group of bomber drones to head to the island's southern tip. He knew what was asked of him, and though he had no say in the matter, he quietly wished that those in *The 212* had made it out and that he wouldn't be responsible for any more unnecessary deaths.

"We're almost there, sir," shouted one of the men. "You've got to push."

"We both know I'm not going to make it," said Kalum, looking down at the several bullet holes in his legs and one in his shoulder. Blood had soaked through his clothes and was pooling into the pile of snow he was sitting on. His back was pressed to the wall of an alley he had run into once the drones had ambushed them.

"There's medics downtown. We have to go."

"My time is done," said Kalum. His breath was shallow, and he turned and spit a mouthful of blood into the snow. "You go. I'll stay and take out as many as I can. Find Alayna. Tell her to stick to the plan."

The man watched as Kalum winced and stood up, grabbing the machine gun and shuffling toward the main street. The man patted him on his shoulder and then turned right, heading to meet up with the others while drones hovered overhead, taking out those still in the street.

Kalum looked up and saw the drones, the black machines that killed without remorse. Some were powered by AI, but others, based on how they moved, Kalum knew there was an operator behind a screen controlling their movement. Cocking the gun, Kalum stepped into the street and fired at one of the drone's, sending it crashing into the street. He quickly sighted another and shot it down as well. The whir of rotary blades filled the air as the swarm flew toward Kalum. He stood there, unmoving until they were in range, and then held up his left hand in the air. He extended two fingers upward, forming the shape of a gun, and then pressed a button on the EMP grenade. A cacophonous sound filled the air as a wave of electricity exploded from Kalum's hand and pulsated through the drones, killing their blades and dropping them from the sky. Kalum fell to his knees and looked up, letting the snow fall on his face, thinking about his childhood, and the days he would spend walking through the soft snow in Japan with his father. He closed his eyes and dropped into the snow, dead to the world but at peace with the person he had become and the cause he had chosen to die for.

Bodies from both sides littered the ground while burning buildings continued to blaze in the distance. The snow continued to fall, but it wasn't enough to cover up the stains of red already permeating the snow nor cover up the smell of burning flesh and sulfur. Men and women continued to fight, bullets from their guns flying through the streets, hoping to find their target. Society had gained the upper hand for a while and seemed to have been pushing back the city's police forces. Once the drones, military hovercraft, and the army had been sent, they knew their chances of victory were slim.

Alayna was standing on a street, her gun pointed to the sky while the others kept an eye on the road ahead. They had taken out three of the city's four major comms units and were now looking for a place to hide. It was night now, and the past several hours had filled with hope, determination, and death. They had encountered little resistance at first, but once the military forces had entered the city, the tide had shifted. During the day, twice her radio had buzzed and twice she had received bad news.

The first was that Kalum had died. The new Blue Team commander had explained what had happened, and before Alayna had a chance to grieve, another voice had broken the silence.

"We're not alone down here," Enzo had said. The demo team had taken out the police HQ from the city's tunnels as well as a few armories and had always radioed about their next target, but now, Enzo sounded worried.

"We're headed for the surface. Downtown area. It's not safe down…" and before Enzo had finished speaking, a deafening sound first roared over the radio, and then Alayna had seen the giant plume of flames and smoke a few blocks in the distance. The demo team was gone, and Alayna couldn't help but think that her time would soon come as well. She watched as the military forces had rappelled from hovercrafts all over the city. Watched as rockets were fired from the ships into buildings, sending bodies and chunks of concrete hurtling to the ground, killing anyone in their way.

She had radioed Dr. Merric, hoping for an update from BioDose HQ, but there was no response. Her next call had been to Magnus and Piper, but all she had received was a fragmented response with no clear information.

"Explosion…" Magnus had shouted. "Alive… Piper… Not safe…" and the radio went silent, with static echoing over the line.

"We have to head downtown," shouted one of her team members, watching as one of the ships came into view in the distance.

"It's a bloodbath," said Alayna. "We'll be of no help. We need to get to safety so we can live to fight another day. We're no good to anyone if we're dead." The team of six listened to her speak, a bulwark of calm amidst the chaos around her. Alayna pointed to her left and the team ran down the street away from the ship, staying in the shadows while the sound of the battle raged in the distance.

The ship shined a bright light down the street and slowly moved forward. A moment later, the sound of a missile cut through the wind and Alayna turned, catching only a glimpse of it before the missile made contact with the building behind her and exploded on impact.

The world went quiet. Dust permeated the air as debris fell and flames rose, licking their way up the walls of nearby buildings. The bodies from the yellow team lay strewn about the street, some with limbs blown off and others seemingly unscathed but motionless on the ground, with Alayna among the latter. The ship hovered over the area, scanning its light on the ground below, and then rose into the sky, heading for another part of the city.

Alayna opened her eyes but couldn't make out anything clearly. The buildings around here were a blur and she didn't know where she was. She could feel the blood from a cut on her head dripping down her face but didn't have the strength to reach up and wipe it away. She kept her eyes open long enough to see snow softly falling on the ground beside her and then she closed her eyes, unable to keep them open any longer.

A Viral State

Chapter 22

September 2072

President Burke sat at his desk looking over the speech he had prepared for today. He looked up and watched as several technicians moved a camera and lighting equipment in front of his desk, and then he looked back down at his speech. Today is of great importance…, he read silently in his head. And indeed, it was. One of the techs held up one finger, and Burke nodded.

He put the notes in a drawer on his desk and saw his speech projected from a holo-screen just above the camera. The camera lights turned on, and a tech nodded at Burke.

"Good afternoon, citizens of The United Federation. Under my Administration, we have achieved great things. For nearly a decade, we have grappled with the Styre virus and its widespread impact on our nation and around the globe. Though many lives have been lost, through my leadership, BioDose has created a way for us to continue to survive and, more importantly, live. Nature has a cunning way of finding our weakest spot, yet, we persevere.

One year ago today, on a cold winter day just like today, a rebellion sought to end the stability of the United Federation, brought about by my Administration. They brutally slaughtered members of our country's military, scientists, innocent bystanders, and Central police officers. They bombed buildings and intended to disrupt the stable supply of doses meant for our country. Today, as I have mentioned time and time again, I would like to remind all of you that there is no threat to our nation's stability that won't be met with swift and merciless justice. Sometimes, you must kill to preserve, and under my orders, all those who took part in the riots are dead."

Burke paused, looking straight into the camera, letting his words sink into all those watching.

"The preterite lives of all those who fought to defend what they so vehemently believed in will never again challenge the stability of our nation. As I'm sure many of you have noticed, heightened security measures have been implemented to ensure the safety and security of government facilities. This protection is also for you. The citizens of this country are our greatest asset, and I will spare no expense to keep you safe.

"Today, we remember the lives lost in the rebellion, and you have my word that no future insurrection will ever take place so long as I am in power. Our Administration is continually working to develop a cure. I'm sorry to say that the rumors of a cure were not true. Our intel discovered that it was nothing more than rebel propaganda used to incite violence and sow chaos. The continued survival of our nation, along with your safety, is my top priority, and I promise you that when a cure is discovered, it will be produced and distributed to the public free of charge.

"Like all of you, I rely on my daily dose to survive, and I would like nothing more than to find a cure. In the meantime, I encourage you to remember the atrocities that took place on this day last year and honor the lives of those who so bravely defended our nation's values and way of life. But also keep in mind that taking time to forget is just as important as taking time to remember. We cannot dwell on what happened, but instead move on and strive for progress.

"What took place one year ago offers a glimpse of the new challenges we all face. To meet them, we must find a new direction, a new path forward. The Administration stands with the people, and for the people. Goodnight."

The camera lights stayed on for a moment and then powered off, leaving Burke alone in the dimly lit room as the technicians packed up the cameras and left his office. The uprising had indeed been a challenge, but Burke knew that any problem could be solved if you threw enough firepower at it. Though in hindsight, he did acknowledge it had been hasty to blow up *The 212* and destroy any political future clout he might need. His new policy, however, of instant death for anyone found guilty of seditious activity was more cost-effective and required less paperwork. He looked out the large window behind his desk and smiled as the snow fell over the city. The city had been maintained and he had, throughout the ordeal, managed to tighten his hold over Central. Burke had always believed in the idea that power, once gained, does not go unused, and he intended to use up every last drop.

———

"What a load of shit," someone said loudly after Burke's address to the nation was shut off. Other voices chimed in, none positive, as the din in the bar got louder. Figures dressed in large jackets and others in dark hoods moved about the open floor, some sitting on wooden benches while others moved together and spoke in hushed tones. That seemed to be a new normal these days - quieter conversations and a way to hide one's face. Burke's new "safety and security measures" had the whole country scared of what might happen to them, despite the repeated attempts by the government-controlled news to shift the narrative that these measures "were in the public's best interests."

A figure in a dark gray jacket, matching beanie, and a black facemask stood up from one of the tables and moved toward the door. The bar was getting louder, and emotions were running high. It was time to go. The door was opened, and the figure headed out, listening to the crunch of snow beneath their feet as the door closed. They headed west, and though it would be a long walk to the warehouse by the river, public transportation was out of the question. It was too dangerous, and with security now tighter than ever, it was best to go on foot.

The city itself hadn't changed much since the rebellion last year. Buildings had been repaired, as had the tunnels that ran beneath the now empty streets. BioDose HQ was still operating, and the Administration had returned to its usual rhetoric that "progress was being made on a cure, though nothing substantial at this time had been found."

Thousands had died in the fight, and obituaries had been written about those that existed. Everyone in *The 212*, either presumed missing, on the run, or dead, was never spoken of, though the government was doing its best to account for all those who had escaped. After *The 212* had been bombed, and Burke had tightened his grip on the country, people had now come to accept that pain and suffering were an inevitable part of the human experience.

Snow continued to fall, and the figure made its way through the streets, maintaining a casual speed but not fast enough to draw the attention of security personnel. The storage facility was a few blocks away, and though the cold was biting through the jacket, it was the only place to go.

Once outside, the figure went to the side of the large building, the grime and rust now frozen in place on its concrete walls, and knocked three times on the door. A moment later, the door partially opened, and the figure was met with the barrel of a gun.

"State your business," a voice said from the darkness.

"I was told this was a safe space," the figure said quietly.

"Are you injured?"

"No."

"Then you aren't welcome," said the voice.

The door began to close. "Not even for a friend of the rebellion?" The figure removed the hood and took off the mask and the gun barrel lowered.

"Alayna?" the voice asked.

"Good to see you again, Darin," she said with a smile. He grabbed her and gave her a hug before pulling her inside and closing the door.

"Where have you been? We all thought you were dead."

"I thought the same about you," she said. "And if I'm being honest, I thought I had died as well."

Alayna looked around the spacious room filled with various furniture covered in dust-covered plastic sheets and then over to Darin.

"What happened to your leg?" she asked, nodding toward the metal prosthetic strapped around his knee.

"Casualty of war," he said with a smile. "I see you didn't make it out unscathed," pointing to her forehead.

She touched the scar running from her temple down to her cheek and smiled.

"Luckier than most. What is this place?"

Darin smiled. "It's what's left. It isn't much, but we're taking care of those in need. I'm glad you found it. We've been flying under the radar since the war and let me tell you, it's not been easy. Follow me."

They walked to the far side of the room and Darin lifted a small hatch in the ground, and they descended into the darkness. Once they reached the bottom, Alayna looked around and realized they were in a large catacomb full of people. There were several beds where people were being looked after, while others sat together at tables and talked. People were rushing by with various supplies and tools and despite the activity, it wasn't noisy down here. At the far end of a room, a dog lay on a dirty blanket and in the soft glow of a nearby candle, she saw the metallic glare and walked toward it.

"Tipper," she said quietly, kneeling down to the pet the dog she had grown so fond of during her time in *The 212*. He looked up at her and both understood the sorrow in the other's eyes, having both someone close to them.

"I'll be back," said Alayna, leaning down to kiss Tipper's head before walking back over to Darin.

"Incredible dog," he said. "I can't express how sorry I am that we lost Finn."

Alayna nodded and remained quiet as Darin continued.

"We've got a makeshift hospital, a team of engineers looking to open a second facility across the city, and enough doses to last us another year. A few guns, but nothing substantial."

"Where'd you get all of them?"

"We managed to hold BioDose HQ for a while and got a shipment of doses over here before we were overrun."

"And Dr. Merric?"

Darin shook his head. "There was nothing we could do. I barely made it out myself. I was shot in the leg, and after the hovercrafts came in, I ran, headed for the sewers. Finally made it here eight months ago, and the sepsis was so bad they had to amputate."

"I'm so sorry," said Alayna quietly.

"Better than being dead."

Alayna looked around again at her surroundings. She had heard about the catacombs under the city but had never been down here herself. For her, things had changed yet were vaguely familiar. The sounds, the energy, the people all remained, but something was missing.

The next few weeks were spent adjusting to living underground, though she was thankful not to be living on the streets or squatting in abandoned buildings any longer. Alayna was set up to join the team of nurses taking care of the injured or sick. The work gave her meaning, and though both she and Darin had taken the cure, they both quietly thought of ways to once again help the masses.

Those questions were answered on a quiet Thursday night. The snow had picked up, and the wind slammed against Central's buildings. There was a faint rasp at the door. Quiet, but enough for the guard on duty to hear. He spoke with the woman at the door and after a few moments. Let her enter. They made their way down the stairs and stood on the landing just as Alayna had done a few weeks ago, taking in the sights. Alayna watched as the new arrival slipped off her hood, revealing a strand of red hair that had made its way out from under her beanie. She continued to watch as she lowered her face mask, and Alayna moved quickly through the sea of people headed toward the young girl.

"Piper?" she said. The young girl turned and smiled. "Piper!"

Alayna grabbed the girl and hugged her, holding her tightly amongst the onlookers.

She pulled back but kept her hands on Piper's shoulders and asked, "How did you...?" but wasn't able to finish the question as she stared in disbelief.

"Magnus and I were together doing recon. A missile hit the building we were in as we were escaping. Magnus..." she began, as tears started to well up in her eyes. "He didn't make it."

Alayna again hugged the young girl and said, "I'm happy you did. Follow me. We'll get you somewhere quieter and give you a change of clothes."

She led Piper down a small corridor, and after she had changed and was given a bowl of hot soup, they sat together at a small table away from all the noise.

"How did you survive out there on your own?" Alayna asked.

"The same as everyone else, I guess. Hid during the day. Scavenged for food. Slept in basements or car parks."

"I'm so sorry," said Alayna. "If I had known you were still alive, I would have looked for you."

"There was no way to know."

"And what did you do for doses?"

Piper shrugged, "For most of last year, when I was 17, I didn't need them. And then, when I turned 18 a few months ago, I didn't need them either. I've felt fine, I mean, despite being hungry and scared every day."

Alayna couldn't say anything. Her mind was trying to process the information as she stared at the young girl in front of her.

"You haven't taken any doses since you've been out?"

"Actually, I never have."

"And you're sure you turned 18?"

"I know my birthday," Piper said with a smile.

"This can't be," said Alayna. "You were there all along, and nobody even thought to..." she trailed off, thinking of everything this meant.

"Alayna," she said quietly. "Is something wrong with me?"

"No, no, no," she said. "Just the opposite. Come with me, right now."

She grabbed Piper by the hand and led them through the throngs of people, many seemingly unaware of their rush among those going about their business.

In the distance, Alayna spotted who she was looking for and shouted, "Darin!"

He turned and saw Alayna, and then Piper behind her. He ran toward them and said, "Piper, I thought you were, well, dead, to be honest."

"We can catch up later," interrupted Alayna. "Darin, we need a lab, somewhere to test her blood. Do you have anything like that down here?"

He looked at her as if wanting to press her on why she needed it, but simply said, "Follow me."

Walking through the catacombs, sliding past people and makeshift furniture, they came to a door built into the walls and Darin opened it with a key. The room had a single light overhead and a microscope as well as a few other medical equipment were sitting on a table on the left wall.

"We didn't have a lot of time to salvage things, but this is better than nothing."

Darin took a seat and prepared a syringe as Piper rolled up her sleeve. He drew the blood from her arm and placed a drop on a glass strip. Sliding it under the microscope, he looked at it for a moment, paused to look up at Alayna, and then looked back down at the blood.

"Does this mean what I think it means?" he asked.

Alayna nodded and then placed her hand on Piper's shoulder who asked, "What's going on?"

"You don't have Styre," Alayna said quietly. "You never have. That's why you didn't need the doses." Piper listened without saying a word and then looked over to Darin who nodded in agreement.

"And we couldn't have known until now because while you were in *The 212*…"

"I was under 18," said Piper. "So, what does it mean?"

Alayna smiled and said, "Against all odds, you're the outlier that can give this country the one thing it needs now most: hope."

"And how are we supposed to do that?" Piper asked. "The surveillance, increased security, a lack of resources. It's impossible."

"A necessary end to things comes when it is most needed," said Alayna. "But more importantly, it's time for a new start. And you're the one person that can make that happen. Finn was the catalyst, and you, whether you like it or not, must continue the fight."

Piper looked from Alayna and then over to Darin. The weight of what they were talking about hadn't yet settled in and although their minds with racing with possibilities, the silence was palpable. Life had become drastically different than anything they could have ever imagined, but like Styre, they knew that nothing was permanent and that change starts with hope. And in that room below the snowy city above, that's exactly what they felt. Hope.

A Viral State

Author Bio

Degen is a travel junkie, gym enthusiast, and avid writer who self-published his first novel *Contraception* in 2018 and has since had four short stories published in literary journals and magazines. He holds an MA in Politics & Foreign Policy from Tsinghua University and works as a news reporter and writer, having published hundreds of news and op-ed articles. He writes dystopian literature in his free time.